W9-CAL-034

Novels by Gerald Brandt
available from DAW Books:

The San Angeles Novels:
THE COURIER
THE OPERATIVE
THE REBEL

GERALD BRANDT

DAW BOOKS, INC.
DONALD A. WOLLHEIM, FOUNDER
375 Hudson Street, New York, NY 10014
ELIZABETH R. WOLLHEIM
SHEILA E. GILBERT
PUBLISHERS
www.dawbooks.com

Jacket art by Cliff Nielsen.

Jacket design by G-Force Design.

Book designed by Alissa Theodor.

DAW Book Collectors No. 1774.

Published by DAW Books, Inc.
375 Hudson Street, New York, NY 10014.

First Printing, November 2017
1 2 3 4 5 6 7 8 9

DAW TRADEMARK REGISTERED
U.S. PAT. AND TM. OFF. AND FOREIGN COUNTRIES
—MARCA REGISTRADA
HECHO EN U.S.A.

PRINTED IN THE U.S.A.

For Robert L. Peters
Friend. Family. Brother.

ACKNOWLEDGMENTS

Where does one start when one reaches the end? It has been a long—and yet remarkably short—journey full of friends both old and new, conventions and readings, and many a fine conversation over coffee or scotch. There are so many people to thank for this wonderful journey.

First are my beta readers. As usual, their feedback proved invaluable: Evan Braun, Troy Bucher, David Fortier, Virginia O'Dine, and Sherry Peters. I have been extraordinarily lucky to have such excellent feedback. These five helped me give you a better book. Mercedes Dobler gave me wonderful feedback on the Japanese scenes, which made me cut out an entire scene and replace it with something much better. Cliff Nielsen's artwork is phenomenal. His vision of my work never ceases to amaze me. When I wrote about the shuttles I pictured an SR-71 Blackbird. At no time did I communicate that to Cliff, yet his imagery is dead on.

I have to once again thank Reg Kovac, who tore down and built my fence while I was finishing edits.

I don't know if I have the words—a strange thing for a writer—to thank the team at DAW for all they have done. Sheila Gilbert took a chance with me, and without her edits, this book would not have been as strong. There are so many people behind the scenes that make what you are holding in your hands such an incredible thing.

Sara Megibow, my literary agent at kt literary, and Jerry Kalajian, my Hollywood agent at IPG, do so much behind-the-scenes work. Thank you so much!

And finally, I get to the teary part. My family has been so supportive I don't even know where to begin. They allowed me to cut down on my full-time job so I could write more, are gentle when I rant and rave on how nothing I'm writing is working, bring me back down to earth when everything I'm writing is glorious, and force me into my office when the inevitable procrastination comes knocking. Jared and Ryan are teenagers now, and still show how proud they are, even when they interrupt my writing when I'm so engrossed in my make-believe world that I don't hear what they are saying. Marnie has read countless copies of this series, catching logic issues, multiple spelling errors, and letting me know when what I have down on paper may not match what is in my head.

one

PASADENA LEVEL 5—MONDAY, JULY 3, 2141 2:00 P.M.

I WALKED PAST THE greenhouses, breathing in air thick with the memories of open sky and soaring peaks—a world away from this damn city that wanted to suffocate me with every step. The smells of flowers and earth, carried in the slight breeze generated by the overhead fans, quelled the uneasiness inside me for the first time in weeks. I could almost imagine there wasn't a ceiling over my head.

Almost.

I stopped to stare past the *shinrin-yoku* sign on my right. It meant "forest bathing," a place to relax, to lose yourself in the trees—in nature—where the worries of the world could fall away for a while. To me, it used to be one of the most beautiful places in San Angeles. Now it held a barely heard whisper of memories. I'd promised myself I wouldn't be distracted, wouldn't let the hurt pull me in. The promise was as empty as I felt.

Past the sign, through the greenhouse's open doors, warm grow lights reflected off the slender white trunks of birch trees, their branches of delicate leaves reaching for the ceiling. A carpet of tender green grass grew between the strong roots, interspersed by gravel paths worn flat by people who could afford to live up here.

We'd buried Ian's ashes in there only two short weeks ago.

I held back a cry. Pain and loss cascaded through me, raw, untempered, tearing down walls I'd barely had a chance to build around open wounds that hadn't had time to heal.

Without realizing, I moved my hands to my belly, resting them there gently. At eight weeks, I was hardly showing, but to me it was obvious. I dragged my hands away, shoving them deep into my pockets.

Pat had told me to wait, told me it was too soon to get back into the field. She didn't know about the baby—no one but Doc Searls did—but she was worried it was too close to Ian's death. I couldn't wait anymore. Sitting alone in the small room the insurgents had given me was slowly turning my brain into mush. The walls pressed in on me, and I had nothing but time. Time to remember, time to dream of what had been lost. Time to go over what I could have done differently. It was all time wasted.

This was my first run for the insurgents since I'd decided to take back control. Seeing the trees, I wasn't sure I had made the right choice. Ian's loss was still too fresh. It was my fault he was gone. What if I made another bad decision? Would someone else die? I wasn't sure I was doing the right thing for the baby either, if I had the right to put him in danger.

A hand touched my hip—a light touch, and then it vanished—followed by a hissed "*Hey.*" I didn't have time to react. Someone from my team—her name couldn't fight through the onslaught of memories—strolled past me as though the touch was accidental. I realized I'd stopped walking. How long had I stood here, staring at the trees?

Now was not the time. *Never* was the time. Not now, not tomorrow. Never. I had work to do, and people—families—on the lower Levels were waiting for the food I would help bring back. What was it that Ian had said to me once? *Fake it till you make it.* Don't let them know you're hurting, don't let them know you're unsure. Just do it.

I turned my back on the greenhouse and crossed the street, mingling with the afternoon crowds going back to work, or maybe just trying to enjoy the day. Our goal was ahead of us, two greenhouses down from the stark white trunks. Unlike the *shinrin-yoku* greenhouse, this one wasn't open to the public. It was SoCal-owned, like most things in San Angeles were, and its interior was shrouded in soft, opaque windows. The buildings went on forever, two rows separated by a parkway with benches and real grass, vibrant under artificial lights. This was one of the hundreds of places where SoCal grew its food for the lower levels. It would end up on grocery store shelves on Levels 4 and 5 until it got too old, then it would be moved to Levels 2 and 3. Level 1 got whatever was left after that. At least that's how it used to work. Now it all went straight to Level 6 to feed the rich. The privileged.

SoCal was one of the big three corporations that owned most of the world's resources and production. They'd built San Angeles and controlled almost everything in it. We were here to hijack one of the trucks loaded with fresh produce and get the food to the lower levels, where it was so desperately needed. Where it belonged.

There was a small loading dock on one end of the SoCal greenhouse that could only fit a couple of trucks at a time, yet there never seemed to be a lineup. A new truck showed up seconds after the old one left. Each one had a single driver that helped load it before driving off. They all took the most direct route to the closest up-ramp, waved through security after a cursory inspection.

The insurgents had sent a small team to grab a truck last week. They'd failed. By the looks of things, their botched attempt had changed the procedure a little. The driver that got out of the vehicle wore a sidearm, and I thought I saw a passenger in the darkened cab. Two people would make it tougher. The guns even more so. I grabbed my comm unit and connected with our team leader.

"Billy's gonna bring a friend and some toys," I said.

"No worries, thanks." The link closed and I tucked the comm unit away.

We had ten minutes before the truck finished loading.

I strolled past the greenhouse, keeping up with everyone else, and pulled the comm unit out of my pocket again. I punched in my access code. The insurgents had guaranteed this corner wasn't monitored—one of the dead spots in the network—and I could change my tracker ID. I made sure there were no drones overhead and cycled the ID. It still seemed strange, knowing I and almost every other person in San Angeles had a tracker embedded in them. They injected us with a vaccine when we were kids. It contained the tracker, which sent out coded signals with every heartbeat. ACE had learned how to cover the technology with their own, making the signals modifiable. Almost no one knew about the trackers. First ACE, the extinct anti-corporate movement, and now the insurgents wanted to keep it a secret. I still didn't understand why.

The new ID made me out to be a simple courier. Once I got on my bike, I'd blend in with the background traffic. I laughed at *simple courier.* It had been a long time, a lifetime, since I'd been that. Everything was simpler back then.

I recrossed the street and walked between the greenhouses to the parkway. The sight of the burned-out hulk ahead reminded me of Janice, when she'd tried to kill me and Pat. My pace slowed for a second before I pushed her from my mind. I didn't have time for that now.

One of the others on my recon team passed by me, heading in the opposite direction. He was a young kid. Too young to be thrust into something like this. The insurgents didn't seem to have any issues with using kids. They'd proven that when they'd used them to blow up water stations on the upper levels. It took me a while to realize he was probably only a year or two younger than I was. We walked by without looking at each other. There were three of us for a reason, and if he'd been identified and monitored by SoCal, we didn't want them to learn about anyone else on the team.

The fact that I'd been placed on recon still stung. The insurgents knew what I could do—what I had done—and threw me in with the rest of the newbies anyway. They couldn't use my pregnancy as an excuse, since they didn't know about it, so I figured it was out of spite for leaving Pat behind when I tried to get Ian. I stopped that line of thought right away. There was no point in going over those events again. I'd done it too often already.

In theory, the only saving grace was the job Pat, Kai, and I were doing for Doc Searls. His son was still missing, and we'd promised the Doc we'd look for him. In truth, I hadn't done much on that either. It was tough to get anything done when you locked yourself in your room.

My task here was to watch the loading of the truck and call ahead as soon as it left the dock. With the tight schedule they kept, it seemed like a waste of time—except that now I'd seen the guns. My job, after the recon, was to follow the truck when it drove out of Pasadena, just to make sure it stayed on route, and then peel off before it reached the intercept point. Like I said, newbie work.

My bike was parked off the main greenhouse and restaurant

strip. I headed that way. The other two on recon would stay behind, verifying that the pattern of trucks stayed the same. If it varied, chances were someone knew the delivery was going to be attacked.

I walked past a small street bistro with a swanky name I couldn't pronounce, surprised it was still open. With most of our food going up to the higher levels, a lot of restaurants had closed. It was tough to sell what you didn't have. A young couple sat at one table, the waiter hovering behind them. They didn't even see me. I was just another courier. The bike was parked a little farther down the street. I grabbed my lid off the handlebars and thumbed the bike's lock. A short ride past the greenhouses and a quick U-turn should put me behind the departing truck.

I was riding by the greenhouse when the truck pulled out. A couple of cars drove between us. I kept my spot and followed it, opening a comm link to let the hijack team know I was in place. The connection was made, but no one spoke. I gave my information and closed the link again.

The truck switched lanes, getting ready to make a left turn. I ended up right on its tail. As it accelerated around the corner heading for the ramp, I passed it on the right, stealing a glance through the passenger window. There were definitely two people in there.

Construction choked the road ahead, diverting traffic coming toward us down a side street, but letting us through. This was it. I raced through the gap and turned right, planning to come back up behind the truck.

The construction had been here all day, put up by the insurgents early this morning, and dozens of trucks had already passed through. This truck and driver would have come through here more than once, taking full loads up and empty ones back.

I zipped around the block, stopping a hundred meters away from the workers. From here, I could see the operation was already unfolding. The truck sat midconstruction waiting for men to carry equipment across the single lane. Almost from nowhere, two masked insurgents ran to the side doors of the truck and yanked them open.

Gunfire pierced the air, and I slammed my bike into gear as the insurgents fell to the ground. By the time I got behind the truck, it was over, and the relative silence of the city descended on us.

I pulled the bike into the construction, stopped, and jumped off, barely giving myself time to put down the kickstand. I sprinted to the driver's door and almost tripped over the bodies of the insurgents. The driver was still alive. His chest was covered in blood and his eyes were out of focus. He kept blinking, looking confused. I yanked him from his seat and let him fall to the ground, climbing in to take his place.

The construction crew had disappeared when the gunfire started—their job was done as soon as the attack began. Tromping on the accelerator, I raced away from the devastation, the forward momentum of the truck slamming the doors shut. I turned down the same corner I'd taken with my bike and made a beeline for the closest down-ramp. The body in the seat beside me shifted. His head fell in my lap. I shivered and pushed it away, leaving a smear of blood on my pants.

The down-ramp was five blocks away. Once I reached the bottom, a support team would pick me up, and I'd have some protection on my way to the next ramp straight down to Level 2.

I had time to think about what had happened. What the hell was I doing? I'd put myself and my son directly in harm's way and hadn't even thought about it. That's not how an expectant mother is supposed to act.

Only two minutes had passed since the first shot, but it felt like an hour. I glanced out the window, banging my helmet against the glass, and scanned the ceiling for drones. The tightness of being boxed in grabbed hold of me and I held back a shudder. On the bike, I would have been able to tell if I'd been picked up. The thin slice of ceiling offered through the truck's window didn't show anything, but how could I really be sure?

When the front tires hit the down-ramp, I breathed a sigh of relief. At the bottom, I'd have others to watch for me. I opened the comm link again and let them know I was on the way. My hands shook as I took the first corner.

SOCAL SAT CITY 2—MONDAY, JULY 3, 2141 2:20 P.M.

Bryson Searls sat in a black chair with webbed backing and some of the best lumbar support he'd ever had. The desk in front of him was the perfect height, allowing him access to the terminal while his elbows were bent at slightly less than ninety degrees. SoCal was doing everything possible to make him feel comfortable.

It wasn't working.

The screen, at an almost exact fifty-two–centimeter distance, had been blank for the last forty minutes. His mind had shut down yet again. There was a time when he'd loved doing the work. He'd enjoyed playing with the equations that floated through his consciousness, visualizing the different combinations to find an optimal solution and then comparing them with what the computer had calculated.

That joy was gone. When he thought about it, which was more often than was probably healthy, he could pinpoint the exact moment in time when it had soured in his gut and turned first to hatred, then to apathy, and finally to fear.

The hatred started when he'd been told the test pilots of the first human flight of his quantum jump drive had died, and his employer didn't care. The apathy started when Meridian had been taken over by Kadokawa, and they'd forced him to continue his work. Meridian had been a smaller corporation with aspirations to be one of the big three. Bryson had worked for them since getting out of university. After the failed flight, Kadokawa had stepped in and taken control of Meridian's assets.

The fear was more recent. He wanted to think it started when he was kidnapped outside the Chinese restaurant, or maybe when he'd met Ms. Peters. He'd been scared then. Who wouldn't have been? But the turning point had come when she called in the guard with the cricket bat to beat the information out of him. His instinct had been to run, to get away as fast as he could. The only problem was, there was no place to go.

Once he'd scurried to do what she'd asked, the guard was sent away. But she made it quite clear he wasn't far. Bryson had sat in the folding metal chair, answering all her questions, holding nothing back. The interview had gone on for hours.

Ms. Peters had taken the memory chip he'd created before escaping from Kadokawa. It contained all of his research and data on the quantum jump drive, including the information on the working system. It had become corrupted somehow. Maybe it had happened when he'd created it—he'd been so panicked about not getting caught that he hadn't double-checked after it had been written. Maybe it happened when he'd been mugged outside the Hotel Ruby.

The screen in front of him flashed back to life. The computer had finished its calculations. Values swam across the screen as the general background noise of the lab cut through Bryson's meandering thoughts. He forced himself to focus on the output until the numbers stopped looking like gibberish.

Without the information on the chip, he had to recreate his

experiments that had led to the data. In theory, the work should have been moving faster, but between trying to get the other people in the lab up to speed and his general feeling of malaise, it was slow going. The delays were turning Ms. Peters into a demon.

As if on cue, the inside airlock door opened and everyone stopped talking.

Bryson didn't turn around to see who it was; only one person had that effect. Instead, he leaned closer to the screen and started tracing columns of numbers with his middle finger. It was his way of giving it to Ms. Peters without, hopefully, her catching on.

The sound of high heels clicking on the raised tiles of the floor stopped behind him. The blood in Bryson's veins turned to ice as the constant fear he lived with ratcheted up a notch. He kept his eyes on the screen.

"Mr. Searls."

The calm voice cut through the silent room like a knife. He let his hand drop and leaned back in his chair, rotating it to face her.

"Mr. Searls," she said again. "My experts say this chip was purposely scrambled. Made that way to stop anyone from being able to read it."

She held the chip between her thumb and forefinger, arm stretched out to where she almost touched his face. Bryson jerked back, rolling the chair into the desk so it pushed through the webbing and into his spine.

"You have nothing to say, Mr. Searls?"

"I . . . I didn't do it." He couldn't keep the whine out of his voice and hated himself for sounding so scared. "It wasn't me."

Ms. Peters arched an eyebrow as if considering what he had said. "No? Then who did it, Mr. Searls? Perhaps someone took it from you, scrambled it, and put it back in your pocket without you noticing?"

"I told you about the mug—"

"We followed up on that. It was just a mugging, plain and simple. The nitwit that did it didn't have the brains for anything more."

Bryson noticed the use of past tense in her words and tried to hide the shiver that went through his frame. What had she done to him? "It could have happened at the restaurant. The old Chinese guy—"

"We don't think so. There wasn't any equipment on-site that could do this kind of damage, and they didn't have the time to take it with them. No, Mr. Searls, we believe you did it before you left the Kadokawa lab. That means you can unscramble it. What is the key?"

"I didn't . . . I wouldn't . . . it wasn't me."

"We'll see." She beckoned over her shoulder and the two guards at the airlock moved to Ms. Peters' side. "Bring him with us."

The guards advanced, and before he could stand on his own, they grabbed his upper arms and hoisted him from the chair. Bryson barely got his feet under him before they dragged him back to the airlock. Ms. Peters was already waiting for them, an impatient look on her face. The door opened at their approach and she spun on her heels to lead the way into the small airlock. He was hauled after her.

As the airlock door closed, one of the guards reached for a cricket bat leaning against the wall. The guard didn't turn, didn't make any excess motion, but Bryson's insides turned to mush. His face flushed with shame as warm fluid ran down his legs.

LOS ANGELES LEVEL 4—MONDAY, JULY 3, 2141 2:23 P.M.

I drove the truck down the ramp, going as fast as I dared without drawing too much attention. It still felt like I was on the edge of losing control as the walls flashed past the windows. The body beside me, now half on the seat and half on the floor, shifted again, wedging against the dashboard. I risked a peek. His neck was bent at a weird angle, smashed against the dash, and was the only thing stopping the body from sliding all the way down. Bile rose in my throat. I swallowed it.

The bright lights of the ramp's exit came into view and I dragged my attention back to the road. As the truck made the transition to level ground and the walls disappeared, I glanced around the cab, avoiding the passenger side. A worn picture sat jammed into a crack on the dashboard, right beside the built-in comm unit. Smiling back at me were the cheery faces of a young boy and girl. I tore my gaze away from the picture when the comm unit built into my helmet crackled to life. I answered it.

"Drive three more blocks to Cant Street. Turn left and head for the transfer elevator."

I did as I was told. The elevator's doors were wide open. I slowed as I approached and was waved in.

Transfer elevators were only supposed to be used by people and emergency vehicles; no other traffic was allowed. It felt wrong to drive right in, but I followed the instructions. The only other time I'd taken one of these had been with Ian, when he'd saved me from Meridian's assassin, Quincy, almost a year ago. Back then we'd ridden in on his motorcycle and gone from Level 2 to Level 4. This time, I was the one driving, and we were heading in the opposite direction. I made sure to keep my visor down to hide my face from the cameras in the elevator. I wasn't sure the insurgents had disabled them, or had the ability to do it.

The elevator ride gave me a chance to examine the picture again. Was the man I'd pulled from the truck's cab their dad? Would two kids be without a parent because of what we had done? There wasn't supposed to have been any shooting. There weren't supposed to have been two people in the truck in the first place, and definitely not one with a gun. They'd brought it on themselves.

I felt bad even thinking it.

Still, we had families to feed as well. We had sick children who weren't getting the medication and the food they needed. What we were doing was right . . . wasn't it?

Ever since the war had started, those of us on the lower levels had paid the price. If we were healthy enough to fight for the corporations, we were pulled off the streets in massive sweeps and drafted. Our kids were left as alone and scared as the truck driver's kids would be if he ended up dying.

It didn't make what we had done to get the food right, but it sure as hell didn't make it wrong either.

The elevator doors opened up behind me, and I slammed the truck in reverse. The cab hadn't even cleared the doors when there was a knock on the window. This guy I recognized. I'd seen him wandering the halls at the building the insurgents used for a base camp. I didn't know his name. I rolled down my window.

"I'll take over from here," he said.

I put the truck in park and opened the door. As I slid off the seat I grabbed the picture of the kids and shoved it into my pocket. If the driver died, maybe there would be something I could do for them.

"Your bike should be here in a few minutes. Thanks for taking over up there. Our backup was too far away to help quickly."

They weren't backup if they were too far away. Before I could respond, he jumped in and drove back into the elevator. The doors began to close and I skipped between them as they clanged shut. I had no idea where the food was going, or how it was to be distributed, but I hoped it would end up in the right place. Where it was needed most. That's what the insurgents were supposed to be about, helping the people.

As promised, someone rode up on my bike and parked around the corner from the elevator. I got on and started the ride back to my room. The blood on my pants had hardened into a shell, and I desperately wanted a shower. I knew I wouldn't get one. The best I would get was a bit of water and a cloth. We'd all rather stink than die of dehydration.

I wished I could have stayed with the truck, to see where it went. There was no point to it, really, but it was a strong urge. I'd learned to not trust people in charge over the last year. First, I'd been sold out by Dispatch, my old boss when I was a courier. Even if she hadn't really been aware of it, she'd still allowed herself to be manipulated by Quincy. And paid for it. After that I'd blindly followed ACE, going through the training and indoctrination, only to be betrayed by them as well.

No one had known Jeremy was at the head of ACE, no one except William and maybe a few others. It didn't matter. Because of ACE, because of the rot that had started the whole damn thing, Ian was dead. The fact that ACE was gone now, destroyed by their own decayed core, didn't make it any better.

I wasn't going to let something like that happen again. The insurgents and I seemed to be on the same side now, but if I even saw a hint of what ACE had become, I would be gone. I didn't know if I could deal with it again.

I rode my bike into the inter-level parking for our building and left it in my assigned spot. The place they'd given me was better than the one I had last time I lived on Level 2, but not by much. At least the bed was more comfortable than the ones at boot camp.

As I climbed the last set of stairs to my fourth-floor room, what I had done finally cut through the anger I always carried with me. What if the drones had seen me get off my bike and pull the driver from the truck? I'd had my helmet on, and I'd changed my ID, but could they trace the bike? And what if the driver had tried to shoot me? Would I be lying on the street in a pool of my own blood instead of him?

What scared me more was that I wasn't sure I cared, except for the baby.

LOS ANGELES LEVEL 2—MONDAY, JULY 3, 2141 2:47 P.M.

Pat could see Kris tense, start to build the wall that had kept her and Kai so far away since Ian Miller had died. She swept down the short hallway outside Kris's room and pulled her into a tight hug, trying to take some of her pain into herself. It wasn't going to work, it never would, but it was what Kris needed. A friend, someone that was there for her. They stood by Kris's door, holding onto each other as if their lives depended on it.

When Kris had finally relinquished control of the truck to another driver, Pat had excused herself from the situation room. She wasn't supposed to be there in the first place. If Jack, the guy in charge of this insurgent cell, had seen her there, she would have been kicked out.

It was bad enough that Kris had insisted on getting back into the field, but when she'd been given a part in the second hijack attempt, Pat had gotten angry. When Kris had taken over the driving of the truck, Pat's anger changed to fury.

Dammit, the girl wasn't even eighteen yet, and she'd lost everybody she ever cared for. Miller had been—still was—the worst loss of them all. Pat didn't even want to think about what it was like to lose your first love like that, and then blame it on yourself. And that was the problem.

What had happened wasn't Kris's fault. It wouldn't have mattered what she did, whether she had decided on the solo or group rescue or to let Miller defend himself, the end result would have been the same. There was nothing Kris could have done to change it, though she'd gotten damn close.

Something else was going on as well. Back at camp Kris had always been the first one to get up in the morning. She'd head out to the cliffs and climb until the rest of the camp had woken up. Now, she locked herself in her room until late in the morning, and when she finally emerged, she looked like shit.

If Pat didn't know better, she would have thought Kris was pregnant. Hell, she did know better. But it didn't matter. Everything pointed to the same conclusion. If it was true, why hadn't Kris told her? Because she was still a kid. She didn't have the tools to know how to deal with it. Hell, most adults wouldn't.

She was in no state to send out on a mission of any kind. That was the reason Pat and Kai had agreed to look for Bryson, to make sure Kris wasn't heading out on her own. To keep an eye on her. That hadn't worked out too well.

Once Kris had her mind set on something, it was tough to change. She was like a dog with a favorite toy, clamping its jaws down tight and fighting with anyone who tried to take it. The problem was, if the dog lost the toy, it could always get another one. If Kris lost her life, that would be it. Some days, Pat was pretty sure that was what Kris wanted, and the thought scared her.

On days like today, the fear only enhanced the anger.

Pat had been ready for a confrontation, ready to yell and scream, to plead with Kris. Take some more time. Get help. Wounds like this don't heal in two weeks. And Pat knew that some never healed. But when Kris had walked out of the stairwell, she'd looked beaten and tired and worn out. There was blood on her jacket and pants. Her helmet swung from her fingertips, looking like it would to slip off and smash onto the floor.

Kris was the first to break off the hug. Her eyes were puffy and some of the dried blood from her coat had flaked off and transferred to Pat's shirt. She brushed off the flakes absently.

"I can stay with you for a while, if . . ."

Kris shook her head. "I just want to get cleaned up, you know. Get into some fresh clothes and maybe lie down for a bit."

Pat knew how Kris felt. There'd been times—but now was not the place for those memories. Now she needed to be here for Kris.

"Will you come down for dinner?" Pat gave a small smile. "We have fresh vegetables."

"I thought that was meant for the families . . ."

Pat saw a flicker of fight in Kris's eyes, a bit of the old Kris coming back. "It is, but we have to eat too. We're no use to anyone if we don't stay healthy. Some of it stayed here, but most of it went back out. I don't think it was enough." She almost said it was good for the baby if Kris ate well.

Kris just nodded and moved to her door.

"So, we'll see you at dinner?"

She leaned her head against the doorframe, and for a moment, Pat didn't think she was going to get an answer.

"Yeah, I'll be there."

Pat put a cheery tone in her voice, hoping it masked her concern. "I'll hold a seat for you!" She watched as Kris unlocked her door and closed it gently behind her.

That girl was in trouble.

LOS ANGELES LEVEL 2—MONDAY, JULY 3, 2141 2:57 P.M.

I shut the door behind me and leaned against it, my ear pressed to the thin material. I stayed there, not moving, until I heard Pat walk back down the hall. She meant well. She always did. At least this time she didn't try to tell me I wasn't ready, that I should take more time. I constantly wavered between thinking she was trying to control my life and that she was a good friend that I didn't deserve.

There were a lot of people dead because of me. Friends, family. People who meant even more than that to me. They were dead either because of something I had done, or something I had failed to do. I'd felt like this before, certainly not for the same reasons, but shitty enough that I wondered why I even bothered to stick around, breathing the recycled air and eating the limited food supply.

In the past, whenever I was in the dumps, I'd always ended up at Northern Dragon Chinese Cuisine. Kai's place. In the few years I'd known him, Kai had become like a grandfather to me. Someone who listened, only offered advice when it was asked for, and made me laugh no matter what the circumstances. That had all changed a couple of weeks ago. I'd found out how he knew my mom and dad, how he had been there when they'd been killed. He'd been their friend.

Through all the time I had called him a friend, he had never once told me. Never even hinted at it. At first I was mad, especially after I'd learned he'd run when my parents had been attacked. Then I realized I'd done the same thing to Ian, leaving him in the rubble for ACE—for Jeremy—to find.

After Ian died, Kai left on a mission for the insurgents while also starting a search for Bryson. Some days I missed Kai desperately, on others he was a faint memory in the back of my mind. Today was definitely one of the miss days. He'd been back; knocking on my door, asking if I was okay. I should have answered him, let him in. Instead I just rolled over in bed and ignored him. He could have tried harder.

Pat and I had become friends at the training compound, but

things had changed here in the city. When we talked, she would offer advice and cajole me into doing something. Usually something I didn't really want to do, and I'd cave in, not willing to put up a fight. It was probably what helped her to get through some of her worst times, but it wasn't what worked for me. I wasn't sure what did.

I drifted into the bathroom, forgetting I'd used all my water that morning. The empty bucket sat in the tub, waiting to catch a stray drip from the tap. I kept the place as clean as I could, but the dark gray ring around the tub from the room's previous occupants refused to come off. I tended to prefer showers anyway, but with the lack of water, all I got was the bucket. The mirror over the sink was cracked but still usable, the reflective coating peeling away from the back of the glass.

The water wouldn't turn on again until after dinner. Everybody would rush to their rooms when they finished eating and wait, their taps already open and maybe an extra bucket available, just in case the flow stayed on longer. It never happened. If we wanted to drink something, we'd have to head down to the kitchen and they'd give us a glass of tepid water or weak tea. Or send us back to our rooms with nothing. The only toilets that worked were on the first floor. Ours had no water, except what we were willing to spare from our buckets. I always tried to save a bit.

The bathroom still held onto the faint smell of vomit—my morning ritual since Ian had died. Maybe it had started before that, I couldn't really remember. It was difficult to remember anything from before. Some of the good times at boot camp shone through, like when he'd come to visit and we'd take off into the surrounding mountains. We'd bring climbing gear, but almost never used it. Every time those memories surfaced, I pushed them back down, deep inside the locked box in my head, where they couldn't hurt me anymore.

I missed the mountains and the freedom I'd had there. The

greenhouses had given me a small hint of that, but I wasn't sure when or even if I'd be able to get back there . . .

I stripped down, leaving my blood-encrusted clothes on the floor, and trudged naked to my bed. The sheets were still crumpled into a ball from this morning, the bed-making part of boot camp training disappearing faster than it had come. The sheets matched the walls and the ring on the tub. Gray on top of gray on top of more gray. I figured they must have been white at one point in their lives, but too many bodies and too many washings had taken that away. I pulled a couple of bobby pins from my hair and put them on the small bedside table.

Lying down, I untangled the sheets and pulled them up to my neck, shivering in the sudden chill, waiting for them to warm up. The mattress was soft. Maybe too soft, but at least it wasn't as lumpy as the compound ones. I sunk in and closed my eyes, resting my hands on my belly. The day's events rolled through my mind and I started tearing them apart. Security would be high after what we did today. We wouldn't be able to get another food truck until SoCal relaxed, which could be never.

There had been three of us on the original recon, each person strolling by the loading dock at different times and from different angles. I don't know if the other two had seen the addition of the passenger, or the guns. We hadn't been allowed to communicate with each other, only the hijack team. The woman touching me to get me back on track was a breach of mission protocol. If no one else saw it, she would be okay. If they had, she would probably be pulled from future missions for a short while. I didn't even know if I was the only one to follow the truck when it drove away. We really weren't much of a team.

I'd told the hijack group about the extra man and the possibility of guns. At least they'd been ready for that, or they were supposed to have been. Doubling back to watch everything go down had been my idea—I expected to be yelled at for that. In the end, everything had gone wrong. Three, maybe four dead. Two of ours and two of theirs. A backup team so far away they were useless.

The man I'd yanked from the truck had been alive, though I didn't know if he'd stayed that way. I'd have to remember to ask about him. Pat might know, especially if she had been in charge of this op. I don't think she was, though. She would have run a tighter operation, and chances were no one would have died. I didn't really know what she did here.

The picture of the two kids swam into my tired brain. I still had it in my jacket pocket. My guess was they were the driver's. Why else would the picture be there? I tried to recall his face, tried to remember how old he was, but once I left my bike, it was all a blur. I hoped he made it, for their sake.

Even though I hadn't pulled the trigger that killed those men, I felt responsible. I told myself this was war. The soldiers on all sides were pawns in the game created by their corporate masters. I was the same, just a pawn. We'd picked or been drafted onto our sides, forced to play by their rules.

The true fault really lay with them. The corporations. Even the insurgent leaders. They were all alike, really. Right now, today, the insurgents were where I wanted—where I needed—to be. The corporations were using and killing the people for their own purposes, and I couldn't stand by and let that happen.

Ian wouldn't have been able to either.

LOS ANGELES LEVEL 2—MONDAY, JULY 3, 2141 2:59 P.M.

Janice Robertson stood in the shadowed alley, hiding behind the heaps of garbage that hadn't been picked up for weeks. She'd almost gotten used to the overpowering smell that felt strong enough to burn holes into her lungs. She'd been here long enough to get a sore throat from it already.

The Ambient overhead had been flickering for days and had finally gone out this morning. Janice didn't care either way, except for the mild headaches she always got from being under the faltering light for so long.

The building across the street from her was a grime-covered dark gray. The thin vertical windows, each one with black stains under it from decades of neglect, gave it a shrouded, secure look. It was a mirror of the buildings to either side of it, and pretty much the rest of the block. The place gave her the creeps.

Despite the similarities, this building was different. Not in its structure or shape, but in the people that went in and out of it. Groups left looking as though they had a purpose or a goal, while most people in the lower levels appeared lost. This wasn't just another tenement on Level 2.

What had attracted Janice here in the first place was simple.

Kris.

Janice had heard about the food lines being set up throughout the lower levels of San Angeles. The closest one for her was in Level 2 Chinatown. They didn't ask questions, and they didn't care where you came from. If you were hungry, they would feed you. That was where she had first seen Kris.

The time between her failed attempt to kill Kris two weeks ago and seeing her at the Chinatown kitchen hadn't been good. Food had been scarce, to the point where she'd fought to eat out of garbage cans. She'd even robbed people on Level 5, looking for anything she could trade for food. She had considered getting caught in SoCal's draft sweeps just so she could get a meal and a bed to sleep in. She didn't know what stopped her from doing exactly that. She had nothing against killing for a living. It's what she had done for Jeremy for the last few years.

She'd succeeded in every mission he'd given her except one.

Kris was the reason she was here instead of on Level 6. Monitoring Kris at the ACE training camp would have finally given her enough money to live more than comfortably up there. She could have quit doing missions. She'd already picked out a nice apartment. It was on the top floor, but that didn't matter as much up there. Now she was stuck down here with no way to get past security, no way to get to the money she had saved. She was fucked.

ACE and Jeremy were gone. Both destroyed by Kris. Janice had found that out early enough. So there was no way to get more work, more money. Getting rid of Kris wasn't an ACE job anymore; it wasn't a Jeremy job anymore. It had become personal.

She'd been following Kris since the sighting in the food lines, mapping her movements and habits. Waiting for the right time.

Kris had ridden her motorcycle into the inter-level parking only moments before. Janice continued to hide behind the garbage, watching the dark windows for any sign of new activity. A light flipped on in one of the thin strips. The timing was late, but it was the first one on. The good thing was it was a window Janice had picked as Kris's, and on the fourth floor. The only other possibility was a room on the second floor, and Kris was too low-level a person to get a premium space like that.

Janice stayed in the shadows for another ten minutes before heading off to Chinatown. She crept deeper in the alley, sliding along the edge of the building, staying between the piles of moldy trash and the fibercrete until she was sure she was out of sight from the main strip. She moved a filthy mattress leaning against the wall to reveal a beat up old motorcycle. She had acquired it only a few days ago, knowing she would need something to follow Kris. Trying to chase a bike on foot was stupid with a capital S. The person who used to own it wouldn't need it anymore. They'd been beaten and robbed for whatever they had before she'd gotten there. She watched him die after she'd taken out two of his attackers. She let the third one get away, dragging a broken ankle. He'd never walk the same again.

She got on the machine and rode the side streets toward Chinatown.

Whatever was in the building she'd been watching, it couldn't have been too big. Janice had easily spotted a couple of guards, but nothing else. A corporation or ACE would have had lookouts in the alley and on the rooftops of the surrounding buildings. These guys had essentially nothing: a lone patrol on the roof that kept a predictable schedule. Amateurs.

Janice parked in a dark corner and walked into the glare of Chinatown. The neon was a constant, no matter what was going on. She pushed past the slow walkers, wanting to be near the front of the food line. It was always good to get into the lines early. The chance of getting more solids in the soup was higher. There weren't many people yet so she could pick her own line. That meant she could flirt with Jason again. Flirting got her more food.

KADOKAWA SAT CITY 2—MONDAY, JULY 3, 2141 3:00 P.M.

Andrew Ito strode into his war room with a confidence he didn't feel. It wouldn't do to show the men what he thought about the war Kadokawa had entered. He had been assigned to his role only a few short weeks ago.

His predecessor had been "let go" in a most unceremonious manner. He had been stripped of his rank and dishonorably discharged. Andrew didn't want to make the same mistake. He didn't want to end his career the same way. Yet what he was being asked to do wasn't what he had signed up for. It wasn't the Kadokawa way.

The loss of the quantum scientist had been a huge blow to Kadokawa. Even though they still had his data and his team, no progress was being made. They remained at a deadlock where, no matter what they did, the outcome on living brain tissue was the same. Whoever they sent through a quantum jump would end up dead.

He knew they had a working jump drive, as long as they didn't transport anything they wanted alive on the other side. That had been proven by Meridian before Kadokawa's hostile takeover. So, instead of trying to fix the jump drive, he switched the team to work on shielding technology. If he could protect the passengers during a jump, it would be a big win to the corporation.

His changes to the Sat City's security had turned the orbiting station into an operational military base. It hadn't taken much. Most of the nonessential personal had been shipped off-site and replaced with military staff, though a few family members had stayed behind. He was working to get them off the satellite as soon as possible. Anyone associated with the jump drive was monitored and escorted by two armed soldiers whenever they weren't in the lab.

At least Andrew had inherited a worthy Sat City. Before Meridian's demise, they had spent huge sums of money on building a larger fleet and adding tremendous amounts of shielding to the city itself. Shielding they hadn't had to use since he'd been here. His teams had tried to pin the single vessel attack on SoCal, but no proof had been found.

Acquiring Meridian and its assets had immediately brought Kadokawa into the war as an aggressor. A massive leap from their usual role as protectors and humanitarians. Since he had taken over, things had escalated from occasional skirmishes with SoCal to prolonged attacks. None of them affecting the city.

Yet.

Lines had been drawn in the proverbial sand and all-out war was only days away. SoCal had attacked Kadokawa's mines on Mars, and Kadokawa had responded in kind. It would take years to bring the mines back up to capacity. But the damage to Kadokawa's reputation could take decades to repair.

Every schoolchild was taught what happened in the last war they'd fought. It had led to the 1947 constitution, in which Japan renounced war as a tool. It was that constitution that had helped form the Japanese military that Andrew had joined. One that was known for its humanitarian goals, for its willingness and ability to help others, no matter what the issue.

Their attack on Meridian had changed all that.

IBC had remained strangely silent. Early on they'd sided with SoCal, going so far as to have the president of the United States stand beside SoCal and declare his dismay at the attacks on the San Angeles water stations. Since the president was owned by IBC, that was a clear signal as to whose side they were on, but they had made no move after that.

Someone in Operations had finally noticed his presence and announced him.

"*Kaishō-ho* in the room."

The men and women not involved in any immediate tasks stood and saluted.

"At ease," Andrew said. "*Kaisa* Mori, what is our current status?"

"We remain at full alert, *Kaishō-ho.* SoCal is maintaining the same number of spacecraft at the front line. They continue to observe us from a distance, but do not dare approach."

"Have we monitored any quantum jumps?"

"None, sir. All vessels portray standard characteristics."

"Good. Expand our perimeter by another thousand kilometers.

Our leaders have asked us to show these *gaijin* that we only tolerate them. Barely." Andrew did his best to hide the revulsion he felt at repeating the order, the choice of words used.

The captain bowed. "Yes, *Kaishō-ho.*"

Andrew watched a screen as the orders were carried out. Expanding the Sat City's borders was completely unnecessary, but he'd ordered it for two reasons. The first and most obvious was to keep poking at SoCal. He'd been ordered to keep them concentrating on what happened here. The more they focused on his station and not on the troops heading out to reinforce the Martian mines, the better the potential outcome. The second reason was to test his captain. He was new at his position and Andrew wanted to find out what kind of soldier he was.

The existing ships expanded their circle, pushing the SoCal forces farther away. When new Kadokawa ships appeared on the display, sent from the Sat City to fill the holes created by the expanding sphere, he allowed himself a tight smile. *Kaisa* Mori knew how to do his job.

Andrew stayed in the room for a few more minutes, observing how Mori handled his team. He didn't need to be there. Meridian had installed surveillance in every corner so that he could watch from his office, but experience had taught him that the people under him reacted differently when he was in Operations than when he was out. Frankly, he was surprised his predecessor hadn't removed the cameras.

When he was away, *Kaisa* Mori ran a more casual room. Talking and moving around was limited, but the people at their stations were relaxed. They still responded to orders quickly. Andrew needed to know if they would react even better under pressure, and with the standoff between the two forces, the only pressure he could provide was his presence.

He turned back to the exit, and as the door opened for him, he sensed the atmosphere in the room change.

This city was ready for war, and his confidence in *Kaisa* Mori had gone up a notch.

Now it was time to check up on the new shielding for the quantum drive.

LOS ANGELES LEVEL 6—MONDAY, JULY 3, 2141 4:02 P.M.

Kai breathed a sigh of relief. He was finally getting somewhere. All it took was to push Kris from his thoughts for half a day so he could concentrate on the task at hand. He felt guilty as hell about it.

Still, it had worked. Doc Searls had finally agreed to help them. He was a great first acquisition. The number of people he had seen in his role as one of ACE's doctors would be a boon to the insurgents. A decade ago, they would not have needed him. Kai's ACE contacts would have been better. But years away from the organization had lowered his value in the area.

Getting Doc Searls still felt like a hollow victory.

Leaving Kris behind was one of the hardest things he had ever done, and he couldn't get the thought out of his head that it was probably the stupidest. She was still in shock and in pain from the failed attempt to get Miller. She probably believed it was all her fault as well. It was easy to forget how young she was sometimes. How she did not have the life experiences to enable her to cope with the kind of pain she was dealing with. Then again, maybe age did not matter.

He should have stayed, no matter what she had said. Even though she did not know it, what she really needed was a friend, not someone who would abandon her when times got tough.

You would figure someone as old as he was would know that.

Now that the first stage of his job was done, he could go back. This time he would not leave until he knew she was ready to deal with the loss.

At least she still had Pat. He sighed again. Kris and Pat had become close during their time together at the ACE training compound, but he was not sure it would be enough. What Kris needed was a shoulder, a helping hand. He saw Pat as more of a take-command type of person. She would probably try to get Kris to talk to a counselor or therapist, try to tell her how to move on. Get past it all.

That was all fine, but it was not what Kris needed. It was not how she dealt with pain and loss and suffering. There would be plenty of time for that later, after she had come to terms with what had happened. She needed time.

Unfortunately, time was a luxury they didn't have. The war was picking up speed. Soon it would reach its tipping point. Other corporations would join in. Sides would be chosen, alliances made and destroyed.

They would be lucky if anyone made it through this time.

He downloaded a newspaper onto his pad and found a place to sit. It was a small corner park with real grass and two trees. He could hear birds singing, probably piped in and played in a loop.

Newspapers, hell, news media of any kind, weren't allowed below Level 6. It was SoCal's way of keeping its citizens in the dark, under control. Even broadcasts were cut off, both comm units and vid screens. The best he could do was look for important articles, memorize them, and pass them on. Taking pictures was out of the question. SoCal had started checking comm units and pads a few days back. It was still a random check, but when the whispers had started moving back through the line he had deleted them all.

The first article he read talked about the state of the rest of the country. The continent-wide drought continued, despite what the experts had predicted. On top of that, massive windstorms across the Dakotas and Minnesota all the way down to Texas had devastated entire crops. Food supplies were going to be a lot thinner, and the prices would skyrocket. No one above Level 5 would even notice, but everyone else would.

Water shortages continued. SoCal had tried to buy more from the east coast, but they refused. Everyone was feeling the pinch in the middle of summer, but no one as bad as San Angeles. The insurgents destroying the pumping stations had hurt them, not that you could tell if you were on Levels 6 or 7. Repairing the damn things was taking too long. SoCal would rather put time and effort into a war than into their own city. Their own people.

So far the war seemed to have stayed between SoCal and Kadokawa. There had been some small fights around the Sat cities. According to the paper, they had all been started by Kadokawa. He had never seen them as the aggressor, but then he had never expected them to take over Meridian.

The last article he read mentioned the fighting on Mars. Again, it had been started by Kadokawa. They had tried to take over SoCal's mines and failed. Casualty counts on the Kadokawa side were high.

It was all bullshit. All propaganda. When you controlled the news and what was allowed into the city, you controlled the population. He couldn't decide what was worse, the total blackout of the lower levels or the lies up here.

He erased the paper from his pad and began the long walk to Level 2.

LOS ANGELES LEVEL 2—MONDAY, JULY 3, 2141 5:35 P.M.

I lay in bed until dinnertime, not wanting to move or see people, wishing I could just stay here forever. The effort to remain pleasant would have taken too much out of me. I may have dozed off for a while, but it didn't feel like it. Exhaustion pulled at my bones, making it tough to find the energy to crawl out of bed. I knew I shouldn't feel this way. I hadn't done anything that would make me this tired. I sighed and kicked the sheets off, forcing myself to get up and take the three steps to my small dresser. In the drawers were a couple of shirts and my last pair of clean pants. At least I had extra underwear. With water at a premium, the insurgents had set up a laundry service. More clothes in less water was their idea. I should be getting some washed clothes back tomorrow or the next day. I was pretty sure if I asked loud enough, I could get extra pants. Especially since I had saved their hijacking plan for them. I got dressed and put the bobby pins back in my hair, buried deep where they couldn't be seen.

I stood by my door listening to the footsteps and the sound of people chattering just outside as they walked to the dining hall. There was laughter and the occasional shout. Life as it should be, considering the circumstances. I dragged myself upright and straightened my shirt. All I had to do was imitate what other people were doing long enough to make it through dinner. I had to try, or Pat would end up pounding on my door wondering why I hadn't kept my promise. I didn't want to go, didn't want to lose it in front of everyone, to lash out at the first thing that hurt me, or worse, see or hear something that reminded me of Ian and break down. That wouldn't be good for anyone.

Missions like the hijacking were easy. I could do my job and not have to interact with people.

When the noises in the hall subsided, I opened the door and merged with the few remaining stragglers. I stared at the feet of the person ahead of me as I walked, attempting to avoid conversation or the inevitable look of sympathy or "how are you doing?" They meant well, but they weren't helping.

Everyone seemed to know me. Or know *of* me. I was the girl that left her team behind to rescue her boyfriend. I was the one that got him killed.

The stairwell was still packed with bodies, and the lack of water created a certain ripeness in the air that filled the enclosed space. I tried to step off to the side, to let the people behind me get through first. Then I could wait until the mass was thinner before I got into the dining hall. I fought the urge to go back to my room.

A hand grabbed my elbow, stopping me from getting out of line.

"Hi, I'm Selma. I was with you on the recon today."

I didn't recognize her.

"You were a little lost out there. I hope you didn't mind me getting your attention. I know it wasn't protocol, but we really needed your eyes. Robert and I both missed the guns you reported. You helped save lives."

"We lost two of ours. Their driver was alive when I pulled him from the truck."

"Yeah. I heard we got him to a walk-in clinic. They shipped him off to a hospital for surgery. He should make a full recovery." Selma shrugged. "I know we're not supposed to care what happens outside our area, but I hate not knowing. Even if we save the life of someone working against us, it makes me feel good, you know?"

For the first time, I looked—really looked—at Selma's face. She was older than me, but still young. Maybe in her twenties. I thought she was making fun of me, or trying to taunt me into an argument, but I didn't see anything in her eyes except honesty and relief. I smiled my first genuine smile in weeks. "Yeah, I do." It felt good to find someone that thought like I did, and my guard came down a notch.

If the insurgents had more people like Selma, especially at the top, things might turn out all right after all. Heck, having more like her in the ranks wouldn't hurt either.

By the time we reached the bottom of the stairs I knew more about Selma than I knew about most people. She had almost gotten married, but her fiancé had been caught up in one of SoCal's draft sweeps. She had managed to get away, but just barely. She'd been holding onto his hand the whole time, but when she turned around to pull him along faster, it was someone else—an older woman. The woman had stopped Selma from running back into the crowd, stopped Selma from being drafted along with him.

That's when she had joined the insurgents. Her goal was to get close enough to SoCal to find her fiancé and get him out. I wished her well, knowing it would never happen. Chances were he was long gone, either in training or already deployed somewhere. If she was lucky, he'd make it and come home to her after the war.

"You know they have quotas to fill?" she asked.

"Quotas?"

"Yeah, the SoCal soldiers. I heard if they get their quota, the rest of the people are let go. If they miss, the soldiers are given an extra shift."

That was news to me. I'd thought they just grabbed as many as they could. It sounded like a hopeful wish, something for people to hold on to if they were caught.

When we entered the dining hall I stopped, searching for Pat and the seat she had offered to save me. Selma misinterpreted my hesitation.

"Come on, you can sit with us. I'll introduce you to Robert."

"No, I . . . I promised a friend I'd join her." I found Pat and pointed her out.

Selma's eyes went wide, and it was as though her face melted.

"Oh," she said. "Oh. You're *that* Kris. I . . . I'm sorry for rambling on like that. I . . . I'm so sorry for your loss."

The will to stand was sucked out of me. For the first time since Ian had died, I'd lowered my defenses and Selma hit me with a hammer. My knees buckled and tears threatened to fall again. For a few moments, Ian had touched me and then been yanked away.

Selma stepped closer, placing a shoulder under my arm before I fell. The room blurred. I struggled to breathe as grief rolled over and through me. I felt myself maneuvered out of the way. A wail built in my chest and I clamped my lips tight, forcing it back down.

Not here. Not now.

My hands shook so badly that Selma grabbed them, wanting to hold them still. She stuttered out a few words, soft, quiet. I didn't hear them.

Demons thundered through my head, grabbing at memories of Ian—our first kiss, the lingering touch of his fingers on my skin—and shredded them before tossing them in shattered heaps back where they had found them. At some point, I felt the presence of Pat.

"Let's get her out of here," Pat said.

She put her arm around my waist and walked me to the exit. Selma trailed behind, not quite sure what to do. People stepped out of our way, staring uncomfortably at the floor as we passed, as though I was diseased.

"What happened?" Pat asked.

"I'm not sure," Selma said. "We were talking when I realized who she was. Then she started collapsing. I don't know. I must have triggered something. She was fine. I'm so sorry."

"Okay. Go get your supper. I'll take care of her. Talk to the cook and have Kris's meal brought up to her room. Please."

Pat didn't wait for a response. Selma faded away as Pat kept walking, supporting me back to the stairs. She didn't say a word.

I didn't have the strength to hold out any longer. The stairwell echoed with the sounds of my pain.

Pat brought me to my room, staying until the food came. I played with it more than I ate, pushing chunks of potatoes and carrots around until she thought enough had made it down my throat. She didn't try to talk to me, didn't try to convince me to get help. She just stayed with me, filling my bucket when the water was turned back on. Mostly we sat. At times it was an uncomfortable silence, and I almost wished she would go back to trying to help me.

She turned to face me before leaving, examining my face as though she could see through to my soul. "How long have you been pregnant?"

Cold fear clutched my heart, and I stuttered out a denial that even I wouldn't have believed. It felt like she had slapped me in the face. Thankfully, she didn't press the issue.

I locked the door behind her when she left and stumbled to bed, my feet dragging across the worn floor. I crawled under the covers without taking my clothes off.

SOCAL SAT CITY 2—MONDAY, JULY 3, 2141 2:45 P.M.

The room was small and quiet, except for the constant background hum of the satellite. The guards had followed Ms. Peters down a hallway to an elevator, gripping Bryson's arms until their knuckles turned white. He would have bruises in the shape of their fingers. The elevator had barely held the four of them. By the look of the narrow hall the doors had opened on, its walls covered in conduits and junction boxes and ventilation pipes, this was a place no one went. Not willingly. Even the air tasted stale and metallic.

Ms. Peters and the guards stood and watched as Bryson changed into dry pants and underwear from a shelf. He wasn't allowed any modesty. The shelf contained nine more pairs, plus an equal number of shirts. All in his size. He tried desperately not to dwell on the implications of that, but failed miserably. The cricket bat leaned against the far wall, beside a desk. Its presence chased away any embarrassment he might have felt changing in front of everyone. What was the point when they could beat him whenever they wanted?

When he was done, Ms. Peters turned to the guards. "Wait outside."

They left, leaving the bat behind, as she pointed to a folding chair leaning against the wall. For a brief moment, he had the crazy idea of grabbing the bat and smashing his way out. But if he did, what then? He had nowhere to go.

"Please, get the chair. Put it there, and sit."

Bryson almost ran as she lowered herself into a chair. She waited until he had done as she had asked, his hands shaking, the chair slipping in his grasp, memories of the last time he'd been questioned by her washing through his mind. Images of the guard and the cricket bat made his vision blur.

"As I told you earlier," Ms. Peters said, "the chip is scrambled. We will find the key eventually, but I thought I would give you a chance to speed up the process."

"You have the encryption key I used. I didn't do anything—" The words came out fast and jumbled.

"You know where lying to me will get you, don't you?"

"I'm not—I—" Bryson's gaze flicked over to the bat and then

studiously returned to Ms. Peters' face. He didn't want to think about that.

"What is the key, Mr. Searls?"

He looked straight at her, trying to appear as open and honest as he could. "I gave you everything."

Ms. Peters rose and perched lightly on the edge of the desk. She leaned in closer to him. He pushed himself deeper in his chair, his entire body suddenly hot and sweaty in the temperature-controlled air.

The chair folded in on itself and he lay sprawled on the floor, unable to inhale.

Ms. Peters stood over him as he struggled to regain control, passively watching his face.

"I don't believe you."

"Please, I'm telling you the truth," he cried.

She sat back in her chair and watched as Bryson picked himself up. Once he was seated again, a guard came in, placing a box in front of her before standing behind him.

"Do you know what this is?" she asked.

Bryson shook his head.

Ms. Peters open the box, revealing a tiny glass bottle and a syringe. Hands clamped onto his shoulders, holding him in his chair.

"This will help us get the truth out of you. There's no need to worry, the effects aren't permanent and only last a short while. Plenty of time to get what we want."

"Truth serum?" Bryson blurted out the words.

"No!" Ms. Peters laughed. "I would have thought someone as intelligent as you would know there's no such thing. This simply helps remove any inhibitions you have. You'll be fully cognizant of what is happening. You'll be able to understand any other inducements we may choose to use." She looked at the bat. "Let's begin, shall we?"

The guard moved an arm around Bryson's neck while the other

arm pushed down on his head. His world faded to gray and he felt a sharp prick on his arm before the guard let go.

She questioned him for another half hour before returning to her seat.

"You appear to be telling the truth, Mr. Searls."

He flinched as she grabbed the bat and walked past him, banging on the door.

"Bring him back to his work area."

The guards were as gentle taking him to his lab as they were in getting him to the room. Bryson didn't relax until he stepped through the airlock. All the tension was replaced with a self-loathing and hatred so intense it threatened to consume him. One day, he would take back what that woman had stolen from him. He didn't know how, and he didn't know when, but it would happen. Or he would die trying.

TWO

LOS ANGELES LEVEL 2—TUESDAY, JULY 4, 2141 12:07 A.M.

PAT STOOD IN the hallway. Kris's denial was proof enough. Damn Ian. He should have known better.

This was the first time she had seen Kris break down and cry, and it tore at her heart. Even though it was something Kris needed and should have done long ago, she wished it hadn't happened in public. Kris would never get over the loss of Miller if she couldn't, or wouldn't, let herself grieve. Someone as young as Kris shouldn't have to deal with something like this. Though it wasn't the first time.

Maybe she thought she was too strong to feel the pain. Maybe she thought it wasn't what people did. Pat remembered the story Kris had told back at the training compound on one of those long, cold winter nights when everyone else was asleep. Kris's parents had been killed and she had been thrown into a halfway house for over a week until they could find her aunt and uncle. A week where she had been left alone. No friends, no family. No shoulder to cry on. Just a dirty crumpled pillow in a smelly room filled with other rejects.

When her aunt and uncle had finally come to pick her up, they were no help, practically strangers to her. Her aunt had told her to stop crying, to get on with her life. They'd put her into a new school and made her work for her keep. How much of that was part of their own grieving process, Pat didn't know. It was no excuse though. No matter how unprepared you were for bringing a thirteen-year-old girl into your home, you figured it out. You helped them get over the pain and the loss, and to heal.

Pat snorted. She'd spent too much time with her own therapist. It didn't matter. She was right, and she knew it. Kris needed more support than Pat was able to give, someone who understood how the human psyche worked. Someone who could help.

Her comm unit beeped in her pocket and she pulled it out. The kitchen, most likely the cook looking for more supplies. A wave of anger swelled in her chest, and she immediately quelled it. She wasn't really mad, and certainly not at the head cook. She was disappointed.

When everything had settled down from the failed attempt to save Miller, she, Kris, and Kai had gone back to Doc Searls, promising to help him find his son. They'd arranged it so that Kris believed she would be a part of it, when really they wanted to give her time.

Maybe it had been a mistake.

After that, they'd returned to the insurgents, and been accepted into the ranks. It hadn't been easy, especially with Kris leaving everyone behind to rescue Miller. The insurgents had needed convincing from Kai to let them join.

They'd been split up almost right away. Kai had been sent off to see if there was anything they could salvage from ACE, human or otherwise.

Kris was given a room and left alone. They didn't trust her. Every interaction she'd had with them had turned out badly.

Pat had been assigned to the food detail. It was an important job, there was no doubt about that, but it wasn't where she had wanted to be. Working with Kris and Kai on Miller's rescue had proven that she had skills in high-level planning of black ops missions. She also learned that managing those ops had helped her PTSD. During the few days they'd spent on the rescue mission, her symptoms had dropped dramatically. It was the closest thing she'd seen to a miracle, considering how far out of control she'd gotten earlier.

She hadn't had any episodes since joining the insurgents, but then she hadn't encountered any of her regular stressors. The planning and monitoring of missions had created all the stressors that normally triggered her PTSD, but somehow being separate from the actual action allowed her to control her symptoms using the mental exercises her therapist had shown her. It wasn't perfect, not yet, but for the first time, she had seen the light at the end of the tunnel.

By placing her in charge of the food, the insurgents were taking that away from her.

She jammed the comm unit back in her pocket, ignoring the call for now. She would deal with it later. Right now, Kris needed all the friends she had. It was bad enough losing your first love like she did. It was even harder when you were carrying his child.

Time to get in touch with Kai and bring him back.

LOS ANGELES LEVEL 2—TUESDAY, JULY 4, 2141 5:09 A.M.

My dreams were of Ian, how his hand felt in mine, the scent of his skin after we made love. The dreams changed into nightmares as I watched him die all over again. As the early morning rolled around, the dreams shifted once more. I wasn't there when my mom and dad had been killed, but in my tortured sleep, I watched the men hit them with fists and boards and pipes until nothing was left.

The Ambients hadn't risen to their daytime levels when I jolted awake, tossing the sheets off me into a puddle on the floor, blurry images of Mom and Dad fading from view. I threw my legs over the side of the bed and stood. My comm unit showed it was a bit after five in the morning.

The water in the bathroom was cool. I dipped my cupped hands into the bucket and drank until it was half gone, using the rest to wash the sleep from my eyes. For the first time since Ian's death, I didn't use any water to wash puke down the toilet. The nausea was staying away, at least for now. When I was done, I left my room, closing the door quietly behind me. Uncertainty rose through me like a thick fog. I didn't know if I wanted to stay here or go out on my own.

The single guard at the parking garage entrance gave me a strange look as I rode out. I guess she wasn't used to seeing anyone leave this early. It bothered me that there was only one person here. Even I knew there needed to be more sentries placed around the building. Maybe there were and I just didn't see them.

Once I was on the street, I turned left, away from Chinatown. Away from anyone who might have known me, almost wishing I could just ride on forever. I had thought I wanted to get back to work, to get out there and help fight the corporations. I wasn't even sure I wanted to find Bryson anymore. All I wanted now was to be left alone.

As I was speeding past the alley across the street from the insurgents' building, movement in the shadows caught my eye. By the time I looked, the alley was behind me and I couldn't see anyone. Another homeless person searching for scraps in the garbage, I thought. Too proud or too weak to take the short walk to the

Chinatown food lines. I made a mental note that if I came back, I would try to find them and help. If they wanted it.

I had no idea where I was going. Up was the only certain thing. Level 1 had never been a place I wanted to be. Not willingly. A destination formed in my head, creeping out from my subconscious at first, then exploding with the sudden intensity of desperation. I wanted—I needed—to visit Ian. To rest against the tree we had buried him beside and just sit. To let the stillness of the forest sink into me. It would be my first time back.

It was still too early to get into the *shinrin-yoku*. All the public greenhouses closed for the night, and I'd have to wait a couple of hours before they opened for the day. I preferred to do that on Level 5.

I rode through Level 2 to an up-ramp as a light mist started falling from the ceiling. It was the only thing the lower levels had for weather. Level 7 would have to have had a full-on thunderstorm overnight for us to get anything. Would the insurgents try to collect any water? It wasn't good for drinking after it had filtered through all the crap above us, but it could be used for other things.

I missed the rain and the sun and the clouds, my time at the ACE compound. They reminded me so much of Ian. Maybe too much.

I shook my head to clear my thoughts and wiped the helmet's visor with the back of my hand, smearing the dirt around until I could see. With my mind made up, I headed for Level 5 to wait for morning to arrive, then sit with Ian for a while. After that, it would be time to move on. I couldn't live in the past forever. The world wouldn't let me.

As I hit the Level 4 up-ramp, two SoCal military vehicles tried to race ahead of me. I hit the throttle and the bike leaped forward, weaving between them. They pulled in behind me and stopped, blocking anyone else from coming up the ramp. One of the drivers jumped out and aimed a scanner toward me, yelling at me to stop and trying to read my tracker ID. I zipped around the corner before he had a chance. I slowed and thought about my options.

They couldn't know who I was, and chances were they didn't care. Still, I could feel the old paranoia setting in. It was Meridian and IBC that had wanted me, and Meridian was gone. That meant this was probably a generic spot check or sweep, and not about me. Maybe they had found out some boarders had taken over the ramp? Maybe they were waiting for them? I doubted it though. Boarders weren't worth the effort.

Maybe they were finally blocking access to the upper levels. A first line of defense before hitting the fortified approach to Level 6. It didn't make sense that they were doing it here. A Level 5 up-ramp would be easier to control . . . closer to reinforcements.

More likely it was another draft. It seemed a bit early in the morning for it, but what else could it be? I didn't have too much choice but to continue up. It didn't dawn on me until I was almost at the top that I didn't have anything to worry about. SoCal had blocked the up-ramp at the bottom. If they were planning something, it would happen on Level 4, not on the ramp. They were blocking a potential escape route.

A shiver swept through me and the bike wobbled. I had just missed being caught in a draft.

There was nothing at the top of the ramp, and I sighed in relief. I rode through the still-sleeping Level 4. More military vehicles sat at the bottom of the Level 5 up-ramp, but they weren't blocking the entrance. Huge prefab fibercrete walls sat on flatbeds, waiting to be deployed. The same kind they'd used to block the hole in the wall on Level 1. I rode past them, and they barely gave me a glance. The closer I got to the greenhouses, the more military and police I saw. The insurgents wouldn't be able to pull off another food heist, not for quite a while.

I slowed down, taking my time. When I rode into Pasadena, the Ambients had reached their full strength and people had started appearing on the sidewalks. I slid the bike into a spot behind one of the many restaurants, most of them closed, and waited for the doors to the *shinrin-yoku* greenhouse to open.

A motorcycle whipped past, too fast even for the nearly empty streets. I took a hasty step back onto the sidewalk. The idiot was going kill someone. On top of that, the rider didn't have a helmet on. All I saw was a flash of brunette hair. The bike leaned around a corner as the greenhouse across the street opened. I double-checked for traffic and crossed.

Walking through the doors yanked me back to the day Pat, Kai, and I had brought Ian's ashes in with us. The small box had been cradled in my hands and I'd been scared of dropping it. I had never felt so alone. This time, the deeper I moved into the trees, the more I felt him beside me, holding my hand. Leading me to where he lay. I took off my boots and walked across the grass barefoot, letting the conflicting feelings of love and loss and pain and remorse course through me. I didn't take a direct route to where we'd buried him, instead wandering in amongst the white trunks of birch until my racing heart slowed to a more manageable pace. When I reached Ian's tree, I almost felt at peace.

The heart I'd carved was still fresh. Sap had leaked out and covered the wound, giving the inside time to heal. The scar would always be there, but the tree itself would continue. I only hoped I would be able to do the same. My back slid down the smooth bark as I sat and closed my eyes, breathing in the calm that seemed to fill the man-made forest. Even the sounds of a city waking became muffled and distant.

I talked to Ian most of the morning, telling him about our unborn son and my daily nausea. About how I'd been fine this morning, and how maybe it was a sign of better days ahead. He listened in silence as I told him how I didn't want to—couldn't—deal with people and their sympathy. They were trying to help, but they didn't know how *I* felt, how *I* was trying to cope with losing him. With losing us.

When I got tired of hearing my own voice, I sat quietly with my eyes closed, remembering the good times we'd had. By the time I was ready to leave, I knew what to do next. That I was better than what I'd let myself become without him. I ran my fingers through the grass that covered his ash-filled box and moved my other hand to my belly. Ian was still with me, and he always would be.

I stilled a quiet laugh. What did normal girls my age do? Probably not sit and talk to their dead boyfriend. Or maybe they did.

I pushed myself into a standing position, leaning against the birch as the blood flowed back into my legs. My knees buckled from sitting so long, and the muscles tingled. I waited until things were normal.

Though it made me uncomfortable, I was heading back to the insurgents. They were the best chance for making the world a better place. But first, there were some loose ends I had to tie up. I needed to see Doc Searls and talk about his son, Bryson. The only way to do that was if he was in his Level 5 offices. Pat, Kai, and I had agreed to search for Bryson, but I hadn't done anything to help. I wanted Doc to know I cared, that I felt bad about losing Bryson that night.

I also wanted to find Kai. I'd treated him like shit the last time I'd seen him. He didn't deserve that.

I'd have to sit down with Pat and figure out what my next steps were, ask why she and Kai hadn't talked to me about Bryson. The conviction I'd felt after we buried Ian was still there, but it was tempered somehow. Pat was a good enough friend to help me with that.

I would have to tell her and the insurgents about my baby. Just the thought of it scared me.

I strode away from the tree, My connection with Ian lessened with every step I took, but I knew I'd be back as soon as I could. When I reached the gravel path, I pulled my boots on and tightened the laces. I was ready. Maybe for the first time since Ian had died. Like the tree, it would take time for me to heal, but it seemed as though the process had finally begun.

The doors to the greenhouse were barely behind me when I saw someone I hadn't expected. My breath caught in my throat.

Janice.

LOS ANGELES LEVEL 2—TUESDAY, JULY 4, 2141 5:52 A.M.

Much like every night since she'd figured out where Kris was living, Janice had watched from the alley across the street. The garbage could be made into a surprisingly comfortable mattress once you got past the smell. She'd managed to get a blanket off of Jason. He was just about ready to ask for more from her, she could feel it. Some things never changed. Even in times of great turmoil and stress, the human life cycle continued. Now it was time for her to decide whether to let him ask and use him for whatever he could offer, or dump him and cultivate another source of extra food.

No matter how comfortable the garbage pile felt at night, by early morning she'd had more than enough. Her back hurt in strange places, and the stench had become even more unbearable. She sat in the shadows with the blanket draped over her shoulders and watched the building Kris was in, keeping an eye on two windows in particular. Patience was the key. It always was on a stakeout. One day, a chance would come. Kris would head out alone or be too preoccupied with something, and Janice would be ready.

One of the windows lit up. It was the one on the fourth floor, only a few doors away from the stairwell and the exit into the parking garage. Janice's pulse quickened and she sat up straighter. Today might be the day. The light from the window flickered, proof that someone was moving around inside. When it turned off, she quickly folded the blanket and hid it a few steps down the alley. If it wasn't there later, she could always get another one.

Her heart raced when the sound of a motorcycle came from the garage. Janice moved to the front of the alley, still keeping to the shadows cast by the failed Ambient. As Kris's bike drove past her, she turned and ran to the street at the other end of the back lane and pulled the moldy mattress off her own bike. Her patience had finally paid off.

She checked the inside of her jacket again, patting the gun Miller had given her when the compound had been attacked. She didn't have many bullets left, but all she needed was one. It gave her an odd sense of satisfaction knowing she would kill Kris with that particular gun, almost as if that's what he had wanted. The bike pulled away from the curb, and she followed Kris to the up-ramp.

Janice hung back as far as she dared. This early in the morning, there wasn't a lot of traffic. Having another bike following you would be pretty obvious. When Kris hit the first ramp, Janice slowed down even more. Ramps were the best place for an ambush. The enclosed space once you reached the inter-level section didn't give you much of a chance to get away.

When she thought she'd waited long enough, Janice raced up the ramp, the back tire of her bike slipping on the greasy road created by the mist. A single taillight flashed up ahead—Kris hitting her brakes before turning. Janice surged forward.

The trouble started on Level 3. Kris zipped between two SoCal military trucks. They pulled in behind her motorcycle, blocking the Level 4 up-ramp.

Shit.

Kris was the least of her worries now. Janice could see only one reason the military would block access, and that was to prepare for another sweep, to find "volunteers" for their army. This wasn't good. She swerved left, the bike sliding in the loose, wet grit. She fought with the balance, jamming her foot to the ground and releasing the throttle, trying to keep the damn thing from slipping out from under her. The bike's rear tire tapped the curb and stood upright, coming to a complete stop before teetering and falling over.

Fear made Janice stronger, and she pulled the bike back up, starting to move before she was fully in the seat again. She couldn't get caught in a draft. Not now. Not when she was so close. Later, after she took care of Kris, she would most likely sign up, even if it was just to get three meals a day and a warm place to sleep. Unless she could find another way to get to Level 6. But now, she had a task to finish.

The front tire lifted off the road as she wrenched the throttle. In front of her, the telltale gray vehicles blocked the way ahead again. She was close enough to see about twenty people in uniform enter an apartment block. Apparently, it wasn't good enough to nab people off the street anymore.

Janice slammed on the brakes, throwing the weight of the motorcycle onto its front tire. She was turning before most of the weight had resettled onto the rear. A thin gap, still dark in the morning light, sat between two buildings. It was barely wide enough for the handlebars to fit. She didn't hesitate.

The bike squeezed through the narrow slot. Gray fibercrete whipped past Janice as she focused on keeping the bike steady, the walls only a handful of centimeters away on either side. She hit a mound of garbage and the bike wallowed and wobbled. Janice twisted the accelerator and kept on going.

Thirty meters later, the motorcycle shot out of the gap, exiting on a narrow street. Janice stepped on the rear brake, locking the tire, and swerved. The street was empty. To her right was the road leading to the up-ramp. It was blocked by military vehicles. She had made it past the blockade. The military had only barricaded a small section off, as though they had a particular goal or person in mind for this sweep.

The only problem was she'd also lost Kris.

She turned left, racing to the next closest up-ramp five kilometers away. It was an express to Level 5, but maybe that was for the better. Kris had been taking the most obvious route up, and Level 5 was as good a destination as any. The bike careened through the quiet streets.

The ramp exited a few blocks from the greenhouses in Pasadena. There was no point in looking for Kris anymore. The number of different routes she could have taken, the number of different destinations, would make it impossible. A few weeks ago, she would have asked Jeremy or ACE for help. Now she was alone. Last time she'd seen Kris up here, she'd been at the other end of the greenhouses. It was worth a shot.

People started appearing on the sidewalk, the early ones that were so full of energy that they had to be up and about. Disgusting, really. She'd never understood the need for early mornings, unless a mission called for it. She slowed down, not wanting to draw too much attention to herself.

With the end of the greenhouses in sight and less than a kilometer to the next down-ramp, Janice decided to wait. There'd been no sign of Kris. This was as close as she was likely to get to Level 6 for a long time, so she might as well enjoy it. She left the main strip, hoping to find a plug-in for the bike. It was getting a little low on power. Behind one of the closed restaurants she saw something she hadn't expected. Kris's motorcycle. Instead of plugging in, she headed back to the main strip. The greenhouses hadn't opened yet, and that meant Kris might still be on the street.

Janice circled the block a few times before she found her. Up ahead, a small figure stood outside one of the cafes that were opening their doors. The figure wore the heavier jacket of a motorcycle rider. Janice turned her face away so Kris wouldn't see it when she passed. At the next corner, she hung a left and stopped.

The question was, what to do next? The approach she had used a couple of weeks ago wouldn't work, since ACE was gone. A surprise attack was the best. As long as Kris knew who was killing her.

Janice rode her bike closer to where she'd seen Kris and parked it, ready for a quick getaway. She still had enough battery left to get somewhere safe if everything went to hell. If it went well, she would take Kris's bike. It was better than hers, anyway.

Drones flitted across the ceiling thirty-five meters above her head, and police and military vehicles were everywhere. Something must have happened here recently to warrant all this. It would make her job tougher.

She forced herself to believe it didn't matter. She was sure she could get the job done and be out before anyone noticed. The public greenhouses themselves were unprotected. Their enclosed ceilings would block the drones, so all she would need to worry about would be other people. The worst-case scenario would be collateral damage. She could live with that.

Janice stood in the shadows as Kris entered the greenhouse filled with trees. Once she was out of sight, Janice edged closer to the door and peered inside. She couldn't see Kris. It would be best to wait here until Kris came out, rather than go in after her and possibly be ambushed.

The wait was longer than she'd expected. Most of the morning had passed before she saw Kris moving through the trees, obviously lost in her own thoughts. Janice stepped in front of her as Kris left the structure.

"Back inside," Janice said.

Kris stared at her. Janice took a step forward, the barrel of the gun pushing against the material of her jacket. Kris glanced down and then back at Janice's face.

"Why?"

"Because I have a gun, you imbecile."

Kris stumbled back. "No, why are you doing this? I never did anything to you."

"I'm just doing my job. Now back inside."

A police cruiser passed by them. Neither Kris nor Janice moved.

"Fine. I'll shoot you here."

Kris bolted into the greenhouse, turning the corner as soon as she cleared the entrance. Janice followed a split second later, the closeness of her target making her throw caution out the window. She made it two steps in before she was clotheslined by Kris's outstretched arm. The impact threw her and she landed flat on her back, the gun falling a meter away.

KADOKAWA SAT CITY 2—TUESDAY, JULY 4, 2141 6:02 A.M.

Fighter craft hung in space, poised to strike. They'd moved into attack formation as Andrew ran into Operations. "Details," he shouted as he closed the last button on his uniform.

"They haven't made a move yet. I've ordered our fighters to prepare," Mori said.

"Have we launched anything for support?"

"Squadron 7 is launching now." As Mori spoke, the SoCal fighters moved.

"How long till they get there?"

"Less than two minutes."

Dammit. This would be over in two minutes. "Bring in our closest fighters."

"Yes, sir." Mori relayed the orders to the pilots.

The attack was blindingly fast. Before reinforcements could arrive, Kadokawa had lost two ships while only crippling one of SoCal's. In all, the skirmish had lasted fifty-three seconds.

"They're withdrawing, sir."

Andrew watched the screens.

"Sir?" asked Mori.

Andrew's shoulders slumped almost imperceptibly. "Let them go. Keep Squadron 7 out there for now. If SoCal makes another move I want three squadrons launched immediately. And double the number of fighters on the perimeter."

"Yes, sir."

"Look for survivors."

"Yes, sir." Mori answered in a softer voice.

They both knew there wouldn't be any.

Andrew understood this was only a test of their perimeter. SoCal now had more accurate data on how long it would take them to launch . . . how long they had before the numbers were balanced. It was over for now. They wouldn't plan another attack until all the data had been analyzed by their experts.

"I'll be in my office." He left Operations, heading to the reports on his desk.

SOCAL SAT CITY 2—TUESDAY, JULY 4, 2141 8:11 A.M.

Bryson stepped out of the shower and grabbed a towel from the rack. SoCal had given him a small suite two floors above his lab. Most of the other lab workers had rooms here as well. They were all kept inside by locked security doors and only got out when SoCal wanted them out. The only difference between this prison and the one at Kadokawa was the constant security that led him everywhere. It was obvious, to him at least, that they didn't want him out in the population. The more cut off he was from the outside world, even just the world of the Sat City, the less chance he had of planning or trying to escape.

The idea made him snort as he dried his hair. He'd lived on Meridian Sat City for a long time before Kadokawa took it over. He knew the ins and outs of the place pretty darn well. It would take him months, if not longer, to get the same knowledge here. SoCal wasn't quite as dumb as Kadokawa though. He doubted that he would ever be alone, even if they did let him out. The girl that had rescued him at the hotel had told him everyone was monitored. For all he knew, the same sensors that tracked people in San Angeles could be installed up here as well.

No, his chances of getting out of here were about zero.

His daydreaming and delaying of the work had gone on as long as he thought was possible. Ms. Peters was starting to get furious and the guards a little rougher every time he came into contact with them. Even thinking of them, of the violence and pain they could bring, made him woozy. The problem was, he wasn't getting the same results he'd seen at his old lab. Sure, things were way better with the shielding than without, but there was something different with the engines or shields that changed their effectiveness. Something they had done during the earlier tests at Kadokawa that changed the way the engine reacted with nonquantum objects. At least that's what he thought.

Bryson couldn't remember what the difference was. His old team on Kadokawa had gone through so many different iterations, he couldn't recall what state the engines had been in when he'd run his original tests. He'd already made the changes that gave the incredible results weeks ago, but they hadn't worked here. It was some combination of his earlier work that had done it. What he really needed was access to the data on the chip he had made.

He'd considered that maybe Ms. Peters was actually able to read the chip, that she was waiting for him to duplicate the experiment to prove the shielding worked. He threw out that idea fairly quick. The longer he took to come up with answers, the more irritated she became, to the point of injecting him with who knows what. And it was in SoCal's best interest to get a ship running as quickly as possible. The quicker they had one, the sooner the war would be over. There was a chance she had another team working on the project, using the data from the chip, but that didn't make much sense either. He plucked the comm unit off the wall and waited. It only connected with one device.

"Yes," Ms. Peters said.

Even the sound of her voice sent a spark of fear through him. "I . . . I need the data on the chip. I can't duplicate the engine configuration that I originally tested with. What I have should work, but it doesn't, not really."

"What do you mean, not really?"

He hesitated. That was a stupid question coming from her. Every night, one of his "colleagues" collected the day's results and sent it somewhere. He was sure it went to Peters.

"I saw protection rates of over ninety-eight percent on my previous test at Kadokawa. I'm only seeing forty-six percent now. The only thing I can think of is the configuration of the engine itself. We tried so many things, I can't remember the exact state it was in when I ran my tests."

"And you believe you can get the information off the chip when my experts weren't able to?"

Exasperation mixed with the anxiety. He tried to keep it out of his voice. "I can't do any worse."

The silence on the other end of the line was long. He sat on his bed, the wet towel still clutched in his hand, and waited. Was she already sending guards? Would she think he wasn't worth the effort? He struggled to get rid of the thoughts by counting his heartbeats. He had problems keeping up.

"I'll have it delivered to your desk at 9:00 A.M."

"Thank you."

The link went down, and he stood to put the comm unit back in its wall cradle. For the first time, he'd been able to push through his intense fear of her and get what he wanted. Maybe things wouldn't go to hell after all. Maybe now he'd get somewhere.

LOS ANGELES LEVEL 2—TUESDAY, JULY 4, 2141 8:27 A.M.

Kai left his place in Chinatown and walked toward the insurgents' building. As he passed the Northern Dragon, he placed his hand on the menu-covered front window. If he made it through this stupid war, he'd reopen the restaurant. No more insurgents, no more corporate espionage, just him and his food and his customers. But especially his friends.

Some of his best memories of the place were when Kris would

come in after a hard day, order some ginger chicken, and eat it at the rickety plastic table he used to keep in the front. Last time she had eaten at that table, it had been moved to the back, and Pat had cooked up some scrambled eggs.

They could not get eggs anymore. Or meat or fresh produce. SoCal wanted them to fight their war, and yet they did not allow in enough food to keep everyone fed. Levels 6 and 7 had more than enough. Fresh fish from the ocean, pineapples from Brazil, olives from Portugal. Whenever he went through the checkpoints, it was like moving to a new world.

One where his friends were not allowed.

The insurgents' building was the same as always. The supposedly inconspicuous guards on the roof and near the doors. Just about anyone with half a brain would know something weird was going on. Since Jack had been promoted to his new position, things had gone downhill. The man was way out of his league. He entered the building.

At this time of day, the communal eating area was packed. No one looked up when he came in, every person lost in their own thoughts or having conversations with their friends. These were supposed to be the fighting force of this insurgent cell, and not a single person cared about who was in their own headquarters. They had become too comfortable, too complacent.

Up near the front, a single person raised their hand. He waved back at Pat and stood in line to get porridge and whatever substitute they had for coffee. By the time he'd gotten to the table, Pat's breakfast was already gone.

"Kris will not be joining us this morning?" he asked.

Pat pushed her tray farther away. "No. I checked her room, and she was already gone."

"Oh, where?"

"I don't know. She . . . she had a breakdown last night, right here, in front of everyone. I'm really scared for her. I don't know how to fix her." Tears made her voice shaky.

"I should never have left." He reached for Pat's hand. She jerked it away and put both her hands under the table.

"I don't know how it would have been different if you'd stayed. The only reason she left her room at all was to go on a mission."

"What?"

"Yeah, I know. I tried to talk her out of it, but she's too damn stubborn. It was supposed to be pretty simple, you know. Just be the eyes for a truck hijack, get some fresh food down here so we don't all die of scurvy."

"It did not go that way?" Kai knew what Kris was like. If there was an opportunity to step up and do more, she would. She was so much like her father that way.

"Of course not. The truck drivers had guns, and she doubled back to see how the hijack was going. By the time the dust settled, she crawled over the dead and drove the truck down herself."

"Is she okay?"

"Physically, sure. Mentally I don't think so. It was too much for her. I should never had insisted she join me for dinner."

"Hmm. I had thought leaving her alone for a while would be best. Perhaps we need to get her more involved instead. Give her some real jobs that will take her mind off of Miller."

"Maybe," Pat said doubtfully.

"I know my Kris. If we do not, she will figure out what to do on her own. That would not be good."

"No, it wouldn't. What do you have in mind?"

"We need to bring her up to speed on Doc Searls and Bryson. We will have to let her come up with ideas on what to do."

"You think it'll work?"

Kai shrugged.

KADOKAWA SAT CITY 2—TUESDAY, JULY 4, 2141 9:30 A.M.

A pad of intelligence and internal reports sat on the desk in front of Andrew. He'd been here since early this morning, carefully reading a report, slowly flipping through the screens, assessing the information it contained, and then moving on to the next file.

There really wasn't any part of the job he hated, but there were a couple he was definitely starting to dislike. He was still new here though, and the best way to get the pulse of what was happening under your command was to read every report, no matter how trivial. The one he had just finished mentioned a minor altercation in the mess. A few people were not happy with the quality of the food. It was something small, but it might be indicative of a growing issue.

His last two postings had been Earthside. The previous one was to bring peace to an uprising in southern India. The Indian military had ousted BEL, Bharat Electronics, from power, trying to restore governmental rule. Naturally, the very poor were hit the hardest, and they didn't like it. Clashes between military and citizens had escalated to the point of civil war, and Kadokawa was sent in to bring aid—and if possible, stability—to the country. They had been at least partially successful. Once the majority of the fighting had stopped, Andrew had been moved up here.

This posting was a bit different. He still had to hit the ground running, but with so many people and the city under his command, he had to do a fair amount of learning as well. The first few weeks of every new posting were always for getting the lay of the land. Since the previous occupants of this position had done a bad job, he wasn't sure how much he could rely on their official reports to know what was going on. He needed to go through as much data as he could get his hands on, test the crew with scenarios, and let his captains understand how he ran his ship. The problem was that the pressure was really on this time. This morning's skirmish with SoCal had proven that. They hadn't liked his expanded perimeter and had pushed back. His men were under orders not to fire unless they were fired upon. SoCal didn't seem to have the same inhibitions.

By the time the fight was over, SoCal had one crippled fighter and he had lost two, both experienced pilots with enough hours behind the controls to have retired years ago. Maybe that was why he was sitting here reading reports instead of in Operations. The loss of seasoned men was a black mark on everyone's record, and he didn't like it.

Andrew rubbed his eyes and sighed, closing the latest report. Instead of opening a new one, he grabbed another information pad that sat alone on the edge of his desk. Flipping it on, he scanned the compact data page.

Santō-kaii Keiji Nagumo. Born January 27, 2102. Thirty-nine years old and a lieutenant for life. A close to impeccable service record. No family, except for a mother living in Nagasaki. Andrew flipped to the last screen and read it—the letter of sorrow for the family. It was as standard as all the others he had seen. He signed the bottom and swiped to open the next file.

It normally wasn't the *Kaishō-ho*'s job to read the records of the deceased, or to sign them personally. His job was to lead the people under him. These were the first deaths since his placement in the city, so he decided to take care of them himself. In the future, he wouldn't even see them. If he did, the pads would cover his desk in stacks so high he wouldn't be able to see the door in the opposite wall. That is what war brought. He sighed again and paid more attention to the pad. *Nitō-kaii* Seiko Nakayama, mother of three. Her husband served as well. He put his formal signature on the document and placed the pad back on the edge of his desk.

He'd lost people under his command before. But whether it was from a collapsed building on an earthquake rescue or by the hand of an enemy at war, the feeling was the same: like he was losing control. His empathy had almost cost him a command position, until he'd been able to show Kadokawa it didn't hamper his ability to lead. Still, each time someone died, even if he didn't know them personally, it felt as though he had lost a piece of himself.

Kadokawa's outlook on the world had made them resist the trend to build high-rise cities, finding them inhumane. Eventually, population growth had forced their hand in that, but the Nippon Islands had stayed as pristine as they could keep them, until the entire area from Wakkanai to Kagoshima had been declared a UNESCO World Heritage site. Kadokawa had purchased what remained of North Korea in 2097, and followed up with South Korea in 2112, building their city between Seoul and Pyongyang, eventually extending along the west coast to Muan. It was only six levels high, but it was open to the outside world at every one of them.

Everything had changed radically when Kadokawa had used military force to acquire Meridian. Andrew wasn't pleased with the direction the new *Kaijō-bakuryōchō*, Sone, was taking them. But what else was to be expected? Kadokawa's military had grown ever since the last corporate war, and the placement of a new president last year, someone as aggressive as she had proven to be, had created a perfect symmetry at the top of the company. War wasn't what Andrew had signed up for, wasn't what many of the men and women under his command had signed up for, but it was now inevitable. He would do his duty to the best of his ability. There was no other choice.

He heard a quiet tap on the door, breaking him from his thoughts.

"Come in."

The steward opened the door and bowed. "*Kaisa* Mori is here as requested, sir."

Andrew checked the clock on his vid screen. He had lost track of the time. He stood as Mori walked in and offered a firm salute.

"Welcome *Kaisa*." He returned the salute. "Thank you for joining me for breakfast."

"Thank you for offering, *Kaishō-ho*."

Andrew walked to a table, already laid out, as his steward bustled in carrying a tray.

"Please, sit. I have both coffee and *gyokuro*. I highly recommend the tea. It was handpicked in the shadow of Mount Fuji."

Mori bowed again. "Tea would be wonderful, thank you."

The steward quickly removed the coffee from the table and fussed with the placement of the cups and utensils. Andrew waved his hand, and the steward faded into the background.

As Andrew sat, he watched Mori's posture and motions. The man came from a good family, according to his personnel file, and it showed in his manners. How much of that was his military training was tough to say.

Andrew poured the steaming water over the tea leaves and let it steep. "I understand you have an interest in twenty-first-century literature."

"Yes, *Kaishō-ho*. I am currently reading *The High Mountains of Portugal* by a Canadian, Yann Martel. He has some interesting interpretations of Agatha Christie mysteries. I am quite enjoying it."

"I have read Agatha Christie, but I've never heard of Yann Martel. Perhaps I will look up his works." He changed tracks. "Your family is currently aboard?"

"No, *Kaishō-ho*. I sent my wife and son to visit her mother when you requested nonmilitary staff to leave two weeks ago. They are in Kyoto."

"I understand the weather there has been quite warm this year. I hope she does not mind." He already knew she had left the station. It was a wise move, considering the recent skirmishes. Some of the officers had kept their families here despite his recommendation.

"Yes, she has always enjoyed the warmer weather."

Andrew finished steeping the tea and poured a cup for Mori before filling his own. The steward entered the room, bringing in grilled fish, white rice and steaming miso soup.

"Any further movement from SoCal this morning?"

"No, *Kaishō-ho*. Their fighters held stationary positions. Even when we rotated squads, they made no move to take advantage of the situation. Perhaps they knew it would be pointless."

"Perhaps. Or perhaps they thought the taking of two lives was enough."

Mori was instantly contrite. "Of course, *Kaishō-ho*. Forgive me for being boastful."

"There is nothing to forgive. A good *Kaisa* always believes the best about his troops. A wise one, however, also knows the worst."

"Yes, *Kaishō-ho*."

They ate the rest of the meal in silence while Andrew contemplated what to do next. When the final piece of fish was eaten, he stood and walked back to his desk. "Please prepare the pilots for an inspection. Before I get there, I'd like a report on their morale after this morning's loss."

Mori nodded and bowed as the steward opened the door for him. If he was upset about the extra work, nothing showed on his face.

This man will move far up the ranks, perhaps even above me, Andrew thought. *I won't keep him waiting for long.*

He picked up the pads of the dead pilots and opened up the last page again, jotting down a personal note to the next of kin. It was a small gesture, but one that no doubt would be appreciated.

PASADENA LEVEL 5—TUESDAY, JULY 4, 2141 10:43 A.M.

I didn't stop to think. There wasn't time. I ran back into the greenhouse and immediately turned the corner, out of Janice's line of sight. She was right behind me. Training told me I had to take the initiative, or I was in serious trouble. Turning around, I raised my arm and swung it toward the door, aiming for her neck but impacting her high across her shoulders. The shock went right through to my chest and my arm went numb. Janice's momentum carried her lower body forward and into the air.

The gun skittered along the gravel path, stopping by the trunk of a tree. I leaped over Janice to try and get to it. Fingers wrapped around my ankle and pulled. I barely had time to twist my body, trying to protect my son, before my back slammed into the path. Kicking with everything I had, my foot impacted on something and I heard her grunt. Her grip loosened. I jerked free and scrambled for the gun again. My hand wrapped around the barrel just as a weight landed on my back, driving me into the ground. I struggled under Janice, bucking her off long enough to roll over.

She straddled me, her knees pressing down on my chest. Her fist flashed toward my face. I swung the butt of the gun. It glanced off the back of her head and flew from my grip. The hit shifted her weight off me, and I writhed out from under her. She dove for the weapon as I sprinted out the greenhouse door.

My bike was across the street and behind the café. I dodged a car, forcing myself through the groups walking on the sidewalk, ignoring the angry shouts of the people I weaved between. I careened around the corner and yanked the helmet off the bike's mirror, jamming it onto my head before unlocking the motor and turning the bike away from the greenhouses. Behind me, I heard more shouting and the high-pitched whine of a motor working hard.

I twisted the accelerator and the torque of the electrics responded, forcing the bike ahead like an impatient beast.

In my mirrors, I saw Janice racing up behind me. I locked my rear tire and shifted my weight, kicking out the back end of the motorcycle, aiming for an alley. My headlight cut through the shadows cast by the offset Ambients overhead. Exiting the alley, I pulled on the left handlebar, my knuckles white. The bike leaned right, throwing sparks as the foot peg scraped on the ground and I swerved around another corner. The light from Janice's bike disappeared from my mirrors for less than a second as she followed me. How had she gotten so close?

The alley ended on a four-lane road with a wide boulevard separating the oncoming lanes. Across the street, a low curb led to a broad set of stairs that opened to a pedestrian plaza. Stores lined either side of the path, and restaurants, shuttered and closed, still had tables and chairs outside. I had no idea where I was, but trying to weave between the traffic would be bad. A gap opened in the line of cars and I shot across the lanes, hoping the plaza would get me closer to a down-ramp, closer to a part of the city I knew.

I jumped the curb and rode the bike up the stairs. Tires squealed as drivers slammed on their brakes, trying not to hit me. Adrenaline flushed through my system and I fought it off. I needed to think, not panic. Thankfully, the plaza was fairly empty. The few people walking leaped closer to the buildings as I whipped past.

I took the next right, barely missing a young mother with a stroller, and stayed on the plaza. Janice's motorcycle screamed behind me. I had to get off this thing and head southwest, back into Los Angeles and down to a lower level. At the very least, I couldn't keep racing where people walked. The ramp I'd taken up was out of the question. I didn't know if it was still being blocked. The military would probably scare off Janice, but I'd be drafted. The thought sent shivers down my spine. Not exactly where I wanted to be.

The plaza ended at another short flight of stairs back to street level. I grabbed the brakes. In her desperation to cut me off, Janice didn't do the same. Out of the edge of my visor, I watched as her bike sped past me, nearly out of control. Her foot slammed on the rear brake, leaving a black smear behind the bike when she saw the stairs. The bike dipped as she pulled on the front brakes. Her back tire lifted off the ground and she took the first step.

I cut behind her as the motorcycle's back end rose higher. As I passed, I saw the mixture of fear and concentration on her face. I could tell she didn't care about me anymore. Not right then. Her bike lifted past the point of no return. Her front tire hopped down another step and the bike began its topple.

She was going to be in pain.

LOS ANGELES LEVEL 2—TUESDAY, JULY 4, 2141 11:27 A.M.

By the time I got back to Level 2, I'd driven through parts of Levels 4 and 5 I'd never seen before. The only thing I knew for sure was that I was heading in the right direction, skipping several down-ramps until I was sure there wasn't any chance of being swept up in one of SoCal's drafts. The ramp I took was on the edge of my old courier territory, an express that skipped Level 3, dropping me into Level 2. I spent most of that ride trying to sort through what had happened, to get my breathing under control. Every time I replayed the event, a new shot of adrenaline kicked in. Where had Janice come from? Had someone taken over for Jeremy, continuing his work? The thought chilled me to my core.

The rest of the ride was routine, but I still remained more vigilant than I had been. If any of my teachers from the ACE training compound had seen how lax I'd become, they would have kicked my ass from here to San Francisco. Hell, I should do it to myself. I started the regular cycle of looking forward and in each of my mirrors, taking note of the vehicles and people around me, making sure I wasn't being followed. Stuff they'd taught us at the compound.

I'd decided to head back to the room the insurgents had given me. I had to let Pat know that Janice was still out there, and still after us. Or at least me. I pulled the bike into the parking garage under the building and found a spot to plug it in.

As soon as I got up to the main floor, I could smell the wet paper bag odor of porridge cooked past any resemblance to food. Despite the aroma, the thought of food worked. I was starving, and the idea of a bowl of porridge made my mouth water, temporarily pushing away the recent incident with Janice.

When I saw the dining room was almost empty, I breathed a sigh of relief. I didn't want to be in a crowded room. The last few stragglers sat randomly around the area. I managed to grab two bowls before the cooks took what was left. I sprinkled some sugar on top and grabbed a spoon, finding a table in the corner. With my back against the wall, I dug into the first bowl, watching as Pat entered and made a beeline for me. I didn't think I was in any condition to argue with her if she brought up my pregnancy again.

"We missed you at breakfast," she said as she sat across from me. The concern on her face almost made me push the food aside.

"I went for a ride. Had some stuff I needed to do, to think about."

I could tell she had a ton of questions, but she didn't ask any of them. Part of me wished she would. Part of me didn't.

"I hope it helped," she said.

I smiled. "Who's the *we* that missed me?"

"Kai."

I stopped, the spoon raised halfway to my mouth and excitement bubbling in my chest. "How's he doing? Does he have more information for us?"

Pat took a quick look around to make sure no one had overheard. "I'll let him answer that. We've got a meeting with Jack in a half hour. They want you there. You'll have time to ask him after that."

A meeting? Weeks of doing nothing, being relegated to lookout duty, and now they wanted me in a meeting? Something was going on.

"They'll fill you in," Pat said. She stood up to leave. "It's good to see you eating."

She was obviously fighting herself, wanting to know how I was, if she could help.

"Stay. Something happened on my ride." I waited until she settled back in and told her about Janice, leaving out my close call with the SoCal drafting squad. That was for another time. She sat there, staring at the wall for a while, her face blank so I couldn't tell what she was thinking.

"I'll pass the information on. She was either waiting for you at the greenhouses, which doesn't really make sense, or she's been following you for a while. The guards will keep an eye out for her here and at the food lines. Maybe you should stay inside for a while."

"Maybe. Thanks."

"I'll come and get you before noon." She stood and left.

Neither Pat nor I had been meeting with the upper echelon since we'd gotten here, despite her capabilities as a strategist. Whatever information Kai had brought back with him must have had something to do with me, or I would have been kept out of the loop. I finished my bowl of oatmeal and started in on the second. It had gone cold.

LOS ANGELES LEVEL 2—TUESDAY, JULY 4, 2141 11:55 A.M.

Pat came to my room a few minutes early, and we walked to the stairs. The oatmeal had turn into a solid lump in my gut.

Two guards stood by the double doors on the main floor. Both had assault weapons. One nodded at Pat and opened the door. As I followed her through, I noticed the safeties were off on the guns.

This hallway was wider than the ones upstairs and the dark brown carpet was soft under my feet. It was as though we had entered a hallowed place. Sounds were muffled, and the air had the distinctive smell of extra purification. There was even room for a few comfy-looking couches against one wall. I'd seen places like this before. Whoever had set this up tried to make it reflect a high-end corporate conference area. A strange choice for a group of insurgents. A door opened down the hall, and a man I'd never seen before stuck his head out. I figured it was Jack.

The grapevine had it that Jack was in charge simply because there wasn't anyone else that could do the job. The top brass had all hopped into a car to watch the water riots personally and been killed for their curiosity. No one thought it had been a true attempt to take out the local insurgent cell though. More like the dumb bastards were at the wrong place at the wrong time.

Jack had been pretty low-level, more of a middle manager-type person than a take-charge kind of guy. They say his day job—before all the shit happened—had been the same, just a midlevel worker bee. Deal with the lower-level flunkies, and get permission from higher ups before doing anything.

Why they didn't bring someone else in to take over was anybody's guess. Maybe the insurgents were less organized than they wanted us to believe.

"Ah! Here they are. We can start." He held the door open for us as we walked in.

Seeing Kai, even though I knew he was here, was a shock. His face was thin and haggard, and dark smudges made his eyes appear sunken.

After we'd buried Ian's ashes, he'd disappeared. I remember having a conversation with him about Bryson Searls, but after that, he was gone. He hadn't said goodbye, hadn't left a note to say where he was going. He'd knocked on my door a couple of times. I didn't respond. As much as I wanted to be alone back then, I had wished he'd taken me with him. Disappearing like a ghost sounded like a blessing. But then I wouldn't have been able to keep my promise to Doc Searls. Not that I really had anyway.

Kai hobbled across the floor and pulled me into a hug. I fought off the tears and hugged him back. He felt as scrawny as he looked, but his arms were strong.

"Please take a seat."

Kai held out a chair and sat down beside me.

"It seems I'm the only one in this room you don't know, Kris. My name is Jack. I'm in charge of this cell in Los Angeles."

"Okay," I said. Jack was a short man, and a little fat. He strutted around the table and sat near the window. I got the impression he didn't think much of me. I sure as hell didn't like him.

"We brought you in on this meeting because of your knowledge and experience in dealing with ACE. Kai?"

Kai cleared his throat, noticeably uncomfortable in the boardroom-style chair. "I have been in touch with some ACE personnel." When I twitched in my seat, he spoke faster and focused on me. "No one from the executive, mainly low-level people. Men and women that joined for the same reason you and I did. They are as lost and as hurt as you would imagine, and they are looking for some way to continue the fight."

As *I* could imagine? I guess they'd had the father of their child killed by ACE. I buried the thought. "How do we know we can trust them?" I asked.

"We're starting with background checks," said Jack, "and bringing in people Kai and Pat know personally. We figure that will give us a good first batch. We'll build a committee that will be dedicated to verifying the others who want to come in."

A committee? With the fake leather chairs and the large table, this was starting to sound and feel more and more corporate to me. Did this guy actually know how to do anything except add layers of management and create meeting agendas? My instinct was to run, to get as far away from anything that looked or felt this way. Instead I gripped my legs under the table, steadying myself, trusting Pat and Kai. "Why am I here?"

"Without a system for vetting applicants, we need to rely on people who worked with them in the past. The first person Kai wants to bring in is someone you've met." He read the paper in his hands. "A Doctor John Searls?"

"Doc Searls? Yeah, I know him." Was he here? My stomach churned. What if he let slip that I was pregnant, or that we were looking for his son?

"Can you vouch for him?"

"What?" Vouch for him? I barely knew him, really. What I did do though, was trust him.

"Can you confirm he wasn't one of the bad apples in ACE?"

"I . . . I guess. I don't . . . I trusted him when I was hurt. He asked me to get his son when Kadokawa was looking for him."

"So he put your life in danger?"

"Not on purpose," I was getting defensive, like this was an inquisition. "He couldn't have known they would be there."

"And where is his son now?"

I stole a glance at Kai. Had he told the insurgents we were searching for him? Somehow I didn't think so. "I haven't seen him since he left Kai's restaurant."

"Just before the building was breached?"

What the fuck was going on? "I guess."

"So you think Doctor Searls and his son had something to do with that?"

"I didn't say that." Hell, I hadn't even thought it. What was the point of even talking to this jackass? My face flushed warmer. "What the fuck is this?" Jack leaned back in his chair and smiled as Kai reached out and put his hand over mine. I jerked it away.

"We're trying to figure out if Doctor Searls can be trusted," said Jack. "That's all."

"By putting words in my mouth?" I stood up, filled with an anger I didn't understand. "Fuck you. If you want my opinion, you can just come out and ask for it. If you want to twist what I say to fit your own ideas, you can piss off." I knew I was overreacting, but now that I was talking, I couldn't stop myself. Doc Searls had done more for me than most people, and I owed him for that.

I opened the door, taking one last look around the office. "Pretty fucking *corporate* of you." I didn't look at Pat or Kai, not trusting what my reaction would be. They followed me out.

"We didn't think . . ." Pat said.

I kept walking.

"We both said Doc Searls should be trusted. I thought you were being brought in to verify."

I stopped before reaching the double doors. "I don't care who that guy is," I said, jabbing my thumb over my shoulder. "I've seen his kind before, and so have both of you. He's corporate. It's written all over him. If he's in charge, if this is what these people are becoming, I'm not sure this is where I belong."

"He is not like that," Kai said. "When you are responsible for a lot of people, you need some structure. Maybe that is why—"

I turned on him. "Why he's an ass? Why this part of the building reeks of corporate greed, while the rest of it barely has room for the people living here? I've seen him at dinner, sitting at a table at the front, his cronies around him. Can't you see he's becoming what we're all fighting against?"

"Kris—"

"No. Something's not right." I walked out past the guards. Who needed guards inside the building when we were all supposed to be on the same side? Put them outside, watching over all of us. Kai hustled after me. Why couldn't he just leave me alone?

"The thing is, Pat and I are thinking it as well. We do not know what to do about it." He paused, glancing at the guards across the foyer. "There is something else though."

Pat joined us by the door to the parking garage.

"I managed to decrypt the chip I took from Bryson," Kai said in a soft voice. "I think we have a bigger issue than just finding him on our hands."

"What do you mean?" asked Pat.

"I know why SoCal wants him so bad. He has designed a ship that can be almost anywhere instantly. The data on the chip called it a quantum jump drive. Meridian, under Jeremy, started building it. Things went wrong and the pilots died on its maiden voyage. When Kadokawa took over Meridian, they continued the work. It looks like Bryson fixed it. Whoever has him now has a weapon more powerful than anything we have seen before. They can destroy whatever corporation they want, take whatever they want."

"You mean they can leave San Angeles and be anywhere in the world with no travel time?" I asked.

"That is the way I understand it."

"It would end the war."

"It would also create an impossible-to-beat corporation," Pat said. "One that could do anything. There would be no one to fight them. No one that could."

Kai nodded. "Could you imagine what SoCal or IBC would do with it?"

I already knew what they were doing, and it would only get worse.

"Have you told Jack or anyone else?" I asked.

"No. I was not sure who to trust with this, besides you two."

"And you think whoever took Bryson is getting him to build one of these things?"

"I do. We need to find out who it is."

I agreed. "Do you have any leads on him?"

"Not yet. I spoke with Doc Searls. He hasn't heard back from his sources either. He did say he wanted to see you."

My face went cold.

"He seemed a bit concerned," Kai said.

"Did he mention why?"

"No. He probably wants to follow up on the rib you broke a couple of weeks ago."

Relief flooded through me, and I hoped it didn't show. What was so hard about telling them the truth? I was carrying Ian's son. I opened my mouth to say the words, and closed it again. *You weren't supposed to tell anyone until three months anyway. Right?*

"Where is he?" I asked.

"He spends most of his time in his offices on Level 5."

That sounded like Doc Searls. "I'll go see him later today," I said. Which was as good enough a reason to leave here as I had. I didn't want to stick around all day.

"You haven't heard? SoCal is starting to block access to Level 5. They are cutting us off more every day."

Shit. Now what was I supposed to do? I turned to leave, already lost in the logistics of getting up there.

Kai touched my cheek, holding his hand there. I leaned into it.

"I missed you," he said.

I forgot all about Level 5, and the familiar anger returned to burn through me. "Why did you leave? Why not at least tell me where you were going?"

"I tried. I truly did, but you locked yourself in your shell so tight, I . . . I could not get through." Tears formed in his eyes and one left a wet track down his wrinkled face.

"You could have tried harder." I wanted to say he *should* have tried harder.

"I know. I did not know how to deal with your pain."

I cupped his hand against my cheek without thinking. The last two weeks had been hard on him. I could see it in his face and the way he moved. Suddenly it was all too much and I let go, pulling away.

"I . . . I need to go. Will you be here when I get back?"

Kai dropped his hand and nodded.

The parking garage door opened easily, and I pushed my way through. I didn't turn around.

THREE

LOS ANGELES LEVEL 2—TUESDAY, JULY 4, 2141 12:01 P.M.

JANICE BLINKED in the onslaught of light when she opened her eyes. Her mind wandered, images of Level 2 Chinatown and a tiny girl riding a big motorcycle flitting in her consciousness. It took a few more minutes for her to remember what had happened. Beside her, the incessant beeping of a machine pushed the last remnants of grogginess away. She rolled her head on the pillow, her hand reaching to rub at her eyes. Something tugged, resisting the movement. A tube was stuck in her arm. Suddenly paying more attention, she examined the room. Besides the medical equipment, it was empty except for a single hard-backed chair by the closed door. There were no windows, no other way out.

She pushed herself upright, the machine beside her picking up its pace. The side of her face was numb, and her left leg ached above the knee. She reached under the covers to feel it, touching bare skin.

Her probing fingers barely registered anything but a bit of pressure. Flicking the covers aside revealed a hospital gown in place of her street clothes. She scanned the room again. They were nowhere in sight. The place smelled and looked like a hospital, but something was off, and she couldn't quite figure out what it was.

As the machine settled back down to a steady beat, someone knocked quietly on the door and opened it. Whoever it was didn't wait for permission to enter. By the clothes the woman was wearing, she was some sort of doctor or nurse. She smiled at Janice, tucking the blankets back into place, and moved to check the bag that fed into her arm.

"Where am I?" Janice asked.

The woman didn't answer.

"What is this place?"

This time, she turned and smiled again. "You've been in an accident. Someone will be here shortly to answer your questions." She left, closing the door firmly behind her. Janice didn't hear a lock click shut.

She got out of bed, placing her bare feet on the cold tiled floor. A shiver ran up her legs. The tube in her arm tugged as she stood, and she yanked it out, pressing her robe over the hole to help stop the blood flow. Her leg felt strange when she put some weight on it. Though there wasn't really any pain, there wasn't too much of anything else either. There was pressure in her calf and hip, but nothing between the two. She limped to the door and tried the handle. It moved.

Bracing herself against the chair, she pulled it open slowly. Janice peeked through the small crack. A face stared back at her only a few centimeters away. She yelped and let go of the knob. The door clicked shut and she scurried into bed, her gown flapping open behind her. She had barely jerked the covers over her again when the door opened and the face became a man of average height.

"Sorry for scaring you like that. Bad timing, I'm afraid. I was coming in to introduce myself. My name is John, John Smith." He grinned as if he saw a look of disbelief cross her face. "Most people don't believe me when I tell them that. It's been happening to me my whole life." He grabbed the chair and dragged it to the bed, spinning it around so the back faced her before sitting down, his arms resting on the back. "You're probably wondering where you are." He contemplated the room as if seeing it for the first time. "Most do when they end up here. You got quite lucky. There was damage to your left cheekbone, and you lost a fair amount of skin on your thigh and hip."

Janice lifted her hand to her cheek. The skin was smooth, though still a little numb. "So, where am I?"

"Right!" His face brightened. "You're in the security wing of Malala Yousafzai Hospital. You were brought here after your high-speed chase through Pasadena. Normally not something that would put you here, but once we found the gun . . ."

Shit. This was not good. "So you're a cop?" Her voice sounded hopeful.

"Oh heavens, no! We wouldn't relegate a weapons possession incident to the police, especially in these times. No, dear girl, you are in far more trouble than that."

"SoCal?" Her whole body went as numb as her cheek.

"Bingo!" The smile disappeared. "It's against the law to have a gun in San Angeles. And for the record, no one knows you're here."

Janice shifted on the bed, unconsciously tugging the sheets higher around her neck. This was definitely not a good place to be. The way she figured it, she was either going to walk out of here SoCal property, or she wasn't going to walk out of here at all. She had no reservations about working for a corporation, and SoCal was the biggest of them. It was what had kept her going for this long.

"Why don't you tell me about yourself? You can start with your name."

She'd already made her decision. There was only one way she'd get out of this place alive, and that was by answering every question they had. "I'm Janice Robertson. I used to work for Meridian, under Jeremy Adams. When Jeremy left Meridian, before the Kadokawa takeover—"

"Jeremy Adams was with Meridian before the takeover? Our sources said he was killed in an attack on Level 5."

"I don't know about that. All I know is he was in San Angeles when Kadokawa took over. He wasn't with Meridian anymore. I followed him when he left. He assigned me to work undercover as an ACE trainee, to keep an eye on someone named Kris Merrill." She couldn't keep the venom out of her voice. "Jeremy contacted me a few weeks ago, telling me to coordinate an extraction on the ACE training facility. That wasn't part of the original plan, I was supposed to be his eyes on the ground. His goal was to capture Kris."

John shook his head and asked her to continue.

"Jeremy wanted Kris bad. I wasn't told what his beef was, and I didn't care. It wasn't my job. I did as he asked and called in the team. The extraction failed, and ACE sent in a transport of their own. Everyone alive was evacuated. My guess is Jeremy had the shuttle taken out. I survived the crash. The only contact I had was ACE. I guess they still thought I was one of their own. They gave me a mission to kill Kris and the cook—"

"The cook?"

"As far as I know, we were the only three to survive the crash. The cook, Pat, used to be ACE black ops, but she had mental issues so they made her a cook at the training compound instead. I figured I'd kill Pat and capture Kris for Jeremy. When I did my regular check-in with him, I'd hand her over. It didn't work out that way."

"When was this?"

"A couple of weeks ago."

John's face lit up as his thoughts lined up and fell into place. "Ah! At the greenhouses in Pasadena? That's who you were chasing this morning?"

"Yeah. So now you know all about me. What are you going to do?" She hated herself for the way her voice wavered.

"What do you think we should do?"

Now was the time. "I'm a free agent. Jeremy missed his last two check-ins. ACE is gone, not that I would have worked for those losers. I'm good at what I do, and I'm looking for work."

"We'll consider it. Why did Meridian want this Kris Merrill?"

"I don't think Meridian did. I think it was all Jeremy."

"The question remains the same. Why?"

"He never said."

John switched tracks. "Do you know where Kris is now?"

"Yeah."

He grilled her for another half hour, bouncing the questions between her time at the training camp, her various jobs with Jeremy, and what she had done since the fall of ACE. She answered every question he asked, told him about every mission she did, twenty-one in five years. All of them but the last requiring undercover work. All but the last successful.

As the door closed behind him, she hoped she'd been able to sell her skills.

LOS ANGELES LEVEL 2—TUESDAY, JULY 4, 2141 12:29 P.M.

The bike was almost fully charged. Checking it was a habit I had gotten into when I was still a courier, and a year in the mountains hadn't changed that. I powered up the ramp out of the inter-level parking. Before I came out of the shadows created by the Level 2 Ambients, I stopped and examined the area. There was no way Janice, or anyone else, would get me by surprise. Not again.

The plan was to grab a quick bite at the food lines in Chinatown, if there was anything left. I was comfortable there, more than I was with the insurgents. I got the feeling that Jack and his cronies thought they were better than the people they were trying to help. It wasn't right. If the people were eating three-day-old leftovers and cheap tofu, then so was I. The insurgents had pasta last week. Pasta! Where the hell did they get all the water to cook it, and what did they do with it afterward?

The tables weren't balanced, and that wasn't the right way to start a revolution. Were all the insurgent cells as inept as this one?

I pulled the bike onto the sidewalk outside of Lee's Fish Market and thumbed the lock, briefly considering checking to see if the old outlet I used to charge the bike at night was still active. I didn't. I'd steal power from the corporations when I could, but not from someone that worked for a living.

The lineups for food were just beginning to build. Workers were manning more than one station, jumping between them for every person that came up. At that rate, they'd be serving when the Ambients dimmed for the night. Instead of waiting in line, I joined the group handing out the seared tofu. The woman gave me a brief smile and ladled vegetables into a bowl. I added a slab of tofu. The sight of it made my stomach do a flop, but I swallowed and kept things under control. I was used to it by now.

A family walked to the tables and my partner slammed a heaping spoonful of overcooked celery and carrots onto their plates. The mother winced when her young daughter let a carrot drop to the road. She bent down and picked it up, placing it on her plate and giving her daughter a clean one. When she caught me watching, I could see the embarrassment flicker across her face before it was replaced with steely resolve. The daughter held her plate out to me. A pool of grungy liquid seeped out from under the vegetables and sloshed around the bottom. I gave each of them a slice of tofu, hunting for the biggest piece I could find for their son—he looked almost my age—and the father took an extra second to make eye contact and say thank you as the rest of the family got rice before trundling off to look for a place to sit.

After a half hour, the faces blurred into a smear of dirt and tears, hope and despair. Some of the hands holding the plates trembled. They probably hadn't eaten in days. For a while, I told them to eat slow, let their systems get used to food again. I don't know how many listened. As more people filed past, my moves became increasingly mechanical: wait for a plate, pick up the now-cold tofu, drop it on the plate. I barely noticed the difference between the adults and the kids anymore.

Someone called my name, the voice sounding like it came from the depths of an elevator shaft echoing through my head more than once before I realized what was happening.

"K . . . Kris? Kris Ballard?" The voice was quiet, hesitant at first, barely registering through the fog I had settled into and the sound of people milling through the street and sitting at the makeshift tables.

"Kris?"

I picked up another piece of tofu. There were only ten or so left. I looked down the line. Some wouldn't get any.

"Kris?"

I focused on the person in front of me, finally realizing the woman had used my real last name. I didn't think there was anyone alive that knew that, except Kai. Her face was wrinkled and her brown eyes sunk into her skull so far it must have been like looking out a tunnel. The world had given her a beating and she'd come out the other end the worse for it. Like most everyone else in the food line.

"Is that you, Kris?"

Through the gaunt cheeks and unruly hair that looked prematurely gray. Through the dirt that stained her face and hands and clothes. Through the tears that coursed down her dry and chapped face. I recognized her. She had the haggard look of a Level 1 worker written all over her—aged beyond her years.

I dropped the tofu. What was *she* doing here? She had no right. I let go of the serving spoon and it clattered into the almost empty container. My heart froze, refusing to beat until the heat rising from the pit of my stomach reached it before creeping through my chest and into my face. My hands shook, my forearms taut and rigid. I gripped the edge of the table, words forming in my mouth of their own accord.

Before they could shape into coherent sounds, the old lady's shaking hand reached out to mine, prying it from the table and turning it palm up. She placed a folded piece of paper into it and closed my fingers. She turned and shambled away, the bottom of her coat tattered and losing its filling, her plate forgotten on the serving table, wedged between the vegetable and tofu bins.

Auntie.

I turned my back on the people left in line, taking two slow steps, and unfolded the paper. By the look of it, the note had been opened and read many times before being folded back up. The edges of the folds were black from years of handling. The paper almost separated in my fingers as I read it, my hands trembling with fear and hate.

Auntie,

I've tried so many times to tell you what Uncle is doing. I know you don't believe me. Don't come looking, you won't find me.

Kris

The handwriting still contained the uncertainty of a thirteen-year-old, the letters rounded and clear and slowly written, instead of the rushed script of an overstressed adult. Written underneath in a shaky hand was the date: *May 3rd, 2137.* In even smaller letters were *Kicked out May 5th* and *Died August 24.*

Tension seeped from my body in a single rush, leaving me hollow and uncertain. I crumpled the note in my hand, grasping for something to lean against. I slid to the ground, only a few feet away from where they were serving, my legs unable to hold me anymore. Hot tears streamed unchecked down my face.

Dead. The bastard was dead and gone. I had given so much of myself to the memories he'd burned into me, so much that lay hidden below the surface. And now it was finished. I stood and stumbled to the sidewalk, whimpering with the rush of emotion, of relief, and oddly, a sense of loss.

In the end, she had believed me. She had chosen me over him, right over wrong. Uncertainty over stability. Only it was too late.

I felt a touch on my shoulder, light, unsure.

"I'm so sorry. I searched everywhere for you."

Something inside me broke. Years—a lifetime—of holding it all in, turning the fear into fuel to keep others away. Suddenly everything merged into one: Ian dying, Mom and Dad, the years of being alone. Being pregnant. It all crumbled into dust. I turned and pulled her into my arms. Her tears soaked through my jacket to my skin, warm and wet. We stood and cried together.

Eventually we separated. Auntie still laughing and crying, holding onto my hand as if she was scared to let go, to lose me again. I helped her over to the lines, and we grabbed whatever food was left and moved to an empty table. We ate in silence, each one of us too embarrassed or too scared to start talking. She broke the silence first.

"I . . . I found your note. I almost threw it away, but I couldn't. I went through your room and found it. Found the red negligee." She stopped and stared at the empty dishes. "I didn't want to believe you, didn't want to know what kind of man he was. I confronted him, showed him the negligee and the emptied bottles. Showed him your note. He denied it all. Told me I was stupid. Worthless."

Her hands shook and I grabbed them. They were cold, too cold even for the temperature of Level 2. She squeezed back, drawing strength.

"I believed him. I . . . I had to. There wasn't any other choice. I threw the damn thing away, along with everything else in your room. When I came home from work the next day, he was passed out. Again. His bottle had tipped and was leaking on the floor. He'd pulled the negligee from the garbage and was holding it, pressing it against his cheek. I . . . I knew then. Hell, I knew before. I just didn't . . . I couldn't . . . I'm so sorry. I should have been there for you. He wouldn't let . . ."

I didn't say anything.

"Something finally flipped. I packed his bags that night and put them in the hall outside. He almost woke up when I dragged him from his chair. It took me a long time to get him out the door. He was so much bigger than me. I bolted it behind him. I didn't know if he had a key, didn't know what he'd do to me if he got back in.

"He shouted and screamed for hours. Kicking and pounding at the door. I called the police, but they don't care about anyone on Level 1. You know that. Jim across the hall had enough, eventually.

His baby girls couldn't sleep. He dragged your uncle outside and beat the crap out of him. I watched from the window."

"He didn't come back?" I asked.

"No. He was too scared of Jim. The next time I heard about him, the police showed up at my door. Too late to be of any use. They told me he'd been killed. Too much to drink, not enough to eat. He had tried to rob a restaurant on Level 3 and the owner had stabbed him. He'd bled out before anyone found him." She paused, obviously reliving the moment, before struggling to move on. "I used most of our money to move up to Level 2. When the food and water shortages hit, I found the nearest kitchen."

The pain of reliving the experience was etched on her face. I knew how she felt, how *I* had felt when I ran away. It was as though someone had jabbed me with a shock stick. For the first time I realized I wasn't the only one that had been abused in that apartment on Level 1. There were two victims there, and we'd both coped the only way we knew how. And we'd both managed to break free.

Everything she did when I lived with them, every action, every word, was wrapped in a layer of self-preservation and fear so thick, she didn't even realize what she was doing to me. How could she have? My image of her shattered into a thousand pieces.

I changed the topic before she could see the reaction her words had on me. "How far do you come each day?"

"I'm not sure. It's about an hour-and-a-half walk. Moving helps my old bones."

I let go of her hands and we got quiet again. She had been alone as long as I had, finally rid of that scumbag. Finally out from under his control.

"I need to go. It's a long way home." She pushed herself up from the table and used it for balance until she could stand on her own. She hadn't had enough to eat.

"Stay. Let me get you some more food."

"I can't. I don't want to walk at night. It's not Level 1, but in times like this, it can get rough."

"I can get you a ride home. I have a motorcycle . . ." Auntie shook her head. "Or I could get a car?"

"No, thank you. I think we both need time to figure things out. I'll be back tomorrow, if you . . . if you want to talk again."

It felt like I was losing her, losing the only real family I had left, but she was right. I had butterflies in my belly and thoughts raced through my head. We both needed time. Healing didn't happen over a single shared meal. It was a good start though.

We hugged again, promising to meet tomorrow. She was reluctant to let go, more afraid than I was that we wouldn't find each other again. I watched as she walked off. Her back seemed a little straighter, her step a bit stronger.

Tomorrow.

LOS ANGELES LEVEL 5—TUESDAY, JULY 4, 2141 1:00 P.M.

After John Smith left, Janice wondered if she had told him too much. She hadn't held anything back, which meant she had no leverage anymore, no more information to give them. From where she sat, there was nothing she had that they wanted. Except maybe her skill set. And honestly, after her performance recently, even that was questionable.

She got out of bed again. The numbness was leaving her leg and a flash of pain made her suck in a breath. Tiptoeing to the door, she cracked it open and peeked out, fully expecting John's face to be looking back at her. She let out a soft sigh when he wasn't there.

From her limited view, the hallway was empty, no guards, no

hospital staff. She opened the door some more and stuck her head out to look in the other direction. It was like a ghost town.

A breeze ran up her spine and she reached back, grabbing the flaps of her gown and holding it closed before stepping into the corridor. Getting out of this place would be a great start, but she knew it wasn't going to happen. John had told her she was in the security wing of the hospital. If no one had been placed outside her room door, that meant they were all at the perimeter.

It didn't really matter anyway. She wasn't about to walk the streets in a thin gown that flapped open in the back. There was no way that would end well.

Instead, she walked the corridor, from her room near the end of the hall to the double doors that, she assumed, led into the hospital itself. She didn't try to open them. With no guards where she could see them, they had to be positioned just outside. The cold white tiles whispered under her feet as she slowed down at every door and opened it. Nine rooms in all, and she was the only one here. By the time she was done, her leg didn't hurt as much.

Where the tenth room should have been was a nurses' station, as empty as the rest of the place. If her clothes were still here, this would be the best spot to start. She began at the desk. Its surface was worn and completely clear except for a terminal. Pressing a key brought the display to life with a small box asking for a name, password, and security number. It was useless to her, unless she could beat the information out of the nurse. She didn't think that would go over too well with John.

Every drawer in the desk was locked, and not with the cheap shit she'd seen on standard office desks. These locks were solid, with a double-edged key slot and heavy construction. The drawers didn't even wiggle when she pulled on them. Janice gave up and moved to the cupboards behind her. They were all the same. Locked.

Her last chance lay with the door at the back of the station. She pressed down on the handle, and it moved with no resistance but didn't open. Locked with a disconnected latch system. No wonder there were no guards. The only places she could get to in here were the other rooms. She decided to go through them one more time. Maybe she could find something to pry open the drawers.

Voices penetrated the double doors outside the station and sent her heart racing. She ran to her room, her bare feet slapping on the floor, the pain in her thigh flaring to barely manageable levels. As she crawled back into bed, the machine beside her began beeping again, its pace frantic.

She lay under the covers, holding her breath and willing her pounding heart to slow down. By the time she heard the knock on the door, Janice had almost decided to get out of bed again. John strode in and repeated the process with the chair.

"Did you enjoy your walkabout?"

"I . . . It was . . . umm."

John laughed. "No need to worry. It shows more initiative than I thought you had, which is a good thing. Though why you didn't try the doors by the nurse's desk is anyone's guess." He paused, looking at the console beside her. "It seems your story about Mr. Adams and Miss Merrill has stirred some interest higher up. Especially Miss Merrill. Did you know they had a bit of difficulty finding records for her? Apparently she fell off the face of the earth for the last year."

"I told you, she was in Canada."

"Ah, at the supposed ACE facility. I see. Well, the decision on what to do with you is no longer mine to make, so we'll be leaving together today. You're lucky. If I'm doing my math correctly, it's been about six months since anyone walked out of this place." His voice lowered. "Most don't get to know when they leave, if you understand my meaning. And if you try anything stupid, you may have the opportunity to find out what we did with them."

Despite John's words, Janice detected a switch in the balance of power. It might be temporary, but he didn't have the same amount of control over her. He couldn't decide whether she lived or died anymore. She could see that he felt it as well as he fidgeted in his seat, his words a cover for his sudden impotence. She had never responded well to threats. They always brought out the nasty in her, and a quick retort was already forming on her lips. She swallowed it, the taste bitter, and just nodded. No one fought against SoCal. If she ever had the chance, though, she would let him know.

"Good." The smile returned. "Since you know your way around, I'll leave you to it. Your clothes will be at the nurses' station, and I'll be back in twenty minutes to pick you up."

Janice waited a few minutes before getting out of bed. This time she didn't bother holding her robe shut. The bastards obviously had cameras everywhere, which meant they'd already had an eyeful. Fuck them. She'd used what she had before. She strode down the corridor, fighting against the limp, not wanting to show weakness. Grabbing her clothes, she walked into the nearest room and locked herself in the bathroom. False bravado could only go so far.

Her pants had a hole torn in the leg above the knee. The frayed edges were covered in dried blood. The shirt was in one piece, but blood had run down the front, making the material stiff. There wasn't much she could do with the pants, but she spent a bit of time washing the blood out of the shirt in the sink, cringing at how much water she used.

Once she was dressed, she jammed the gown into the toilet tank, forcing the intake valve open. It would take them a while to find it, she hoped. It was a petty act, but it still made her feel better. Fuck the water. She waited by the nurses' station, sitting in the chair behind the worn desk. The double doors swung inwards and John walked in, still alone. He told her to come around the counter and to face it, her arms on the surface and her legs spread apart. He shackled her legs first, then pulled her arms behind her back, one at a time, and zip-tied them together.

There were no guards outside.

"I don't know if today is your lucky day or not. You're going on a 36,000 kilometer trip."

Shit.

LOS ANGELES LEVEL 5—TUESDAY, JULY 4, 2141 1:42 P.M.

The first up-ramp I rode to had a line at least a hundred cars long waiting to go through the new security checkpoints SoCal had set up. I wasn't in the mood for hanging around and went back down to Level 3 to find an express up-ramp that, with some luck, had a shorter line. As I rode I kept looking down side streets for SoCal military. With all of the drafts going on, I was constantly on edge. Working for SoCal wasn't on the top of my list of things to do.

Some late lunch traffic slowed me down—people pretending there was nothing wrong. That they or someone they knew couldn't be drafted at any time. That the world was normal.

I was still uneasy about this morning's close call. It had been out of the ordinary, mainly because of its location. The thought of being locked down here, away from Ian, burned like a fire in my chest, and my vision blurred. I blinked and shook my head in an attempt to push the feelings away.

It didn't work.

Forcing my grip to loosen on the handlebars, I twisted the throttle and accelerated toward the up-ramp. SoCal had set up here as well. I'd expected that. The line only held a few vehicles though. I stopped before I got there and double-checked my tracker ID using my comm unit, just to make sure it was set to show me as a standard courier.

When I hit the line, they scanned me and asked where I was going. I gave them an address on Level 5 I knew was a SoCal one. If they thought I was on a run for their bosses, I figured it would be easier for me to get through. They made notes on their pads before letting me pass. If they had asked to look at my paperwork, I would have been screwed. How long would it be before they stopped couriers from going through?

I had kept up my regular scans in the mirrors, always calculating the traffic around me. Had I seen that silver car before? Did the driver of the one passing me look familiar? It was exhausting, keeping up the hypervigilance, but it had become a habit well before I went through the checkpoint.

There was no use in hiding where I was going, so I rode the most direct route and turned onto the right street to Doc Searls' office.

Even though I wasn't a courier anymore, the bike and the changed tracker ID helped me get into places without a second glance. A blue compact car got closer, staying in the curb lane. I was pretty sure I'd seen it before, but how many blue compacts were on the road? I pulled over and watched it drive past. The passenger was on his comm unit and the driver kept her eyes straight ahead. I honked the bike's horn, but the driver's stare never wavered. She was either obsessive about keeping her eyes on the truck in front of her, or she was studiously trying not to look in my direction.

I rode past the office, watching the parking lot, before doing a U-turn and pulling in. It was the same thing Ian had done last year at Doc's Level 6 offices, and what I had been taught to do by ACE. Survey the area before committing.

There was a small spot right by the front door. I zipped in, turning the bike so it faced outward, ready for a fast exit if I needed it. I thumbed the lock and walked in.

The building was a single floor, a simple strip mall with one section converted to a doctor's office. A waste of vertical space, which meant it wasn't cheap. I was surprised there was a receptionist behind the front desk. I'd never seen one in the Doc's offices before, but then, I was never there when there could have been one. I guess I didn't expect him to have regular patients.

The receptionist peered over her desk as the door closed, a quizzical expression on her face.

"I'm sorry, but we don't have any packages to pick up."

"I'm here to see Doc Searls," I said.

"Oh, of course. I'm sorry. What's your name?"

"Kris Merrill."

The receptionist read the display in front of her, scrolling through whatever she saw there. "Did you have an appointment?"

"Oh, no. Sorry. I thought I could . . ."

She smiled. "We don't take walk-ins. There's a clinic down Clint Drive. They're not usually too busy."

"He wanted me to come by."

She gave me another look, this one starting at my face and moving to my feet, then back up again. "What was your name again?"

"Kris Merrill."

Another reading of the display. "You're not listed as a patient."

"No, this is—"

"Kris!" Doc Searls walked around the corner, a pad in his hand. "I wasn't expecting you. Please come into the back." He handed the pad to the receptionist and led the way. Once we were in his office, he made me sit on the examination table. "Let's take a quick peek at that rib, before we get on to other things. Lift your shirt for me?"

I did as he asked and his fingers probed where the rib had fractured.

"No pain?"

I shook my head.

"Good. Good." He sat and pulled his glasses off, rubbing the bridge of his nose. "I had a conversation with Kai recently. He wants me to join the insurgents. Do for them what I did for ACE. Do you think that's a good idea?"

Why would he ask me? I was a nobody in the insurgents' organization. "I dunno. On one hand they seem unorganized, on the other way too corporate. But I think their heart is in the right place. I hope it is."

"Hmm. I know you do things for them. Can you see yourself doing it long term?"

"I . . . I'm not sure. They seem to be getting more corporate all the time, I don't know if I can do that."

"I've been thinking about saying yes. I'll have to consider it some more now. Thanks, your opinion helped."

I didn't know what to say.

"But that's not why I called you in. Kai didn't know you were pregnant—"

I jumped off the table. "You told him?"

He was obviously surprised by the question. "No, of course not. That would be unethical."

"Then how?"

"It's amazing what people will talk to a doctor about, especially when it concerns someone they care deeply for." He paused. "It's your choice whether to tell your friends or not, but single mothers usually need all the help they can get."

"I'll tell them. Just not yet."

"Okay. Best guess is you're right around the two-month mark

now and hardly showing. It'll get more noticeable as things move further along."

"I know. I'm not ready yet. I thought it was smart to wait until three months, anyway."

"Sometimes." Doc Searls stood. "We'll take a urine sample today and weigh you, and I want you to book an appointment for next week. We'll make sure mom and baby are healthy, and see if we can't predict a due date. Okay?"

I nodded.

"Good. You're getting enough to eat?"

Another nod.

"Okay. You look a little thin, so try to get more. If you're having issues finding food, come and see me. Or better yet, talk to your friends. They'll want to help."

Before I could answer, he handed me a cup and pointed me down the hall. When I was done, he weighed and measured me before bringing up Bryson.

"I wanted to thank you for helping my son. When I found he'd left your care I had some friends hunt him down. Besides you, I mean. They heard of a project being headed up by a physicist. They didn't get a name, but the description sounds like him."

"Where is he?"

"SoCal Sat City 2." His voice lowered and I could hear sadness creep in. "Out of our reach." It looked like he was trying to hold back the tears and I struggled to contain my own.

"The insurgents are keeping me out of everything, but I can talk to the people I know, try to find out for sure if it's him or not." Doc Searls' face brightened with hope.

"Would you? You won't get in trouble?"

"I don't think so."

He nodded, the look on his face expressing gratitude more than words could. "Thank you. I'll try to do the same from my end." The tone of his voice changed back to that of a professional as he stood. "Remember to book an appointment."

SOCAL SAT CITY 2—TUESDAY, JULY 4, 2141 1:57 P.M.

Bryson shifted in his chair again. He hadn't gotten anything done since his call to Ms. Peters this morning. Now he was considering calling her again. It was after lunch, and he still didn't have the memory chip, as she had promised. He picked up the comm unit on his desk and started making the connection. The swish of the opening airlock followed by the sudden hush of voices around him made him stop midconnect and close the link.

He watched her approach. When she had caved in, deciding to give him the memory chip, something had changed, like a switch had been flicked in his head.

Gone was the constant background burr of fear, gone was the urge to never cause trouble, to do as he was told. He wasn't sure how long his sudden sense of courage would last, but it had passed the first test. Her approach didn't send him into a panic, didn't make him feel like he was about to spew his lunch all over the floor.

Ms. Peters got closer, the ever-present guards right behind her.

"Here is the chip." She handed it to him.

Bryson let her lay it in the palm of his hand and looked at it. This one was SoCal branded. "It's not the original."

"We made a copy. The original stays with us."

"So, you can't read it, but you figure you can copy it cleanly?" He shocked himself with the quick retort.

"It's a bit-for-bit duplicate."

Was that surprise in her voice? Bryson rewarded himself with an imaginary pat on the back and sat straighter in the chair. "And if part of the encryption is the onboard controller? If it is, you've handed me garbage."

"Don't you think we thought of that?"

She turned harsh and defensive. The guards took a step closer. Bryson's heart skipped a beat and his face flushed with heat. Had he pushed too far? He didn't care. His newfound control overrode the fear that threatened to creep up and grab him and he drove forward.

"Maybe. But then again, maybe you missed it."

"Don't push your luck, Mr. Searls. You caught me in a good mood this morning, and I agreed to give you the chip." She sidled closer and whispered into his ear. "You don't want to get on my bad side. I keep telling people we don't really need you. We already have a weapon that can drop a bomb anywhere."

The words sent a chill up his spine, but he knew he couldn't back down now. Besides, he'd learned something new. Ms. Peters had a boss, and that boss didn't want him dead. "I'm already on your bad side." He rotated his chair to face the desk and picked up the chip from his palm with two fingers, pretending to examine it as if it was somehow tainted. All of his attention was focused on what was happening behind him. He could feel the heat of her anger on his back, half expecting the guards to haul him from the chair and drag him from the lab.

After what felt like an hour but couldn't have been more than a few seconds, he heard the tapping of her heels as she walked away. The airlock door swished again, and he relaxed, slouching forward and cradling his head in his hands. He let out a slow, ragged breath. The chattering in the lab increased beyond the regular background noise. It seemed he had made an impression on more than Ms. Peters.

Despite his attempt at courage, he still fought the compulsion to run after her, to apologize for his attitude, how he had acted. When the urge finally dissipated, he realized he actually felt pretty good. In fact, he was proud of how he'd handled the situation. His first step into retaining at least a semblance of control had been a huge one, but it had worked. As long as they needed him, he would continue to push at the boundaries they had set, and he figured he would most likely get away with it.

He examined the chip in his hands again. It hadn't been a joke when he'd suggested the controller may have been modified. It could have been something simple, like having the computer request a sequential read, and the controller randomizing it instead. That would have been a fairly easy one to find, though. There were ways to hack a controller so it appeared to be doing what was asked, but in reality it did something completely different. If it *had* been hacked that way, there was a chance it was too subtle for Ms. Peters and her people.

It didn't matter anyway. This memory chip was a copy, and wouldn't have a hacked controller. If there was one. Either the data on it was a duplicate of the original, or it wasn't. He'd still have to run the same tests.

Back in Meridian and Kadokawa, his computers had been some of the most powerful on the Sat City; superfast optical backplanes and memory, available online storage in the petabyte range, and a few hundred processors to bring it all together. They were even better here. Back then, he'd developed algorithms that would find patterns in mass quantities of data, a must when dealing with the quantum information of the engines. Applying those algorithms to the chip would require some changes, but they weren't insurmountable.

He inserted the blue square into the reader on his computer and took a preliminary glance at what it contained. As Ms. Peters had said, it was garbage. Certainly not what he had written to it a few weeks ago. Whatever had scrambled the data, it had done a good job. He cracked his knuckles. Time to get to work.

Modifying the code took him longer than expected. He'd done some quick work and had the software parse the data, but it was still too messed up for it to make sense of what it saw. That's when he got serious, and the changed code flew from his brain to his fingertips to the computer in front of him. Even the noise of the lab disappeared. It was the first time since he'd been brought here that he lost himself in a problem.

When he was finished, an exact copy of the chip was in his computer's memory, and the new software began its job of making sense of the garbage he saw. It would take a while. He left his station and grabbed a cup of tea. The algorithms didn't work any faster if he was watching them.

He'd already finished his second cup and started working with one of the other people in the lab on the alignment on the nanofilaments in the shielding when the lights flickered. At first he thought he'd imagined it. Someone in the far corner gave a little shriek and everyone stopped what they were doing, staring upward at the embedded fixtures. When it didn't happen again, they continued their work.

Bryson had spent most of his life after university on a Sat City, and he had never seen something like that before. Individual lights burned out, but never a room-wide failure. No matter how short. It was as though the entire grid had lost power for a split second.

He was still uneasy by the time he got back to his station. To his surprise, the software had finished running. The vid screen was blank except for a single line of text at the top, the cursor blinking lazily behind it.

Information retrieval aborted by ACE. Have a nice day.

He drew in a sharp breath as he focused on the words.

Fingers flying over the keyboard again, he modified the code and reran it. Since the computer had the basic patterns of the data already stored, the algorithms ran significantly faster. He did it three more times, with each result showing the same single line of text on the screen. Each pass deepened the hollow pit in his stomach. There was a small chance if he cleared the data and started the tests from scratch, it would come up with a different result, but each time he changed the code and tested again, the chance grew smaller and smaller. He tried it anyway, with the same results.

Somehow, ACE had gotten hold of his chip.

His hands were shaking as he picked up the comm unit and called Ms. Peters.

It wasn't until he closed the link that he realized what he had done. She knew everything that had happened after he'd left Kadokawa, and there were only two places the chip could have been switched. The mugger outside the crappy hotel, or when that girl, Kris, had rescued him and brought him to the old man's restaurant. He had no way to warn her. Ms. Peters had said they'd already ruled out both of them, especially the mugger. What if the girl and the old Chinese guy *had* done it?

That meant they had everything they needed to build a quantum jump ship. Once they had that they could travel almost anywhere instantaneously. All they needed was a corporation to fund them.

He may have just gotten her killed. Or worse.

FOUR

LOS ANGELES LEVEL 5—TUESDAY, JULY 4, 2141 2:14 P.M.

THE BLUE COMPACT car was nowhere to be seen when I left Doc Searls, and none of the other cars had anyone in them that looked like the woman driver. I hadn't seen the passenger—the man on the comm unit—too clearly, but if the driver wasn't around, he wouldn't be either. That's what I hoped anyway.

I shook my head. Nerves were making me see things where there wasn't anything to see.

Ian had always been vigilant, always been aware of what was going on around him. Was this what it was like for him? Constantly second guessing yourself? Trying to find possible patterns where none existed? I didn't think so, but if it was, I had no idea how he hadn't gone fucking crazy from it. It's how I was starting to feel, jumping at shadows that had probably been there my whole life. If I had bothered to take notice.

A small voice in the back of my mind started talking, the one ACE had cultivated in me during training. *That didn't mean no one was following me.* I tried to shut it up. Turning into a paranoid freak wasn't on my to-do list. I rolled my shoulders in an attempt to get the tense muscles to relax.

The only person who had reason to look for me would have been Janice, and I only knew that because she'd almost gotten me. That had ended with her going over the handlebars of her motorcycle. There was no way she'd walked away from that. So really, there was no reason for anyone to follow me. Right?

Despite trying to convince myself, I kept up the standard rotation of left mirror, right mirror, and straight ahead. Knowing I was about to be home helped me relax, but I didn't ease off on the vigilance.

In between the scans, I thought of Doc Searls and Bryson. It was obvious Doc wished his relationship with Bryson was better. Stronger. The look on his face when he talked about his son was one of sadness and remorse mixed with hope and pride. The effect his jumbled emotions had on me was immediate and powerful. I was barely hanging on as it was, and Doc had pushed me even closer to the edge. I opened the helmet's visor and let the wind dry off my new onset of tears. At least he still had a chance to reunite his family. I didn't.

The down-ramp back to Level 4 was virtually unprotected. A couple of SoCal soldiers patrolled at the entrance to the ramp, scanning me as I went down, but that was about it. They were treating the ramp the same as they did the Level 6 access ones, making it tough to get up, but easy to get down.

I passed a small bunch of skateboarders lounging at the top of the down-ramp to Level 2. Most of the buckles on their armor were undone and they were sitting on the barrier by the ramp entrance.

By the look of it, they'd either missed a group going down or were waiting for more of their friends to join them.

The boarders had become more aggressive since last year. Almost as if the constant threat of SoCal military drafts had given them even more of a reason to be assholes. I couldn't blame them, really.

If a bunch were heading down, I could probably stay behind them until they reached the bottom. If I met them on their way up instead, my best bet was to ride back up against traffic and pick a different ramp to go down. I figured it was worth the risk and entered the down-ramp, passing a few slow-moving cars.

I caught up with the boarders about halfway down. There were two dozen at least, hitting speeds of fifty kilometers an hour as they zigzagged down the ramp between the dark fibercrete walls. I was pretty sure that if they had decided to ride the center line, they would've hit speeds of ninety or more. But then they couldn't have bothered any vehicles coming down after them, and bothering people was always their goal.

I slowed down and stayed a good couple hundred meters back, giving me enough space to turn around if they decided to stop. A car hugged the wall on my right and passed me, looking for a gap to get through the boarders. It was a stupid move. As it got close to them, one boarder swerved, leaving an opening for the car to take. I dropped farther back. I'd seen this ploy before. It wasn't going to end well.

The car nosed into the opening and the boarders gave it more room. As it pushed in deeper, a few of them fell back and rode in behind it. Before the driver knew what was happening, the car couldn't go forward without running someone over, and couldn't slow down without one of them running into it. The brake lights flickered with indecision. That was when the boarders moved in.

Two of them ollied, jumping their boards and grabbing them

with one hand while placing the other one on the front of the car. The car's forward speed popped them right onto its hood. They landed on their feet with their boards in hand and at the ready. Both of them swung at the windshield at the same time and the glass cracked in a spiderweb of lines.

The driver finally made a decision and slammed on the brakes, stopping in the middle of the ramp. I stayed well back, the bike angled in case I needed to take off.

The two boarders on the hood rolled off onto the fibercrete, their armor taking the brunt of the impact. They'd done this before. They were back on their feet before the driver could figure out what to do next.

Boarders swarmed the car. A half dozen of them reached under the molded front bumper to the frame behind it and lifted, jamming their boards under it before letting go. It didn't matter what the driver did now, the drive wheels were off the ground. The car wasn't going anywhere.

In the sudden silence, I heard the thunk of the car doors locking. It didn't really matter. The boarders smashed at every window until the glass crystallized in a latticework of confusion. They all exploded inwards. A total of twenty seconds had passed, and they were grabbing the driver and pulling her out through the shattered glass.

I couldn't let this happen. I dropped the bike into gear.

Before I could move, a huge truck rounded the corner below the attack. Gray on gray. There was only one type of vehicle that color, only one that would drive up a down-ramp. SoCal military. I popped the clutch, racing up the ramp and leaving the boarders and their victim in a frozen tableau as they watched the truck approach them.

I rushed past the stopped traffic, my breath coming in short bursts. Horns honked as I fought to fit through cars that had almost collided while trying to pass everyone else. Squeezing against the wall, I weaved between chunks of fibercrete, the knobby edge of my tires gripping in the loose grit. The top of the ramp came into view.

The boarders at the entrance weren't there anymore. In their place sat another truck. Gray on gray, its matte black logo of the California coastline barely visible. Soldiers with guns stood in front of it. No traffic entered the ramp behind the last car. I let go of the throttle, my hand numb and fingers tingling from gripping so tight. Deep in my chest, I felt the too-familiar sensation of fear reaching for my thumping heart, squeezing the life out to silence the steady beat.

I turned around and sped back down, leaving a black streak of rubber behind me. As I weaved through the standstill traffic, drivers got out of their cars, wondering what had happened below to stall the flow. I could use them. It might be my only chance.

I eased back on the throttle and the bike slowed. At every quizzical look, every open window or door, I yelled as loud as possible. *Draft!* Fear spread like a ripple in a scummy pond, racing ahead of me as I continued my descent. More people stepped out, hesitant until my momentum caused them to move in the same direction—a mass of humanity pouring down the ramp, the pace picking up, until they ran full speed. My message reached ahead like the hand of death.

People stumbled and fell. Some were picked up. Some were trampled. Some managed to roll under a car. No one seemed to care. The moving mass was no longer human, no longer sane and rational creatures that helped one another. They were animals with no sense of herd. Human self-preservation at its worst.

They surged past the busted-up car, pushing the boarders ahead of them. The people in front finally realized their way was blocked and tried to slow down. The horde behind them kept on moving. People screamed. There was no stopping the momentum. In only a few more steps, bodies would be crushed against the SoCal truck and the row of soldiers stretched across the ramp. A siren blared in the enclosed space, the echo louder than original, bouncing along the walls in an attempt to escape. Another blast and the panicked crowd faltered.

A gap opened and I swerved left, racing beside the wall, dodging people and accelerating as the siren screamed again. A body slammed into the back of the bike, sending me into a slide. I hit the ground hard, my helmet cracking against the road as the bike skidded below me. My eyes lost focus. I rotated onto my back, keeping my feet pointing downward. The bike smashed through the soldiers, taking a couple of them out. Their linked line of armor and weapons broke. I slid through the crack, followed by anyone close enough to see what I had done and alert enough to take advantage of it.

The bike collided with the wall and spun before coming to a stop. I pushed off the still-rotating rear tire, moving farther into the road. People ran past me, over me. I rolled onto my feet and stumbled away. I had to lose myself in the chaos. Gunshots echoed off the ceiling and the crowd wavered again. The confusion helped me. I was going to make it.

I had to make it.

SOCAL SAT CITY 2—TUESDAY, JULY 4, 2141 3:06 P.M.

Janice had been on shuttles before, even visited a Sat City back when she was still working for Jeremy, so it was nothing new. It was rare enough for her that normally she would have felt a little excited, but not knowing what her future was going to be squashed that. They'd landed on some sort of military deck of SoCal 2 instead of the main terminal. That was new.

She'd been hauled down plain composite hallways by military police until they had gotten here.

Now she sat in what she could only call a prison cell. Sure, it was a higher-class one than she had ever seen before—and she'd seen quite a few—but it was still a cell. Four walls, a table bolted to the wall with two chairs, and a locked door. She double-checked the lock, thinking it looked like a simple push-button mechanism. She was right. With a lock that simple, she could be out of the room in less than five seconds. The problem was, where would she go after that?

SoCal Sat City 2 was huge, but it didn't matter. When you were floating in space in a fucking tin can, there weren't too many places to hide. Correction, there were a lot of places you could hide, just not for long. So she sat in her tiny, weak prison cell and waited until someone came to get her. That had lasted long enough for her to have to pee so bad, she had considered going in the corner. Instead, she finally decided to pop the lock.

There wasn't much to see on the other side of the door. Just a hallway with a few more doors like hers along one side. There was a single door at the end—the one they had brought her through on the way in—and she headed for that. No lock. No guard. No bathroom. She was jogging through the interconnected rooms, trying to keep her steps smooth so she wouldn't jostle her bladder and hoping she would find someone who could point her in the right direction. Her need pushed aside the discomfort in her leg.

Were they trying to test her? That didn't make sense. Were they so sure of themselves that they didn't care? Again, that didn't make sense either. So what the fuck was going on? She dashed around for ten minutes before she found a bathroom, sprinting to the door and barely making it. When she walked out, a woman with a stun gun waited for her. Where the hell was she when Janice had almost peed herself?

SoCal implemented the same rules in their Sat cities as they did in San Angeles. No guns. Janice found it interesting that they also applied the rule to their security forces up here. The woman didn't say anything, instead simply pointing back in the direction Janice had come.

It was only when they got to the room outside the prison hallway that Janice noticed the floor change from carpet to plain white tile. John Smith sat waiting for them. He stood and smiled, as though her getting out of the locked room and being led back by a guard was an everyday occurrence and nothing to be concerned over.

"Ah, there you are! Time to meet your new best friend. Follow me." He beckoned with his hand and the guard fell in behind them.

The elevator they got on went up several floors before it came to a stop, the doors opening into a hallway with a security desk. They were let through and took another elevator up. This time when the doors opened, the view left Janice breathless and a bit giddy. It took everything she had not to gape at what she saw. The far wall was covered in mossy green plants, and in the center was a waterfall splashing into a small pool at the base. Brilliantly colored flowers punctuated the space.

The floor was plush, covered in a carpet that matched the greenery without taking away from it. Wood grain covering wrapped the other three walls, and a reception desk blended in, almost hidden from view. A man stood from behind the desk and smiled.

"Go right in. She's expecting you."

John led Janice to the living wall. As they got closer, she noticed it was overlapped in one place, creating an almost hidden passage. If you didn't know it was there, you'd have to be at the right angle to see it. Security through obscurity? She let her fingers touch the moss as she walked past, and the guard slapped her hand away.

John walked beside her now, waving at the guard to stay behind them. The hallway was lined with the same wood grain material as the reception area. Just to show the guard what she thought, Janice slid her fingers along it.

"Mahogany and cherry wood. I believe it's real," John said.

She jerked her hand back.

He laughed. "A common reaction. Your fingers won't hurt it though."

A waterfall, real wood. Enough of it to fill a forest, Janice thought. She'd never really seen a forest, besides the scrappy pine outside the compound, but she had a pretty good idea of how many trees were in one. If this was all designed to put visitors at ease, it wasn't working on her. The unimaginable amount of money on display was too much. Still, she wanted this kind of life for herself—although maybe not this extravagant—and would do whatever it took to get it.

John stopped at a door and knocked, only opening it when Janice heard a faint "Come in."

In stark contrast to the richness of the reception area and the hallway, this room was white and gray. Simple furniture made the room seem bigger than it was. One entire wall was covered in bookcases, filled to almost overflowing but never getting to the point where it looked messy or out of control. It was the only thing in the room that spoke of money, and the understated aspect of it made it even more apparent.

A man, dressed simply in a black dress shirt and pants with creases so sharp Janice was sure she could use them as a weapon, turned from the bookcase. He didn't acknowledge them or even look in their direction. Instead, he moved to a small table that contained a sweating carafe of water. Without asking, he poured three large glasses, handing two of them to John and Janice.

John nodded his head in thanks while Janice took a sip of the cold liquid.

"Ms. Peters will be with you soon." The man glanced at Janice in distaste.

John nodded again, still not drinking. When the man left the room, leaving the third glass on the table with the carafe, John visibly relaxed. Janice tried for another sip and he touched her arm, shaking his head.

She still wasn't sure why she'd been brought up here.

A door opened in the side wall and John stood straighter, his movements became more formal.

The woman walking in went straight for the water glass and took a sip before turning back to them. She walked to her desk and sat, motioning toward the two empty chairs in front of her. "Please, sit. Enjoy your water."

Only after John was in the chair did he drink from his glass, cradling it in his other hand when he was done. Janice copied him. Normally, she was pretty relaxed. Wherever she was, whoever she was with, they could take her or leave her. Even in front of Jeremy, she had always been relaxed. Vigilant, but relaxed. But this whole environment made her feel uncomfortable and out of her depth. She shifted in her chair, earning a quick glance from John.

Ms. Peters put her glass on a small coaster on the desk. "Tell me what you told John. Leave nothing out."

The glass Janice held was suddenly heavy and slippery, but she didn't have any place to put it down. Instead, she gripped it with both hands and for the second time told a complete stranger everything she knew about Jeremy, ACE, and Kris.

LOS ANGELES LEVEL 2—TUESDAY, JULY 4, 2141 3:15 P.M.

Pat walked out of what she called the cold storage room in the subbasement, a pad in her hand and a frown on her face. They were still low on food, and what they had was already beginning to go bad.

This room was originally designed to store what the tenants of the building above couldn't put in their apartments. When Pat had first seen the room, it was separated into small areas with chain-link fencing that reached from the ceiling to the floor. She had turned it into food storage, and it wasn't cold enough to keep things fresh for long. Not even with the cooler Level 2 temperatures.

Today, the people would be able to eat more than their normal share. It was better to use all the food than let it sit and go to rot. She passed her pad to one of the other people in the hallway. Her orders were already written on it.

"Use anything that is starting to go bad. Give the street kitchens as much as they can take."

The man nodded, walking away as her comm unit beeped. She pulled it from her pocket and read the display. It was Jack. Either he was fast, or something new had come up. She wished it was something new, but knowing Jack, he was already getting ready to countermand her food orders.

Someone had already told him what she was doing.

When Jack had been moved into his position, he'd filled his staff with people he knew, people he'd worked with, surrounding himself with people he trusted, no matter what their skill set. He'd ended up with a bunch of lackeys and yes men. She answered the comm unit.

"What?"

"You're using twice as much food today as yesterday."

"Yeah, it's starting to go bad." Jackass. It figured he was already trying to second-guess her.

"We're running low," Jack said.

"It's going bad. By tomorrow, the lettuce and tomatoes will be brown goo. I need food that can hold better, or a proper refrigerator to store them in."

There was silence on the link before Jack spoke again. "Exchange what is going bad with something less perishable from the Chinatown and the Skid Row kitchens. Make sure our people are fed."

Pat frowned. "That will work for today and maybe tomorrow. What about after that?"

"Your orders are to keep our people fed. We need our strength for what's coming up."

"So you're willing to hurt the people we're trying to protect? And what *is* coming up? You've kept me out of the loop ever since Kris and I went out the hole in the wall."

"That cost us a lot of resources with no return."

"So I'm being punished? Is that why you put me on food? You told us the only thing you wanted was to get your people back. We did that."

There was another pause. "Come up to my office."

The link went dead.

Pat jammed the comm unit into her pocket. Food was running out. The people they were supposed to be helping were starving. Water was at a premium. Between SoCal rationing the water and Jack rationing the food, people were going to start dying. That wasn't how this was supposed to go.

The last run on the greenhouses had been great, and they had some vegetables that would last, even if they weren't properly refrigerated. Everyone would be eating potatoes and carrots for quite a while. But what they really needed were nonperishables. And a lot of them. SoCal still used trucks to get food from the Level 1 docks to Level 7. If they could get a couple of those . . . There was no point. It was too well protected. Pat left the sub-basement and crossed the lobby.

The two guards were still standing at the double doors. They let her in without a word. Jack's office door was open, and she could smell food in the hallway. She walked in without knocking. Jack and one of his cronies sat at the meeting table, with two plates of food and a pitcher of water on it. Her blood began to boil.

Enough was enough.

Pat grabbed the crony by his shirt and hauled him out of his chair. She had him out the door before he even knew what was happening, slamming it in his face and locking it before turning back to Jack. His face was bright red.

"What the—"

"Shut up and sit down." Pat yanked his plate away and turned it over on top of the other one. Mashed potatoes with gravy squished out from between the plates and plopped onto the table, followed by small chunks of meatloaf and pieces of carrot. Pat sat and stared at the still standing Jack until he finally sat down as well. "People are starving."

"I was talking to the cooks today. Everyone is getting more than enough."

"I'm talking about out there." She pointed to the wall facing the street. "When was the last time you left this building?"

Jack examined his fingernails. "I've been busy. We're planning an offensive to take back portions of Level 3 and 4. Places where we can control more of the water and gain access to the food warehouses. Winning that will help everyone."

"In the meantime, you eat meat and potatoes while the people out there have vegetable flavored water and soft tofu?"

Someone pounded on the door. Pat didn't move. She was so angry every muscle twitched. They pounded again.

"I'm fine," Jack yelled, exasperated. The pounding stopped. "We need our strength," he said in a softer voice. "The people inside this building and others like it are the ones who will be on the front lines next week."

"I agree, we need our strength, but if the people we are supposedly doing this for are dead, what's the point? You have to see how the food distribution isn't fair, never mind the water. What did you do with the spaghetti water from last week's dinner? Did you dump it? Recycle it? Or maybe, just maybe, you gave it to the street kitchens to add a bit more flavor to their meals. I'm sure they'll be forever grateful." She couldn't keep the sarcasm out of her voice.

"I'll ask the cook."

"I don't expect you to know everything that goes on around here, but food and water are the big topics, and not just inside this building. You need to keep on top of that."

Jack stopped cleaning under his fingernails. "That's why I gave you the job."

"Sure. And I'm doing it the best I can. When I say we're running low, you send out teams to collect perishable goods. And why? Because it makes a statement to SoCal, not because it's what we can use to feed people for more than a week."

Jack sighed and leaned back in his chair. His whole body looked exhausted. "I didn't want to be here, you know?"

"What?"

"All of this," he waved his hands around the room. "I didn't want it. I enjoyed my job. Talking to informants, coordinating medical care, talking about plans with Kai so I could write a report and make myself look good. I wasn't cut out to lead. This was supposed to be temporary, and now they can't afford to send someone else. They're as fucked up as we are."

"So? It's time to step up. Work with what you've been handed. You can start by coming with me to see what everyone else is putting up with. These people are your responsibility now."

Jack's posture changed, and he looked nervous and uncomfortable. "I read your reports."

"That's obviously not working."

He spread his hands on the table, eyeing the upside down plate. "What is it that you want from me?"

"Come to the Chinatown kitchens with me. Today. Now. You've seen what we feed *our* people. Come and see what we feed them." She stood and waited by the door.

"I have a meeting right away—"

"Fuck the meeting. You've been in here so long that everything has been relegated to a report or a column on a spreadsheet. Come with me and really remember why we're doing this."

"I know why we're doing this."

"Do you?" Pat opened the door. Outside stood one of the guards. Behind him was Jack's dinner guest.

"That's her. Arrest her!"

The guard moved forward.

Pat had enough. She ignored Jack and stared into the guard's eyes. "If you touch me, you'll wake up in the hospital next week."

The guard hesitated before moving to reach for her again.

"It's okay," Jack stood behind her in the doorway. "Pat and I are . . . are going out. Get a security team ready."

"Alone," Pat said.

"I can't. It's . . . Look what happened to my predecessors . . ." He stopped, looking at the faces staring back at him from the doorway. Suddenly slouching, he sighed and nodded. "I'm going to the Chinatown street kitchen."

The guard followed them to the double doors and went back to his position. Pat had already forgotten about the crony as they left the building.

LOS ANGELES LEVEL 3—TUESDAY, JULY 4, 2141 3:43 P.M.

I took the risk of peeking over my shoulder. Behind us, the soldiers had regrouped their lines and were slowly advancing on the people still trapped in front of them. I looked forward in time to see the man in front of me falter and trip. Jumping over him, my foot caught his raised arm. I lost my balance, careening until my legs could catch up with my body. The people behind me drove me forward until the man was out of sight.

SoCal wasn't stupid. They would know that some people could make it past the soldiers. That left two possible situations. One, they didn't care. They would catch more the next time they tried. Or two, and more likely, they had soldiers waiting at the bottom of the ramp.

All the ramps had access panels to the inter-level equipment, similar to the one in the parking garage Ian had pulled me into when he had rescued me from Quincy. Ian had a key to open his door. I didn't have anything.

The group was thinner by the walls, with most of the people who made it through choosing to clump in the middle of the ramp. Typical crowd mentality, and something SoCal would be expecting. I started edging toward the wall, fighting against the steady pressure of bodies trying to merge with the crowd. By the time I'd reached it, the bottom of the ramp was in sight.

Below the point where the wall turned into a barrier, another row of soldiers stood across the entire ramp. Behind them were a collection of panel trucks, the doors open, ready to accept the captives. The sight of them almost made me stop.

The barrier here was fifteen meters above the ground. They started it about five meters below the level of the ceiling—no point in giving anyone easy access to that—but high enough so if I decided to take that route, I'd be badly hurt when I hit the bottom. I didn't know if they'd come and collect me from the floor, or let me lie there until some locals found me.

The thought of lying under a Level 2 down-ramp, too hurt to move, filled me with as much dread as being caught by SoCal. At least they would want to keep me alive. I couldn't say the same for the people who lived here. Both my son and I would live if I chose SoCal. There really wasn't much of a decision to make, but I wasn't going down without a fight.

I stopped, my back pressed to the wall, and pulled out my comm unit. First things first, I had to make sure my tracker was set to something valid. It wasn't. I'd programmed the comm unit to change the tracker ID every five minutes, so I couldn't be traced. That was usually safer than programming to no ID. I changed back to my Kris Merrill ID and quickly switched to sending a text message. I typed in a single word, attached my coordinates, and sent it off to Pat.

Drafted.

Then I dropped the phone and smashed it with the heel of my shoe, scattering the pieces over the road. Standard procedure. *Don't let SoCal know I can change my ID.* If they found out, my life expectancy dropped. A lot. The way I saw it, I still had a chance to get away, but it was slim. ACE had drilled into me to always be prepared, and that's what the text to Pat was all about.

Following protocol, even if it was ACE protocol, helped calm me down. I slowed my breathing and watched the flow of the group ahead of me.

The people had thinned. Some, like me, had stopped on the ramp, watching as the soldiers below corralled anyone who was the right age. Old people and young kids were separated, the kids moved to another group of SoCal soldiers, the old ones let go. From farther up the ramp, I could hear more people approaching.

It was now or never.

I slid along the barrier, my shoulders slumped and my feet dragging in the grit left behind from crumbling walls and passing vehicles. This is where my height helped, and my posture made me seem even smaller and weaker. I could almost see the soldier in front of me relax as I got closer. I didn't think I'd be mistaken for being too young, but I could be overlooked as too weak.

When I was two feet away from the line, I exploded outwards, kicking forward with the heel of my foot into the soldier's knee. She fell, collapsing forward onto her hands. She didn't even have time to scream from the pain. Her knee would never be the same. She'd probably get a desk job. I leaped over her crumpled form.

I was midair when something slammed into my back. Air exploded from my lungs.

I fell on top of the woman, and the world disappeared.

LOS ANGELES LEVEL 2—TUESDAY, JULY 4, 2141 3:27 P.M.

The food lines were still going strong, even this late in the afternoon. Pat and Jack weren't close yet, and they could already hear the noise from all the people. Hundreds of quiet conversations echoed between the buildings and the ceiling. At every sharp noise, Jack twitched and looked like he wanted to run for cover.

He had been slowing down the closer they had gotten to the food tables, and stopped a few feet away. His head swiveled, and Pat could see his eyes darting from face to face, never quite stopping to focus on the details, but taking it all in. A scowl replaced the look of fear on his face.

"Christ! I've read the numbers on how many people we feed, but seeing it is completely different."

Pat stayed silent.

"With this many people, we need more security details. If a fight broke out, it could turn into a complete riot. We need a team of people to manage and liaison with the workers here. I'll order—"

"No. Stop." Pat's voice was sharp. "We don't need security teams, or people with guns, or managers. Don't you see that would only raise the level of tension? Bringing in guards or soldiers would guarantee a riot instead of prevent one. Look at these people. For some, this may be their only meal today. The water they take home with them will have to last until they can come back. Do you see any shoving or pushing in line? Do you see any anger at all? Look over there." Pat pointed about midway down the line on the right. "That man let a family of four get in front of him. This time of day, there's a really good chance he gave up his meal so those kids could eat. And if that's the case, there's an even better chance the mother and father will split their meals with him and their kids."

"You mean . . . we can't feed them all?"

"No, we can't. Even your numbers should have shown you that. Some of the reason we can't feed them all is because we still get our three meals a day. Half the people in our building don't even know this exists, but isn't this what we are supposed to be fighting for?"

Jack nodded.

"This isn't just happening here. The entire city is like this. Between the fucking drafts and the rationing by SoCal, we are dying. It may not seem like it to us, but why don't you go and ask them? How many buildings like ours do the insurgents have? How many people are getting all the food and water they need while these people starve?"

"So, what's your plan?" He kept staring at the family of four as though they had torn out his heart and were holding it on display.

"The first is to cut our rations and bring the surplus here, to the kitchens. That will extend our ability to feed *everyone*. The second is to get more food. Something less perishable, something that will last if SoCal decides to let us all just fucking die. Don't you see? We're replaceable. As far as they're concerned, we breed like vermin, and in another couple of generations, everyone will forget what SoCal did to us. They'll find someone else to blame, so if there is another corporate war, if this one doesn't kill us all, they'll have more people to recruit or draft."

"And where do we get more food?"

This was where she could get in trouble. She drew in a deep breath. "I don't know. You keep me in the kitchens and storage areas, I don't get access to the information I need to come up with a plan."

Jack nodded again. "I can't tell you what will happen at the other insurgent compounds, but we start rationing tomorrow. We'll keep to three meals a day, but make the portions smaller. It's the best I can do. I'll pass the word up the line to see what the other cells are doing. Maybe they can help. I'll get you access so you can find another source of food."

Pat grinned, barely able to get the words out. He was giving her more than she'd hoped for. "Thank you." The comm unit in her pocket vibrated. She pulled it out, expecting to see another message from the head cook. Instead the display showed Kris's name. Pat opened the message and shuffled back a few steps.

"What's wrong?"

"Kris has been drafted." She was getting lightheaded and leaned against Jack's outstretched arm for support.

"Are you sure? Call her back."

Pat's hands went cold and she almost dropped the comm unit. "There's no point. ACE training says she should reset her tracker ID to its default and destroy the phone in order to limit SoCal's knowledge on our ability to change the tracker."

"She didn't finish training. Maybe she—"

"She finished, out here on the streets. Kris is smart and she knows what would happen if they found out she could change her ID."

"Do we know where she is?"

Pat reread the message. It contained the coordinates of Kris's location. "Level 2 down-ramp, north of Chinatown. She's close!"

Jack grabbed his own comm unit and created a link. Pat heard him order a team out to the site. Her numb brain made the words sound a million kilometers away. She fought the pull of memories, trying to root herself into the present.

"We're preparing a team. If we can get her out, we will. If we can't, we'll do whatever we need to make sure she doesn't talk."

Pat nodded and turned away, leaving Jack at the tables. The threat in his words reverberated in her ears. Would he think the same way if he knew Kris was pregnant? She closed her eyes and breathed deep, forcing her brain to function normally, to not be pulled back into the war in her head. Fighting the urge to take out Jack where he stood. When she opened her eyes, he was standing in front of her, concern written all over his face. She didn't believe it for a second.

"You okay?"

She nodded again, wondering how the bastard could even ask her that question. "Yeah." Another deep breath. "Yeah. We can't coordinate the team from here. Come on let's go." She'd have to find a way to be in charge of the team to make sure Jack wasn't able to follow through on his threat.

He started jogging back to the insurgents' building. Pat grabbed his arm, holding him back.

"You have hundreds of people behind you living in fear. Don't push them to the edge of panic. They've all seen you here. They may not know who you are, but they look at the way you dress, how the people serving the food treat you. If you run, they'll panic." Just saying the words helped calm Pat. She wanted to bolt to the insurgents' building, get in with the crew going out to the coordinates. But she fought against the urge.

Instead she just walked, as if the only person she really cared about wasn't about to become a foot soldier in a war she despised.

She punched in Kai's number on her comm unit.

FIVE

SOCAL SAT CITY 2—TUESDAY, JULY 4, 2141 9:05 P.M.

BRYSON SLUMPED BEHIND his vid screen, his head resting in his hands as he rocked back and forth. The other people in the lab had been escorted out hours ago, leaving him alone to figure out where things were going wrong. The quiet seeped into his bones, and he shivered.

The copied memory chip was essentially empty—one of the reasons Ms. Peters and her group couldn't decrypt the damn thing. There wasn't anything to decrypt. It was pretty much random gibberish except for the message from ACE, and one other thing. There was a single packet that looked different than the rest, at least to his algorithms. He doubted anyone else would have been able to see the difference. After a few hours of poking around and tearing it apart, the only conclusion he could come to was the packet contained a virus. A mean one that had already been deployed.

His first reaction had been to unplug his computer, but at that point it was probably already too late. The chances the virus had escaped onto the lab network were near enough to one hundred percent that it was guaranteed. The good news was that the chance of it having left the lab was significantly less. The lab's network was pretty much isolated from the rest of the city. But not completely. He knew his data was backed up every night, and that Ms. Peters could see anything on his computer at any time. That implied some sort of connectivity. He didn't have access to any of that, and couldn't trace it.

If the virus was as dangerous as it seemed, it would find those holes.

He'd thought about contacting Ms. Peters again. She obviously hadn't been watching him in real time when the virus unpacked itself, or she would have been down here long before now. Unless the damn thing had taken care of that as well. Or maybe she had no clue what she was looking at. He didn't even pick up the comm unit, mostly out of spite. If they thought they could kidnap him and force him to work without any repercussions, who was he to try and stop a virus from infiltrating SoCal's systems? With the protections they would have in place, it wouldn't live long anyway. Maybe some of the information it would grab would tell people he was up here. A prisoner. Maybe they would come and get him. It only made sense that *they* had to be ACE, and ACE had some people who could come and help. Didn't they?

He studied the chip sitting on the stainless steel countertop. It seemed simple enough, an unlabeled blue square that looked almost like the one he had dumped the quantum drive information onto. There wasn't anything special about it. Strange how something so small might be the only way someone on the outside would know where he was.

He kept staring at the chip. Blue on top of silver. Something in his brain niggled. Blue on top of silver. Color. Frequencies. Quanta. The thought snapped into place and his fingers raced over the keyboard in front of him, the virus forgotten. A detailed three-dimensional image of Meridian's quantum ship popped up on the screen, and he zoomed in. The outer shell, or shield, of the habitable area contained hundreds of millions of quantum wells and transmitters. The wells converted and stored ultraviolet photons for later use. The frequency of ultraviolet light fell between 130 and 140 nanometers. The problem was, the frequency was wrong. Using the 100–120 spectrum was what they needed. The different range prevented the quantum eddies from penetrating into the living space of the vessel. How the hell had he forgotten that? Coupled with the engine design fix he'd done on Kadokawa, that had solved the protection issue.

He moved the formulas into the proper part of the spectrum and started more tests. It would take some time for the simulation to find the exact frequency, but he expected positive results by the morning.

He stared at the screen, watching the simulation run through its steps, everything else pushed aside in the thrill of discovery.

LOS ANGELES LEVEL 3—TUESDAY, JULY 4, 2141 4:02 P.M.

Two people stood on either side of me, supporting most of my weight as we waited in line among the others captured in the sweep. The one on my left was so tall he had to crouch so he didn't lift me off the ground. As soon as the line moved, he let me go and I almost dropped. The woman on the right grunted and took most of my weight. I struggled to get my feet under me.

"How you doing?" she asked.

I shook my head, staring at the ground as everything came into focus.

"You took quite a hit. It took three soldiers to stop the one soldier from tearing you apart. I'm still not quite sure why they did it."

"I tried to get out. I thought I'd broken her knee." The line moved forward and I shuffled my feet to keep up.

"That explains the woman, but why would the other soldiers stop her?"

"Quotas," I mumbled. I tried to put some more weight on my feet. My legs shook, but they held me.

"What?"

"Quotas." My voice was stronger. "The soldiers have draft quotas to fill. If they don't fill them, they get extra shifts."

The woman stared at me, squinting. "How do you know that?"

Shit. How did I know that? Only because I'd heard it before dinner at the insurgents' building. The fact that it wasn't common knowledge didn't even occur to me. Until now. "Umm, I don't know. I overheard some guys talking on Level 5 before they closed it off. It may not be true."

"Huh." The woman shifted as I took more weight off of her. "You okay to stand on your own now?"

"Yeah, I think so."

She lifted my arm from around her shoulders and took a small step away, her arms still outstretched to catch me in case I fell. I wavered, but stayed up under my own power. I wasn't sure about moving yet.

"Thanks," I said. "I'm Kris."

"Carlene."

"Thanks, Carlene."

"Don't thank me. Those bastards threw you onto us. We didn't have no choice."

"Thanks anyway." I finally got a good look at her. She was a larger woman, and her face showed signs of age with the hard lines of a difficult life. Despite that impression, her eyes were soft and concern flashed through them. She seemed to be too old for SoCal to want her. Why hadn't she been separated out with the others?

"You'll be okay," she said.

"I'm about to be drafted in a war I don't believe in, made to fight for people I hate. I don't think it's going to be okay." With the words came a deep-rooted fury. I swallowed it, hoarding it for later. I would need everything I had if I wanted to get out of this. I couldn't stop the tears.

Carlene's looked softened and she put a hand on my arm. "You're young yet. They don't draft no one under eighteen. How old are you, sixteen, maybe?"

"Seventeen, but my birthday is at the end of August." Looking younger than I was would have helped me if I didn't have this damn tracker ID. I should have set to an ID younger than I really was.

"Maybe they'll let you go and hope to catch you in the next one, when you're older."

"Quotas."

"If they're real," Carlene said. There wasn't much hope in her voice.

The line shuffled forward, the soldiers keeping us tightly packed. Carlene and I stood in silence. I watched the soldiers. They weren't young, and they had the air of people who had been doing their jobs for a long time and knew how to do it well. The ones at the perimeter of the ad hoc drafting station stood in a rough circle with their backs to the tables and waiting trucks, trusting the ones monitoring the line to keep us in our place. A few of them were chatting with the soldier next to them. Relaxed. Like they'd done this many times before.

It was obvious they didn't use draftees for this job; they used professional enlisted men and women, veterans. Maybe they were worried anyone drafted would have too much sympathy and wouldn't do a good job. Maybe they thought the draftees would try to escape. I knew I would if given the chance.

The line shuffled forward again.

Carlene sighed. "This is your first draft, isn't it?"

"Yeah."

"You're pretty skittish, always looking at the soldiers and fidgeting with your hands."

"You're not," I said.

"Nah. This ain't my first time. Won't be my last."

"What do you mean?"

"I've been in five of these now," Carlene said. "I ran at the first one too, but these old, fat legs don't carry me too far or too fast. Not anymore. They let me go every time. Old and fat ain't what they want. I don't know why they even bother with me, unless it's quotas, like you say. Maybe I'm just borderline fat." She chuckled at that. "Now I wait for them to come and get me. I don't run no more, but I don't help them any neither."

Five? I'd seen a couple of drafts and managed to avoid them, but if one person had been in five, they were a lot more prevalent than I thought. "You're lucky."

"I don't feel lucky. I'm fifty years old, worked hard my whole life to give my kids the best I could. Two, sometimes three jobs to keep them in school with clothes on their backs and food in their bellies. Worked too! I got two boys, both done better than me or their old man ever did. They went to college. One was a plumber, the other wanted to be a teacher. They're both gone now, lord knows where. Both caught in the same draft. I haven't heard from them since, and it's been over a month." Her voice hitched and she took a quick wipe at her eyes. She grabbed my arm and her voice became harsh. "Never let those bastards know they're getting to you. When we get to the front of the line, you stand as tall as you can, and don't you blink.

Show them that you ain't scared. Show them that they got no power over you, over who you are." She paused and glared straight ahead between the few people left between us and them. "It's what I do. I wish I could do more."

I didn't know what to say, so I stayed quiet and grabbed her hand, giving it a tight squeeze before letting it go. We were one person away from the front of the line when she spoke again.

"If you see my boys, Dwane and Markell Porter, you tell them I love them and think about them, okay? Dwane and Markell Porter."

"I will."

"Say their names so you remember them."

"Dwane and Markell Porter."

She nodded fiercely and looked forward again, pushing me behind her as she stepped up to the table. Her back stayed ramrod straight, even as they led her past the circle of soldiers to her freedom.

Then it was my turn. I did as she said, looking the man sitting at the table right in the eye. He was the first to turn away. It was a hollow victory.

"Name."

"Kris Merrill."

"Age."

"Seventeen."

"Take off your jacket and hold out your arm, with your sleeve rolled up."

As I moved to do what he asked, I noticed a woman off to the side, about three meters away. She held a scanner in her hands and moved it up and down my body. "What's she doing?" I knew, of course. She was scanning my ID. I just wanted to see what they would say.

"Jacket and sleeve."

"Not until you tell me what she's doing."

Two soldiers stepped from the sides of the table and stood facing me, one on either side. One of them smelled like he hadn't showered in a week. Was this the fight I wanted to pick? I reached for the zipper on my jacket.

"She's scanning for weapons. Jacket and sleeve, or these two will make it happen for you." He couldn't have sounded more bored.

I shrugged and took off the jacket. It would be obvious to anyone who knew about the IDs what she was doing. I didn't want to be caught with knowledge I shouldn't have.

Once she had a scan, the information would be shown on the display on the table. What would have happened if it didn't match what I'd said? I rolled up my sleeve and felt the jab of a needle in my arm. They didn't take much blood.

Carlene had been told to go left. I was told to go right. They printed out a wristband and wrapped it tightly around my arm. It had a single barcode on it. No text, no numbers. I walked around the corner of a van and stopped. The line in front of me was shorter than the one I'd left, and by the looks of things, the age of everyone in it was younger. Men and women in worn-out suits, boarders in their protective gear, the jackets removed and carried in their hands. I seemed to be the youngest here. No one cared.

We were grouped in batches of twenty and herded into the backs of the large trucks. There were no windows, and the only way out was the same way we had gotten in. Two soldiers followed us and closed the doors behind them. I heard a bar drop.

We were on our way.

LOS ANGELES LEVEL 3—TUESDAY, JULY 4, 2141 4:29 P.M.

"They're gone." Pat closed the link on the comm unit and threw it onto the dashboard. They were still a kilometer away from the draft site. Her insides churned and she thought she might throw up. It had taken them too long to get a team and a truck. Kai had heard what was happening and managed to get a ride with them.

In the back of the tarp-covered truck sat eight men and women. Seven of them had K-3700s, fully prepared for an extraction. The last one had a C14 Timberwolf, an old Canadian sniper rifle. Sandy was the only person Pat trusted, besides Kai. And she wasn't about to send him out with a sniper rifle. Sandy was also the only person that had orders to take out Kris if they couldn't get to her. Orders that wouldn't be followed. Pat would be in debt for a long time to pay off the favor.

"What do we do now?" the driver asked.

"Wait for an update. There's no way we can get her out of a SoCal base. Our best bet is to ambush them on their way to wherever they're going." Almost impossible, she thought. They already had a head start. "There are two places they could take them: southwest to Hawthorne, or north to Burbank."

"My guess is Hawthorne," said Kai. "There is no place big enough to train all the people they are grabbing in San Angeles, so they have to be shipping them out of here. The air base is the quickest way to do that."

"That means they're heading through Level 6 security," the driver said.

"We won't even get to Level 5 with the new checkpoints in place. Our only chance is to stop them from going through. Let's move," said Kai.

The driver stepped on the accelerator and the motor whined in response. He swerved around a slow-moving car, throwing Kai into Pat. "We'll never make it."

"Just fucking drive. Faster!" said Pat.

The truck sped up, the worn and pitted Level 3 road tossing it on its suspension like a rag doll. From the back, Pat heard a curse.

Even strapped in, the people back there were all being thrown around pretty good.

They slowed down again as they approached the up-ramp. Traffic was thin. News of the ramp draft had gotten around pretty quick, and people were scared of getting trapped. No one wanted to be in SoCal's army.

If SoCal was trying to limit movement, what they had done had worked. The truck nosed up the ramp, passing one or two cars on the way, and sped up again. Pat's comm unit rang.

She grabbed it off the dash, reaching almost in front of the driver to where it had bounced. "Pat here." She listened and hung up, gripping the phone tight. "They're heading toward Hawthorne."

Kai smiled, though there wasn't any humor in it.

Traffic was heavier on Level 4, and drones hugged the roof below the Ambients. The driver slowed to the speed of everyone else. Pat knew why he did it—they were already conspicuous with the damn truck as it was. Speeding on top of that would draw more attention. Each person in the back had a temporary blocker under their clothes so they couldn't be tracked. That helped a bit. If the drones scanned the truck and found eight IDs, they would have been stopped and arrested already.

Each slow kilometer that passed drove Pat deeper into frustration. Kai gripped her shoulder, trying to give her some extra strength. A headache was starting to form behind her left ear from clenching her jaw so tight. They stopped the truck less than a kilometer from the Hawthorne Level 5 up-ramp. Pat banged on the back, and the sniper jumped out, running into a building that almost touched the ceiling. Someone inside held the door open and closed it behind her.

Everyone else waited in the truck. After what felt like an eternity, Pat's comm rang again. She put it on speaker.

"Yeah."

"I've got them. Five trucks heading toward the up-ramp. They're bypassing the checkpoint."

"Can you see anyone inside?" Kai asked.

"No. The best I can do is take out a tire and stop the line."

Pat didn't hesitate. "Do it."

Her driver left the curb and continued to the up-ramp just as Pat heard a sharp crack.

"This is going to be suicide," he said in a shaky voice.

A half a second later the voice came over her comm unit again. "Shit. Missed. There's a pretty stiff breeze coming down the ramp."

"Can you compensate?"

"Yes."

"Then try again." Pat knew why she was trying so hard to get Kris back. Kris had become the only family she had. Jack's goal was the safety of the insurgents. Even if it cost Kris her life.

If they got close enough, the extraction team would get her out. It's what they trained—what they lived—for. The real question was how much did she trust the sniper? There was only one answer that worked: she trusted her with Kris's life.

"Missed again. They've mobilized vehicles. Two battle drones heading our way."

Fuck. "Get off the roof. Now. We'll pick you up later tonight." The comm link closed. She turned to the driver. "Get us off the street."

"No can do, no place to go."

"Fuck. Then let's get rid of our cargo."

"I had better go with them," Kai said. "I will see if I can find out what they will do with her after Hawthorne. It is not a training facility, so they won't be keeping them for long."

The truck slowed and seven people jumped out the back, their K-3700s jammed under jackets and stuck down pant legs. They dispersed, each heading in a separate direction. As Kai climbed out of the cab, she gave him a quick smile. How did he keep his cool so easily? The door closed and the truck picked up speed again until the next corner, slowing to turn away from the up-ramp.

"We're going to be stopped," Pat said. "They'll want to know what we're doing. Stick to the story. There's no way for them to tie us in with shooting at the up-ramp. Hell, they may not have even figured out it was a sniper yet. Hopefully we'll just be a mandatory check for them."

The driver's face had gone white. He had a death grip on the steering wheel.

"Breathe, and stick with the cover. We'll get out of this just fine."

A battle drone dropped from the ceiling and hovered in front of the truck, its dual .50-caliber weapons pointing straight at the driver. Its speakers came to life. *Stop the vehicle and get out with your hands up.*

Pat's door was open before the truck had stopped. They both got out and stood between the drone and the truck's grill, waiting. She could hear the driver's raspy breath. If he wasn't careful, he was going to pass out. At least it would still be realistic.

It took only a few minutes for the SoCal ground crew to arrive.

"Lay on the ground, hands behind your back."

The driver responded so quickly, he scraped his cheek on the rough surface of the road. Two men approached and zip-tied their hands and feet. Four more went around the back of the truck.

"Clear."

Pat and the driver were rolled over, staring into the deadly end of machine guns.

"Names."

"Pat Nelson." She added a slight waver to her voice, trying to appear meek and scared.

"D—Dave Fowler."

"What are you doing with the truck?"

"Scavenging," Pat replied. "The lower levels are hurting pretty bad. We figured if we found anything up here, we could sell it to them."

The soldier's boot lashed out, hitting Dave in the chest. "Fucking profit mongers. Willing to rake over your own people for a dollar. If I catch you up here again, I'll shoot you." He turned away. "Let them go."

Pat lay still as they cut the zip ties. These guys were idiots calling her and Dave profit mongers. The corporations ravaged the common people every day, and they'd been doing it for decades. Their bosses were the assholes here.

Before she got to her feet, the soldiers had piled back into their truck and drove off. The drone was nowhere to be seen.

Pat sat back in the truck as Dave slowly picked himself up off the road. She could see he'd been rattled by what had happened. Good. It was experience he could use later. They didn't have near enough of it in the insurgents.

When they rounded the corner she picked up her comm unit again, connecting to the sniper.

"You okay?" she asked.

"Yup. Just packed up and ready to head home."

"Good. Thanks for sticking around."

"No problem."

Pat closed the link and slipped the comm unit into her pocket.

"Who was that?" asked Dave.

"Sandy."

"She's just getting out?"

"Yeah. She covered us during the stop."

"She was watching the whole time?"

"You bet. Never leave anything to chance. If we got into serious trouble, she was ready to cover our escape."

"We would never have made it."

"We had less of a chance without her."

They both got quiet as they drove back down to Level 2. Pat was lost in her own thoughts.

Kris was gone.

LOS ANGELES LEVEL 3—TUESDAY, JULY 4, 2141 4:11 P.M.

The van had no windows, no way to view the outside world. I sat in the semidarkness created by a single strip light along the center of the roof, protected by a thick black cage, stopping anyone from using it as some sort of weapon. The truck was otherwise bare, save us and the seats we sat on. We'd been driving for ten minutes and gone up a level before the people around me began to whisper to each other, trying to find comfort in the sound of voices other than the ones in their heads. The voices harbored the same fear and uncertainty I felt.

My ACE training kicked in, and I started mapping the drive. I closed my eyes and stayed quiet, feeling the motion of the van under me, counting my breaths, keeping track on my hand using unseen motions of my fingers. Whenever I stole a peek, the soldiers were sitting by the door, staring into nothing as the time passed.

By my calculations, we drove for about thirty-five minutes before we hit another up-ramp. Using my best estimation of speed and the number of stops we had made for traffic and lights, I figured we had traveled a little more than twenty kilometers. When we'd been pushed into the trucks, they had been facing south. Based on the turns, we had headed mainly west, toward the ocean.

As the trucks rolled up the second ramp I thought I heard the distinctive sound of a high-speed ricochet. The soldiers didn't seem to notice. Ten minutes later, we hit another up-ramp. That meant we were heading through security. The lack of delay meant we were being expedited through.

We hit another up-ramp. Level 7. If the people in the van could see outside, they would have gone into shock. I doubted a single draftee in any of the trucks had ever been exposed to open sky. We stopped briefly and I heard a gate open, before driving for another couple of minutes. The sound coming from outside changed and we dropped down. Not far enough to go down a level. Underground parking. Keep the draftees in an environment they knew and understood.

The trucks stopped and the rear doors were thrown open. Even in the parking garage, the air felt different than where we had come from. It had lost the permeating scent of the huddled masses, of recycled air being blown through old and dirty ventilation systems. There was a tang that I immediately associated with the ocean. As we got out, I watched the other draftees, emulating their reactions to the differences. I didn't want to stand out.

Soldiers herded us into a cargo elevator that lowered us farther into the depths of our prison. Before the door closed, I heard the distant roar of a shuttle taking off. Everyone else ignored it. Maybe they thought it was a damaged filtration system, not knowing what a shuttle sounded like. But I listened to what it told me.

The sound meant we had traveled far enough west to be close to the shuttle port. We weren't in it, though, it wasn't loud enough. I couldn't place direction from the noise—it had echoed down the ramp leading back to the surface. Even with that, I knew where we were, without a doubt. There could only be one place. We were at the SoCal Air Force Base south of the shuttle port. I also knew this wouldn't be our final destination. This was an interim spot before they shipped us somewhere for training and brainwashing.

I knew all about that. ACE had done their share to me.

The elevator doors opened onto a fibercrete tunnel and with it the familiar scent of recycled air. This time without the stench of the lower levels. Only thirty meters farther in, a huge door swung on massive hinges, opening into even more tunnel. Armed soldiers stood outside the door on full alert, rifles held at the ready. Inside were three women in white lab coats, waiting for us.

No one moved until the soldiers started pulling us out. Then, like obedient children, we followed them. The only sound was of our feet on the floor. The door became more impressive the closer we got. It was thick, almost ninety centimeters by the look of it. The frame had three deep holes in it, matched by three huge cylinders embedded into the door itself. Once that thing closed, there was no getting out unless they wanted you to.

Someone shouted from the front of the group, their voice filled with dread. Panic spread like unventilated smoke on Level 2, and the tide of bodies turned, pushing back on those of us following. I fought against the sudden surge and slipped to the side wall, followed by a couple of other people, watching as the horde tried to get back to the elevators.

They didn't know it was already too late.

A single shot sliced through the air over our heads, and a hole appeared in the back of the elevator. For the first time, I noticed it was home to more than just one. People had panicked here before, and been brought back under control with the threat of violence or death. Everybody froze and the tunnel fell into an eerie silence. A single voice cut through the stillness.

"Welcome to SoCal Basic Training. Starting today, your mind, your body, and your very soul belong to us. You will maintain control of yourself, and follow these three people to your quarters for the night. Tomorrow, you will be shipped to Snied Parker Base to begin your training." The voice paused, then rose in volume. "Move. Now!"

Once again, the only sound was that of shuffling feet. When we were finally all through the massive door, it closed silently behind us. The only signs of its movement were a rush of air before it closed and the sound of three cylinders driving home.

We followed the people in lab coats to the first regular-sized door I had seen. A small sign above it read "Decontamination." We were herded inside and ordered to line up in three rows. I stayed in the back, trying to remain small and inconspicuous. The feeling of being trapped threatened to overtake me. I fought it as the line of bodies in front of me pressed me into the wall. The only other exit in the room was a set of double doors opposite the ones we had come in through. The soldiers stayed with us, standing along the opposite wall.

One of the people in lab coats, the tallest one with the bright red lipstick and a beak for a nose, started talking. "Welcome to Hawthorne Air Force Base. You've all come from various walks of life. In order to allow you to mix with the other trainees tomorrow, we have to make sure you are clean and healthy. First row, strip. Leave your clothes in a pile where you are and walk through the double doors. New clothes will be provided once you are done. We'll get your bloodwork results back tomorrow before you ship out."

No one moved.

The same voice from outside the elevators boomed across the silent room. "First row. Strip and move through the doors to your right. Now."

In a sudden flurry of motion, the front row started to remove their jackets and shirts. Everyone hesitated before they stripped off their underwear, trying to cover themselves in modesty. They were led silently to the double doors.

KADOKAWA SAT CITY 2—TUESDAY, JULY 4, 2141 5:40 P.M.

SoCal was up to something. The problem was, Andrew couldn't figure out what. Even the intelligence reports were vague when they mentioned the Sat Cities. His forces, and SoCal's, had spent the day eyeing each other warily across the thousands of kilometers that made up the front line. None of the ships had moved.

The battle on Mars had intensified. SoCal had brought in new troops, barely trained and barely controllable. It should have been a bad move, but it had worked. They'd regained control of the mines. Kadokawa troops, or what was left of them, were huddled to the north waiting for air rescue. So far SoCal had left them alone.

Things were changing within Kadokawa as well. All because *Kaijō-bakuryōchō* Sone and Kadokawa's president had gotten control of the once-peaceful corporation and turned it into a warmongering one . . .

Andrew caught himself before the thought could fully complete. Even thinking it felt like treason to him. He was a soldier. He knew that the day he signed up. When he was told to do something, he did it to the best of his ability.

And yet . . .

He'd received a private communiqué just before lunch from Natsumi. He corrected himself, *Kaishō-ho* Kadokawa. The note had troubled him to his very core. He and *Kaishō-ho* Kadokawa had been childhood friends. They'd joined at the same time, attended the same training camps, and moved up the ranks in synchronicity, until she had reached *Kaishō-ho*. He had been held back at *Kaisa*, simply because he was needed where he was. There had been no one to promote into his position, to fill his space.

His plan had been to ask for her hand when they both reached *Kaisa*, but circumstances had placed them on the opposite side of the globe for more than a year. *Kaisa* was the first step into admiralty, and allowed a bit more freedom, a chance to have a life outside of the military.

Her outranking him put a stop to those plans. It wouldn't have been proper for him to ask anymore. They were both *Kaishō-ho* now, but the distance between them remained. He was in the field, and she was in Okinawa. Her position had more responsibilities than his did. Soon she would be *Kaishō*, and even further out of reach.

The communiqué was encoded with nothing the military normally used, and it had left him stumped for most of the day. Only after an early dinner with the enlisted, which he tried to make a daily habit, did he realize what was going on. The code was actually quite simplistic, but difficult to break at the same time. Natsumi had found it in an old text in the library at Nagasaki when they went to school there, and they had both memorized the encryption and decryption routines, running through them daily to make sure they had everything right. They'd used the code throughout high school, passing notes to each other about whatever topic came up. With her, it had almost always been math or geography. For him, physics and calligraphy. She'd never really understood the beauty of either.

It took him some time to decode the message—the old routines were only a memory, and he hadn't used them in decades. When he had finished and read the complete message, he'd immediately deleted its receipt from the logs and destroyed the pad he'd decrypted it on.

She had spoken of the old Kadokawa, of how they'd worked together to bring the necessities of life to the people of Korea after an earthquake had devastated the east coast. How they'd helped protect Machu Picchu when civil war had threatened to destroy the ancient city. Together, they had helped rebuild cities and bring joy back into people's lives. The new president and *Kaijō-bakuryōchō* were destroying all of that. She wrote what she was going to do about it.

She spoke of treason.

Andrew had sat in his room, going over the message word for word, searching for a different meaning behind them. Perhaps he had memorized them wrong. Perhaps someone else had written the words, or forced her to do so. He sighed, knowing none of that was true. She'd signed the letter using her given name. He hadn't spoken it out loud since she'd outranked him, though in his thoughts she would always be Natsumi.

The note had come from her.

Trouble was brewing in Kadokawa, and she had picked a side. She had just told him why, and asked him to join her. He yearned to be with her, to help her any way he could.

But duty . . .

LOS ANGELES LEVEL 7—TUESDAY, JULY 4, 2141 5:35 P.M.

It was my row's turn.

I had never been comfortable being naked, and was even less so with other people around. Watching the first rows strip down and march through the doors didn't relieve any of my discomfort. Gender didn't really matter, I preferred staying clothed around everyone. I was sweating as I took off my clothes, even in the cold room. The last of us stood and waited, keeping our eyes on the ground.

We didn't need to be told to start moving. As soon as the double doors opened, we walked single file across the room and through them. I resisted the urge to cover up and kept my eyes on the feet of the man in front of me. The soldiers had watched the previous groups, their gaze lingering when they saw something they liked. I could feel them watching me. My belly protruded a bit, and I tried to suck in my gut. I wasn't sure why.

The doors opened to a short hallway. There was another exit at the other end, clearly labeled with a lit green sign, and two doors in the left wall. The one closest to us was open and we were led in. One of the women in the lab coats stood nearby. I peered over her shoulder and saw a wet trail exiting the other door, stray footprints discernible near the edges.

The floor of the room was soaking wet. Three people in rubber boots and ponchos stood against one wall with hoses in their hands. We were told to stand against the other, our arms raised above our head, facing out.

The person in the lab coat stood in the doorway. "If you have any sores or open cuts, this will hurt a bit. The water contains antibiotics and various chemicals for killing lice or anything else that may be on you. As the water sprays, you will duck your head into the stream and wash your hair. You will do the same with your armpits and groin. If we think anyone is not doing an adequate job, we will do it for you. We won't enjoy doing that, therefore neither will you. When the water stops, turn to face the wall and repeat the process. You will be told when to exit through the far door."

The water turned on. It seemed like the assholes got pleasure from humiliating us like this. Treating us like animals with no respect as people. The first spray was right in my face, held there until I couldn't breathe before moving on to the next person. I washed my hair, trying to look like I was doing a thorough job while still being careful to keep my bobby pins in place. By the time we were told to turn, my skin was bright red from the rubbing and the water pressure.

"Bend over."

I was too slow. All three hoses aimed at the back of my head, forcing my face into the wet, slimy wall. When the pressure stopped, I was bent over like everyone else. I hated the men with the hoses, hated the soldiers and the lab coats. Hated SoCal, with every part of who I was.

I shivered as they corralled us through the doors into the hallway and through the next set of double doors. We were separated into two groups, men and women, and forced to stand against another wall, still wet and cold, as they stuck fingers into our mouths and other places. At least this time they had the decency to have a woman search our group.

We were finally given towels. They had been used and washed so often they barely worked anymore. I did the best I could and wrapped the towel around me. It was so small I had to hold it together with my hands. Some of the larger men and women held their towels clutched in front of them.

The man with the loud voice stood in front of us again. "You will be given clothes and a place to sleep tonight. Tomorrow, we'll go over your blood test results and send you to training. You'll have six weeks to become the soldiers we want you to be. Those that don't make it will not be returned home. There will be water available after you're dressed." He smiled. "Drink as much as you want. It's all you're getting until tomorrow. Do you understand?"

Most of the people just mumbled. I stood silent, dreaming of the different ways I would kill him.

"When I ask a question, you will respond with a '*Yes, sir.*' Do you understand?"

Several of the group replied with soft answers.

"I can't hear you." The soldier took a step closer to the nearest person and yelled only centimeters from his face. "Do you understand?" Spit flew from his lips.

This time, everyone responded, including me. I would bide my time, but when it was right, I would kill him.

The clothes came in two sizes, medium and large, with no differentiation between men's and women's. Except for the underwear. The military gray material was stiff and coarse. I ended up rolling up the bottom of the pants and the sleeves of a shirt that I tucked in down to my knees.

Everyone drank water. As many glasses as they could, thrilled by how much was available. I watched from the sidelines until I noticed the soldiers paying more attention to me. Then I stood in line and pretended to drink.

ACE had taught us to never accept food or drink from the enemy. I knew I couldn't hold out forever, but I could last a while. Long enough to tell if SoCal put something in it.

They marched us single file down a long hall with doors on either side. None of them had windows, and under the doorknob was a ten-digit keypad. The light on each pad glowed red. We went into the sixth door at the end of the hall.

The room was spartan at best. The walls, ceiling, and floor were bare fibercrete and the beds simple plastic frames with thin mattresses. On the end of each bed were a pillow and a couple of thin blankets. The far end of the room was an open washroom. Toilets and showerheads lined the walls, and a single large sink separated them from the beds. There was zero chance of privacy. I managed to get a bed by the door, laying the first blanket down as a sheet and using the second for its intended purpose. I'd slept in enough disgusting places to want something between me and the mattress.

"Lights out in two minutes."

It couldn't have been much past 6 P.M., but exhaustion swept through me. I lay on my bed and watched the others. Several of the men sat in a small group, talking quietly and waving their hands. I didn't know what they were going on about. I didn't want to know. The others simply commandeered the beds near the front of the room. Most of them were already under the blankets before the lights went out.

I could hear the men cursing as they tried to find a place to sleep in the dark. Eventually the room quieted down. I lay there until all I could hear were the sounds of sleep from the humiliated and exhausted people around me. I shivered and pulled the single blanket tighter before finally closing my eyes.

Despite my exhaustion, I was wide awake.

SIX

LOS ANGELES LEVEL 2—TUESDAY, JULY 4, 2141 7:00 P.M.

THINGS HAD GONE all wrong. Pat and Kai sat in the dining hall, alone in the large space. Neither of them spoke. Rows and rows of empty tables spread across the room, waiting for the morning crowd to turn the silence into noise. The place used to be an auditorium for the residents of the block, but had been converted into the hall.

They had tossed around ideas, come up with plans, figured out ways to get Kris back. None of it mattered. Levels 6 and 7 were sewn up so tight it would take weeks just to find a way through. If they could find a way. None of Kai's contacts had responded to his pleas. If Doc Searls still had access, they could have used him. But he'd lost that. Getting up to Level 5 would be possible using the inter-level corridors . . . as long as they could avoid the military patrols.

Even if they could get access, unless they could get Kris outside the base, they didn't have a hope.

"We have lost her," Kai said. "We both know the base is only a temporary stop. They will fly her out to the SoCal training camps and brainwash her into being whatever they want."

"She's smarter than that. She won't fall for it."

"She did at the compound."

Pat stayed quiet. She had believed in ACE for so long that she was still uncomfortable when someone said negative things about it. She'd been brainwashed along with the rest of them during basic training, and her years of work had added to the loyalty. That was why she still wanted to defend them, even after she knew what they had become. Was it bad that all she really wanted right now was to go back to being a camp cook?

She nodded in response to Kai's statement.

"The insurgents have people in SoCal. No one in the military, but once she comes out of training, we should be able to find her," he said.

"And what will we be able to do then? What if they send her to Mars, or up to one of the Sat Cities? How do we get her back? Will she want to come back? What about Jack? He doesn't trust her now. It'll be worse if we can get her."

Kai shrugged.

The man sometimes infuriated her. He was sitting here as calm as could be while all she could feel were her insides being torn to shreds. The sense of helplessness reminded her too much of her time in France when she had been a prisoner. She jumped to her feet, pushing the plastic chair away from the table. Her body couldn't take being stationary anymore, she had to move, had to do *something*.

Kai reached a hand up and placed it on her arm. "We have no choice but to wait."

"I can't wait. It's not how I was designed. We have to get up to Level 7 tonight and find a way to get her out of there."

"You want to sneak into Level 7, break into a military base of one of the largest corporations in the world while they are on war standing, scour the place until you find where they are keeping Kris, and get back out again? Do you know how impossible that is?"

Kai's words were a knife in her heart. Of course she knew it was impossible. She collapsed back in her chair and placed her head in her hands. For the first time in years, the tears that flowed down her face weren't from reliving memories of the past, but from what was happening in the present.

"Come. We are both exhausted. Tomorrow, our minds will be fresh and perhaps we will figure something out. We will talk with Doc Searls, and have more ideas to work with." He stood and waited.

She knew he was right. There was nothing they could do. Even if they slept for weeks, nothing could be done until she came out of basic training. Then, if they got her, they could begin the process of bringing back the real Kris. The one who had been there before SoCal changed her. They *would* change her. No one was strong enough to resist what they could do. ACE had managed to bring Pat back from the edge of insanity. If they could fix her, there would be a way to fix what was left of Kris. There had to be.

She rose from her chair, bracing her hand on the back to help lift her, and dragged herself to the door. Kai put his arm around her, preparing for the slow climb up to her room.

LOS ANGELES LEVEL 7—WEDNESDAY, JULY 5, 2141 3:28 A.M.

The door to the room opened and light flooded the center aisle between the beds. I had only been half-asleep, and the noise of the lock opening pulled me wide awake. I lay as still as I could.

Two soldiers entered the room and I saw the shadow of a third still in the hall. Through my eyelashes, I watched as the soldiers pulled shock sticks from their belts. When they started yelling and banging on the sides of the bed frames, I almost jumped. Forcing myself to stay still, I watched as they repeated the procedure down the entire room. No one moved. No one woke up.

When they reached the end, the tips of their shock sticks came to life, glowing in the dim light. As they walked back, they pressed the sticks into the mattresses of every sleeping person.

"Looks like they're out."

"We're not done yet."

"Yeah, yeah. I've done this with every batch. You want to know how many I've found? None. I think the whole spy thing is a load of crap. They just don't want us to sleep on our shift. This is your first night, you'll figure it out."

"Shut up and keep going."

Two beds away from me, someone made a sound when they touched the mattress.

"Well, what do we have here? Someone that isn't asleep when he's supposed to be."

The soldier pulled a man from the lower bunk. It was one of the guys that had stayed up talking when the lights were turned out.

"Spy crap, eh? You think this guy didn't drink the water because he wasn't thirsty?"

The man swung, connecting with the soldier's jaw and dropping him on the spot. The second soldier didn't hesitate, clubbing the man with the shock stick. The third soldier stayed at the doorway. By the time the man was down, the first soldier was back on his feet. He hoofed the man in the chest, pulling his foot back for another kick.

"Stop." The voice from the door was calm. The soldier stopped. "Check the other beds and let's get him out of here."

The soldiers continued their search. My bed was next. I tensed, exhaling all the air in my lungs and waited. The shock stick touched my mattress.

All I felt was a slight tingle.

The soldiers grabbed the man on the floor and dragged him out, leaving the door unlocked behind them. I guess there was no need when everyone was drugged.

I sucked in a long slow breath. What had just happened? I waited, listening to the sounds of sleeping people. When I was sure no one else was faking it, I hung my feet over the edge and dropped to the floor.

The first thing I did was check the man's bed. He hadn't placed one of the blankets under him, choosing to stay warm and to sleep directly on the mattress. I ran my hand over top, feeling a metal lining under the thin material. It wasn't much, but it would pass the shock from the stick to whomever was lying on it.

I crept to the door. I couldn't hear a thing. We were the last room in the hallway, so it stood to reason that we would be the last room searched. I pulled open the door and waited.

Nothing happened.

That huge door they brought us in through couldn't be the only way in or out of this place. My guess was they used it as a psychological tool to keep us in line. There had to be another way. I walked down the hallway in my bare feet, hugging the wall. Each door's keypad was green. Unlocked. Did that mean they'd be coming back?

I went down the first hallway I found that I didn't recognize. It ended in a single door. Another electronic lock glowed red. Through the small window, I watched as soldiers threw a man into a room. They came back my way.

The sound of my feet slapping the floor bounced down the

hallway as I tried to find a place to hide. I rounded the corner barely ahead of the door opening.

"Okay. Let's collect the doc and get these guys ready for tomorrow."

I ran back to the room on tiptoe, closing the door behind me and climbing back into bed.

It took them another half hour to get back to my room. The soldiers were more relaxed, standing by the door as the doctor went to the first bed across from me and injected something into the man sleeping there. He moved to the next bunk.

"How long you been working here?" a soldier asked.

"Four weeks. I've got two more before my next rotation. Where were you before you came here?"

"Protection detail on Level 1. We watched over the food trucks being loaded at the ports and covered them on the way up here."

"Level 1? Must have been a crap job."

"Nah, it wasn't bad. You're not on Level 1 for too long. The ports are way better than anything else down there, just like a base up here really. On the way back, you're riding in the trucks. Used to be better though. There would be three of us in a truck. Now with everyone going off to fight, we don't have the manpower anymore. Now it's the driver and a couple of mannequins to make it look like we have a full complement. Makes the trip pretty boring."

"Sounds like a stupid idea to me."

"Nah. They're not that smart on the lower levels. Besides, we were augmented with extra drones. They flew above the Ambients where no one could see them."

"I thought that was impossible."

"Just shows what you know. Won't last long anyhow, they're moving to transports to fly everything up. Less risky."

I tuned them out when the doctor reached me. I didn't want anything to do with his injection, but there wasn't anything I could do about it, unless I was willing to get beaten up and thrown in a cell like the guy. I didn't flinch when the needle went in.

This time when the soldiers left, they locked the door.

LOS ANGELES LEVEL 7—WEDNESDAY, JULY 5, 2141 6:00 A.M.

I spent the rest of the night tossing and turning in the narrow bed, fading between sleep and a half-awake state where my brain churned at light speed, fed by my subconscious to create vivid dreams of blood and dead soldiers. Whatever I'd been injected with was making me go into overdrive. My best guess was it was an antidote to whatever they tried to make us drink last night.

The sound of an electric buzz and a lock chunking back dragged me from the latest vision of a loud boisterous man having his face peeled off in a single jelly-like piece while he begged for mercy.

The lights came on and half the people in the dorm groaned.

"Everybody up." It was the man that had yelled at us the night before, still loud and commanding. "You have ten minutes to get ready. Your beds will be made and you will be standing at the end of it when I get back. Is that understood?"

Everybody responded in unison. "Yes, sir!" I lay on my bed with my mouth shut.

Once we were locked in, people began to stand, shuffling off to the business end of the room. I followed.

Everyone milled around for a few seconds, not quite sure what to do, before one woman walked up, pulled down her pants, and sat on a toilet. She didn't make eye contact with anyone. Soon there were lines as everyone waited their turn.

I went to the sinks between the beds and the toilets and turned the tap. Fresh water flowed cool and clear. It was more of a catalyst to the people in the room than the exposed toilets had been. Those near the end of the lines followed me, running their fingers through the cool liquid, cupping their hands and drinking as much as they could hold, until some of them threw up. I restrained myself, taking only what I thought I needed. SoCal would steal from the lower levels to make sure we had enough.

I wasn't worried about being drugged this time. They'd want us on our feet so we'd be easier to move.

When I was done, one of the toilets was empty. I went as quickly as I could, staring at my knees the whole time.

We were all back in the main room by the time the door buzzed again. Every one of us made our beds, some too scared not to, others doing what they were told, already resigned to their fate. I made mine because it was the best way to stay under the radar, inconspicuous as I tried to figure out how to get out of this mess, or at the very least, how to get through it in one piece.

Habit almost made me make the bed the way I had been taught at the ACE compound, but after watching some of the others, I realized I couldn't do that. Some pulled their blankets up, placing the pillow on top of it. Others at least tucked the blanket in at the bottom. Very few tucked it in all the way around. No one made neat, square hospital corners. I discreetly pulled my blankets apart again, making sure to be messy.

At the sound of the door opening, we all scrambled to stand at the ends of our beds. A woman stood in the doorway, one I hadn't seen before. Her uniform looked like it had been starched that morning. She didn't even bother to walk in the room.

"You will now have breakfast," she said, her voice projected to the back wall. "We will give you twenty minutes to get your food, eat it, and return your tray to containers at the front of the mess hall. After that, you will line up single file with the rest of your group. Do you understand?"

"Yes, sir!"

"Follow me."

We walked back down the hallway I'd snuck through last night, except this time each of the doors was open. As we left the barracks area, the smell of bacon wafted through the air. Despite myself, my stomach grumbled in response. The insurgents had fed us, but bacon hadn't been on the menu. Maybe we could have eggs and toast!

The mess hall reminded me of the one in the insurgents' building, except for the lack of chairs. Each table had a built-in bench on either side, permanently attached. Another group of draftees was finishing up at the food line as we walked in.

Everyone was talking, some to the people at the table they were at, others to tables across the way, comparing notes on how they had gotten here and what had been done to them. I grabbed a tray and a plate, waiting my turn in line. The place was packed. There were more men and women here than had been picked up with me. Lots more. I figured there were at least five hundred, all of them sitting twenty to a table, just like us. I ignored them and started examining the food in front of me.

It looked and smelled really good. There were scrambled eggs, bacon, pancakes with syrup, fresh fruits, and fried potatoes. More food than I or anyone else in the room had seen in a long time. People loaded up their plates and were given plastic spoons. I moved some bacon and eggs and a couple of pancakes onto my plate. At the end of the food line was coffee. I filled two cups and balanced them on my tray before sitting at a long table with the rest of my group.

As we were eating, soldiers walked the room, one per aisle, and two extra at each wall. Their guns were holstered and a clip held them in place. If I'd tried to get to one, I'd have to undo the clip before pulling the weapon out. By that time, any of the other soldiers would have had time to put a bullet in my back. I'd have to wait.

When we were done and our trays returned to the bins at the front, we all went back to our tables and waited. The woman who had led us here stood at the front.

"Line up."

Each of the soldiers monitoring the room stood at the back wall. Behind the woman, by the doors we walked in through, was the man that ordered us around last night. Each table was led out one at a time.

When it was our turn, we followed the woman again. One of the soldiers at the back wall came after us. The woman led us down yet another hall that ended at a single door and made us stand up against the wall. The first person was let through the door while the rest of us waited. When they came out, the next one went in. The woman on my left leaned to whisper in my ear.

"What do you think they're doing in there?"

"Maybe the doctor they told us about last—"

The soldier who had followed us jumped in front of me. "No talking."

He leaned in closer, trying to threaten me by being taller. I smiled and looked away. After a while, he just left.

I waited for my turn, walking through the door without really knowing what to expect.

The inside was a regular office with a single small desk and an examination table. The man behind the desk pointed to an empty chair and read from a pad.

"Kris Merrill?" He sounded bored.

"Yes."

"You're seventeen?"

"Yes."

"According to your chart, your birthday is in two months, is that correct?"

"Yes."

He put the pad down and leaned on the desk. "Too young to be in the military, I'm surprised they kept you. They must have figured you were close enough that it didn't matter." He paused. "Did you know you were pregnant?"

"Yes."

"And you didn't tell anyone when they picked you up?"

I snorted. "Have you ever been through a draft? They don't give you much time for talking."

He stared at me before responding. "I guess not. I'd kick you out of here on your age alone, though I'm not sure they would let me. They don't have a choice about your pregnancy."

Tears welled up in my eyes and I slumped back in the chair. I hadn't realized how much getting out of here meant to me, until there was a chance it could happen.

"Now how about you get up on the table and we check on you and the baby? I'm guessing you don't have a doctor, most from the lower levels don't." His voice had switched to all professional.

I kept my mouth shut and wiped the tears away.

SOCAL SAT CITY 2—WEDNESDAY, JULY 5, 2141 9:00 A.M.

Last night's simulation runs had all worked perfectly, narrowing the critical band down to a few nanometers. The results were even better than they had been last time he'd run them on Kadokawa. Bryson rubbed the sleep from his eyes and let out a huge yawn. He had finished testing around one in the morning, and when he was finally escorted back to his quarters and crawled into bed, sleep became an evasive beast, constantly shifting and moving, forcing him to chase after it. It had taken him at least a couple of hours of tossing and turning before he fell into a sleep filled with equations and test results.

He had woken up exhausted and on the edge of burnout. His alarm went off at the same time it always did, and he'd forced himself out of bed and into a warm shower. It didn't help. He was on his second cup of tea when the alarm went off again. It was time to go to work.

The atmosphere in the lab was as quiet as it ever was. No one knew about the test results, how the world was about to change. Hopefully for the better, but he was too jaded to believe that for even a minute. Not this time. He sat in his chair and stared at the blank screen before calling over one of the other physicists in the room. His interactions with everyone here had shown her to be the quickest study, the one he could rely on to double-check everything, and do it right.

"Ailsa, could you come here please?" The entire lab went quiet. He rarely called anyone over to his desk.

"What can I do for ye?" Her Scottish accent was quiet, but definitely there.

"I need you to check these results. Make sure I didn't miss anything." He handed her a memory chip with the base data. "You'll need to set up your own tests and run it through the simulator."

"I can do that." She took the chip and went back to her desk.

It would take her a few hours to complete. Bryson went to the corner of the lab that contained a small kitchen and poured himself a cup of coffee. He wasn't normally a coffee drinker, but the tea wasn't working. He sat on one of the small couches and sipped the hot liquid. Bringing food or drinks back to his desk was against lab policies, and rules were important.

He'd just drifted off when the lab door whooshed open and silence fell, bringing him back to full wakefulness.

"Where is he?" Ms. Peters' voice cut through the silence.

No one answered, but he saw a single hand point in the direction of the kitchen. He stood and waited for her.

She walked across the lab, the familiar sound of her heels clicking on the raised tile floor. "Tell me about last night." The regular pair of soldiers followed her.

"I made some changes and ran some tests."

"I know that. Tell me about the results. Are they valid?"

He shrugged. "I'm having Ailsa redo my tests from the base data. If she can duplicate them, I can tell you if they are valid. Or not." Her question proved one thing at least . . . the lab network was being monitored. That brought the virus to the front of his thoughts. If she could look into the lab network, then there was a potential path back out the virus could use. It would all depend on how well the path was firewalled, and how good the network virus scanners were. He imagined they would be very good. But from what he could understand of the virus, so was it.

"How long will that take?"

Bryson read the clock on the wall. "Maybe another forty-five minutes?" He must have done more than drift off.

"Good." Ms. Peters' comm unit rang and she pulled it out of her jacket pocket. "Hello?"

"Are you sure?" she asked, waiting for the reply. From her body language, he could tell something was wrong. "And they let her go?" More waiting. Her entire body had tensed up and she turned slightly away from him, her movements stiff and unnatural. "I sent out that memo yesterday afternoon. They should have known—"

Bryson smirked. Even with her back turned, he could tell she was furious. She wasn't used to being cut off.

"I don't care. Get her back and do it now." She closed the link and faced Bryson. He stopped smiling. "You have an hour to get a report to me."

"That won't give me—"

"I don't care. Start writing it now. Two versions if you have to, one for if that girl's tests duplicate yours, and one if they don't."

With that she turned and stormed out of the lab, her two goons following her.

It bothered Bryson that she had called Ailsa *that girl*. Ailsa had a doctorate in quantum physics, just like him, and that alone should earn her more respect.

LOS ANGELES LEVEL 7—WEDNESDAY, JULY 5, 2141 12:05 P.M.

The back of the truck was almost empty. There were no soldiers with guns guarding the door, just empty seats and the same single strip of light in the middle of the roof. The only other occupant besides me was a man hacking up a lung. He kept talking to me and apologizing. I moved to the far corner.

We were told SoCal was letting us go—they didn't want us. I don't think I'd ever been so relieved not to be wanted in my life. We didn't get our clothes back; they'd been destroyed. We did get to keep the ones they gave us. I was already chafing from the bra that didn't fit.

The relief didn't last long. The truck turned the wrong way when it left the down-ramp on Level 6. I remembered the route we'd taken to get up, and I was sure we had taken a different turn. Was it my memory that was wrong?

The guy in the corner couldn't stop coughing. He'd given up all pretense of covering his mouth. His face was haggard, with sunken eyes and pallid, yellowish skin. I'd seen this before. This was the severe withdrawal of a Sweat addict. I was told it was a hell of a high, but when you came down, things got really tough. Without warning, his hacking turned into choking, and whatever he'd managed to get down his throat during breakfast came back up. The truck braked and then accelerated. I lifted my feet away from the putrid stream that slid down the length of the floor.

It didn't take long before we hit another down-ramp. Level 5. We stopped almost right away and the back door opened. The soldier reeled away from the stench and held the door open at arm's length. I jumped out without looking back, wondering why they dropped us off behind their checkpoints. I guess since we'd scanned clean, they weren't too worried. That was good to know . . . they trusted their data. Maybe too much.

They had dropped us off at McConnell Park. The place looked worse than it had a year ago. There was gray scum over the little water left in the pond. It looked thick enough to walk on. I couldn't believe I'd used it to clean myself up last time I was here.

The trees had lost most of their leaves, and the grass—if you could still call it that—churned more gray dust into the air with every step. I sat on a bench by the water and watched an old couple on the path across from it. There were no mothers with baby strollers, no people walking and enjoying what little nature this part of the city had to offer.

I missed my mountains and blue sky with a ferocity that was completely unexpected. My *soul* yearned for the hard, warm rock pressing against my skin with Ian beside me. Talking about the little things that barely mattered then, and now mattered so much. Tears coursed down my cheeks and I bent over, my arms wrapped around my knees, and rocked, holding in the pain and the memories.

How I wanted to lock the memories away with the others. How I wanted to forget everything. His soft, gentle touches. The taste of his lips. The blood in the back seat of the car.

But not this time. Not for Ian. I would remember all of it, let it shape me into a mother who told stories to her son. Stories of how great his dad had been, how strong, how loving. We couldn't be a family, but he would still know his dad.

I wiped my nose with the rough sleeve of my shirt and rubbed my face free of the tears. I had a son to fight for, and the next step of that fight was getting home.

I walked from the park past the statues of men on horses. They were always men, never women. I guess women were never important enough to get a statue.

The restaurant Mikey had dragged me through when we'd been trying to lose Quincy was gone, its windows boarded up and the sign cracked and missing pieces so I could see the light fixtures behind it. Keeping a restaurant open when food was scarce was a stupid idea. I hoped the owners had gotten out before they lost everything. It had happened so fast, I doubted it.

Walking to the transfer elevator would take me about a half hour, and that would get me down to Level 3. If it was open. For all I knew, they closed all access to the elevators when they installed the new checkpoints.

From there, it would take most of the day to walk to Level 2 Chinatown. At least it was daytime. The streets had gotten worse at night; desperate people often did desperate things. The proliferation of drugs had expanded, everything from everyday Sweat to whatever could get people high.

I guess it was easier than facing the new reality for some.

SOCAL SAT CITY 2—WEDNESDAY, JULY 5, 2141 8:30 A.M.

Janice woke up from one of the best sleeps she'd had in a long time. The bed was firm, but comfortable, and the sheets were clean. It was a far cry from the alley outside of Chinatown. The first thing she had done when they put her in the room was double-check the door. They had locked her in from the outside, and this lock was a good one. The second thing she did was strip down and take a shower. They had cleaned her up in the hospital a bit, but not as well as fresh hot running water and soap would. She'd stood under the flowing bliss until her skin wrinkled, using more water in thirty minutes than she had seen in months.

Life in the Sat Cities wasn't too bad. She could get used to it.

She had dried off and padded to the double bed, wriggling under the cool sheets until they were up to her neck. Sleep took over before she'd realized.

The clock on the bedside table showed 8:30 in the morning. The table in the corner held a thermos and fresh fruits and vegetables. Someone had been in the room as she'd slept. Janice knew it should have bothered her, but it really didn't. In fact, they were treating her pretty good. Today she would find out what SoCal planned to do with her. The way she saw it, they would give her three options: start working for them, put her back in the hell that was San Angeles, or kill her.

Killing her seemed to be a distant third. There was no way they would waste water and food on someone they were planning on getting rid of. She didn't want to be dumped back into San Angeles with the rest of the garbage. Out of all three, the first option was the best scenario she could think of. She'd be employed again, and maybe, just maybe, she'd be able to get above Level 5 and get to follow through on her retirement plan. Things were looking good.

Her outlook changed when her door opened. She'd gotten dressed in her old dirty clothes and eaten breakfast when the two soldiers walked right in. Both had holstered stun guns and batons. One stood by the door while the other grabbed her and walked her out of the room. They didn't say anything.

"Where are you taking me?"

They didn't even look like they heard her.

"I want to see John Smith."

She tried to pull her arm away, and the other soldier grabbed her as well. They closed the door and marched her down the hall. What was going on? Her fingers tightened into fists with her arms locked to her sides.

The hall was as empty as last night. It looked like an apartment complex, but each door had an external lock, just like hers, and the exit at the end was guarded.

John met her past the door.

"Let her go," he said. When the soldiers hesitated he turned to them. "Let her go. Now."

They did as they were told.

"Now, Miss Robertson, come with me."

Janice didn't hesitate. Anything was better than being hauled around by the soldiers like a common criminal. "Where are we going? Back to see Ms. Peters?"

John smiled. "No. If you ever see her again, you will either be in serious trouble or exceptionally high on the corporate ladder. I don't think you would like to be either of those."

Little did he know. Her goal in life was to get comfortable enough that she would never have to do anybody else's dirty work for them. No more contracts, no more guns. Just some peace and quiet under the Level 6 roof. She had never liked the open sky. If she needed to go full corporate to do that, so be it.

"So where—"

"All in good time." He walked faster, forcing her to pick up her pace until they reached an elevator.

They got off on a floor that looked like every office building she had ever been in. Sconces reflected light off a ceiling painted white or light gray, and the floor was tiled with something easy to clean. Every few feet, a closed and unlabeled door led off into parts unknown. She counted the doors they passed until John stopped in front of one that was like all the others. Number thirty-four.

"Go on in," he said. "I have some other errands to run. If all goes well, I'll see you again."

"And if it doesn't?"

He opened the door and placed a hand between her shoulders, pushing her in. The door shut automatically behind her.

The room was small, set up for a single interview. Behind the scrawny man with a shirt that billowed around him was a mirror, no doubt two-way. She'd been in enough interrogation rooms to recognize one. Her best guess was that John was behind it, watching everything. Maybe even Ms. Peters. The man sat behind a small table permanently attached to the floor. She took the only other chair without being asked, anxiety rising through her. She tried not to show it, but her leg bounced despite her attempts to stop it.

The interview was short. The man knew more about her than she knew about herself, everything from where and when she was born up to the day she had started working for Jeremy. He read it off like a litany of offenses, something to be atoned for at all costs. He ended it with an offer. Work for SoCal.

She grabbed at it like it was life preserver. It probably was. It was also far too easy.

"Good," he said, standing up and reaching out to shake her hand. "Normally we have a training stage, but with your time at Meridian and ACE, we'll bypass that. Instead, you'll be working with a more seasoned person. Your job will be to find and monitor Kris Merrill and the insurgents. Nothing more. Your partner will be in charge. Consider this your only chance. If you screw it up . . ."

"So you're sending me down to Level 2?" It was a stupid question to ask.

He picked the pad off the table. "You may go."

"Where?"

It seemed as though the question puzzled him. "Out the door, of course. I have work to do."

She shrugged and left the room the same way she'd walked in. He followed her out, the door closing behind him, and walked down the hall, away from the elevator. Should she follow him? Was that what he wanted? She was saved the decision by John coming out of the door beside her interview room.

"Good. Let's go. I'll introduce you to your partner and send you on your way."

LOS ANGELES LEVEL 2—WEDNESDAY, JULY 5, 2141 9:35 P.M.

I walked through the bright flickering neon of Chinatown. What once felt like home now felt like a stranger's place you had visited once before. Everything you expected was there, but it was somehow different and foreign. It took me a while before I figured out exactly what it was. Sure, there were more homeless people on the street, and it was quieter than I ever remembered it being. But what was really different was the smell. Gone were the wonderful odors of cooking and the fragrances from the open markets. The smells I had always associated with home, the reason I had moved back here as soon as I could.

The quietness of the street was disconcerting. There was no hustling of people shopping, living, laughing. The place was a ghost town despite the lights and the homeless. I was a stranger where once I had belonged.

The after-dinner lineups were gone, and the food tables had been moved off the road. The Ambients had already dimmed for the day, further slowing the long walk from Level 5. At least the elevator had been open, though no one was allowed on when the doors opened on Level 3.

I continued through Chinatown to the home base of the Los Angeles insurgents.

Security had been beefed up since I had last been here. Shadows of people on the rooftops slid outside my vision, and inside the main entrance were two extra guards, and the gate to the parking garage was closed. Something had changed. Was it because of Janice finding me at the greenhouses, or had something else happened? I was stopped at the door.

"What are you doing here?"

The woman's question surprised me and I took a half step back. I knew I should have recognized her, but her name refused to bubble to the surface. I wanted my bed. It had been a long day of walking.

"You were caught in a draft. How did you get out?"

I still didn't respond, too exhausted to care.

"Kris, it's me, Selma. We met at dinner."

"Right, Selma." The memories of the last time I'd met her flooded through me and my face got hot. "I just want to go to my room and sleep."

"I can't let you in." Her voice was apologetic. She turned to the other guard. "Go get Pat Nelson."

"Where is she?"

"I don't know, just go find her." The second guard took off. "You need to wait here. I can't let you in. I'm sorry, I . . ." She pulled me over to a wall. "Here. Sit and rest. I'm sure Pat will be here right away."

I put my back to the wall and slid to the floor. What the hell was going on? Why was I being treated like the enemy? It felt like an hour had passed before Pat and Kai came running into the lobby.

"Kris? Oh my god, Kris." Pat pulled me to my feet, and they grabbed me in a three-way hug. "We thought you were caught in the draft. We tried to get you, but the trucks went through to Level 5 before we could do anything."

I untangled myself from their grasp. "I was. They let me go. I walked down from Level 5."

"They let you go?" asked Kai. "Why?"

I just shrugged.

"They had to have given you a reason."

Pat had already guessed why, but she was staying quiet. It was because I was pregnant. Did she really expect me to say that in front of Kai and everyone? Fuck that. "I'm underage."

They both looked at me as though I wasn't fooling anyone, especially Pat. "You won't be in a month or so. They really let you go because of that?"

"Not just because of that." I knew it was time to let them know the truth, just not here. I started walking to the stairs.

"Hey! I can't let you go up there," Selma said. She moved to step in front of me.

I must have seemed ready to take a swing at her. She took a step back and apologized.

"I'm sorry. I'm just doing what I was told."

"You were told to keep me out?"

"No! No, just to keep anyone out that didn't belong. I mean, you were drafted, and—"

Pat stepped in. "I've got this one. Come on upstairs. We didn't reassign your room yet, so it's still yours."

Kai started to follow us, but she held him back and whispered something to him. He looked hurt, but stopped following.

We were quiet as we walked up the four flights of stairs to my room. Pat stayed behind me, one hand on my back as I plodded up each step. She followed me into my room.

"Talk to me," she said.

I lay on the bed, too worn out to even get under the covers. Pat came over and took off her jacket, placing it over me, and sat on the edge. She brushed hair from my face, but didn't say anything more.

I closed my eyes and started talking, reliving what had happened. I told her about getting caught in the draft, what I knew of the route we'd taken, the process we'd gone through when we got there. I paused when I got to the quantity of water and food they had, letting it sink in for both of us. A full debriefing.

It was time to tell her more.

"Do you remember when I went to Doc Searls for my fractured rib?"

She seemed a bit taken aback by the sudden switch. "Yeah."

"He did some extra tests, and . . ." I didn't know why I was still hesitating. I blurted it out, opening my eyes to see her reaction. "You were right. I'm pregnant."

I don't know what I expected. Anger, an outburst, quiet resignation. What I got was a knowing nod.

"Why didn't you want to tell me?" She shook her head as if changing her mind and caressed my cheek before grabbing both my hands. "Are you okay?"

"Yeah. I am. It's a boy."

"How far along?"

"About eight weeks."

She was quiet for a while longer. "I guess that's why you've been looking like shit in the mornings?"

I chuckled.

"Tomorrow we'll change your diet, make sure the baby's getting everything he needs."

"This is between you and me, okay? I . . . I don't want everyone to know. Not yet. It's . . . it's too soon anyway. You're supposed to wait until three months, right?" It was turning into a protective mantra.

"What about Kai?"

"I'll tell him." Pat's eyes widened and I could tell she didn't believe me. "I will. I don't want anyone else to know. It's too soon."

"We'll have to tell Jack, at least. Maybe get you off the more dangerous jobs, into something less stressful. He needs to know why they let you go."

I laughed at that. "Less stressful? I work the food lines and do the occasional surveillance. How less stressful do you want it to get? Any less stressful and I may as well stay in bed. Besides, shouldn't that be my choice?"

She paused again, staring at the wall before coming back to me. "Okay. It is your choice. But you need to remember you're thinking for two now. It's not just you anymore."

"I know that."

"You'll start to show pretty soon. Everyone will know then."

"I know that, too."

"Okay." She grabbed her jacket. "You get into bed and get some rest. I'll come and check on you later."

"Wait! I overheard some of the soldiers talking about the food trucks from the military ports on Level 1."

She listened as I told her what I had heard.

"You think it's true?"

"Why would the guy lie? Neither of them knew I was awake."

Pat rested a hand on the doorknob. "I agree. Now go to bed."

I reached for her and held her back. "Thanks."

"Get some rest," she said with a smile.

seven

KADOKAWA SAT CITY 2—WEDNESDAY, JULY 5, 2141 10:00 P.M.

ANDREW COULDN'T SLEEP. He lay in his bunk staring at the ceiling, going over Natsumi's coded message, rolling every sentence through his mind, searching for nuances and hidden meanings. He'd memorized the note and destroyed the original. What if he had missed something? Should he have kept the damn thing so he could go over every piece of it? No, that was only looking for trouble.

The note listed the humanitarian programs that had been canceled, as well as the new military actions taking place. The takeover of Meridian had been only one of them. At the end, Natsumi had spoken of the old corporation, the one her family had created. She had closed by saying she planned to bring the corporation back to its roots. Back to being a humanitarian organization instead of a military one.

She didn't believe the new *Kaijō-bakuryōchō* and president were the right people for the job. The new president had replaced her father last year. He no longer had the will to run Kadokawa. The death of his son Gorō had changed him. The first thing the new president had done was replace the head of the military with Sone. Together they had turned Kadokawa into a money-hungry, warmongering corporation. Just like SoCal and IBC.

When Andrew had joined Kadokawa, his first job as a private had been digging through the rubble in Korea, finding bodies after an earthquake devastated the region. He remembered Natsumi digging beside him, working harder than most of the men. They had paused for a brief rest and a sip of water when they'd heard the noise. It had sounded like a cat meowing deep in the rubble.

They had dug methodically, careful to not collapse anything below, and followed the sound. First with picks and shovels, and then with their bare hands. The crying had gotten louder as they got closer, turning into the distinctive sounds of young child, hurt and alone. This was seven days after the earthquake had struck.

Then the crying stopped.

The digging became frantic, both of them with their heads in the hole, their arms reaching down and scooping out dirt and broken concrete. The first thing they had seen was a foot, so tiny and filthy they had almost missed it. They had slowed down then, anxious yet unwilling to rush to the point where they might cause a cave-in.

They had followed the foot to a knee, then to a waist. The child's second leg was broken midthigh, angled away from the body. They brought the leg together with the other one as carefully as they could. The child screamed in pain, and they both smiled. The scream meant it was still alive. Once they got the legs together, he'd held them as firmly as he dared while Natsumi grabbed the child's hips and pulled.

That boy had been the only one they'd found alive. His only family an older sister that had been visiting a friend out of the city. At the end of every day, when all he and Natsumi had found was the dead, they both spoke of the one boy. The survivor. The boy and his sister had tried to sign up with Kadokawa when they were old enough, but his leg had never healed right. The sister now served under Andrew as *Kaisa*.

Kadokawa had helped rebuild, replacing the old concrete and steel structures with reinforced fibercrete, bringing the old city into the twenty-second century. There had been talk of creating another megacity, but it was quickly voted down.

Andrew knew Kadokawa wouldn't do that today. There was no money in it, no way to make a profit. Even if it helped their own people. It had taken the new president only a year to transition the corporation into what it had become.

After Natsumi had been promoted, they had still kept in touch, mostly on a professional level, but occasionally a dinner or lunch if he happened to be in Okinawa. They had been civil, but not much more than that. Each time they had parted, his heart had broken a little more. Each time, he had tried to harden it against the feelings he could no longer display.

And now this.

It wasn't the note that had gotten to him, though its contents were keeping him awake. It was how she had signed it. The use of her given name had torn down all the walls he had taken years to build.

He pushed as much of it off to the side as he could and concentrated on the letter itself. It all boiled down to one item. The one thing he couldn't even contemplate. To help her in treason.

And yet, she had asked.

He pushed the sheets aside and climbed out of bed. The chill of the room sunk into his skin. He slipped into a pair of slippers and pulled on a robe.

Kadokawa kept the Sat City's time synchronized with Japanese Standard Time, which meant he could catch the late news summary. Normally his information was far more accurate than what the news channels got, but his didn't have anything local. He wasn't getting any sleep, so maybe a distraction would help. He turned on the vid screen and switched to NHK.

The first item up was about SoCal. His reports had talked about mandatory drafts for several weeks, and it had finally gotten out to the general press. The video showed people lining up, chatting to each other, some of them smiling. It stunk like the propaganda it was. His reports had shown the reality of it, large-scale military sweeps grabbing people off the streets. It wasn't humane. It was worth fighting against.

The story ended with a mention of Kadokawa tentatively planning to do the same thing.

Andrew's mouth hung open, and he slowly closed it. They had to have gotten it wrong. He hadn't seen anything in his reports. If it was true . . . He'd been in the Kadokawa military for most of his life, joining when he was nineteen, and for the first time, he thought he may have made a huge mistake.

The next piece of news only drove the feeling deeper.

Kadokawa had pulled its humanitarian aid out of Russia. The country had gone through a massive political upheaval months before, and the new regime was worse than the old one. During the battle, both sides had destroyed hospitals and bombed neighborhoods full of families on simply the rumor of dissidents collecting there.

Canada had been the first to arrive with doctors and food and water. Kadokawa took a few extra days, waiting for reports from the Canadians to see what was needed the most, and where. They had arrived with platoons of helpers and supplies, all coordinated by Natsumi. She must have known this was happening weeks ago. Knowing her as well as he did, he was certain it would have torn her apart.

This, then, was the reason for the message. This was why she would go so far as to talk treason. He couldn't deny the reasons were valid. He didn't have the investment in the aid program she did, but he had the deeply bound morals and training that had been driven into him by his family and the military. The military before Sone.

He closed his eyes and went over the note again. She was right, dammit.

She was right.

LOS ANGELES LEVEL 2—WEDNESDAY, JULY 5, 2141 10:30 P.M.

The door closed behind Pat with a soft click, and she leaned her forehead against the frame. Miller was an idiot. You weren't an operative for ACE and a parent at the same time. It didn't work. Kris was proof of that, she had been a young kid with no parents. What the hell had he been thinking?

She heaved herself off the frame and walked down the hall back to the stairs. This was going to change everything for Kris. She had no idea how much work having a baby was, how much care and attention they needed. She was still a child herself! The girl was in for a world-changing experience.

The first thing they would have to do was find a quieter place for Kris to live. A small room on the fourth floor of this building was out of the question. Her neighbors on either side, and possibly all of them in a hundred-meter radius, would get pretty tired of a screaming baby at all hours of the day and night. This was no place to raise a kid.

They'd have to find a crib and clothes and toys, and when the time came, baby food. There would be bottles and wipes and diapers. It almost seemed more complex than a mission. But maybe she was getting ahead of herself.

Kris didn't say she wanted to keep the baby. Pat sighed. She didn't say she wanted to get rid of it either. She had said the baby was a boy. He was the only thing she had left of Ian. She wasn't going to lose that.

Pat pulled her comm unit out of her pocket. She had a meeting with Kai and Jack in a few minutes. Keeping this away from Jack would be easy. Kai, however, seemed to have a sixth sense sometimes. Especially around Kris. Knowing him, it would come out tonight, and he'd question and needle her until she either told him or punched him. As long as she stayed focused on the task at hand, maybe he wouldn't notice.

They met in Jack's office, the same as they always did, but this time it was different. The guards weren't at the double doors leading into the sanctified halls of the upper echelon; they'd been moved to the front door. The floor was still carpeted, but the extra-wide hallway had changed. In place of the comfy chairs and tables were desks, one for every two or three offices, except for Jack's. His office had a desk all to itself.

Behind each one sat someone studiously staring at a vid screen, typing at something, or shuffling through pads of information. It was obvious they were assistants. The place looked more like a working facility than the prestigious offices of a large corporation. It was a move in the right direction. Visually, at least.

Jack stepped out of his office with a pad in his hand. He passed it to his assistant.

"Kai's not here yet. We won't start without him, but why don't you come in now?" He glanced at his assistant. "When Kai shows up, let him right in."

"Yes, sir."

Jack shut the door behind them and settled into his chair. "I wanted to thank you for yesterday. I . . . I know I'm not great at this job. I didn't want it before all this happened, and I don't want it now. We all have to do what we have to do. Thanks for keeping me on my toes."

"You needed a kick in the ass." Changes were happening, but she wasn't willing to give in yet. She couldn't shake the small kernel of doubt that had nestled into her brain. Everything had moved too fast and seemed too perfect.

"I sent messages to the other cells I know about. I don't know if they'll do anything or even if they'll pass the message to the sections they know."

The insurgents had always been a disorganized group, but from what she was hearing, it was worse than she, or anyone else, had thought.

Kai knocked on the door and walked in, breaking the awkwardness building in the room.

"Good, we're all here." Jack joined them at the round meeting table in the corner, looking almost apologetic for the agenda he held in his hand. "There's two items we want to talk about today. The first is the acquisition of ex-ACE staff, and the other is about solidifying our food chain. Kai, let's start with you."

"I had a conversation with Doc Searls again. He is more than willing to help us out in the same capacity he did for ACE. He is also making a permanent move to Level 5, closing his Level 6 offices."

"Damn," Jack said. "Our resources on Level 6 are extremely thin. He could really have been useful to us. He wouldn't have had to come down to Level 4. We have people that know their way through the service corridors between Levels 4 and 5."

"I had that conversation with him. He really wants to limit what he does for us to the medical area. He certainly has no interest in becoming a spy. If information comes to him via his patients, he is willing to pass it on, but he will not dig for it, and he will not become a middleman or broker for information."

"That limits his usefulness," Pat said.

"It does," Jack said, "but if he's willing to stay there, we could use him. Even being on Level 5, he could at least bring us news of the outside world."

"No," Kai said. "He will not do anything that jeopardizes his practice beyond medical care. Besides, the new checkpoints stop us from getting whatever he could bring with him."

"As I said, we have ways around that," said Jack. "We'll need doctors, but if he's not willing to do much more than that, why are we trying to recruit him this hard?"

"He can give us more ACE operatives than Pat or I combined. He has either patched up or modified the trackers of almost every operative ACE has had in the last twenty years."

Jack sat quiet for a while, thinking. "How will he contact them?"

"He has records of every modified tracker he has ever worked on."

"That's not smart. What if they were found? It's a huge back door."

"They are encrypted."

"That doesn't mean shit. You know that. Can we get the records ourselves? Get rid of the loophole, the potential back door in our security?" Jack asked.

"You can't—" Pat said.

Jack held up his hand to stop her and watched Kai shift in his seat.

"He is a good doctor," Kai said.

Jack smiled as if Kai's response answered all his questions. "That works for me. Let's get this moving and on the payroll as soon as we can. If things go wrong, we'll look into it again. Now, onto our food problem. We don't have enough to feed us and the people. Something has to give. That being said, we're going on immediate rationing, which will give us a couple of extra weeks. What else can we do?"

"The Pasadena greenhouses are out of the question," Pat said. "We don't have access and basically botched the first job, and were saved by Kris . . ." She hesitated. " . . . the last time."

Kai gave her a quick glance.

"What we need are nonperishables. I thought the insurgents had stockpiles of food and equipment for just this situation," Pat said.

"We do, and they do include food, but not enough for everyone. We need to supplement and store all we can."

"There are regular shipments of food coming in by ship from South America and China. They transport those by trucks up to Level 6 almost every day, for now. If we could take one of those, maybe a couple of dozen trucks at once, we'd be okay for a while. From what I understand, every port along the SoCal coast gets regular food shipments. If we can coordinate with the others, we could get enough food to last a long time. The same thing happens on the landward side of the city, but those deliveries get direct access to Levels 6 and 7."

"Yes," said Kai. "And every port is also a SoCal military base. We would never get close enough to get anything."

"We wouldn't attack near the base."

Jack studied the back of his hands before replying. "Okay. You have two days to come up with a plan. I'll try to get you a list of contacts near the other ports. Coordinate with them and give me something I can bring to the other cells."

Pat nodded. Two days wasn't a lot of time, but it might be all they had anyway . . . even less if they dumped the trucks for air transport.

"If that's it, I think we'll call it a night."

"Umm, no. I have one more thing." Here it was. The part Pat didn't want to talk about. Unfortunately, she didn't have a choice. As long as she kept Kris's pregnancy a secret, it should be okay. Though even that felt wrong. "Kris came back today," Pat said.

"Kris? The same Kris who got drafted yesterday?"

"Yes."

"How did she escape?"

"She didn't. They let her go because of her age." Pat swallowed the half-truth. It was easier than she'd thought it would be.

"How old is she?" Jack asked.

"Seventeen."

"How close to eighteen?"

"A couple of months."

He shook his head. "I can't see that happening. I've heard of kids being drafted and trained if they were close enough to their birthday. What's so special about her?"

"She was exhausted when she came in, I didn't want to ask too many questions. I brought her up to her room and let her sleep."

"You left her alone?"

"Yes."

Jack got up and opened the hallway door. "Have a guard put on Kris Merrill's room immediately. Make sure they verify that she is still in there. They are not to let her out."

Pat heard a mumbled reply.

"You do not have to do that," Kai said. "Kris would never do anything that would harm us."

Somehow, Pat knew he was referring to her and himself.

"It's too odd to leave alone," Jack said. "A lot of people depend on me for their safety. I can't let it slip because you know her. SoCal never lets people go."

"I know, but—"

"There's no discussion, Kai. Until we can figure out what's going on, she's under house arrest."

Kai just nodded.

"Good. Get in touch with Doc Searls, and Pat, get me a working plan in two days."

He held the door open for them and they left.

Kai stopped Pat partway down the hall. "Why did they let her go?"

She pressed her lips together.

"Tell me."

"No."

"No? Why not?"

"I can't. It's not my place."

"Is she in trouble? Did she make some sort of deal with SoCal?"

Pat gave him a disgusted look. "You know better than that." She slipped her arm from his grasp and walked through the double doors, relieved to be left alone.

LOS ANGELES LEVEL 2—THURSDAY, JULY 6, 2141 2:27 A.M.

I woke up to a dark room, shadows chasing demons into the black corners. My heart hammered in my chest and a silent scream fell from my lips. At least I hoped it was silent. My eyes slowly focused, and the light from the dimmed Ambients filtering through the window helped push the demons away, helped me remember where I was. It was still night. The long walk from where SoCal had let me go to my room on Level 2 came back in dribbles, and my heart settled down, my body eventually relaxing back into the warm bed.

We'd all heard the horror stories of how SoCal got the draftees to fight, whispered over meals in the mess hall. Some of it was straightforward. Give them basic training and throw them in the field against the enemy. They either fight or die. Or both. Some of it included brainwashing, sleep deprivation, drugs. The list went on. I knew I was lucky to get out.

It dawned on me as I lay in bed that I hadn't felt sick the last few mornings. Maybe that was finally done with and I could get back to being a bit more normal. I had no idea how long morning sickness was supposed to last. I should have asked Doc Searls.

I had told Pat about the baby last night. Even as I thought the words, a massive weight lifted off my shoulders. I was finally able to share and talk about it with someone. Sure, Doc Searls had always known, but telling Pat was different. More personal. More of a relief.

Now, though, things would change. Pat would keep her promise about not telling anyone, at least I hoped so, but that didn't mean she wouldn't do anything she could to keep me out of the field. She'd been trying her best since Ian had died, and I knew she would triple her efforts.

Maybe it was for the best.

No! I couldn't let myself think that way. If I did, there was a chance I would never get back out there, and that was where I wanted—needed—to be. Sitting back and letting others do the work wasn't who I was.

There were so many unanswered questions and so many decisions to make. I pushed them away. One thing living on Levels 1 and 2 had taught me was to take life one day at a time. Long-term plans were good to have, but the day-to-day was what kept you alive, kept you moving.

I rolled onto my side and closed my eyes. Tonight I would sleep. Tomorrow would be a new day.

Fifteen minutes later I turned over, trying to get comfortable. Ten minutes after that I did it again. After tossing and turning for an hour or more, I finally got up. I wasn't going to sleep. It was too fucking early in the morning to be awake, that was for sure. Maybe I could get a bite to eat from the kitchen. I hadn't had anything during my walk yesterday, and I was famished. I tried to straighten out my crumpled clothes, still from SoCal, and opened the door.

"I'm sorry, you'll have to stay in the room."

I gasped and jumped back about three feet, ready to fight.

"Close the door and wait till someone comes to get you in the morning."

A guard! They had placed a guard by my door. Why the hell would they . . . Because SoCal had let me go and the only person who really knew why was Pat. I closed the door and went into panic mode. My breathing was shallow and quick. I wasn't ready to let *everyone* know. It was too soon. How was I supposed to get out of this mess?

For the second time tonight, I felt lightheaded. This time it wasn't from relief. I was scared, truly scared of what the insurgents would do to me. Would they kick me out? Move me to the sidelines where I would be more useless than I already was? I'd thought of leaving them many times, but it was different when the choice was out of my control.

I stood behind the closed door for few minutes before crawling back into bed.

Sleep finally came, but with it came the dreams of Ian and me, and then the nightmares that had kept me segregated at boot camp. I hadn't had them since I found out I was pregnant. Maybe their brief absence made them feel worse. Maybe the turmoil I felt amplified the emotions. The panic of the closed box, of the bullets entering my body, were the worst they had ever been.

I woke up screaming, my throat raw and Pat leaning over me, holding me down, trying to let me know everything was all right.

Faces peeked in through the open door until the guard shoved everyone back and closed it. He'd been gawking as much as everyone else. I cried in Pat's arms until there was no strength left in me, no more tears to release into the world. I must have fallen asleep again, waking up alone in a brightly lit room to the sound of tapping at the door.

I sat up groggily, rubbing the sleep from my eyes. Every part of me ached and protested at the sudden movement. "Come in."

The door opened and a head stuck through. "Hey." It was Selma. "I've been asked to bring you to Jack's office, if you were awake."

I stared at her.

"I can tell them you were still sleeping, if you want." I could almost feel the concern emanating from her. Was she one of the people who had stuck their head in the door last night? It didn't matter. The story would have gotten around by now.

"No," I sighed. "Just give me a couple of minutes to change and clean up." I had forgotten to check if my buckets were full yesterday.

"Take as much time as you need."

"Thanks."

She left me alone. I crawled out of bed, looking for clean clothes in the dresser. I would stick out like a sore thumb wearing the clothes SoCal had given me. They looked too much like what the military wore. Someone must have come in and put my clothes away. The dresser had two of my pants and shirts in it, plus some clean underwear. I stripped down and got dressed, leaving the SoCal clothes in a pile in the middle of the room. They could burn them as far as I was concerned.

One bucket had a bit of water in it, enough to wash the crud from my eyes and rinse out my mouth. When I was done, I opened the door. Selma was waiting for me.

"You ready?"

"I guess."

"Okay, come on."

I followed her down to Jack's office, and the guard followed me.

LOS ANGELES LEVEL 2—THURSDAY, JULY 6, 2141 12:17 P.M.

By the time the interview was done, I was more tired than the night before. My eyelids were heavy and I slouched in the chair Jack had offered me. I don't know if he simply didn't believe I was pregnant, or if he thought it was something SoCal and I had dreamed up in order to reinsert myself as a mole into his organization. At least he'd brought in food so I could eat.

At some point, I gave up and walked out, telling him to get his own damn doctor to check me out if he wanted. Fuck him. I didn't need that shit in my life. The insurgent guards left me alone once I walked out of the building.

I left, not knowing where to go. I just knew I didn't want to be there right now. It was tiring being treated like I was the bad guy, and I already missed my bike. By the time the insurgents had gotten back to the scene of the draft, it was gone. Probably stripped for parts and sold off to put food on someone's table. I couldn't blame them. But without it, I felt exposed and vulnerable. I didn't like it.

I turned toward Chinatown, staying by the buildings that lined the streets, my old haunts pulling at me like I was a puppet. I didn't know what I was going to do until I got there. The street kitchen was still setting up. From what I had heard, they had cut the meals down to one a day. Even though the food was supplied by the insurgents, it wasn't run or staffed by them. I would come back when the food was ready and at least help serve it. I still had to get my mind off of the distrust that had oozed from Jack, so I walked into the Lee's fish market, wanting a reminder of where I had come from. It worked.

The second I walked through the door, I was transported back to last year, when I had lived here. Though the shelves were almost empty, the smell of raw fish filled my nose and the oils soaked into my skin.

It lasted no more than a minute before I realized I could never—would never—go back to the person I had been. Too much had happened since I was a courier. I had gained and lost so much. I walked out, uncomfortable and feeling like I needed to shower for a week. It had reminded me of a life I wasn't part of anymore. Though I had enjoyed it at the time, I had been forced to move on, had lived a lifetime since I'd left.

I walked down to Kai's old restaurant, faded menus still covering the windows. He had put them up only a couple of weeks ago to stop people from looking in, from seeing us in there. I cupped my hands to peer through the gaps. The inside was dark. I barely made out the counter separating the kitchen from the public area. Despite the covered windows, the restaurant still looked ready to open, ready to serve lunch to hungry people. The chances of it happening were pretty much zero.

As I pulled away from the window, a reflection in the glass grabbed my attention. I leaned back in, pretending to take another look inside.

Though the glass rippled the image, I was fairly certain of what I had seen. It was Janice, pulling on the arm of a man I didn't know. He was tall and thin, and for the briefest moment I thought it was Quincy. My insides loosened in fear, turning into a blob of jelly. I knew it couldn't be him. Even if they'd gotten him to a hospital, there wasn't a chance of bringing life back into his body. Not after what I had done. I watched Janice and the man for a few seconds before casually turning around and staring right at them.

I had to be one hundred percent sure it was her. I'd seen her fly over the handlebars of her bike, which meant if she was here, she wasn't working alone. Someone had gotten her to a hospital and fixed her up. The image in the glass was too wavy to be certain. Turning may not have been the smartest move though. On one hand, if they knew I had seen them, they might give up and go away. Though I didn't think that would happen. She had been too persistent for too long. It was more likely that they'd be extra careful, making it even more difficult to see them.

But I had to be sure.

The moment I made eye contact, a voice called out to me. I recognized it immediately. My aunt. I caught Janice staring at her, memorizing her face, her walk, her posture, and my heart fell. Suddenly, I wished I'd never met my aunt again. Knowing Janice had seen her ripped away the certainty that if anything happened, it would happen to me. That no one else would be dragged into what was coming.

Before I could turn away, before I could warn my aunt, she came up to me and gave me a hug. If Janice had paid attention to half the training she'd gotten at the ACE compound, she would have spotted the weakness. I didn't think she was stupid enough to have missed it. If she did, her partner would have caught it instead. Even dressed in clothes worse than most people on Level 2, he gave off an aura of danger.

Suddenly, it wasn't just me in trouble. I raised an involuntary hand to my abdomen. I guess it never really had been.

LOS ANGELES LEVEL 2—THURSDAY, JULY 6, 2141 12:10 P.M.

Despite her initial misgivings, Janice's new partner seemed good. Very good. When she had first met him, when John had introduced them, she was worried. Manfred was dressed in a crisp steel blue three-piece suit with the thin lapel and high vest that was all the rage. He looked more like a fashion model than an operative of any sort.

She still wasn't sure why they had sent her back down. They'd barely questioned her. Maybe there was something in her records that had helped. More likely, they were testing her. Trying to figure out whose side she was on, and whether her skill set matched what they had read. She figured she wasn't hanging on by more than a thread. One mistake and Manfred's orders were probably to kill her and dump the body.

The whole shuttle ride down, she tried to figure Manfred out. He was quiet, not responding to her questions. At one point, he told her to shut up. She'd stopped trying then.

They hadn't given her the gun back. Instead they'd given her a stun gun. It could only be used to incapacitate, not kill. SoCal wasn't taking any chances.

By the time the shuttle landed, Manfred had already changed into something more casual. The same button-up shirt, but with a more relaxed pair of pants and comfortable-looking shoes. He'd blend in on Levels 6 and 7 with that, but stick out like an intruder on the lower levels.

They got a car to drive from long-term parking. Another thing that made them stand out. It was too new and too clean to be of any real use. It reeked of money and wealth beyond what anyone, even on Level 5, could afford. Even an amateur would be able to recognize the car and realize they were being followed, that it didn't belong.

When they reached Level 5, he locked her into the car and left. She tried to unlock the doors, even groping under the dash for any wires. She struggled to remove the front seat headrest, hoping to use it to break the glass, or at the very least pry off the inside of the door so she could fiddle with the locks. They didn't budge, and she gave up. Twenty minutes later, a beat-up old thing pulled in beside her.

The driver looked worn out, tired, but not too badly off. His clothes, though somewhat clean, were frayed and patched. It took her a few seconds to realize it was Manfred. He unlocked the car she was in and pulled her out, shoving her into the front seat of the one he had driven up in. They still hadn't spoken more than a few words.

On Level 3 he made another switch, dressing more like the homeless and destitute on Level 2 than she did. It was ridiculous how often he changed. It would have been easier to do one switch on Level 5 and stay with it.

They left the car in a parking garage in the Italian sector and walked down the ramp to Level 2, blending in with everyone else heading to the food in Chinatown.

Manfred shuffled his feet, as though he barely had the energy to move them, to get to the only thing that might keep him alive for another day. It was all a bit much, the costume and posture changes. Even his skin was dirtier than when they had left orbit. She wasn't sure if the effort was for her benefit, or if this was something he always did.

They walked into Chinatown side-by-side, his hand on her shoulder, as though he needed her support to walk. The tightness of his grip told her otherwise.

"I can't be seen here. We need to move off the main strip," she said.

"Try to blend in."

"If Kris is here, she'll recognize me."

He stopped across from a shut-down Chinese restaurant and looked her up and down, as if really seeing her for the first time. "We don't need to get you different clothes. These ones look like shit already. Not much we can do about the hair. I can hack it off a bit, make it shorter and rougher. Maybe rub some dirt in it. It looks too clean."

Janice bit back a sharp retort. She balked at the idea of chopping off her hair, but knew he was right. "We could stay in the alleys," she offered instead.

"No. If the insurgents have people on guard here, and they should, they'll be on the lookout for anybody who doesn't fit, and skulking in alleys will trigger them. Not good."

Janice froze. Someone had stopped to look in the window of the Chinese restaurant across the street, and from the back it looked a hell of a lot like Kris. She grabbed Manfred's arm and started dragging him away.

He stopped, staring in the same direction as her.

The person turned and looked right at them. Janice let go of Manfred's arm. It was her. It was Kris.

A woman's voice called out, and Kris turned. Manfred stepped back, behind a family heading toward the tables set up for the street kitchen. He turned and walked with them, slouching to change his profile, dragging Janice behind him. She tried to do the same. She was too slow for him and he jerked her closer, almost pulling her off her feet.

An old woman walked in the opposite direction, heading straight for Kris and called out her name again. She raised a frail arm, all skin and bones, and waved. Kris didn't wave back. The woman approached Kris and gave her a hug before pulling away.

Janice followed Manfred, doing her best to blend in, while keeping an eye on Kris and the old woman. She memorized her face. It might come in handy one day.

Her job wasn't to kill Kris anymore, and that really bothered her. She was supposed to monitor and find any patterns, document the people Kris hung out with. SoCal knew Kris was part of the insurgent cell that had been pestering them, stealing their food, had staged the protests outside the water distribution centers weeks ago. Maybe even supplied some people with guns.

Their hope was that Kris would show them where the insurgents were. Janice had given them the location outside Chinatown, but there were more insurgent buildings scattered throughout San Angeles. Follow Kris, find out some of the higher-ups, follow them, repeat, and eventually figure out the infrastructure of the entire faction. Standard surveillance. If she did what SoCal wanted, she'd come out of this alive.

They'd blown it right off the bat.

KADOKAWA SAT CITY 2—THURSDAY, JULY 6, 2141 12:20 P.M.

Andrew drank tea alone in his room. Even the warmth of the golden *Hachijūhachiya Sencha* failed to boost his spirits. He had left Operations on the pretense of needing to catch up on some paperwork, but in truth, he was exhausted. He hadn't slept much the night before, tossing and turning, waking with a hollow feeling in his chest, his pulse racing. Strange dreams of being caught doing something he shouldn't—chopping down his father's prize bamboo to make a play sword when he was eleven years old, stealing his sister's *konpeitō* when she wouldn't share with him—filled any sleep he did get.

It had been a while since he'd had an anxiety attack, even one as small as the couple he'd had last night. He knew what had brought them on. What he didn't know was what to do about them.

The reports he'd brought with him sat on the table mostly unread. Some of them were simple things to do with allocations of personnel. It was one of the other ones that intrigued him the most.

The main docking bay lights on SoCal Sat City 2 had gone out for two minutes that morning. Shuttles had been forced to stay in holding patterns until they came back on. His intelligence officers were trying to figure out exactly what was going on. Had the city experienced some sort of malfunction, unheard of in recent history, or were they trying to hide some activity in the darkness? Some of his officers had even tossed the idea of malcontents messing with the systems. Interestingly, the lights on the military bay hadn't gone out.

He picked up the pad and scanned it for the third time. Earlier in the day, a strong location beacon had gone off on the SoCal satellite as well. It had lasted for one-point-two seconds and abruptly cut off. They hadn't intercepted any communications from SoCal about the incident.

Some of the scenarios in the report tied the two together, almost going so far as to describe a potential stealth vessel that had been rumored for years. The vessel put out no signals of its own, using only passive devices, and would therefore require an active signal to target its docking site. For some, that led directly to the docking bay lights going out. Hide the ship at all costs. If that was what truly had happened, it was a huge risk on SoCal's part. Andrew didn't believe that, though. Why use the commercial docking bay to hide the arrival of a stealth vessel? If you worked to keep something a secret, you didn't have a big public display.

It was all guesswork at this point. No one knew for sure what was going on, and their moles hadn't gotten a message through. Tough to do during a time of war.

Moles or infiltrators were a constant problem between corporations. Their entire existence was predicated on finding out more about their competitors than anyone else. Even Kadokawa in the better days had people planted everywhere. The Kadokawa corporate arm, which financed the military and humanitarian side of the operations, still had to be competitive in the global markets.

Kadokawa had stayed out of the first corporate war—as much as they could anyway, preferring, once again, to help the people hurt by the fighting. This time around, they were taking a more aggressive stance. The hostile takeover of Meridian had positioned them into one of the lead instigators.

Andrew threw the pad back onto the table in disgust. He took the last sip of his tea, already gone cold and bitter. He'd tossed around the implications of Natsumi's message and the new Kadokawa actions all night. He wasn't getting anywhere except frustrated and mad. He had a job to do, and that was that. SoCal's fleet was still holding its position, but they could move at any time, and he needed to be ready. He would do what he had done when she had been promoted. Lose himself in his work and his duty.

It wasn't until he was walking out of his office that he realized he had used a modifier when referring to Kadokawa. The *new* Kadokawa. When had he started doing that?

EIGHT

LOS ANGELES LEVEL 2—THURSDAY, JULY 6, 2141 12:20 P.M.

JANICE AND THE MAN she was with had disappeared. I scanned the crowd over my aunt's shoulder as she hugged me, but couldn't see them anywhere. Where the fuck had they gone?

My aunt let me go and gave me a confused smile. She could tell something was wrong, but didn't know what it was. She grabbed me and pulled me to the tables, obviously thrilled to have reconnected with me. The more I thought about it, the more *I* wasn't sure. Four years was a long time to carry around the hatred I'd had for her, and it wasn't something I could get rid of overnight.

So, out of spite, I told her how I had survived. What I had done in order to eat and put clothes on my back. I didn't hold anything back, even when I saw her flinch. When I wasn't looking for Janice,

I didn't move, sitting like one of the statues in McConnell Park as I parceled out my life in words. Part of me was pleased with her reaction. Most of me was mortified.

She cried. She held my hand, squeezing it tight. She stared in my eyes as if she could see the horrors I'd faced flashing across them. All she could say was *I'm sorry* over and over again. I stopped talking when I reached the point of getting the courier job at Internuncio. She didn't need to know the rest. Didn't need to know about ACE, about Ian. About the baby.

I reached for my comm unit out of habit, forgetting for a moment that I had destroyed it. I'd have to find some way to replace it. Getting hold of Pat or Kai would be an issue. There was no way I wanted to walk through the front door of the insurgents' building.

It was surprising how naked I felt without the comm unit. I'd become so used to having access to all the data, but more than that, I'd gotten very used to being able to change—to hide—who I was from the SoCal scanners.

"Is everything all right?" Auntie asked.

I pulled myself out of my reverie. "Yeah, but I gotta go."

The look on my aunt's face said she didn't believe me. "Will I see you later?"

"Yeah, I'll be around here a lot, working the food tables." We stood and I turned my back on her, heading for nowhere. I needed somewhere to stay tonight.

I had nowhere to sleep.

The thought hit me like an unexpected punch to the gut. The safest move was to suck in my pride and go back to my room. I just couldn't do it. Not now. I saw my aunt walking past Kai's old restaurant and knew what I had to do.

LOS ANGELES LEVEL 2—THURSDAY, JULY 6, 2141 12:48 P.M.

I waited until my aunt had passed the front windows of the restaurant before I started heading back in that direction. Several of the people preparing to serve food stopped what they were doing and waved at me. I waved back, trying to appear nonchalant and relaxed. Trying to reinforce the idea that this was what I always did, every day.

I made it through the seating area, already starting to fill up, and around the serving tables before someone tried to talk to me. I told them I didn't have time, but I'd be back later in the day.

As soon as I reached the side street by the restaurant, I zipped around the corner and up the back alley. I stopped there, waiting and watching in case someone had followed me. When no one approached, I moved over to Kai's back door. I gave it five sharp taps and two bangs with my foot. Kai's special knock. If you knew it, it was easier to get in. There was no answer. I really wasn't expecting one. I'd have to break in.

The door was freshly clad in metal, impossible to break through, and its hinges were on the inside. It had been reinforced since the break-in two weeks ago. Getting through the door would be next to impossible. The front windows would be the easiest, but far too noticeable. I moved to the connection between the restaurant and the next building, stepping over bags of garbage, ripped open with their contents strewn everywhere. The gap between the two buildings was about five centimeters wide, easy enough to jam in a hand or two, as well as the tips of my shoes. I'd be able to climb up the one story to the roof in no time.

I reached high, putting my flattened hand into the crack and cupping it. The fibercrete was textured enough for me to get friction.

I jammed in a shoe and stood, pulling on my hand at the same time. I only had to repeat the process a few more times before I was able to reach the top of the building. I grabbed onto the lip and walked my feet up until I could swing a leg over.

The roof was disgusting. It was obvious no one had been up here since the place was built. With no wind or rain to help keep it clean, it was layered in grease from the vents over the woks below me. Each layer had absorbed the dirt and grime constantly in the air, creating a morass of slime. When my shoe first broke the surface of the sludge, it released a stench so powerful I almost fell over. I had thought that maybe I could use the vents to get into the restaurant, but I quickly changed my mind.

Grease layered the bottoms of my shoes, and some of the thick crud had been pushed up the sides, almost over the top and onto my socks. I pivoted to get out of the mess and slipped. My stomach flopped like I was in a high-speed elevator going down. I teetered forward, trying to keep my feet under me and only slipping more, until I couldn't keep my balance.

I landed on my hands and knees.

The viscous gunk seeped into my pants and oozed between my fingers. I struggled to stand up, and ended up crawling to where the pool ended, heaving from the stench that enveloped me. I used the edge of the roof to scrape as much of the ooze off of me as I could. I stunk so bad I had to stop to retch.

All I'd wanted was a place to sleep, and now I'd turned into a walking sewage tank. I ground my teeth together and felt the anger, all too familiar recently, seep through me. How could I have been so stupid? Kai had worked out of the building for years, had used it as a hospital for the insurgents. He'd even had an escape route built in, just in case. We'd used it. What made me think getting in would be easy? I was an idiot, that's what.

Maybe I should have broken a window. Who cared if it was obvious? At least I wouldn't stink like I'd been rolling in piles of oily shit. It wouldn't have been any less stupid than what I had done.

I tried to draw in a calming breath and ended up gagging instead. The smell was getting worse. I moved back to the edge of the roof by the alley and lay on my belly, sliding my feet over. I tried to stick my toes into the crack, but they slipped back out again. I shimmied lower, my gut on the edge, and kicked off my shoes. What did I think I was doing? Eight weeks pregnant and lying on a roof three meters off the ground.

Without my shoes on, my toes stayed in the crack and I slid over the edge, releasing the pressure on my belly. I don't know if he felt better about it, but I sure as hell did. I gave my hands one more wipe on the fibercrete and lowered myself, repeating the same moves I'd done to get up. My grip wasn't as secure and I put more pressure on them, hoping they would hold. They did until I was about a meter above the back alley. My left hand popped without warning. Instinctively, I tensed my right hand more, creating a better hold between it and the buildings. It didn't matter. I peeled over backward, my toes doing nothing to hold me against the wall.

I didn't have time to suck in a breath for a scream before I landed flat on my back, the wind knocked out of me. I rolled over, getting onto my hands and knees, trying to pull in some air. The garbage under me shifted. It had broken my fall, saving me from being seriously hurt.

"Kris!"

The shout cut through the alley.

"Oh, Kris. Are you all right?"

It was a stupid question. One I didn't have enough air to answer. My aunt was climbing over the refuse, trying to reach me. I held up a hand for her to stop at the same time I took my first breath. It took me another couple of seconds before I could talk.

"Yeah, I'm good." I stood and leaned against the back of the restaurant. "I'm good." The concern on her face eased, but didn't vanish.

"What on earth were you trying to do? I was coming back to wait at the tables when I saw you duck into the side street. It didn't seem right, so I followed you. I was looking down here when I saw you fall."

"I was just . . ." What was I doing? Trying to break into a friend's place so I wouldn't have to sleep on the street. "I was trying to get an overview of the place. I didn't think . . ."

"No doubt you didn't think." Her voice held the edge I remembered from when I was a kid, and bile rose in my throat. She took a whiff and lifted the back of her hand to her nose, taking a step away. "What is that godawful smell?"

"Me. The roof was covered in grease from the restaurant. A fucking fire hazard if you ask me." I found my shoes and put them on.

"Yes, well, do you live near here? We need to get you some clean clothes and maybe a bit washed up."

I sighed. Here it was. "I was kicked out of my place."

"You have nowhere to stay?"

I shook my head.

She paused for a split second. Barely long enough for me to notice, though I didn't think she did it on purpose. "Well, you'll stay with me. My place is small, but it's better than the street. I still have some water from this morning. It won't get you a hundred percent clean, but it'll help."

I was about to protest when she took a step closer, ignoring the smell, and grabbed my elbow, dragging me across the garbage.

"It's outside Chinatown. A bit of a walk, really."

I followed her, shaking my head slowly. If you would have asked the Kris of two days ago if she would ever live with her aunt again, you would have heard a string of obscenities a kilometer long. Now here I was, following her back to her place.

Life had a strange way of going full circle.

LOS ANGELES LEVEL 2—THURSDAY, JULY 6, 2141 12:32 P.M.

"What the fuck do you think you were doing?" Manfred pulled Janice into a side street and slammed her against a wall. "You don't grab me. Ever. Especially when the person we're trying to monitor is right in front of us."

Janice pushed back, her shoulders hurt from the impact. "You weren't listening to me. I tried to get your attention. It almost seemed like once you knew who she was, you did everything you could to be seen."

Manfred scoffed. "You have no idea what you're talking about."

Janice leaned against the wall, shocked by what she now knew. "You *wanted* to be seen. You wanted her to know we were together. You wanted it." She paused, her voice soft and shaky. "You *need* it, don't you? You need to make everything more of a challenge."

Manfred placed both his hands on her shoulders and pressed her into the fibercrete. He leaned in until his face was centimeters from hers. "You have no idea what you're talking about, so it would be best to keep your mouth shut."

Janice slipped a shoulder out from his grasp and hit his elbow while she spun away from the wall. He barely caught himself before smacking into the rough fibercrete. When he turned around, his face had contorted into a mask of anger.

"That's it, isn't it?" Janice said. "The change of clothes at almost every level, the vehicle switches, all of it is just a sham. You almost want to get caught. What good is the chase if the target never knows you're there, right?" The absolute hatred written all over his face sent shivers up her spine, but she stayed on the attack. "Is what I'm saying making you mad? Does the truth hurt, Manfred?"

"You don't know when to shut up."

"I know exactly when to do everything, and it's not when some asshole tells me to."

Manfred lunged for her, his fingers snagging at the neck of her shirt as she rotated away. It was enough. He pulled her back toward him.

Janice's training kicked in and she spun, using Manfred's grip as a pivot point. Her fist swung out, the pivot driving her fist faster, using the strength from her shoulder and the sudden rush of adrenaline. The back of her hand impacted his cheek and she felt bones crack. She wasn't sure if it was hers or his. Right now, it didn't matter.

Manfred's head spun, moving his body with it. His fingers loosened and released their grip on her shirt. He ended up on his hands and knees, blood dripping off the tip of his nose from his split cheek. Janice reeled away as he swept out his leg. He hit just above her ankles, kicking her legs out from under her. She fell forward, throwing out her arms to break her fall. Her right arm twisted, her hand gripping the butt of her stun gun.

He was on her before she had time to move, jumping on her back, driving his knees into her kidneys and the air from her lungs. His hands wrapped around her neck, and he leaned in to whisper in her ear.

"I knew this was a bad idea. Maybe that's why they told me I could kill you if you fucked up."

Janice's vision blurred as the blood flow to her brain was squeezed shut. She arched her back and rolled, bringing her elbow up. The blow wasn't hard, but it was enough. Manfred fell off her.

She rolled onto her back, grabbing her stun gun from her pocket as she did the move. Manfred pushed to his feet at the same time she did. His eye was swollen shut.

She surged toward him, aiming for his blind side. The stun gun drove forward, hitting the first piece of exposed skin she could find. The tip of the gun slid off his cheek, driving into his swollen eye with enough force to sink in. She pulled the trigger and held it there until Manfred's body convulsed away and fell in a mound on the ground.

She stood over him, panting as he continued to twitch while the lingering charge slowly drained from his body. It wasn't enough for her. Kicking him onto his back, she leaned down and pressed the gun into the center of his chest. She held the trigger until there was nothing left in the device.

Janice walked away from his still form, away from the main street to somewhere a bit quieter. She'd fucked up really bad. She'd let her anger take control. If SoCal found out what she had done . . .

She saw Kris on the street, the old lady leading, and followed them, Manfred almost forgotten.

LOS ANGELES LEVEL 2—THURSDAY, JULY 6, 2141 12:49 P.M.

Despite the smell, my aunt helped me out of the garbage-strewn alley. I limped a bit, but the dull ache in my thigh diminished with every step I took. She turned toward the main street of Chinatown. We were almost at the corner before I stopped her. I didn't want to be out amongst the people I had worked with. Not looking and smelling like this. I didn't want to be seen by Janice either.

"Can we go down a quieter street?"

She took one look at me and nodded, leading me in the other direction to a parallel street. How had this woman, frail beyond her years, someone I had hated for too long to keep track of, become someone I was relying on? How had she become someone I *could* rely on?

Despite how I felt, I kept a vigilant look out for Janice and her friend. The last thing I wanted to do was get into a fight. After training with her, I was pretty sure I would win, but it would be a tough battle. Throw in her companion and having my aunt there would make it more difficult. Who was I fooling? It would be impossible. If Janice used my aunt—and I knew she would—what would I do? I wasn't sure.

When we finally made it through Chinatown and into the nondescript area just outside, I relaxed a little. Ten blocks with no sight of her, farther from the kitchens and even farther away from the insurgents, was a good place to be.

"How long?" I asked.

"Another hour or so. You'll have to slow down. I can't walk as fast as I used to."

I was going slow. My thigh still hurt and I'd slowed down for her. "Let's stop for a second."

She breathed a sigh of relief and lowered herself to the curb. I sat beside her until I got a fresh waft from my clothes. I stood and moved a bit away.

"You wouldn't happen to have some extra clothes, would you?" I asked.

"Nothing you'd like, or would fit. I have a dress I can't wear anymore. I could take it in a bit."

I grimaced.

"It would be better than what you're wearing. I did some laundry yesterday, so I won't have enough water for another couple of weeks." She gave a quiet little laugh. "I'm not sure I'd have enough water or detergent to get rid of that smell anyway. It's horrible."

"It is, isn't it?" I started laughing with her. The tension of the last few days flowed out. Without warning, my laughter turned to tears. I swiped at my eyes.

"What's wrong?"

"It's nothing I can talk about." The look on her face was one of pure hurt. "I'm sorry, it's just . . ."

"No. It's all right. I . . . I'm not in any position to have earned your trust. I understand. It's okay." She stood and faced away from Chinatown, turning her back on me. "Should we continue?"

I hesitated before answering. "Sure."

We finished the rest of the walk in silence. Alone, I could have done it in half the time. When we finally got there, she was breathing hard.

Her apartment was on the bottom floor of an old building. It looked like someone had tried to keep it up long ago, but now filth and cobwebs clung to the corners. A light came on in the foyer when we walked in and cockroaches scurried away, trying to find safety in the shadows. I'd seen worse, but this was pretty bad.

Auntie must have seen the distaste on my face.

"It's the best I can afford."

"But your place on Level 1 was better than this."

"It had its own problems. And it was Level 1. I would live in worse than this to be out of that hellhole. To be rid of the memories."

She shuffled down the hall, unlocking a door at the end with a key hung around her neck. When I walked in, it was like a different world. The walls were clean and the floor uncluttered. Along the edges of the walls were roach traps.

"It helps, but it's not perfect."

"Your place is great."

"Thanks. The bathroom is down there. I'll get a bag for your clothes. You'll find a housecoat behind the door, until we can get you fitted into the dress."

I grimaced again.

"It's all I have to offer."

"It'll be great, thanks." I hated dresses. I always had. Dresses made me look like a girl, and a girl was a target on the streets I'd lived in. I'd switch it out as soon as I could.

"Use as much of the water and soap as you need, please."

I smiled as I closed the door to the bathroom. There was a lock on it, an improvement from when I had lived with her—with them—on Level 1. I stripped out of my pants and shirt and socks, holding them in my hands until the bag came. Auntie knocked on the door and slipped the bag through to me. Once the clothes were sealed and outside the bathroom, the smell got better. I washed up as best I could without using all the water and walked out wearing a frilly pink housecoat that swept the floor.

"Feeling better?"

"Much, thank you."

"This is the dress." She held up a plain navy blue shift. It was obviously too big for me, dragging on the floor and billowing at the waist. "Let's get some measurements and I'll see what I can do."

I hesitated.

"If you have nothing on under the robe, you can wear one of my shirts before I measure. If you're not, there is nothing to be afraid of." She paused, making eye contact with me. "There's no one here to hurt you. Not this time."

No one ever would. I'd learned how to take care of myself. It wasn't the only reason I hesitated though . . . I was pregnant. I slipped the robe off my shoulders and shivered in the sudden cold.

"I'll be quick."

Auntie took her measurements, not saying anything if she noticed my bump. She hadn't seen me for a long time, so maybe she thought this was the way I was.

"You can put the robe back on."

I put it on and retreated to a couch in the corner. Auntie stayed by the kitchen table humming happily to herself. I'd never seen this side of her. When I'd lived with them, she'd always been going off to work or cleaning or shopping. In hindsight, she'd probably kept that busy just to stay away from her husband. She had been a bitter woman back then.

I woke up when a shadow fell across my face, jumping to my feet and almost knocking Auntie over, not realizing I'd fallen asleep. I apologized and stood there like an idiot. She handed me the dress.

"I took one of my old shirts and sewed it in as a liner. It should keep you warmer. I kept it a bit loose-fitting as well. I didn't think you would mind."

"No . . . I . . . thanks." I took the dress. The stitches, all hand sewn, were perfect. "How long was I asleep?"

"It looked like you needed it."

"How long?"

"Most of the afternoon."

I went to the bathroom and dropped the robe, replacing it on the hook by the door. The dress slipped easily over my head. The shoulder straps had been shortened, so most of me was covered. It still showed my shape despite the loose fit. Too much. The dress let me move, but I still felt exposed.

I walked out of the bathroom, heat rising in my cheeks.

"There! Almost perfect. I could take in the sides a bit more—"

"No. No, thank you. It'll be fine."

"Until you find some pants."

I grinned. "Until I find some pants. I'm sorry for taking you away from the kitchens. We could still get some food. I know some people."

"I have a little left in my freezer. I try to take some home every day, just in case I can't make it one time. I'll thaw out a couple of plates."

I sat back on the couch in my dress, trying to remember to keep my knees together, and watched my aunt prepare us supper.

LOS ANGELES LEVEL 2—THURSDAY, JULY 6, 2141 4:57 P.M.

It took a while to get dinner ready. We sat at her small kitchen table, covered in an old lace tablecloth, and chatted while we waited, getting to know each for the first time. The more we spoke, the more she reminded me of my dad.

Dinner itself was barely passable. The freezing and thawing cycle hadn't added anything to the free kitchen's food, and she must have grabbed this stuff from a really bad day. The end result was a grainy soup that slid down your throat in a gelatinous lump.

"I always go out for an evening walk before the Ambients dim," my aunt said. "Even with the distance to the food, I still need more exercise than I get. These bones aren't getting any younger. The air seems cleaner at this time of day as well. I know I'm too slow for you, but would you want to join me?"

"Of course!" The thought of heading out in the dress made me feel vulnerable and exposed, but how could I say no? She had offered me a roof over my head, and put food, if you could call it that, into my stomach.

Before we opened the door, a loud bang and swearing came from the hall. I froze, gripping the doorknob. Auntie put her hand on my arm, her shrunken muscles pushing hard through the thinning skin.

"That's Jackson from down the hall. He comes in drunk and cursing most nights. If you wait a bit, he'll get himself into his rooms and quiet down."

Her voice stayed soft, hiding the tension I saw so clearly in her arm. We waited for a couple of minutes, listening to the noise. A door slammed and the yelling became muffled.

Auntie visibly relaxed, and it drove the point home that I wasn't the only one being abused in that old apartment on Level 1. She had been as well. Maybe not physically like I was, but she had been emotionally battered, and still showed the scars from those years.

Did we ever really lose them?

"We can go now." She opened the door and closed it behind us, locking it.

"How do you put up with it?" I asked, nodding my head toward a closed door. I could still hear him cursing.

"I know he lives alone . . . that his lack of control, his addiction, isn't harming anyone else. I stay out of his way."

That was more than she'd been able to do when it was her husband. As we walked past Jackson's apartment, she picked up her pace, slowing only when we reached the door heading outside. I could almost feel the connection between us forming. There wasn't anything she could have done to help me all those years ago.

He wouldn't have let her.

The strength she would have needed when she kicked him out. The fear she must have felt. The same as mine. All I wanted to do was pull her into my arms and hold her until we both could let go of what that man had done to us. I held the door open for her instead.

The air felt fresher than when we had come in, but that could have been my imagination. For one, I didn't smell as bad anymore, and the dress let me feel the air swirl around my legs with every step. Auntie looped her arm over mine, and we strolled around the block, not saying anything, each of us lost in our own thoughts and memories.

From nowhere, a body slammed into me.

We fell in a pile of arms and legs, intertwined and writhing in a hope for freedom. I could see Auntie, she had been thrown into the wall of the apartment block and lay still. I slashed out with an elbow, happy with the solid impact and the feeling of less weight holding me down.

Before I could stand, a foot arced toward my head. I rolled to the left and the heavy booted foot scraped my cheek. Blood splashed in my ears. I didn't know who had attacked us. My world was a flurry of arms and hands and feet and knees.

I jumped up, risking a glance at my aunt. She had moved to a sitting position by the wall and watched, her eyes wide, her face a sickly white. Looking was a mistake. A fist snaked toward my face. I ducked, blocking it with a forearm and swinging back in return.

It was then I recognized Janice.

How had she found me, and where was her partner? I stumbled back, away from my aunt. The move created more space between us, and we stood there, both of us ready for another attack. I had to finish this quickly, before her partner could join the fray.

"Why?" I panted. "Why are you doing this?"

"Because I was told to." She circled to the right, trying to get me between the building and her, with my back to my aunt.

"By who?" I stepped backward instead, out onto the street.

"William, from ACE. Jeremy would have wanted it too."

"Jeremy is dead and William has disappeared. You don't need to do this."

"You're right. This is for me." Her last words sounded more like a snarl.

I didn't know what to say. Before I could, she was on me again, her foot lashing out at my knee.

I blocked it, pain shooting through my shin. The momentum of her kick spun her partway around. She was out of control. I took advantage and jumped, hammering my elbow into the base of her skull. She collapsed and lay still. I stood over her, struggling to catch my breath before grabbing and dragging her to the side of the road. I dropped her in the gutter and grabbed her hair, raising her head over the curb, and slammed down with everything I had left. Her forehead glanced off the corner and smashed into street. I picked up her head again.

"Kris!"

I let go and rushed up to my aunt, pain shooting up my leg at every step and my breath coming in sharp ragged gasps. "Are you okay?"

"I can't move my leg. You . . . you were trying to kill her."

"She was trying to kill me. We need to go. Last time I saw her, I think she had a partner."

"Okay."

I heard the fear in her voice.

Auntie tried to stand and collapsed back down with a whimper. "I can't."

"Where does it hurt? Let me see."

"My hip, I think. As soon as I put weight on it, I start to feel weak."

"Is it bad?"

"I don't think so. I can make it."

"Okay. Put your arm over my shoulder. I'll help you up." I crouched under her arm and stood. She cried out in agony. "I know where I need to take you. We need to find a car."

nine

LOS ANGELES LEVEL 2—THURSDAY, JULY 6, 2141 5:22 P.M.

JANICE TWITCHED ON the ground. The curb, only a few centimeters from her face, came into focus. She watched a cockroach skitter in the corner, disappearing inside a tiny crack. The back of her head ached and her face was numb. She pushed up to her hands and knees, and the ache turned into a sharp pain, making everything blur. Kris and her friend were gone. Though she knew which building Kris's friend lived in, it wasn't worth checking out. Kris was too smart to head back in there. This wasn't over yet.

Her world spun as she struggled to get to her feet, eventually crawling over to the wall the old woman had leaned against and using it to brace herself. When she finally made it up, she rested, pressing her cheek against the cool, moist fibercrete, closing her eyes against the spin. She stayed that way, trying to focus her thoughts. Blood ran down her face from a gash.

Before she could move on, her comm unit rang.

She fumbled through her pockets, her coordination still uncertain. The buzzing stopped. She focused her eyes on the screen. Damn. It was SoCal. The thought barely formed before the unit starting buzzing again.

"Hello?" Her head pounded with the sound of her own voice.

"Where are you?" John asked.

"I . . . I followed the old woman. Like Manfred told me." Lying was her best plan at this point.

"Manfred told you?"

"Yeah. We lost Kris and decided to split up, then call each other if we found her."

"Fine. Where are you?"

"I'm west of Chinatown, a little over thirty minutes away by foot."

"You'll have to be more specific than that."

"Okay, let me find a street sign." Janice lurched from the wall and wiped the blood from her eye. She wandered around the back of the building, each step sending shards of pain into her head. She stuffed her empty stun gun into a drainpipe. Better to get rid of the evidence. "There are no signs here. It's on the main road leading out of Chinatown. I'll start walking back."

"No. Stay with the old woman."

"There's no point in that," she said. "Kris jumped me. Took me by surprise and knocked me out cold. I doubt they're still in the neighborhood. I wouldn't be."

There was silence at the end of the link. Janice continued to walk away from the building.

"Damn. Okay. I'm heading west. I'll pick you up."

"Okay."

The link went dead and Janice tried to pick up her pace. The throbbing in her head kept time with her footsteps, but she struggled through it as best she could. It was better to be as far away from where she had hidden the stun gun as she could get. Ten minutes later, a black sedan slowed down and did a U-turn, pulling up beside her. It was John.

"Get in."

She reached for the door handle, missing it on the first try, and slid into the passenger seat. There was no one in the back. "Where's Manfred?" she asked.

"Manfred's dead. Christ, you look like shit."

"What? How did . . . when?"

"I need to see your weapon."

"My stun gun?"

"Hand it over."

Janice reached into her pocket and paused before frantically searching her other pockets. "It's gone."

"Gone?"

"Kris must have taken it after she attacked me. I'm pretty sure there wasn't anything on the ground when I got up. Things are kind of fuzzy." At least she was telling the truth about that.

"She took your stun gun and left your comm unit?" Manfred continued, not giving her a chance to answer. "We'll go take a look."

Janice's heart plummeted. "Yeah, okay. It's back that way a few blocks."

She made him turn off a block before the old woman's apartment, finding another that was similar. "It was right here. I was standing here waiting for the old lady to come back out, and I was hit from behind." Her hand reached up to the goose egg on the back of her head and she winced.

John pushed her down in the seat and moved her hair. "That's quite the lump. She got you front and back. Why didn't she kill you?"

Janice stayed quiet. John watched her face as he drove.

"Where were you?" he asked.

"Over there." She pointed to a spot by the exterior wall of the building.

"Not a great place to be waiting."

"I was moving to get a better position on the front door."

He didn't respond. "Wait here. I'm going to look." He got out of the car and wandered around the corner of the building. The doors locked behind him. When he came back, he wasn't happy. "There's no sign of a fight or blood."

"I . . . I can't explain that. I was hit from behind."

"So you say."

"What's that supposed to mean?"

"You don't think it's weird that Manfred was killed with a stun gun and yours is missing? That you look like you were in the worst fight of your life and losing? That I can't see any traces of a fight here?"

Cold sunk into her chest. "Weird, yes. But if you're asking if I killed him, then no. I'm pretty messed up. I need a doctor. Maybe I got the wrong building."

"We'll see. Ms. Peters has some questions for you as well. Manfred was her favorite."

Janice leaned back in the seat. Shit. She tried to memorize every piece of the lie she had told. If she got something wrong, maybe she could use the hit on her head as an excuse.

Every part of her hurt.

LOS ANGELES LEVEL 4—THURSDAY, JULY 6, 2141 5:15 P.M.

I carried Auntie as best I could. I didn't want her to be anywhere near Janice when she came to. I should have killed the bitch instead of leaving her behind.

The pain must have been close to unbearable for Auntie, but she took it without a sound. When we finally stopped, I lowered her to the ground and made her as comfortable as possible.

"I need to get you to a doctor."

"I can't afford one. A broken hip at my age is a death sentence down here. Especially if you're not working."

"I know someone. I just need to get you there." There were no cars in sight. "You wait here, I'll be back as soon as I can."

She laughed, stopping with a burst of pain on her face. "I'm not going anywhere."

I took off as fast as I could, wind whipping around my bare legs. Leaving Auntie alone on Level 2 wasn't what I wanted to do, but I had no choice. I slowed once I rounded the corner, limping from Janice's kick. I needed to find a vehicle. The older the better—it would be easier to hot-wire. It didn't take long, not down here. The car was at the side of the road with the driver getting out. I waited until he was almost at the building before I took him out. One jab to the kidneys and he was down. I snatched the keys from his hand and unlocked his car.

The driver struggled to his feet, and I suddenly felt guilty.

"I need to borrow your car."

"No! You can't." He hobbled to the street as I closed the door.

I yelled through the windshield, "You'll get it back."

He was practically climbing on the hood by the time I'd unlocked the motor. I threw the car into reverse and tromped on the pedal.

Even these old buckets had impressive torque. A side effect of being electric. The car cannoned backward, leaving its rightful owner lying on the ground again. I felt bad for the guy, but I didn't have much choice.

Turning in the middle of the road, I raced back to my aunt, breathing a sigh of relief when I found her where I'd left her. I helped her into the car and we sped away.

"You said you didn't have a car," she said.

"I don't. I stole it."

She gave me a sideways glance. "You steal cars like it's nothing. You fight like a demon. If I wasn't there, you would have killed that girl. I don't think I got the whole story back at the kitchen."

She must have been hurting. Her voice was strained but calm as she tried to fight her way through the pain.

"You didn't. And the guy will get his car back. At some point."

"What is it you're not telling me, Kris?"

"Lots." I zipped up to Level 3, keeping my foot steady on the accelerator.

"Are you going to tell me?"

"I don't think so."

She sighed, trying to keep the weight off her hip and failing. "You've gotten into the same nonsense your dad did, haven't you?"

I didn't answer.

"You know it's what got them killed, don't you?"

I turned savagely down a street to the next ramp, hearing a sharp inhale from my aunt. "I know what got them killed."

"Do you?"

"More than you know. Now let me drive, dammit."

I drove to an up-ramp, hoping to get to Doc's Level 5 offices, but the checkpoint was shut down and completely blocked. There wasn't any way to get up there.

Shit.

Now what was I supposed to do? I didn't have my comm unit anymore, I'd destroyed it when I was picked up for the draft. I had no way to contact him. What I did have was his number memorized. All I needed was a comm unit.

What the fuck. I'd already stolen a car tonight. What was a small mugging? I told my aunt to stay in the car and took off at a run. I didn't want her to see what I was about to do.

The first person I met was an older lady. She reminded me of the one who had given me a ride to the greenhouses not too long ago. I planned my angles and timing, hoping to push her into an alley as she walked past it. When the time came, I couldn't do it.

I drew in a shaky breath and straightened the damn dress. Stealing and mugging wasn't who I was. It wasn't the legacy I wanted to leave behind for my son.

I walked across the street and approached the lady from the front. "I'm sorry to bother you, but—"

The lady walked around me.

I danced back in front of her, my body complaining in protest. "I just—"

"I ain't got no money," she said. Her knuckles were white she was holding her purse so tight.

"I'm not looking for money. I just need to make a quick call. My aunt is hurt, and I need to call her doctor."

The woman stopped, actually seeing me for the first time. "A likely story." She still looked uncertain, but at least she'd stopped.

"It's true. You don't even have to give me your comm unit. I can give you the number and you can call."

"I don't think—"

It was my turn to interrupt her. "Please. It'll take less time than it did to talk to me."

She pondered the question for a while before finally nodding. "What's the number?"

I recited the one Doc Searls had me memorize. Surprise crossed her face when it was answered right away.

"I have a girl here says you're a doctor." She listened for a while. "What's your name, girl?"

"Kris Merrill." The name still felt uncomfortable when I said it.

The woman repeated it and nodded. "He wants to know if you can get up to his office?"

I shook my head no.

"She says no." The woman watched me as she listened to Doc's reply. She closed the link. "He says to meet him at the Newman Street elevator. He has a friend with a clinic close to there."

"Thank you."

"You can thank me by telling me your doctor's name. It takes me months to get an appointment, and they never come to me."

"He's family," I said. "We get special treatment."

"Figures."

I raced away, feeling her eyes boring into my back. I felt good. I had actually used my brains instead of forcing my way through something. I didn't have to steal a phone from a poor defenseless old woman. I got back to the car and told Auntie we'd meet the doctor soon before I put the car into gear and accelerated to the elevator. She nodded and breathed through gritted teeth.

We didn't even have to wait fifteen minutes before the elevator doors opened. Doc hurried out and I saw three SoCal soldiers with rifles before they closed again.

"I was just about to go through security to Level 6 when you called. They were just telling me to turn around. It seems I don't have clearance to be up there anymore." He looked at my aunt through the passenger window, "What's the problem?"

"I was attacked on Level 2. It was Janice, the same one who tried a couple of weeks ago."

My auntie kept looking at us. She didn't say anything.

"Okay. So what happened here?" He opened the back door of the car and eased into the seat.

I noticed he didn't ask where I got the car from.

"She was knocked over pretty hard. Her hip is hurt." He didn't asked who she was. I was already in Doc's debt. This was going to make the debt even bigger. I didn't mind . . . he didn't seem like the kind of guy that would force me to do something I wouldn't want to.

"Probably broken. Drive two blocks that way," he pointed behind the car, "and turn right. It's about half a kilometer to the clinic."

We pulled into a strip mall parking lot and I stopped just outside the clinic doors. Doc got out and unlocked them, coming back to help Auntie inside. He locked the door behind us.

"Kris, could you get the gurney from the second room down the hall?"

I did as I was asked, returning as he got her to shift closer to the edge of the examining table.

"This'll hurt a bit, but I promise it's the last time we move you, okay?"

She just nodded.

"Okay. Kris, get her feet and move them to the gurney. Not too fast. Move at the same speed as her body." He got an arm under her hips and one under her shoulders. "On the count of three. One, two, three."

We lifted and moved her over. A small whimper escaped before she held it in, her face turning red.

"You can breathe now," Doc Searls said. "The worst is over. We'll get you X-rayed and fixed up in no time." He wheeled her out of the room for the X-ray, coming back a few minutes later. When he pulled them up on his vid screen, it didn't look good. "Definitely broken. In more than one place." He turned to my aunt. "If it's okay with you, I'm going to put you under before I fix it. If I don't, it's not going to be a comfortable experience."

She nodded again and he injected something in her arm. She was out in seconds.

"That'll hold her for a while. You'd better fill me in while I work on this."

I did, leaving nothing out.

"And this woman, Janice, wants you dead why?" he asked.

I shrugged.

He nodded. "Let me finish up here. I'll take a look at you and the baby. Then we need to talk."

LOS ANGELES LEVEL 4—THURSDAY, JULY 6, 2141 6:32 P.M.

"Is this on or off the books?" Doc Searls asked.

We'd left his examination room and stood in the hallway. He looked more tired than I'd ever seen him. "I don't know. On the books, I guess." I paused. "I'm not really part of the insurgents anymore."

"Why not?"

"They're making choices for me they have no right to."

"The baby?"

I nodded.

"They care about you."

"Bullshit. If they cared, then they should have talked with me instead of about me. I should have been allowed to make my own choices."

"Ah, the age-old argument. You're right, of course. Would you have made the same decision they forced on you?" He waited for an answer.

"I don't know." My voice was soft and quiet.

"Well, enough of that then. What's done is done. Come into my office and tell me what you know about Bryson."

There wasn't much to tell. I barely knew anyone I could get information from. Even Pat hadn't gotten back to me with anything. I wasn't about to mention the decrypted chip. It turned out I was really crappy at this part of my job. "Let me call Pat, see if she found anything out." Doc Searls handed me his comm unit. I made the connection and waited.

"Hey Doc." She actually sounded chipper. I perched on the edge of the examination table.

"It's me."

"Kris? Where have you been? We were so worried. Are you okay? Why are you using Doc's phone?"

"Take a breath. I'm fine. I destroyed mine before the draft, remember? I'm calling to see if you found any information about Bryson." There was silence on the link for a few seconds. "Hello?"

"Yeah. Okay. I haven't heard anything yet. I know ACE used to have a couple of people up there, but who knows if that's still true. I wouldn't even know how to contact them."

"Okay, thanks. I gotta go."

"Kris—"

"I'll call you back later." I closed the link and handed the comm unit back. The second it was in his hand, it rang again. He read the display.

"It's Pat."

I shook my head. All she would do was quiz me on why I went to Doc Searls instead of back to her. It was a story I didn't want to get into right now.

"She's worried. You know that. Don't let your anger change who you are."

"You talk to her then. I'm going to check up on Auntie." When I slid off the table the dress rode up my legs and I had to pull it down. I hated the damn thing. As I left the room, Doc Searls answered his phone.

Auntie was still asleep. Here, on the gurney, she appeared even thinner and more frail than she had when I had run into her on

Level 2. Five years ago, she had been strong and capable. Living on Level 1 took a lot out of you, especially with someone like her husband. I could see what it had done to her in every line on her face.

I took her hand and held it, brushing a stray length of gray hair away.

There was a soft knock at the door and it opened.

"What did you tell her?" I asked.

"The truth," Doc said. "It's easier to remember. She says you need to head back down. Jack's been asking questions."

"He can fuck off."

"O . . . okay." He settled himself into a chair with a sigh. "Time to tell you what I know. There's an old ACE team up there. I asked them to check if it was Bryson I was hearing about. They confirmed it."

So he didn't really need me. So why ask me what I knew? "An ACE team? Do you trust them?"

"Miller did. Most of them were people he trained when they first got into the field."

That was good enough for me.

SOCAL SAT CITY 2—THURSDAY, JULY 6, 2141 6:30 P.M.

Bryson poured over the test results from Ailsa. She had been even more thorough than he'd expected, and the test had taken all day. He hadn't heard anything from Ms. Peters.

He didn't have to block out the background buzz of the lab—there wasn't any. Everyone had eventually found out what she had been testing, and the results she had gotten. Now they were hovering at their stations, staring at Bryson's back as he hunched over his stainless steel work area, instead of back in their rooms.

There were slight variances in the final results, some of them indicative of incorrect data entry, though he had picked Ailsa for a reason. Her work was the most precise of anyone's in the lab. His included. She never entered data from memory, even if it was the thousandth time she'd had to do it. She always cross-referenced from the original source. It was more likely that he had incorrectly input something during his tests.

Besides the variations, both tests showed the same result: a ninety-nine percent reduction in harmful radiation and outside interference during the quantum jump. Slightly better than the results he had gotten before leaving Kadokawa.

The chances of someone being hurt making a jump had dropped dramatically. He just needed to figure out the chances and possible effects of the remaining one percent. He didn't think Ms. Peters would care.

Bryson completed the thought with mixed emotions. The loss of the two pilots on the first jump was still personal to him. It didn't matter that Jeremy had forced the test, it was still his research, his technology, that had failed them. And he knew what SoCal's plans were—the same as Meridian's had been. To fight and win a war. The ability to have troops and weaponry anywhere at any time was a world changer.

He leaned back in his chair and stretched, suddenly realizing how quiet the lab was. He spun in his chair, expecting to see Ms. Peters hovering behind him. All he saw were the faces of everyone else in the lab.

He gave a quick nod and watched the range of emotions of the people in front of him. Some, like him, were uncertain. Others cheered and clapped the backs of those near them. Ailsa walked over.

"That's it then," she said.

"Yes."

"At least the war will be over before it's even started."

Bryson smiled. "Do you always try to look at the bright side of things?"

"It's the only thing that gets me through the day."

"I should try it, then."

"You should. Maybe we can work on it together."

A thrill ran through him, quickly squashed by logic. "Maybe. I'm not allowed out much."

"None of us are, but we're trying to look on the bright side, remember?"

"I do! I'll check with my keeper. I expect she'll be wanting the results." He watched the celebrating staff. "If she doesn't already have them."

The airlock hissed open. "I expect she does, but I don't think it'll stop her from checking," Ailsa said. She went back to her terminal, leaving him alone to face Ms. Peters.

"Come with me." Ms. Peters didn't bother asking him if the tests had worked or not.

They walked out of the airlock, Bryson flanked by the two guards. They were different every day, and he hadn't yet seen the same person twice. He figured it was to stop him from being too friendly and maybe find a soft spot in SoCal's plans for him.

"Where are we going?"

Ms. Peters didn't answer. She walked to the elevator, already held open by a third soldier, and they rode it up in silence.

They stopped two levels below the promenade Bryson had arrived on a few weeks ago, the doors opening into a bustling hallway. Everyone here wore the standard gray uniforms of the SoCal military, making him in his white lab coat and Ms. Peters in her red business suit the odd ones out. The composite walls and exposed conduits were gone on this floor, but this place was obviously designed for expedience over comfort. They walked for a few minutes before coming to an unmarked door. Ms. Peters flashed her hand over a plaque in the wall and the door swung open. She stepped through and he followed, the guards remaining in the hallway.

The room was a simple security checkpoint. As soon as they walked in, the soldier behind the desk stood, his hand on his weapon. The taser wasn't clipped in. He didn't say anything, didn't make any move. The only other exit was a door in the opposite wall. Above it, a light glowed soft white.

"Peters, five four zero six three. Accompanied by Dr. Bryson Searls."

The light above the door shifted hue to yellow and pulsed. Bryson counted each on-off cycle. A cycle lasted a second, and he counted ten before the light shifted again to green and the door clicked. The guard relaxed. With everything automated, Bryson figured the only reason the guard was there was to take them out if the authorization didn't work.

"Welcome back, Ms. Peters. Admiral Hamil is expecting you and Dr. Searls," he said.

She didn't answer, moving to the unlocked door. The soldier scrambled to get there ahead of her and hold it open. The second they stepped through, two new soldiers trailed Bryson, leaving him to walk beside Ms. Peters.

They had entered a massive hangar. The craft in the center seemed small in comparison, yet it was about the same size as the executive class cruiser Meridian had done their quantum jump test with last year. Bryson stopped in his tracks, suddenly realizing what he was looking at. The soldiers pushed him forward. Ms. Peters didn't notice.

"You . . . you already built one?"

"We made the assumption that the plans we had were accurate, and moved ahead. Since you've been here, we've modified the engines to your latest specifications. Ah, Admiral Hamil. What's our status?"

"It's good to see you again too, Ms. Peters." His voice boomed out across the nearly empty hangar.

The admiral's response seemed to fluster her. "Yes . . . of course. Good to see you."

"We've received your latest changes. The engines are complete, and you only want us to modify the shielding?"

She glanced at Bryson, expecting him to answer the question.

"Umm, yes," Bryson said. "We haven't made any changes to the engines for two days."

Admiral Hamil's eyes lit up. "Ah! The great Dr. Bryson Searls. Your work has given our builders quite a few migraines over the last year."

"I . . . umm . . . okay."

"Ha! Spoken like a true nerd, eh?" He slapped Bryson on the back, propelling him forward a step before turning back to Ms. Peters. "It'll take us a couple of days to do the modifications. More if our systems go down again. Damnedest thing. I've been up here for over a decade, and I've never seen so many back-to-back issues."

Bryson tried to hide the shock from his face. Could the virus he'd freed in his lab be causing the issues? If the Sat City's protections couldn't stop the virus, they should have at least slowed it down. Breaking through to the military systems showed that it hadn't. Whoever had written the virus knew what they were doing. He had to admire that.

"SoCal One has been having issues as well," the admiral said.

"Enough about that, Admiral. Will we be able to do a test on July tenth, then?"

"We should. We're holding a lottery with our pilots this afternoon. They all want the maiden voyage."

"Good. Dr. Searls will be taking a look at your work, to verify it's ready."

"Of course. This way, Doctor."

LOS ANGELES LEVEL 4—THURSDAY, JULY 6, 2141 7:11 P.M.

I left my aunt with Doc Searls. Though he had repaired her hip, the drugs he had given her would keep her out for the rest of the night, and I had a car I had promised to return.

After that I would get in touch with Pat and Kai and we'd see if the information we had on Bryson formed any sort of cohesive picture. I was tired of not getting anywhere. Even separated from the insurgents, it felt good to know I had people I could still rely on.

The doc had helped me out a lot during the past year or so. Add to that the huge risk he'd taken coming down to Level 4 to do it again. I owed him not only my life, but so much more. Now that he was down here, the chances of his getting back up to Level 5 would be slim. With luck, the insurgents would help him get through the inter-level corridors and back up there.

The car was where I'd left it, the keys still in the motor lock. A sure sign I was on a higher level, though I'd still gotten lucky. If I'd done the same on Level 2 or 3, the car would already have been gone. On Level 1, it would have been stripped down to nothing, keys or no keys. I got in and rested my head against the steering wheel.

What would Ian do if he was alone, isolated, had no way to get in touch with anyone? I sighed. He'd call in favors. Get his friends to help him. The same thing I was planning on doing.

I unlocked the motor and backed the car out of its spot. There was a man on Level 2 who needed it back. I know he didn't believe me when I told him I'd return it, but it was the least I could do.

The streets were empty. Everyone was too scared to be out, scared they would be drafted. People almost always felt safer at home. I could understand that. I went on autopilot, navigating the streets down to Level 2 without really knowing where I was. Even then, though, I kept up the vigilant sweep I'd used on my bike, keeping an eye open for anything out of place.

I still couldn't figure out why Janice hated me so much. What had I done that had turned her against me? Was it really about finishing what William had told her to do? That felt wrong. It had to be more.

It wasn't something I was going to be able to figure out.

I started paying more attention to the road. I'd picked up another car a few blocks back, and it had followed me around the last two corners. I had been sticking to the most direct route down to Level 2, so there was a chance it was just heading in the same direction. I swept through the next intersection before the light changed and turned right, away from the down-ramp. The car didn't follow. It didn't even try to beat the light to keep up with me. I looped around anyway, coming up behind him.

The car was a standard IBC design, about as cheap as you could get. Even the piece of shit I was driving was a step up from that. If they were trying to keep me under surveillance, they were going to extremes. That thing was more likely to fail than to keep up with me.

I'd never been this paranoid, even when I was living alone on Level 1. Sure, I had been scared all the time, but I'd never thought everyone was out to get me.

The closer I got to where I'd borrowed the car, the more careful I became. I wasn't worried about the police. Even if the owner had reported his car stolen, no one would do anything about it. Not on Level 2.

I was worried about Janice and her partner. She had a weird way of showing up in unexpected places: the greenhouse, my aunt's building. I didn't want to be surprised. The insurgents had never given me a weapon, so if she really wanted to kill me, I'd have nothing to protect myself with. Having a gun, or even my old taser, would make my life easier right about now.

I pulled up in front of the block where I'd gotten the car. A young boy sat on the low front stairs. As soon as he saw me, he ran inside. I'd barely gotten out when the owner came. He had a length of pipe in his hands, plastic from the look of it, but it would still do some damage. When he got within three meters of me, I tossed him the car keys and took a step back. He caught them and stopped advancing.

"I told you I'd bring it back."

He didn't answer.

"I'm sorry, but it was an emergency." I turned and ran around the corner. I still had the problem of getting back to my aunt, and I wasn't about to walk up two Levels at night. I was back to the where I'd started, needing to find a place to sleep.

I considered the room the insurgents had given me. I was pretty sure I had a change of clothes there, so at least I could get out of this stupid dress. I hadn't planned on going back, but beggars couldn't be choosers. It was the best chance I had. I could sneak in, grab my clothes, and sleep on the street tonight.

It wouldn't be the first time.

Ten

LOS ANGELES LEVEL 2—THURSDAY, JULY 6, 2141 8:47 P.M.

THE BACK OF the insurgents' building was dark, the dimmed Ambients creating deep shadows where the light tried to reach over the structure. I'd scoped out this back alley more than once. The insurgents kept people on the roof on a ten-minute circuit. I waited until I saw the patrol leave and crept into the alley. The door was halfway down. I tripped over some garbage; my eyes hadn't adjusted yet. I didn't have time to wait.

The door itself was at the edge of the shadow. I crouched in front of it and grabbed the two bobby pins from my hair, biting off the bulbed ends and bending them into shape. I had six minutes left.

The first pin slid in and I could feel it lift the locks. I slid in the second and twisted. The bobby pin bent and the door stayed locked.

Five minutes.

Pulling the pin out, I doubled it over and reinserted it, using the first bobby pin to lift the locks again. This time when I twisted, the cylinder turned.

Four minutes left and I was in.

I had barely closed the door behind me when I was grabbed. Two insurgents took an arm each and marched me to a wall. I struggled, loosening the grip on my right arm before they held even tighter. One of them twisted my arm behind my back and pressed me against the cold fibercrete.

"What the—"

"Kris Merrill?"

"Get your hands off me." I twisted in their grip.

The woman searched me while the man held me still. I didn't know what she was looking for. The stupid dress didn't give much opportunity to hide anything.

"Come with us."

They didn't give me any choice, almost dragging me down the hall to the foyer and through the double doors to Jack's office. One of them got on her comm unit.

"Tell him we have her."

She put the comm unit back in her pocket and pushed me into a chair. I kicked, taking out her leg. She collapsed on the floor. Her partner pulled out his gun, pointing it at my face.

"Sit!"

I stared at the barrel and lowered myself back down. He didn't check on his partner, didn't lean down to help her. His entire focus was on me, the gun shaking slightly in his hands. I couldn't take my eyes off of it.

The woman got back up and limped to the far wall, staying behind her partner. I heard the doors at the end of the hall swing open. The sound of running feet finally pulled my attention away from the wavering pistol. I risked a glance toward the doors.

Pat ran down the carpeted hall.

"What do you think you're doing?" she asked.

"She broke in through the rear door. Jack's orders were to bring her here."

"He ordered you to stand here and point a gun at her? Put that damn thing away before you accidentally shoot someone."

The woman spoke up. "She attacked me."

"What, and you wouldn't have done the same if you were dragged here against your will?" She turned back to the man. "Put your fucking gun away."

"She tried to break in." He didn't budge.

"I just wanted to get my clothes, I—"

"If you don't put the gun away," Pat interrupted. "I'll take it from you."

"You'll do nothing of the sort." The woman had pulled out her own weapon and was aiming it at Pat.

"How dare—"

"Shut up and sit beside her."

For a microsecond, Pat's eyes lost focus and a flash of pain crossed her face. It disappeared so quickly, I wasn't sure I'd even seen it.

She moved faster than I'd ever seen her move before, stepping toward the man, grabbing his pistol hand and driving her hip into his groin. He was on the ground, weaponless, before his partner could even move. Pat aimed the gun at him.

"Now we have a problem," she said.

I stood up and moved behind Pat, out of the woman's line of sight. Limiting potential targets meant Pat would only have to concentrate on one thing. The woman with the gun.

"I just came in to get some clothes. I didn't want to see anyone, so I came in the back," I said.

"I don't care what you did, holding you at gunpoint isn't right."

Pat moved her gun off of the man on the floor and pointed it at the woman. "Drop it."

"I can't do that."

"Drop it and let us walk out of here."

I watched as Pat's back tensed. She was getting ready to pull the trigger.

The double doors flew open.

"What the hell?" Jack yelled down the hallway.

"Call off your goons, Jack."

"Everybody put those damn things away and explain to me what the hell is going on."

The woman didn't move.

"Put your gun down! That's an order."

As soon as the woman's gun lowered, I could see Pat begin to relax. She didn't move hers until the woman's gun was holstered.

Jack looked at Pat and me. "Both of you, in my office. And you two. Wait here until I call you in."

"Yes, sir."

The man on the floor stood and reached to get his gun from Pat. She turned her back on him and walked into Jack's office. The moment she was inside, she dropped the gun on the desk like it was pure acid and collapsed into a chair.

I'd seen this before. Seen when her memories came back to haunt her. Seen how debilitating they could be. Jack closed the door and sat down, ignoring Pat.

"What the fuck do you think you're doing?"

I shrugged.

"You break into my building, fight with my guards, and don't answer my questions. That's not going to help you." He paused. "Okay, let's try a different question then. You're using *my* people for your own agenda, and that's not the way we do things here. Why are you asking about personnel on SoCal Sat City 2?"

I didn't answer, leaning over Pat instead. She reached out a hand and grabbed my forearm, giving it a tight squeeze. She would be all right.

"Answer the question, Kris," Jack said. When I hesitated, he looked at Pat. "And you ask me why I don't trust her? Why I send out a crew to make sure she doesn't get taken by SoCal? She won't even answer my questions. This is—"

"Doc Searls said he thought his son was up there," I interrupted. "I was trying to find out for sure."

"And do what with the information?"

I really didn't know. Go up there and get him out? Tell Pat and see if she could plan a rescue? Certainly tell Doc Searls that he was right. He'd discovered that on his own anyway. "I just wanted to confirm to Doc Searls that his son was okay." An idea was starting to take shape in the back of my mind, and I wasn't sure I liked it.

Jack shook his head. "Our resources are spread so thin, we can't afford to have these kinds of distractions. You should have come to me."

"And say what?" I leaned over his desk. "Tell you that Doc Searls' son may be up there? What would you have done? Anything? More than likely, you'd push me away and tell me to stick to what I know. What if I told you Doc was on Level 4 and needed to get back up to Level 5? Would you help him?"

Jack paused as if considering my last question before he decided to ignore it.

"You have a year's training with ACE, and you think you're ready to take on a Sat City?"

"I have no idea what I can do, and neither do you. You won't let me. You've been putting me on the same jobs you would give anybody off the street. You haven't trusted me since day one."

"Trust? Trust is earned around here, young lady. The first time you worked with one of my teams, you pulled your gun on them, and almost destroyed the mission trying to get your fucking boyfriend out. The second time, you left your own partner to try a stupid rescue. How am I supposed to trust that? You're just a kid."

"I saved the Pasadena mission. I gave you the information on the Level 1 food trucks."

Pat sat up straight. "Jack, she—"

He raised his hand, telling her to stop. "This isn't about you. I'll get to you pulling a gun on one of my men later."

Pat stood beside me. Her entire body was vibrating, though I didn't think Jack would see it. "She's right. Kris and I joined you because ACE was gone. You've never really trusted us. You should have teamed Kris up with one of your own men so she could get field experience. You should have pulled Kai and me into your planning sessions instead of giving us the lowest job you dared."

"Pulling in old ACE people isn't a low-end job."

"No? Then how about food management? You had me counting apples in the bloody basement."

"It's an important job."

"Yes, it is," Pat said. "But it's not the best use of the resources you have."

"I haven't worked with my teams for too long," Jack sighed. "But I know what they can and can't do. You two were unknowns. I wanted you someplace I could keep an eye on you. I had no idea what to do with Kai. He wanted out, you know. He didn't want to have any part of this. The only reason he stayed is because he wanted to be close to her."

"So you ship him as far away as you can, looking for other people you're not sure you can trust?" I asked.

"You don't understand."

"No, I don't." I turned to go. "I need to get my stuff, then I'll be out of here."

Pat followed me out. Jack stayed quiet.

KADOKAWA SAT CITY 2—THURSDAY, JULY 6, 2141 8:37 P.M.

Andrew stood at attention, his *Kaisa* beside him. Around them the general noise and activity of the docking area continued. An unscheduled shuttle had arrived from Okinawa. The doors opened and Andrew pulled himself even straighter.

The moment *Kaishō-ho* Kadokawa stepped out of the dark interior of the shuttle, he knew why she had come. He let out a shaky breath and Mori gave him a quick glance before staring ahead again. Perhaps he would chalk it up to a Kadokawa coming to the station. Andrew left the line and met her at the bottom of the stairs. He bowed. "Welcome to Kadokawa 2." He always got butterflies in his stomach when she was around.

"It is good to be here, *Kaishō-ho* Ito. Please forgive my unexpected arrival. I was inspecting our efforts in Mexico. They have had some recent flooding and many people are homeless."

"You are a long way from Mexico."

"Yes, I am."

He led her back to the line. "Please, may I introduce *Kaisa* Mori? He has proven to be an excellent leader, and has helped me immensely." He caught a slight flicker of surprise crossing Mori's face, followed by a deepening of his skin color.

Mori saluted. She returned it. "I have heard good things about you, *Kaisa*. Your name has come up more than once in Okinawa."

Mori's skin turned even darker. "Thank you, *Kaishō-ho*. You are too kind."

"Not at all. I have learned to give credit where credit is due."

Mori bowed low.

She turned to Andrew. "I cannot stay long. Will you honor me with a small tour of the city?"

"Of course."

Mori bowed again. "Please excuse me. I should be in Operations." He left the two alone.

"It has been a long time, Andrew. You seem to make it a habit to only visit Okinawa when I am not there."

"I . . ."

She smiled, her face gentle and kind. "I only wish that this time we could have met under better circumstances."

"As do I."

"Ah, Andrew. You have never been able to lie to me. I see it too clearly in your eyes."

"Then you know it is true when I say that I have missed you." He shocked himself with his abrupt honesty.

"I do."

He turned and followed the path Mori had taken off the flight deck. "Your message came as a surprise to me."

"Yes. I wish it could have waited till I was here, but my visit wasn't a certainty. You did not respond."

He held open a door for her, closing it softly behind them. Almost immediately the noise of the flight deck disappeared, replaced with the normal sounds of air recyclers and the background hum of electronics. "As I said, it took me by surprise."

"Have you thought about it?"

"I have found it difficult to do much else."

She placed her hand on his arm, stopping him in the empty hallway. Her touch was hot, even through his uniform. "I know this is not easy, Andrew. Duty and honor have always been strong for you. But you have to think about where that sense of duty is placed. Is it with the people we help every day? Is it with the men and women under you who will die if this war continues? Or is it with our new leaders and the way they are changing Kadokawa? Changing it away from the reason we both signed up. Together."

A private walked down the hall toward them, and she removed her hand.

"This is not the proper place for this discussion," he said. They continued walking. The private hugged the wall and stood at attention, giving a crisp salute as they walked by. "Would you like some tea?"

"I would, thank you."

He led her to his office, instructing his steward to bring in tea and a small bite to eat.

"Please come inside. It will take him a few moments to bring everything."

Once the door was closed, she sank into a chair, rubbing her eyes with her thumb and forefinger. "Andrew, things are changing so fast. I wonder from moment to moment if we are doing the right thing."

He noticed her use of *we*. Was she already including him, or were there others? Perhaps someone she cared deeply about. The thought stilled him to his core. He pushed it aside. It wasn't worthy. "Do you believe with your heart it is right, or with your head?"

"Both. Our new leaders are creating a Kadokawa that revels in war, that does not care about the loss of sons or daughters, but only cares that they get more power, more control. More profit. Do you not see it?"

"I see it every day. I have already sent two letters back to families who will never see their loved ones again, to husbands and wives who now must raise their children alone. I have sent those letters before, but never because of a pointless war."

"Then you know why we do this."

"I do. I . . ." He stuttered and looked into her eyes. "I do not yet know if I can be part of it."

A soft knock at the door brought her back to her feet. The steward brought in a tray with tea and freshly made rolls, placing it at the conference table.

As he moved the cups from the tray to the table, she stepped forward. "I will do it."

If he was surprised, he didn't show it. He verified everything that was needed was on the tray, and backed out of the room.

They sat at the table, not across from each other as rank and protocol dictated, but beside each other as friends. She picked up the pot and poured the black tea into a cup. The pot returned to the tray and she handed him his steaming tea before pouring her own.

"I have missed you as well," she said softly, almost too low for him to hear. "I long for the days when we worked beside each other. When we spoke freely of our hopes and dreams. Of our desires."

"I could no longer do that when you were made *Kaishō-ho*. You outranked me, and it would not have been proper."

"That was a long time ago, Andrew. Do you really believe something as silly as rank should have taken away what we had?"

Andrew sat silent, sipping the hot tea.

"When this is done, what will you do?" she asked.

"If I live through the war, I will retire," he said. "My family home has been sitting vacant for too long. I want nothing more than to sit and listen to the wind rustle through my father's bamboo."

"Nothing more?"

He shifted, a flush coming to his cheeks. "I cannot ask for more."

"Cannot or will not?"

"Perhaps a little too much of both."

Another knock on the door halted her hand from reaching for him again. The door opened.

"Sorry, sir. SoCal Sat City 1 is showing some of the strange behavior we are seeing in SoCal 2."

"Thank you. I'll be in Operations shortly."

"Yes, sir."

Before the door fully closed, she was already standing, the moment gone and back to business. "I read your reports. Do we know what is causing the disruptions?"

"No. My officers each have their own ideas, but nothing that can be proven."

"Is it possible they are purposely confusing us, hoping to distract us from an attack?"

"Anything is possible, Natsumi, nothing is known." When he looked at her, there were tears in her eyes.

"I have waited a long time for you to call me that again."

"I . . . I am sorry, *Kaishō-ho*. I should have been more careful."

At his switch to her formal title, she wiped her eyes and took a step to the door. "I understand. Come, let us see the strange occurrences for ourselves. Then I must return to Okinawa."

"Of course, this way."

LOS ANGELES LEVEL 2—THURSDAY, JULY 6, 2141 8:58 P.M.

Pat walked me all the way to my room. When I opened my door, she followed me in and closed it behind her.

"Do you mind if I stay?" she asked. "I don't like what happened downstairs, and I . . . I just want to make sure it doesn't happen again."

"So now you care? Why, because I'm pregnant?" As soon as I saw the pain my words caused I felt horrible. I knew she'd always been here for me.

"Things have been tough since Miller died. I didn't always know how to help you. I saw how much pain you were in, how you tried to hide it, and nothing I did worked. You did your best to push me away. I always cared."

"I know. I'm sorry."

"Me too. We're both to blame. You know Kai stayed with the insurgents because of you. Sometimes I think you mean more to him than his own family."

I turned my back to her, speaking over my shoulder. "Is that why he's never here? So he can keep an eye on me?"

"Even Kai has his limits, Kris. When Jack asked him to find ex-ACE operatives, he refused. He believed you needed him here. Your walls went up pretty high, and pretty fast. It pushed him away too."

"Pushed him away? It's barely been two weeks, and he decided he'd had enough? Some friend." I didn't know why I was being so mean. It wasn't good, or right, but I didn't apologize.

"Don't do that."

"Do what?"

"You're trying to push us away again." She put her hand on my shoulder. "We've all lost someone."

I spun around, breaking the contact she had made. "I lost the man I loved. You lost a partner." I didn't see her hand before it landed on my cheek. The force of her slap pushed me onto the bed. I lay there stunned before the tears came.

"Oh Kris, I'm so sorry. I didn't mean to." She rushed to the bed, sitting beside me. Reaching for me.

Everything came crashing in at the same time. I wanted Ian to be alive so bad, I could feel it in every part of me. He'd been stolen from me, and I couldn't do anything to get him back. I couldn't even hurt the people who had done this to us.

Instead, I hurt my family.

I pulled Pat into a hug so tight that I didn't ever want to let go. For the first time, I allowed the pain to become part of me, I let it soak through my armor and into *me*. We shook and cried until we had nothing left to give. I held on to Pat, listening to the steady rhythm of her heart.

We pulled apart. Her shirt was wet through to her skin and clumps of stringy snot ran down it. My dress was the same. We sat in silence for another few minutes, wiping our faces with the backs of our hands. Pat reached over and pulled at my dress.

"That's pretty gross, sorry."

She made a face, and we laughed until we cried again.

"Thanks," I said.

"I think we both needed that."

"Yeah, I think we did. I really miss him, you know?"

"I do."

"I'm sorry about what I said earlier. About your partner."

"I know."

We sat in silence, each lost in our own memories. I moved to the edge of the bed. "I really need to get out of this dress. It's not my thing."

"You look good, though."

"I doubt it." I opened up the drawer, finding a single pair of pants and a t-shirt. I pulled them out and went to the bathroom to change.

"You wouldn't happen to have a shirt for me, would you?"

"Nothing that would even remotely fit. You can try the dress when I'm out if you want. I won't be needing it again."

I heard her laugh through the closed door. "It's okay. I'd never squeeze into that thing. I'll be fine."

It felt good to be in real clothes. I shoved new bobby pins deep in my hair and left the bathroom, going back to the bed.

"I know you want to leave," Pat said. "But a night's sleep will do you good."

I didn't argue.

Pat had already picked a spot on the floor. The bed was too small for the both of us. I stripped the blanket off and handed her my pillow before crawling under the sheets.

I was asleep almost instantly.

Morning came before I was ready. The Ambients shone their harsh light through a crack in the curtain, bringing me to full wakefulness. I lay in bed for a few more minutes. Comfortable. Hungry. I stretched, realizing I'd had one of the best sleeps I could remember. It had been a long time. I crawled out from under the covers and found Pat huddled in a corner still fast asleep. She jumped awake when my feet hit the floor.

"Morning already?"

"Yeah."

She got up, all traces of sleep already gone. "So what's your plan?"

"I don't know. I can't stay here, but I don't know where else I can go. I've seen what the corporations do, what they get away with. I can't pretend it's not happening."

Pat sat on the edge of the bed, silent.

"I want to help so much," I said. "But the insurgents seem to be making things worse instead of better. They started a civil war with their tactics and their guns. Sure, they set up the kitchens, but would that have been necessary if they hadn't caused the water shortage? The more I see, the more I think they want to be another corporation."

"I've started thinking the same thing."

"So how can I help the people who are being hurt by this? How can I help work toward weakening the corporation's grip over us? I used to think ACE was the answer. So did Ian."

"Well. How about we start with family? You said your aunt was with Doc Searls. I can get Kai to meet us there."

We talked a bit longer before Pat went down and grabbed us some breakfast. I waited in the room, lost in my own thoughts about family, about how much I would give to be reunited with Ian. With Mom and Dad. About how Doc Searls must be feeling, knowing where his son was and the amount of danger he was in. This damn city seemed to create broken families as though that's what it was built to do.

Maybe it was.

By the time Pat knocked, I had washed most of the sleep from my eyes. We ate and headed down to the parking garage.

"Your motorcycle is gone, but I should still have access to a car. I'll drive you."

"And if you don't?"

"Then we'll walk. Together."

It was good to have a friend again.

LOS ANGELES LEVEL 4—FRIDAY, JULY 7, 2141 8:42 A.M.

Either Jack had had a change of heart, or he hadn't thought of cutting Pat's access to a vehicle. She grabbed a sporty two-door and drove toward the exit of the parking garage, where security opened the door and waved us through. Pat drove past Kai's place and I crawled into the tiny back seat to make room for him. We got to the clinic before it was open. Pat pulled out her comm unit and called in.

The doctor unlocked the door from the inside and held it open for us. He'd stayed the night. I guess he really had nowhere else to go.

"How's my aunt?"

"Still sleeping. She woke up an hour ago wondering where you were. I told her you were asleep in another room. I didn't want her to worry."

"Thanks. How's her hip?"

"It should be fine, even at her age. The fractures weren't too bad. Once she's fully healed, you'll barely be able to see it on X-rays, so I doubt it'll be a bother to her. She'll be able to walk normally in a week or so."

That was a relief. It was my fault she'd been hurt in the first place. I should never have gone back to her apartment. The good news was that I hadn't seen Janice since last night, and I'd been looking the entire drive up here. I was on a roll for apologizing, so I figured I'd better get one more out of the way.

"I don't think I ever apologized for not bringing Bryson back to you." I thought I saw a flash of pain cross his face, quickly replaced with what looked like professional detachment. A skill every doctor needed.

"You did. I know you did your best. It's not your fault he took off like he did. Besides, you had a lot more to worry about."

"Thanks, Doc. You've been one of the stable points through all of this, you know? You fixed my tracker, you patched up my ribs. Now you took care of my aunt. I think I'll owe you when this is done." I didn't mention the baby. I still hadn't told Kai.

He glanced past me at Pat and Kai. "I think so too." When he looked back at me, he was more serious. "I think I know how you can balance the books. I know I'm asking for a lot, but right now you three are the only ones I know in the insurgents."

"Do not ask for what we cannot give," said Kai.

"I'm scared," Doc said. "I'm scared I'll never see my son again. Scared that I'll never be able to tell him how proud I am. You know, we never really saw eye-to-eye. Instead of getting to know each other, we argued. Even when he was a boy, I spent so much time helping my patients, I missed out on getting to know *him*."

We stayed quiet, letting him finish.

"I just want the opportunity to let him know that . . . that I'm proud. That I'm sorry. I . . . I don't want to . . . With the war, where I am, where he is. I don't want lose the chance to let him know."

"So what are you asking us to do?" Pat asked.

"I . . . I want the insurgents to send someone up there. I want them to get him out and bring him down. If . . . If they do that for me, I'll do whatever they want. I'll bring whatever information I can from the higher levels down to them. I'll be a courier or a spy or a killer, if that's what they want from me."

The idea that had been forming in the back of my mind solidified, and it scared the shit out of me.

"The insurgents don't have the manpower or the connections to get someone up there," said Pat. "Hell, they barely get information from above Level 5, never mind people. I don't think they can do what you're asking."

"That doesn't matter." Doc paused, looking between us as if he was still trying to figure something out. "I've been in touch with some of the people I knew from ACE. At first, it was just to help Kai get me in with the insurgents, but after a while, I realized why I wanted to join them. My son is the only thing that matters to me. The only thing I have left since his mother passed. They can help."

"If they can get an insurgent through, why can't they do it for you?" I asked.

"I asked them that. They say it's too dangerous. They want someone that's been trained to deal with anything that might come up. Look at me," Doc said. "I'm old and slow. If I went up there and something went wrong, I'd be useless."

He sighed and slumped against the wall. It was the first time I'd seen him drained and tired. Old. My heart felt heavy. Is this how my dad would have felt if he'd been shoved into this situation? Would he have done anything to find me, to get to me? I wanted—needed—to believe he would.

Pat stepped closer, placing her hand on his shoulder. "I don't know what the insurgents can do."

"They need better access to the upper levels. We will ask them," said Kai.

"That's all I can ask for." Doc Searls nodded, quickly turning toward the examination rooms to hide the tears that had started forming in his eyes. "I'll check on your aunt."

Even the professional detachment couldn't hide the shakiness of his voice. When he was gone, I pulled Kai and Pat toward the front door.

"I need to stay with my aunt. Jack wouldn't listen to me anyway. You have a better chance. Why don't you head back?"

"You'll stay here?"

"I've got nowhere else to go."

They looked at me as though they were trying to read my mind before they nodded and opened the outside door.

I followed them into the parking lot. "He can't get to Level 6 anymore. What are the chances Jack is going to help?" I was pretty sure I knew what the answer was.

Kai shuffled forward. "It is not good. If he was asking ACE instead, there would be no hesitation. They owed him a lot. Jack does not."

"I don't think it would matter," said Pat. "The man's an ass."

Kai just nodded.

eleven

KADOKAWA SAT CITY 2—FRIDAY, JULY 7, 2141 9:00 A.M.

THE VID SCREEN on Andrew's desk flashed again. This was the second time in an hour SoCal's navigational beacon had gone quiet. This wasn't on SoCal 2. It had had issues for most of last night and the early morning, but from what the Kadokawa sensors could pick up, things were stable now. The failing navigational beacon was on SoCal 1.

What was happening wasn't normal. Sure, every satellite had issues once in a while, but not of this magnitude or for this length of time. The fact that the failures were moving between the two cities was strange as well. He'd finally gotten a message from one of his moles on SoCal Sat City 1, and the report hadn't helped clear up the situation. Apparently, life support on the flight decks had shut down for twenty minutes, and the executive offices had reached almost thirty degrees Celsius before coming back under control. Those were the big ones. Not too many people knew of the minor power surge that blew out the lights in engineering, or the spoiled food from when a freezer lost power long enough to get warm without its sensors throwing a warning.

Those who did know were trying to find the fastest way back to Earth. It had gotten so bad that extra security was put in place to keep the crowds away from the shuttle ports. If things kept going the way they were, SoCal would have a mass panic on their hands.

Both cities were having massive systemwide failures. That was never good when you were 36,000 kilometers out in space. How long would it be before major systems failed in large public places?

He touched a button on the screen.

"Hai, *Kaishō-ho*."

"Get me *Kaishō* Aiko." He closed the link before he got a reply.

Something was going on, and SoCal was in trouble. *Kaishō* Aiko was responsible for the near-Earth military zone, and the only one that could give Andrew permission to do what he wanted. His comm unit rang. He grabbed it off his desk.

"Sir, *Kaishō* Aiko for you."

"Thank you." The background tone of the call changed. "*Kaishō* Aiko?"

"The *Kaishō* is very busy, *Kaishō-ho* Ito. Perhaps you can leave a message. I will be sure he gets it."

"The matter is quite urgent. If I could speak with—"

"That will not be possible."

Andrew stayed quiet a little longer than courtesy allowed before speaking again. "I have sent in my reports about SoCal 2. Similar events are now happening on SoCal 1. I would like to offer assistance. They appear to be in trouble, and I don't believe they have enough shuttles to do a full evacuation . . . should the need arise."

He still wasn't sure he was making the right choice, but at least it felt right.

"We are at war with SoCal."

"But not with all the people in the cities. We have never failed to offer aid when needed—even to those Kadokawa considered its greatest rivals."

"We are no longer the same corporation. Being a rival is different than being an enemy, *Kaishō-ho*."

"Not to those who need our help."

"I will pass your request on to *Kaishō* Aiko, as you asked."

"Time may be critical. The incidents aboard both satellites appear to be increasing."

"I will pass along your request."

Andrew held back the retort forming on his lips. "Thank you."

The link went dead, the distinctive background sound of a call from orbit replaced with silence. Kadokawa had never refused aid to anyone. True, SoCal hadn't requested any, but something was obviously failing aboard the cities, and it wasn't minor. Whatever it was seemed to be affecting almost every system.

A career built on offering aid to those who needed it, and now his hands were tied by greed. It wasn't right. Andrew was trapped between his and Natsumi's view of Kadokawa and the one his superiors had changed it to. He couldn't shake the feeling that everything was wrong.

The message light on his vid screen lit up. Andrew touched it, already afraid of what he would see.

The message was from *Kaishō* Aiko.

No help is to be offered to SoCal at any time, under any circumstances.

His finger hesitated over the screen again, hovering over a

contact list. He slowed his breathing before pushing firmly over the name Natsumi Kadokawa.

"*Moshi moshi.*"

"Sorry to bother you at home."

"Andrew! It is nice to hear your voice. Let me call you back on your direct line."

"Of course."

Thirty seconds later, his comm unit rang. The blinking red circle in the top right corner of the screen indicating a bidirectional encrypted link.

"Hello."

"Ah, Andrew. You have been away too long, you even answer a call like a foreigner now."

"It has been long."

"But you did not call me to talk about the little things, have you?"

"I have not." He repeated the contents of his call to *Kaishō* Aiko.

"Yes, Aiko is one of Sone's placements," she said. "Has been for many years, before Sone was made *Kaijō-bakuryōchō*. Aiko joined only ten years ago, and was quickly promoted."

"What am I to do? My heart tells me I must help, yet my superior tells me I cannot."

Her voice got softer. "You have always had a difficult time following your heart, Andrew. Often choosing the easier path of honor and orders. Perhaps it is time to let your heart decide?"

"I don't know if I can." He knew it wasn't always the easier decision, as she had stated.

"Neither do I. Did you call me so that I could make the decision for you? That is something *I* cannot do. Not for you, and not for this. As in your past, there are choices only you can make."

"Natsumi, I—" He didn't know what to say.

"I will honor your choice, Andrew. I always have. I only pray it will not tear us further apart. I need to go."

"Thank you."

"For what?"

"For being my Natsumi. Even after all these years."

"I could not be anything else. Goodbye, Andrew."

For the second time that morning, he listened to the silence of a dead line. He closed the link and wiped at his eyes.

LOS ANGELES LEVEL 4—WEDNESDAY, JULY 7, 2141 9:14 A.M.

I watched them drive away, placing a hand on the door handle to the clinic to make it look like I was going back inside. What I really needed was time to think, and what I was thinking about was fucking crazy.

As soon as the car was out of sight, I left the clinic, taking the first corner to get off the main strip. I kept looking over my shoulder, feeling Pat's eyes burning a hole between my shoulder blades, right where my scar used to be. She was never there.

What I was feeling was guilt, and I knew why. Pat wasn't my partner on a mission anymore, but the feeling I had was the same. I was thinking about leaving her behind, and I didn't like it. I'd promised her I would never do it again, but I knew she wouldn't let me go. I tried to rationalize the danger I was putting myself—my unborn son—into by going to SoCal 2. By asking what was more important: the two of us, or the man that could change how the entire game was played?

But I knew it was so much more than that.

I tried to use logic. Kai had told me about the quantum drive, about what it could do. I knew Bryson was the one behind it, either building or designing the damn thing. If SoCal or any other corporation got their hands on working technology like that, it would be the end of everything. How long would it be before one of them controlled the world? Before they destroyed all the competition?

Long enough to kill too many people. To break too many families apart.

That's what it all boiled down to. Family. I had lost mine. Twice. Once when my parents had been killed, and again when Meridian had taken Ian. My hand rubbed my belly as I walked, almost feeling the life growing inside of me. I finally had family again; my aunt, Kai and Pat. My son. I had been given another chance, but what did it matter if there wasn't a world to bring him up in? If all he could be in life was a slave to a massive corporation—or worse—would that be any life at all?

I slowed my pace looking for a place to sit, suddenly exhausted. I'd wandered into a more residential neighborhood, instinctively wanting somewhere quieter where I could do my thinking alone. I breathed deep, hoping to capture the faint scent from the grass covering some of the tiny front lawns. I didn't even get a hint. This place was pretty upscale for Level 4, but not *that* upscale. Most the lawns were either painted fibercrete or fake grass. I turned to walk back to the main street I'd left behind, remembering one of the office buildings had a bench.

A body hurtled toward me. I sidestepped, half expecting to see Janice, and they rushed past. If I hadn't turned, they would have plowed straight into me. I'd been so deep in my own world, I'd forgotten about surveillance. I glanced toward the main street and noticed more people running my way. They were leaving the main street like cockroaches on Level 2 left a burning building. It didn't take too long before I saw why. Figures in mottled gray clothing chased them.

Another SoCal sweep.

I had two choices. I could run with the rest of them, or wait and use my age and pregnancy as a way to get out. The decision took only a split second. Maybe it was more instinct than choice. I ran, ducking into a back yard, leaving the others to run down the street.

The yard was small, and only one of the neighbors had a short fence. I took it, scrambling over the meter-tall structure into a well-tended garden. It wasn't just flowers, but potatoes and carrots and lettuce growing in aboveground boxes.

Shouts from the front street kept me moving. My pulse raced and I ran. If the soldiers were following the running people, maybe my best bet was to go in the opposite direction. I climbed the next fence onto another fibercrete pad painted dark green. A small shed took up a quarter of the space. I ran to it, pulling at the door. The damn thing didn't budge. I kept on running, this time angling toward the yard that faced the next street.

These houses didn't have fences. Instead, yellow lines marked the yard boundaries, indicating what part of the Level 4 floor came with the house. I slid down beside a set of back stairs and crawled to the corner. Squeezing my eyes shut and holding my breath, I cracked them open enough to peer around the edge of the house. I lay low, keeping my head as close to the fibercrete ground as I could. Through the space between the houses, I saw a couple of people lying on the ground, soldiers holding them in place while more soldiers continued to run past.

I had no place to go. Sweat pooled in the small of my back and my breathing was short and shallow. A shout from behind me made me spin around. Nothing was there.

A dozen options ran through my head. None of them good. In the end, I decided the shed was my best bet. If I could get inside and lock it behind me . . . I sprinted back to it, already winded from the short burst of speed I'd used. A quick look showed the thing had no windows. I went back to the door. The lock was a simple key system. If I had time I could have opened it.

I switched gears and sprinted back to the yard with the fence. The gardens were all aboveground boxes filled with synthetic soil and water drip feeders, just like the greenhouses. The plants looked like they could use some more moisture.

Using the edge of the box as a footstep, I leaned over the garden until I could use the fence as balance. The boxes didn't touch it. The gap was small. Too small for me to fit. I followed the fence around the corner to the back until I reached some plants that were tall and thick with large leaves. Hopefully it would be enough to hide me. I slid down the fence and jammed myself as far into the gap as I could. Only my lower leg and arm fit. It was the best I could do. I tried to slow my breathing so I wouldn't be heard and peered through the tall plants.

More shouting came from the street. The soldiers were checking yards. The door on the shed rattled. Through the leaves, I saw feet stepping into the flowerbed. They would see the damage I did when I jumped the fence. Maybe they'd think it was from someone leaving the yard. I heard a comm unit.

We've got quota.

The soldiers in the yard immediately started talking, obviously more relaxed.

"I hate chasing 'em down."

"Yeah. This was better than yesterday though. I don't know who picked the area, but almost no one was there. Somewhere on Level 3. We ended up chasing the bastards for blocks."

"What a pain in the ass."

"Yeah. They paid for it though. No one gets rejected for having a few extra bruises."

The return laughter got quieter as the soldiers left the yard. They were as mean as the rest of the corporation.

San Angeles was turning to shit, and if it was so easy for SoCal to do this to us now, how easy would it be for them to do this to this rest of the world? Once they had the quantum jump drive, there wouldn't be anything that could stand in their way. But there was something now.

I was going in.

LOS ANGELES LEVEL 4—WEDNESDAY, JULY 7, 2141 9:32 A.M.

"No, I won't let you." Doc Searls' face was turning a deep red as anger rushed to the surface. Gone was the professional detachment he'd used when I'd first told him I was going.

I waited him out as he continued, bringing up the baby and everything else he could think of. He ended by telling me he couldn't live with himself if something went wrong. If I never came back. I felt my own blood pressure rise as he continued. It wasn't his place to tell me what to do, and he knew it.

"I'm not giving you the choice, Doc. I'm going to find some way up there whether you help me out or not. It'll be a lot tougher if I have to do it on my own, but that's a risk I have to take." I'd already used all of the arguments I'd used to convince myself it was a good idea. None of them seemed to have as much effect as my last statement. He slumped into his chair.

"You'll never get up to Level 5. They have it all blocked."

"You had some sort of plan for the insurgents. What was that?"

"What about your aunt? Are you just going to leave her behind?"

Instead of answering my question, he was still trying to keep me from going. I'd already told him why I had to go when he brought up my unborn son, and again when he asked about Kai and Pat. I didn't bother answering this time. I stayed where I was and just stared at him. I could tell he'd given up and was just making a last-ditch attempt.

"I have a map of a safe route through the inter-level passages to Level 5."

"You're sure it's accurate?" I asked.

Doc shrugged. "My contacts seem to think so."

"And what happens when I get up there?"

He hesitated again and I stared him down until he couldn't look me in the eye anymore.

"You meet up with a water truck at the top of the Level 5 up-ramp. The truck's got a modified baffle you can hide in. They'll get you into Level 7."

I guess that had to be good enough for me. He reluctantly handed me the map and a comm unit, calibrating it for my tracker, and left the room. He was already making a connection on his own comm unit before the door closed behind him. It didn't matter who he called.

The closest entrance to the inter-level support corridors was in an apartment block about two minutes away, and the up-ramp for the water truck was only three blocks from the exit. I'd be in and out before Pat or Kai or the insurgents could do anything about it.

I had about thirty minutes before the truck exited the up-ramp. The timing was going to be tight. I bolted from the clinic and sprinted all the way to the apartment block, suddenly glad for all the running they'd made us do at the compound. I stopped only once I'd reached the entrance of the apartment blocks. My breath came in short gasps as I tried to slow down the mad beating of my heart. It had only been two weeks, but I was already out of shape.

The map had the building's security code on it. I typed it in and heard the faint buzz of the lock releasing. The hardest part was waiting for the elevator to arrive. I could have taken the stairs, but with the way the run had winded me, I didn't think I'd be able to run up twelve flights. I might have been able to get there, but I'd definitely have nothing left for the corridors.

The elevator let me out on the top floor. I glanced at the comm unit. Seven minutes already. Fuck, I wasn't going to make it. It dawned on me that might have been Doc Searls' plan, and anger flared through me, giving me a shot of adrenaline. He wanted to delay me until I wouldn't be able to catch the damn truck.

The laundry room was right beside the elevator. I breathed a sigh of relief when I found it empty. A locked door faced the elevator shaft wall. I found the key right where Doc Searls said it would be, taped to the inside of the cabinet holding the sink, jammed in near the top where no one would accidentally find it. I unlocked the door and replaced the key. Someone might need it in the future.

SoCal wasn't dumb. They knew the inter-level corridors were a security risk. It was the main reason they didn't have any between Levels 5 and 6. But there were a lot of different routes through, and they couldn't monitor them all. I was counting on it. The best they would be able to do was timed patrols all along the corridors. All I had to do was miss them, and I'd be fine. Easier said than done.

It worked until I'd almost reached my destination.

According to the times on the map, there weren't supposed to be any patrols in the area. They were all at the Level 4 entrance points. I guessed they didn't much care if people came down, only that they didn't want anyone to go up. I was wrong.

They must have heard me coming. I blundered around the final corner, so eager to be out of the warren of corridors that I wasn't being careful enough. The only thing that stopped me from having my brains splattered against a wall by a baton was that I flinched in the right direction.

A body slammed me into the wall, pushing me farther from my exit. They weren't even asking any questions. If you were in here, it was for all the wrong reasons.

The back of my head followed my shoulders into the wall and stars swam in front of my eyes. I couldn't see anything else. I lashed out low with my foot, pushing against the wall to get more power, hearing the impact more than feeling it. My vision slowly came back.

Over my gasping for air, I heard the sound of a shock stick slice past my ear. I lunged in the opposite direction, falling over the legs of my first attacker. Weak hands grabbed at my ankles and I kicked them away. Rolling onto my back, I saw the second soldier step over her fallen comrade. I scrambled backward, trying to put more space between us. She was too fast. Her boot slammed down onto my hip, glancing off. I faked more pain than I felt.

The second kick barely missed my head. The moment it swung past me, I rolled in, closing the distance between us. She couldn't kick me anymore, but she still had the shock stick. I kept the roll going, impacting her legs so hard she bounced against the wall and fell on top of me. I heard her baton rattle across the floor.

She was well trained. The first thing she did was scramble between my legs, trapping them with her feet and raising herself to pummel me with her fists.

Before she could straighten all the way I reached up and grabbed her head, pulling it toward me and weakening any punches she tried to throw. She did exactly what she wasn't supposed to do, fighting to gain distance. I let her head up, grabbing her ears as she lifted. I felt them tear, followed by an uncontrolled scream. Pushing her off, I scrambled to my feet and ran toward the exit.

I knew they had radios and would call it in. Unless their training had completely faded, they'd memorized what I looked like, my clothes, how tall I was.

If I didn't reach the water truck in time, I was dead.

LOS ANGELES LEVEL 5—FRIDAY, JULY 7, 2141 10:04 A.M.

The run to the up-ramp was chaotic. Every pedestrian, every car or truck, was a potential enemy. I left the sidewalk, hitting an alley behind the office buildings. There were no people down here, but I had to slow down every time I came across a street, walking across as if I belonged. As if I hadn't just taken out two SoCal soldiers. My hands shook and I couldn't slow down my racing heart.

I looked at the comm unit Doc Searls had given me. It showed two missed calls. I recognized one number as his. The other was Pat. It vibrated as I was holding it. Kai.

The clock said 10:04. I had a minute to get into position. I sped up, darting across the street as horns blared and tires squealed, reaching the up-ramp with only twenty seconds to spare.

It was too quiet. Had I missed the truck? I dashed down anyway. I had to be around the corner so the truck could stop without anyone seeing it. From below, I heard the rumble of tires and the whine of a motor struggling under a heavy load and I sped up, relief flowing through me. I turned the corner just before the truck did. If it hadn't had been going slow, it would have run me down. The tanker was bigger than the one I rode on top of a couple of weeks back. This one was at least twelve meters long and made of metal.

The passenger jumped out. "Kris?"

I nodded.

He grabbed my arm and almost dragged me up the ladder to the top of the tank, pulling open one of the large hatches used to fill it. He looked down the ramp and motioned for me to get inside.

The dark swirling water was only a foot below me. The entrance to the baffle was small. I wasn't sure who they'd planned to sneak in using it, but it didn't look like a grown man would have been able to fit. The sight of it made me catch my breath and fight off the panic I could feel growing inside of me.

There wasn't enough time to get it under control.

I lowered my feet in, finding a step only a few inches into the blackness. The man closed the hatch behind me. I was locked in the dark with no way out. My chest tightened, threatening to cut off all oxygen. I couldn't breathe. The bottom of the space wasn't flat. Instead, it narrowed to a V shape, the last few inches filled with water. I could feel the weight of it around me, hear it sliding over the plastic walls. In the darkness, it became a beast searching for its dinner. The lack of air made me dizzy and I slipped, wedging myself into the bottom of the baffle.

I bit off a scream, not sure if it could be heard outside the tanker. I was sucking in air faster than I needed it. Spots flew before my eyes, the only thing I could see in the pitch black. My hands groped in the dark, sliding off the smooth wet walls of my prison before finally finding one of the steps I'd used to get down. I yanked myself to my feet.

The truck braked, and fresh water fell into the baffle, starting the panic all over again.

I wasn't sure how long I stayed in that hell. At one point I had the clarity to turn on the comm unit to light up the space. It was a mistake. Suddenly everything became smaller, tighter, and the water swirling centimeters from my face filled me with terror. I turned off the light and cried until the truck stopped.

The hatch above me opened and daylight spilled into the tanker.

I lurched up the steps, almost throwing myself off the top of the truck in an effort be free. A hand steadied me, not letting go until I'd stopped moving. It wasn't the same guy who put me into the hatch.

"You must be Kris."

I couldn't do anything but nod. It must have been enough.

"I've seen some of the toughest people I know come out of there quivering. You're doing good. We don't have much time. I've got a pair of SoCal shuttle port coveralls and ID for you. Make sure you upload the signature to your tracker. We leave in five minutes."

He climbed down the truck, leaving me with a bundle of clothes and a lanyard with a barcode on it.

"Come on. In the car."

I followed him and changed in the car, pulling the coveralls over my wet clothes. My hands were still shaking.

"So what's the process from here?" I asked, surprised at how steady my voice was.

"We'll meet up with Sarah outside the shuttle port. You'll follow her in through security and she'll get you to the right shuttle. The attendant will get you on board, into the crew space under the cockpit. You'll be comfortable enough. Pilots and crew use the space to rest on longer trips. Get rid of the coveralls before you go through the SoCal 2 shuttle port. Once you're in the common area, a big guy with the name Cecil will meet you. He'll give you the lay of the land and help you as much as he can."

"How will I recognize him?"

"Like I said, he's a big guy, around two meters tall and easily 122 kilograms. He knows your name."

We drove the rest of the way in silence, my wet clothes uncomfortable under the coveralls. I watched the clouds move across the sky. It felt like forever since I'd seen one.

Sarah and I walked through security with barely a second look.

They scanned my security pass and presumably matched it up with my tracker ID. I was on the shuttle and buckled in no more than fifteen minutes later. I made sure I didn't look out the viewport while we were stationary, crew wouldn't be here before takeoff. Once we started moving, I risked a look out.

I kept my face glued to it for the entire flight.

The beginning part of the trip was normal, except we used a runway instead of the vertical lifters. From what I remembered, taking off vertically used significantly more fuel than allowing the stubby wings of the craft to generate some lift for you. Acceleration pressed me back into my seat, and we lifted off, shooting into the sky before breaking through the thin layer of clouds. The sun glared off the window and the glass darkened to compensate.

The shuttle continued to climb and the sky turned darker blue and then to black. The horizon curved and glowed as we rose into space. The SoCal coast spread below me with no sign of the hell that lived alongside it. Above me, stars shone. I was filled with a sudden rush of freedom. It was as if everything fell away from me. Every worry, every pain, every bad memory. I even forgot how uncomfortable my clothes were. As the shuttle slowed to match the Sat City's course, I became weightless. The only thing holding me down was the seatbelt.

The station came into view through my window, a huge globe floating in space, ringed with lights that outlined it against the blackness. Our shuttle rotated, facing the city, and my view changed to the satellite curving into the distance.

The shuttle's engines suddenly fired and we veered off, acceleration pressing me against my seatbelt. My window filled with the view of the massive shuttle port. The interior shone with lights bright enough to chase away the darkness of space. The shuttle continued its turn and made another approach. Why had we aborted our landing?

Our second attempt was smooth. The outside of the city loomed into view once again before we entered the dock. We coasted to the far wall, small corrections in our heading and speed shifting the shuttle slightly, until we sat stationary. A large tube extended outward. When it touched the shuttle the entire thing shook, but we didn't move. A few minutes after that, gravity came back.

The attendant came down to get me. I took off the coveralls and she quickly opened a carry-on bag and tossed me some dry clothes. They were too big, but they were better than what I'd had. They would also blend in better with the people on the Sat City. I left the shuttle like a normal passenger.

I didn't even make it past the gate before I was stopped.

The soldier was waiting outside the boarding ramp, stepping in behind me and zip-tying my hands together before I knew what was happening. He didn't say anything, simply leading me through to the exit.

I hadn't even made it into the city. My heart fell and I plodded along beside him. Somewhere along the chain, someone had told SoCal there was a stowaway on the shuttle. Whether they had said why I was there, I didn't know. I didn't think it would take too long before I found out.

The city's shuttle port was utilitarian at best, designed to move people in and out with a minimum of fuss. When we finally left the docking area, my mouth dropped open.

We'd exited in a giant mall, at least three stories tall. Trees, some of the largest I'd ever seen, grew from the ground floor, reaching to the ceiling almost ten meters up. What I first thought were birds flitting amongst the branches turned out to be drones darting through the sky. High above, white clouds were painted on a blue background.

Everyone walked at a leisurely pace, moving in and out of the shops and restaurants that lined the outer walls. Even the brief time I'd spent on Levels 6 and 7 paled in comparison to what I saw. There was more money here than in all the Levels of San Angeles combined.

Though there was no sunlight, the space was brightly lit in a warm, soothing light. I couldn't find the source of it. If even a small portion of the money and technology used to build this was reinvested into San Angeles, everyone's lives would get better.

I gawked like a little girl as we walked through, barely noticing the wrinkled noses and quiet whispers of the people around us. I had never in my wildest imagination believed something like this could exist.

My guard pulled us off the main strip and into a wide hallway. A bank of elevators sat waiting. We got on the first available one and rode it down. Some things never changed, and for a second I was back to being a courier when techno-fusion pop music spilled from the hidden speakers.

The elevator opened into a narrow hallway, the composite of the walls painted a dull gray. I was led to a small room and pushed inside. The door closed behind me with the sound of a lock driving home. I sat in one of the two chairs, putting a desk between me and the door where the guard stood. I didn't have to wait very long.

The door opened and a woman walked in, her red suit looking out of place. She sat in the other chair looking cold and professional. Corporate. She was dressed too fancy to be low-level. This one was pretty high up.

"Miss Merrill." She glanced at the pad in her hand. "Or should I say Miss Ballard?"

A jagged chunk of ice filled my chest. How could she know that? ACE was supposed to have deleted my real name when they created Kris Merrill. I didn't answer.

"I do need to know what to call you. It will help as we get further along. I'm Ms. Peters."

Rule one when being interrogated: don't answer questions, even if they seem simple and safe. I kept my mouth shut. She spent the next ten minutes telling me my life story, starting from when my parents had died to yesterday. Her voice became rough when she mentioned I was pregnant. My mind went numb.

"I have some blank spots where you seem to disappear, so I imagine you can change your tracker ID."

It wasn't a question. She wasn't trying to hide anything from me. What the hell was up?

"Will you be answering any of my questions?" She waited for a response. "We have some time. Maybe tomorrow you'll be more cooperative." She looked at the guard who accompanied her. "Put her in a holding cell. Water only, no food and no blankets. Bring her back here tomorrow for seven A.M."

The guard nodded and turned to open the door. He hid the panel with his body and punched in a number. The door stayed locked. He punched in the number again with no success.

"Oh for . . . I'll do it." Ms. Peters pushed him back and entered a code, still blocked by the guard's back. The lock opened and she stormed out. The door banged shut behind her.

To me, it looked like Ms. Peters had helped it.

The guard swore. He tried the door five more times before it finally unlocked. He stood in the doorway, holding it open.

"Come on."

As I stood up, an arm reached around the door and grabbed him, slamming his head into the edge. He fell, and I jumped over the table, landing on his chest. I felt his ribcage give and break just as a knife cut his throat.

A soldier stepped around the corner and wiped the blade clean on the guard's shirt. "I'm Cecil, your contact. I didn't think that bitch was ever going to leave."

SOCAL SAT CITY 2—FRIDAY, JULY 7, 2141 12:02 P.M.

Bryson was scared. He'd been scared before. In fact very recently, but this was something new. This he felt emanating from his bones until it numbed his face. Here he was, sitting in a tin can in space, surrounded by nothing but vacuum and death, and things were going very wrong.

Even in the sheltered environment of the lab and his rooms, the rumors were starting to filter through. Key systems shutting down and coming back up. Simple things like primary lighting in a hallway or vid screens in one of the bars on the promenade. And scary things like environmental control and the attitude jets. A huge thing like the city didn't stay in orbit on its own. Even something as simple as docking a shuttle could affect its position—nothing that could be detected by a human, but things could move over the course of a thousand dockings.

He was scared of dying up here, alone in his lab, while the rest of the station evacuated or panicked. He knew he had released the virus into the systems. It was that damn memory chip the ice queen had given him. His routines had awakened the virus and spread it to the internal systems. He wasn't happy about it anymore. This was no ordinary virus that would cause some problems before being eradicated. This one was destructive, and if left unchecked, would bring the station down. And it was moving fast! It needed to be stopped. He hoped SoCal's scanners and firewalls were up to the task.

The door to the airlock opened and Bryson turned around in his chair to look. The only thing he saw were the guards standing outside staring in. Both the inside and outside doors of the lock had opened at the same time, allowing unfiltered city air into the lab. An impossibility. The interior airlock shut and his view of the guards disappeared.

He faced his screen again, his entire body tense and the blood running cold in his veins. He *was* going to die down here, along with everyone else in his lab. His first thought went to Ailsa.

If they got out of here, the first thing he would do was get to the closest escape station and use it. He—they—had been walked down the hallways to their rooms enough times to know there weren't any along the way. Their best bet at finding one was to go somewhere they hadn't been before—if they got the chance. It was also the best way of getting lost.

The airlock doors opened again. This time it was only the inside one, and a guard stood on the other side.

"They've ordered everyone to their quarters," the guard said. "Let's get moving. Same routine as always, three at a time." He pointed at Bryson. "You're in the first group."

Bryson filed out with Ailsa and a tech. They were herded into the elevator and rode the two floors to their living spaces. The doors refused to open for a full thirty seconds when they reached their floor. When they finally did, Ailsa scrambled ahead of the guard to get out and sat panting on the floor.

"Come on, Ailsa," Bryson said. "I'll help you to your room."

"They're just gonna let us die here, you know. The city will shut down and they'll leave us behind."

"We're too important for them to do that." He wasn't sure he believed it, but it was what she needed to hear. He put an arm around her back and under her arm, helping her to her feet.

"You are. I'm not."

"Then we stick together, okay? If they evacuate me, they'll have to take you too. Okay?" He watched as relief flooded through her eyes.

"O . . . okay."

"Good. Now come on."

When they got to their quarters, the guards didn't even put up a fuss when he helped her into his room. He heard the familiar sound of the door closing and locking.

TWELVE

SOCAL SAT CITY 2—FRIDAY, JULY 7, 2141 12:11 P.M.

TOGETHER WE PUSHED the body back into the room and closed the door. There wasn't anything we could do about the blood on the floor.

"How did you find me?"

"I was waiting for you to get out of the shuttle when I saw the soldiers head in. When they escorted you out, I figured it was my job to try and get to you."

"And you're a SoCal soldier?"

"Nah. It's a great cover up here, though. One of the most common articles of clothing in the city these days." He led me from the room, my hands still zip-tied together. "I've been up here since ACE fell. Good thing I stayed. I think."

"When do I get these things off me?" I lifted my hands behind my back, even though he couldn't see them.

"As soon as we get off this floor. Not a good place to be."

He led me to the end of the hall, stopping at a panel flush with the wall. It had a single round keyhole in it. No electronic locks here.

"Come on. They build these things to get easy access to everything for maintenance. Easy is a relative term though. You won't have any issues, but the place is a bit small for me."

Great. More small places. It seemed to be a constant that ran through my life. Cecil fished a key from his pocket and opened the access way.

"Took me three weeks to get a key." He pushed me ahead and closed the door behind him. "Nice and quiet," he whispered. "These places have been crawling with people since the city started having issues. Follow me."

The space was narrow. I could walk facing forward with my shoulders barely touching the outer walls, but Cecil had to do a sideways crabwalk. The walls were plain composite and covered in pipes and ducting. Dust blew up with every step. I struggled to hold back a sneeze, finally giving up and trying to bury my nose into my shoulder. It didn't work. Cecil looked at me, motioning for me to turn around. I saw the flash of a blade in the light, tensing at the sight. The freedom from the zip tie felt wonderful. He struggled to pick up the tie from the floor.

"No use leaving this here to tell people where we've been," he said. He shoved the zip tie into his pocket.

There was light in here, but it wasn't much. A simple square patch of cold blue light every four feet on the ceiling. With Cecil walking in front, all my light came from behind me. His head blocked everything until we had passed it.

The corridor split into two. We turned right until we got to a simple ladder embedded into the composite. He started climbing without a word. I followed, careful not to get too close to his feet.

We skipped the next corridor, continuing up one more floor. Cecil stepped off the ladder and waited for me. Voices echoed up from below. He held his finger to his lips and motioned for me to follow again. The door we stopped at looked like the one we'd used to get into the maintenance corridors.

"The other side of this door is living space for some of the tradespeople who keep this city running. It's the best place for us to emerge. They've been running around all day, trying to solve the issues that are cropping up. Walk around like you belong, and we should go unnoticed." He took off his guard jacket and reversed it, hiding any trace of its military aspects.

"Where are we going?"

"My room. From there we can figure out what to do next. Come on, let's go."

Pulling a spring-loaded lever on the door released the catch, and the door swung open. We walked out. A few people looked at us as we emerged, but he started talking about electrical problems on E-17 that had disappeared by the time he got there. I nodded and the interest waned. We were just a couple more people chasing down ghosts.

The conversation was the perfect cover. From what I overheard, everyone around us had had similar experiences over the last few hours. Things were getting worse. We passed through the residential area into what looked like a monitoring center. Vid screens were lit up, text scrolling red. Half of the text would turn green and disappear only to be quickly replaced by new problems.

"They control everything from here?" I asked.

"Nah. We'd never get into that section. Security is so tight, you need eight levels of clearance just to know where it is." He winked. "Dead center of the city, actually. Same place all the computer equipment that runs this place is. It's no big secret. Protected like nobody's business though. This is a monitoring station. They put it close to where the tradespeople live so they can see what's happening. This is a display of this segment. There are seven more."

All the text on the boards suddenly went green and one by one fell off the display. Nothing red came to replace it. Within seconds, the screens were blank. There was a palpable sigh in the room.

"See, told ya," one man said loud enough for others to hear. "It's a bloody computer glitch. If they would have rebooted the damn thing hours ago, we could have all had regular days. Bastards don't care about us working folk, do they?"

His question was answered by a quiet murmur. Everyone still watched the screens, waiting for them to suddenly jump back to life.

"Come on," Cecil said.

We walked side by side out of the monitoring room, following the slow trickle of others doing the same.

"How many of you are up here?" I asked.

"Just a handful. I think there's a couple of people from the insurgents that are creating havoc in San Angeles, but I don't know who they are. Above my pay grade, I guess."

"I know I'm here to get Bryson, but I really want to know how Ms. Peters knew so much about me. ACE was supposed to have created new records for my new name. How is it possible that she—that SoCal—managed to put the two personas together?"

"You have no idea how big and how powerful SoCal really is, do you?"

"I'm beginning to. I still want to know how she found out. Is there any way I can get into her office while she's not there? Get a look at her files?"

"I don't think so. She's about as high up in SoCal as you can get and still be on Sat City 2. She's higher than some on SoCal 1, but they say she likes it here."

"So, how do I get in?"

"Not easily."

"Not even through the maintenance corridors?"

"Sure, but you'll never get out of them without being checked for ID."

"Let that be my problem." I rested my hand on my belly again. *Sorry kiddo,* I said to myself. *But if they have all that information, we'll never be safe. I gotta see what they know and if I can get rid of it, or we'll never be free.*

SOCAL SAT CITY 2—FRIDAY, JULY 7, 2141 12:20 P.M.

The last thing Janice had expected was another ride up to SoCal 2, but that was exactly where John had taken her. They'd driven directly to the shuttle port on Level 7 and boarded the next commercial flight up. She didn't get a private one this time.

The incoming shuttle had been packed to capacity. She'd watched as people streamed off almost like they would never stop. The look of relief on their faces was confusing. Something was going on. She didn't dare ask John. He looked ready to snap as it was.

They boarded the shuttle with five other people and rode up to SoCal Sat City 2. Why was no one heading up with them? When they got there, there was no waiting. The shuttle landed and docked. The crowd trying to get on the departing shuttle was massive and bordering on unruly. They had to fight their way through.

From the shuttle port, it was a brisk walk across the promenade to the elevators, exiting at the top floor. They stopped at the security checkpoint before they reached their destination.

Ms. Peters' office was the same as the last time Janice had been here. The same man offered them both glasses of water. This time, she waited for Ms. Peters to arrive and have a sip before she drank. She had always been a quick study.

"I had a conversation with your friend," Ms. Peters said, looking straight at Janice.

"My friend?"

"Yes, Kris Merrill."

Janice stood, almost spilling her water. "Where is she?"

"Sit. Down." It was the first time Janice had heard emotion in Ms. Peters' voice, and it scared the hell out of her. She gently lowered herself back into the chair. John hadn't moved.

"But never mind that now." Ms. Peters went on as if nothing had happened. "I believe I placed too much trust in you. Sending you back to monitor the girl was obviously a mistake."

"I was attacked from behind."

"So I've been told. And Manfred? Where were you when he was attacked?"

Janice reiterated her story. Ms. Peters didn't interrupt her.

"And where is your stun gun?"

"She says the girl took it," John said, speaking for the first time.

Ms. Peters never took her eyes off Janice. "I believe I asked you the question."

From the corner of her eye, Janice saw John shift deeper into his chair. "What he said. It was in my hand when Kris attacked me from behind. When I came to, it was gone."

"I see. You do know that Manfred was one of my best?"

Janice thought it was better not to answer. If he was one of her best, it was a miracle SoCal got anything done.

"John. Take her to medical. Have her completely checked out to see if it can corroborate her story." She looked back at Janice. "I'll check our data feeds. Let's see what the cameras and sound pickups have to say about it."

Janice shivered and the water in her glass formed concentric circles over the previously still surface.

Ms. Peters smiled.

John led Janice from the office. When they exited into the hallway he turned to her. "You better hope you're telling the truth."

"I am."

What she really hoped was that there had been no cameras or audio pickups anywhere near the place. It was pretty unlikely. What she needed was a plan to get out of here. If the crowds kept up around the shuttle bay, it could help her. She followed John, trying to walk with more confidence than she felt.

SOCAL SAT CITY 2—FRIDAY, JULY 7, 2141 12:28 P.M.

"I'm telling you, you'll never make it. The maintenance shafts don't go all the way there. You have to pop out and go through security to get back to maintenance," Cecil said.

"Shit. Their very own fucking Level 6."

"I never thought of it that way, but yeah."

"People from maintenance go through all the time though, right?"

"Yeah, with special orders. They have to show the paperwork and get scanned before they're allowed through."

That had me stumped. There was no hiding under the back seats of cars or in tanker trucks filled with water to sneak through this one. "Is there any way you can fake the forms?"

"Not well enough to get through."

"But enough to make them think I'm legitimate for a few seconds?"

"What are you planning?"

"If they always let through the trades with the proper paperwork, then as long as I can fool them long enough to get their guard down—"

"Then we can take them out when they're not expecting it."

"Right." I noticed he had used *we* instead of just *me*.

"These guys are highly trained, it won't be easy."

"Better trained than us?"

"Yes. And they have years of experience before they get a post like that. Someone with no field experience won't have any hope of getting past them at all."

"Not alone."

Cecil paused. "No, not alone. Dammit. We'll have to get you a weapon. Guns aren't allowed up here, same rules that they have in San Angeles. They're a bit more strict up here, though. Even security doesn't have guns."

"So what do they use?"

"Stun guns, tasers, shock sticks. That kind of stuff."

Great. "I have experience with tasers and stun guns, and we trained on the shock stick in camp."

"Any field experience?"

"With a taser. I guess you could call it that." He looked at me sideways, but didn't ask any questions.

"A shock stick is too big and bulky. They'd see it right away. A taser or a stun gun you can keep in your pocket. I have a couple stashed we could use."

"You wouldn't happen to have the taser and stun gun combo, would you?" May as well stick with what you know.

"Yeah, but I hate those things."

"I love them." That got me another sideways look.

We got back to the monitoring station. All the screens were still blank, and the place was almost deserted. Cecil had hidden his stuff in a maintenance corridor, so we were heading back into them the same way we'd come out. He stuck his key in the lock and we got back inside while the hallway was empty.

"Which way?" I whispered.

Cecil pointed left and up. I followed the corridor to another set of rungs in the wall. When I pointed, he nodded.

He held up three fingers. "Three floors," he said softly.

I climbed, slowing down before I stuck my head up to look at the next floor. I didn't hear any voices. At the third floor, I moved off to the side, waiting for Cecil to squeeze through the opening.

"They've got a map at a junction about two hundred meters that way." He pointed to what I thought was deeper into the city. "I'll show you the route up."

The map was etched right into the composite. It looked like it had been painted over and then wiped clean, leaving the etching a different color than the surrounding wall.

"Okay, we're here." Cecil pointed to the midpoint of the map. "My stash is over here. We'll get there, and then take these ladders up seventeen floors. That's where we'll need to exit."

I counted the floors on the map. Seventeen up from the stash was where it ended. "Is there a map for above it?"

"I have no idea. I think it's only two or three floors though, so it shouldn't be too tough to find our way."

"And you know where Ms. Peters' office is?"

"Nope."

"Will the guards know?"

"They should, but it'll be tough to get the information out of them. We're right at the top of the city. If it's anything like the bottom, the floors are fairly small. Some of the upper echelon may even have a floor to themselves for offices and a place to live."

"You said Ms. Peters was the highest-level person in the city?"

"Yeah, I think so."

"So chances are she'll be on the top floor?"

"It's a good bet."

"Okay then, let's move."

SOCAL SAT CITY 2—FRIDAY, JULY 7, 2141 12:52 P.M.

We only had to backtrack once after hearing voices in the corridor ahead, moving to a tee section until they started fading again. I looked at Cecil and he nodded. We retraced our path and continued up.

Sections of the corridor looked like they almost never got used. The areas we were walking through were dusty, but at least you could see footprints on the floor where tradespeople had used the corridor in the past. A couple of the offshoots had dust bunnies the size of my motorcycle in them.

"What's down these?" I asked.

"Usually just shortcuts between corridors. Most people would rather walk outside than stay in these twisty things, though."

"You think we can get away with it?"

"Walk outside? Maybe. You want to risk it?"

I thought about it, wondering how many people we'd run into. "Not really."

"Me neither. Take a left here, then up one more floor."

I followed his directions, reaching a section of corridor that was darker than the rest. The light had gone out. It was probably on purpose. Cecil reached above and behind some ducts, pulling out a gray duffel bag.

"Wouldn't they see that when they fix the light?"

"It blends in pretty well. Besides, maintenance corridor lights are low priority. Even more so if there's nothing important near them.

This is just a straight run. The last junction box was two lights back, and the next one is farther down. The chance of having this light replaced this year is pretty slim."

He reached into the bag, handing me the taser/stun gun combo. It was bigger than the old one I'd had. There was no way this would stick to the back of my jacket and go unnoticed, but it would fit in my pocket. My heartbeat picked up as I looked at it.

"You okay?"

I nodded.

"You sure you want to go through with this?"

"Yeah. If they have that kind of information on me, what else do they have? Maybe everyone who used to work for ACE has that kind of detail in their files." If they did, that would make Pat and Kai vulnerable. It looked like Cecil finally realized that meant him as well.

"Okay. Let's go then."

We found the next closest ladder and started climbing. They went up three floors at the most before you had to walk a bit to get to the next one. I wasn't sure why they had been built that way, but I didn't much care either. It gave my arms a chance to rest before I had to go up another three floors.

Partway there, my stomach growled loud enough to get a look from Cecil. "You got anything to eat?" I asked.

"Nope."

"Shit." I pushed through the hunger.

The seventeenth floor came before I knew it. We followed the corridor to an exit close to where Cecil thought the security checkpoint was.

"You ready?" he asked.

"Nope." I purposely changed my voice to sound like him. It earned me a small smile.

"Act natural. We'll chat and look at the pad as we walk up to them. No need to look them in the eye or anything. This is just another job we need to get done. Okay?"

I sucked in a breath. "Okay."

Cecil pulled the latch and walked out, dust clinging to his shoes. The hallway was wide and carpeted, the composite walls covered in a fabric that softened the edges. Except for the constant background noise of the satellite itself, you would almost believe you weren't in space.

We passed an elevator and rounded a corner. The security desk was only a few steps away. I almost stopped, suddenly unsure of what I was doing.

"I hope this ain't another stupid glitch," Cecil said.

"Yeah," I said. "I'm getting tired of running around and finding the problem has fixed itself."

Security stopped us. "Can we see your papers?" Cecil handed the pad over. I reached for my pocket, and the guard's eyes followed the motion. I scratched my nose instead, and on the way down slipped my hand into the pocket over the taser. It helped stop the shaking I was sure they'd noticed. I didn't grab it—he would have seen my fingers tightening around something.

"You had anybody else up here chasing ghosts?" Cecil asked.

The guard laughed while his partner watched. "More than I can count. I'll check the order number against the computer."

"If the damn thing is working," I said. I had both guards looking at me now. Maybe I should have kept my mouth shut. I pulled my hand from my pocket and scratched my nose again.

"Everything's been acting up. Even these stupid terminals." The guard leaned over the keyboard and started typing in the numbers.

That was our cue to move.

I'd barely gotten my hand around the taser before Cecil launched over the desk, driving the guard's face through the vid screen. The second guard reached for his shock stick and swung. He wasn't aiming for me.

The stick barely missed Cecil's arm. The guard with his face through the vid screen shifted and mumbled. Damn, they were both still up. The shock stick made another swing, and when it reached its zenith, I lunged, driving the prongs of my stun gun into the guard's neck. He dropped to his knees. I followed with a side kick to his throat, crushing his trachea. Cecil reached for the man by the vid screen, lifted his head, and smashed it back into the desk.

The entire thing had taken ten seconds. Too long. Cecil grabbed the shock stick and we raced past the security station and entered the next maintenance door.

"Somebody paid attention in class," Cecil said.

Damn right I did. I was shorter and smaller than anyone else. I had to be better.

"We have fifteen minutes, tops. Less if someone happens to want up here."

We found a ladder and climbed. The exit door was right there. Cecil popped it open and stuck his head out.

"Hey!" I heard a voice from inside the room.

"Sorry, sir." Cecil stepped out all the way. "I'm following a glitch and it led me here. Have you noticed the lights going on and off?"

"Practically all day. The last guys up here couldn't find anything."

"That's why we're here, sir. Trying to follow up, see what they missed."

"Ms. Peters will be back in ten minutes. You'll be done and gone before then."

"That's the plan," Cecil said.

I stepped out, my taser ready, and fired. The two prongs ejected and pierced the man's shirt, embedding into his skin. When the shock entered his body, he couldn't even scream. Cecil stepped forward, and when I let go of the trigger he swung the shock stick at the man's head. The groaning stopped, and he lay still.

I looked around. One wall was covered entirely in moss, and the sound of water trickling through it filled the room with a gentle background noise. The other walls were covered in wood. It looked and felt real. The room screamed of money.

The furniture was comfortable, but showed this to be just a waiting area. If Ms. Peters had an office, it had to be close by. Cecil began walking the wall.

"Hey, over here," he whispered.

He took another step and disappeared behind the moss. I jogged after him, entering a short hallway with a room at the end. The room was a simple white and gray with bookcases along the wall. I didn't care about them. I cared about the desk with the terminal on it. I ran past Cecil and hit the keyboard.

The image of a young boy appeared on the display. He couldn't have been more than three years old. Did Ms. Peters have a son? I found that hard to believe. Overlaying the image was a plain white rectangle.

Password locked.

I guess I should have expected that. There was only one pad on the desk. I lifted it and the screen turned on, an image of my face plastered across the display. I showed it to Cecil.

We spent a precious two minutes looking for anything else and came up empty handed. It was time to go. We ran back to the maintenance entrance and climbed back down to the bottom, entering the hallway where the guards were. The one Cecil had attacked was still down, but not out. He was slowly trying to reach the terminal. Cecil tromped on the guard's back. As we ran past I grabbed the pad off the desk.

We got back in the maintenance corridors.

THIRTEEN

KADOKAWA SAT CITY 2—FRIDAY, JULY 7, 2141 1:15 P.M.

SOMETHING WASN'T RIGHT.

The report that came across Andrew's desk said the strange disruptions on SoCal Sat City 2 had completely stopped. Again, no one could explain why, which wasn't really unexpected, considering no one knew why they had started. SoCal 1 had followed shortly after, and both cities appeared to be stable. So far, it had lasted over an hour.

It didn't make any sense to him. The types of issues they had seen didn't just disappear like that. Even though it saved him from a decision he didn't want to make, he couldn't help but wonder when the next barrage would start.

As far as he knew, Natsumi was the only person who was talking of overthrowing Kadokawa's leadership. What if it was just her, and she was fishing for more people to join? He sighed. That wasn't the

Natsumi Kadokawa he knew. She would have been quietly gathering forces around her for a long time, probably ever since the new president took control and assigned Sone to lead the military. He was looking for excuses. As she had said, looking for the supposedly easier road of orders and honor.

A beep from his vid screen interrupted his thoughts. He touched a flashing icon in the lower right corner. "Yes?"

"Sir, SoCal has sent another twelve ships to our front line."

Twelve was an odd number. "Is it a rotation of pilots?" Sitting in space took power as well, and the fighter craft either needed refueling or to return back to SoCal 2.

"It doesn't look that way."

"Get ready to launch another squadron. I'm on my way. And keep an eye on SoCal 1 and 2. This could be a diversion." He closed the connection and rubbed his eyes. SoCal seemed prepared to push their standoff into an actual battle. His heart rate sped up as he left for Operations.

The lights were dimmed when he walked in, and everyone was looking at their displays. As soon as the door closed behind him, *Kaisa* Mori approached.

"The ships have lined up behind their existing line. Fairly spread out, but it increases their number above ours."

"The squadron is ready?"

"Waiting for your command, sir."

Andrew leaned over the shoulder of a person he hadn't met, looking at the heat signatures and patterns of the SoCal fighters. A dozen of them glowed hotter than the rest—the new arrivals. They had positioned themselves evenly, making the overall effect look like a waste of manpower. What were they planning?

"When was SoCal's last shift change?"

"Only an hour ago sir."

That made it at least another four hours before replacements were supposed to come. The display glowed bright and the dozen ships powered away, back to SoCal 2. What the hell was going on?

He stood, easing the kink that had developed in his back from bending over. Getting old was never fun. "Could this be another glitch in their systems?" If it was, it was a major step up from failing lights and environmental control.

"I don't know, sir."

"Of course you don't—" Andrew interrupted himself. He hadn't meant to raise his voice. "It was a rhetorical question. Pass the information on to intelligence. I want their opinion in fifteen minutes."

"Yes, sir." Mori turned to go but changed his mind. "And our people ready to launch?"

"Keep them at ready." They wouldn't like it, but that wasn't his problem.

"Yes, sir."

Mori strode across the room and talked to a young woman in the corner. She almost ran from the control room.

Andrew paced back and forth behind the backs of those watching the monitors. "Bring SoCal 2 on the main screen."

The city filled the display.

"Pull back a bit."

The city got smaller, finally looking like a globe floating in space. From here, it all looked so serene. There was no indication of the technology and computational power required to keep it stationary, to keep the nearly quarter of a million people living on it alive. The city was almost entirely self-sufficient, growing its own food, recycling all of its water. Despite that, shipments were still needed from Earth. Mainly in the form of fresh water and delicacies the upper echelon wanted.

Without warning, half of SoCal 2 went dark. All the exterior lights had shut off on the Earth side, and the composite material reflected the planet's light. Andrew's chest tightened. This wasn't over, then.

Mori ran up. "It looks like it's exterior lights only, sir. We have no indication of internal systems failing at this time."

Andrew nodded. The city was falling apart, and whatever had affected it was also having its way with SoCal 1. He paced furiously across the floor, more confident as the decision started to take a firm grip in his mind. He was about to disobey a direct order, and it would ruin his career.

"Open a direct line to SoCal 2."

Mori hesitated before asking "To who?"

"As high up the military ladder as we can get."

"Yes, sir."

The connection was made and the room went absolutely quiet.

"Rear Admiral Hamil's office," a voice answered.

Damn. The best they could do was a secretary?

"This is *Kaishō-ho* Andrew Ito from Kadokawa Sat City 2. I wish to speak to Admiral Hamil."

"One moment please." The secretary was good. Andrew hadn't heard the slightest waver in his voice. It would take them a minute or so to trace back the line.

It took a minute and thirty-two seconds.

"What can I do for you, *Kaishō-ho*?" The voice was gruff, but he had pronounced *Kaishō-ho* almost perfectly.

"Admiral, your city seems to be having some issues. Kadokawa," he paused. "*I* would like to extend an offer to help."

"We're at war. What kind of help do you think we would accept?"

Andrew took a step forward as if he could close the gap between them. His voice softened. "There is a time for fighting, and there is a time for helping. You have 250,000 people in your city, less the ones who have already evacuated. Let me do what we are known for. Let me help."

The pause on the link was longer than he'd expected. Maybe there was some hope for a peaceful ending to this after all. The response cut through the silence.

"I'm sorry, *Kaishō-ho* Ito. I can't allow that. Any movement toward us will be considered hostile."

"I am sorry to hear that."

"Me too, *Kaishō-ho*, me too."

The line went dead. Mori stared at Andrew. "What now?" he asked.

"Now we wait. Again. I imagine we shall soon hear from Okinawa. I'll be in my quarters waiting on the call. You will, no doubt, be placed in charge until they can find my replacement. Keep the squadron at ready for another hour. If nothing happens, let them get some rest."

"Yes, sir."

As Andrew walked to the door, almost every person stood and bowed as he passed them.

SOCAL SAT CITY 2—FRIDAY, JULY 7, 2141 1:22 P.M.

The pad I'd taken from Ms. Peters' office contained three files. I sat in the only chair in Cecil's room, munching on a chocolate bar he'd had. Cecil sat on the edge of his bed, looking uncomfortable.

One of the files was on me and contained everything Ms. Peters knew about me plus our conversation in the interrogation room. The other two were more interesting. One was on Bryson Searls and the other on Janice. I had some trouble deciding which one to look at first. I finally decided on Bryson since he was up here with me.

His file was excruciatingly detailed, beginning with his university years. I skipped to the end. They had him holed up in a lab on the lower floors during the day, and in a secure living space a few floors above that at night.

The next thing that caught my eye was what he had accomplished. The data Kai had decrypted was accurate. Being able to travel over vast distances in the blink of an eye. The first thought that entered my head was maybe we could find a place to live that we wouldn't fuck up as bad as this one.

"Where's floor C3 and C5?" I asked.

Cecil looked surprised I had said something. "Oh. Um, way down. Right near the bottom. It may be as low as you can go before everything turns into support infrastructure. Why?"

"Bryson Searls is down there."

"So what do we do about it?"

"Nothing, yet." I went back to reading and the room got quiet again.

Janice's file wasn't as big, but way more interesting. She'd been trained by Meridian well before I met her in ACE boot camp. No wonder she'd picked everything up so quickly. Jeremy had put her in the compound to keep an eye on me. When I reached the part where she had called in the attack, I almost threw the pad across the room. The bitch. I knew she was behind it somehow.

The attack at the greenhouses against Pat and me had been planned by William. The report didn't say why, but I figured I could piece it together pretty well.

After her motorcycle accident and capture, SoCal had teamed Janice up with one of their top operatives to watch me. Ms. Peters had made a note in the margins: *K.M. responsible for Meridian and ACE downfall?* I had to stop and think about that for a second.

In the end, I didn't really believe it. Jeremy had been the reason

Meridian had fallen, and William had helped him with ACE. I had been trying to find a way to stay alive and get Ian.

The last note said that Janice had been brought to the city and sent to see a doctor. Apparently I had jumped her from behind and knocked her out, stealing her stun gun, and they wanted to see if her wounds were consistent with that. Janice was playing some sort of game with Ms. Peters, and I was being dragged into it.

Now we were both up here. Fuck. The last thing I wanted to do was tangle with her again. It was a big city, so the chances of meeting her were slim to none.

I put the pad down on the tiny desk and stared at the wall.

"Find anything interesting?" Cecil asked.

"Yeah. Some pieces of the puzzle finally fit. A lot more still don't." I paused. "Is there a way to get to Bryson?"

"He's on C Level? Not really. The maintenance corridors don't go down that far. There's no need for them there, all the mechanicals are in the regular hallways."

"So we'd have to walk in the open. Any security checkpoints?"

"Not the last time I went. But last time, there wasn't a lab either. There's no reason to have a lab down there unless you're trying to keep it a secret. Whatever they're doing, SoCal doesn't want anyone to know."

"We could use the same trick, get past any security."

"I doubt it would work again. The guys upstairs had to have been found by now. They'll put two and two together pretty fast."

"Then how do I get down there?"

"You sure you want to? Most of it is sewage disposal and water treatment. Holding cells are just above that. Usually, if you go down there, you're in a bad place."

"Holding cells? What if you went back to being a guard and brought me down there?"

He thought about it. "Maybe. I'd have to zip-tie your hands again, and fake some orders. They're a lot tougher to do than maintenance ones."

"You think we'll need them?"

"Absolutely."

"How long will that take?" I asked.

"I could have them in a couple of days, but that won't work for you. Our window to get you back down to San Angeles closes when the last shuttle leaves tonight at 18:00 hours."

"Why?"

"Crew rotation on the shuttles. We lose our crew and we lose the chance to sneak you on board."

"Doc Searls said I would have three days."

"Normally, that would be true. With the war, SoCal has accelerated the schedules."

I was so close. "So basically, we need to get Bryson and off this thing in five hours."

"Yeah."

"Then I'm going down now." I was surprised at how fast I'd made the decision. "If I get caught, I'm fucked anyway. Ms. Peters already has me."

"Not now she doesn't. And when we get you on the shuttle, you're on your way home. Do you really want to throw that opportunity away?"

"I have a mission to complete."

"Sometimes you have to know when to abort."

"Maybe, but not yet. Get me back into the maintenance tunnels and I'll go down as far as I can. After that, I'll play it by ear. Can you get me a uniform?"

"Nothing that'll fit. I'll come with you."

I breathed a silent sigh of relief. Someone in a uniform would make things way easier.

Cecil pushed himself off the bed and reached past me, opening the door. He took a sudden step back, a look of shock on his face. A soldier followed him in.

"Cecil Howe. We have some questions about your whereabouts for the last—" The soldier looked my way, and I saw the realization hit him. It was all Cecil needed. He rushed forward, slamming the back of the soldier's head into the doorframe. The body dropped like it had no bones.

Cecil grabbed my hand.

"Come on."

Two steps out the door, he fell, his hand letting me go. More soldiers ran down the hall. I stared at Cecil as his blood soaked into the carpeted floor, the handle of a knife embedded in his neck.

"Miss Merrill!"

Ms. Peters followed the men. One of them took a swing at me. I ducked, pulling the blade from Cecil's body.

"That's enough. She's not to be harmed. Not yet."

The soldier stepped away, the effort it required visible all over his body. Ms. Peters stepped over Cecil as two wires shot into my chest. My back arched and I fell.

"Thinking of going somewhere?" She plucked the pad from my hand and kicked away the knife. "Maybe to kill some more people?"

My mouth moved but no sound came out.

"Shut up, dear. It's better that way." She turned to the soldiers. "Throw her into the smallest cell we have."

The soldier who'd almost hit me smiled. "Yes, ma'am."

"And don't harm her. If I see so much as a bruise . . ." She let the sentence trail off.

The look of disappointment on the soldier was swift and brief. I gave him my sweetest smile.

SOCAL SAT CITY 2—FRIDAY, JULY 7, 2141 1:35 P.M.

Even though the soldiers were told not to hurt me, it didn't make them gentle. They put zip ties on my wrists and looped three together for my feet, two tight around my ankles and a long one connecting them together. It let me move, but not much. My hands were tied in front this time, which gave me a fighting chance. Once Ms. Peters was gone, they tightened the ones on my wrists until I could feel them cutting into my skin. I was in pretty deep, and had no idea how to get out.

We went down three different elevators to get to where we were going. The final one opened in a corridor painted flat gray and covered in the machines required to run the city. This was what Cecil had described. No maintenance corridors needed down here. The sound of machines pumping air and the hum of electrical circuits pushed to their maximum filled the tight space.

I was led to a door with a single guard standing outside. She opened it and the three of us went through, entering a short hallway. Evenly spaced reinforced doors lined the walls. Holding cells. They were pushing me faster than my bound feet would allow, and I almost toppled forward before one of them caught me.

"It wouldn't do to get hurt, would it?" The soldier grinned viciously and ground his thumb into my armpit. Pain shot through my shoulder and down my arm until I gasped. When he let go, only numbness was left behind. "It wouldn't do at all." His partner laughed.

They opened a door and he shoved me through it. I stumbled and fell on a bed in the corner. I was up before the door closed, hopping back to it. The door locked before I got there. I banged on it.

"Hey, aren't you going to untie me?" I banged some more and yelled. No one answered. I stared at the door, filled with a sudden fatigue. How I wanted to be back in the compound with Ian and not a care in the world.

I hobbled back to the bed and examined the zip ties. They were standard military and police issue, plastic with embedded strands of steel running through the length, giving the tie a tensile strength of over five hundred pounds.

The locking tab was good as well, thick and buried deep into the grooves of the zip tie, hidden by a sheath that prevented someone releasing the tab with their fingernails. This wasn't going to be easy.

I reached down to untie my shoelace from my right shoe, and fed some of it out of the eyeholes. When I had about half of the shoelace out, I undid the other one. I fed the long end through the ties around my wrist and knotted it to the other lace. The zip ties around my feet limited my motion, only giving me ten or twelve centimeters on either side. It had to be enough.

Lying on my back on the bed, I pumped my legs as though riding a bicycle, drawing the shoelace tightly against the plastic. I pulled on my hands, creating more pressure. It didn't take long before the heat from the friction melted the plastic and tore through the thin metal strands. My hands popped free. I lay there and breathed for a while, rubbing my wrists. I was halfway there.

I untied the knot and pulled the shoelace completely out, this time using my hands to move it and melt through the tie connecting my feet. I left the ones around my ankles. I didn't want to destroy my shoelace and end up running around with a shoe that was falling off, or worse, in bare feet.

The first thing I did after putting my shoelace back was explore the room they had put me in. It was a glorified prison, though it didn't look like it was initially designed to be one. A single room with a bed firmly attached to one wall, and a toilet and sink attached to the other. Water flowed from the tap when I turned it on. I was hungry, but if I couldn't eat, I could at least drink as much as I could hold.

The walls were composite, the same stuff everything else was made of up here. Fibercrete wasn't nearly strong or flexible enough for something this massive in orbit. There was no way I was going to break through the walls.

I tested the door, just in case. Always check everything. You never know what your enemy might have forgotten. That was How to Escape 101. The door was definitely locked. I searched under the bed, then tried to follow the plumbing back into the wall. Even the door hinges were on the hallway side. Despite all that, this still wasn't a prison. The keyhole went straight through the door. If I'd had a key, I could have just unlocked it and walked out. This was definitely a temporary place. I had to get out before they decided to move me somewhere more permanent.

I reached into my hair and pulled out the bobby pins.

The lock looked like it was an ASSA six-pin cylinder lock. They'd been making these for centuries, but the basics of a mechanical lock hadn't changed. This would be difficult to do with a full pick set, never mind a couple of bobby pins. I bent the pins into shape and got to work. I lost the friction a couple of times before finally picking it open twenty minutes later.

There was no one in the hall, just more closed doors like mine. I had no idea if anyone was in them, and I didn't have time to find out.

The lights in the hallway flickered and turned off. I stood in the dark for a full minute, groping for the walls before they came back on.

I had to find Bryson and get him out. To do that, I had to go through the guard at the door and get to the elevator. I would check the living quarters first, and if he wasn't there, I'd try to get down to the lab on C3.

The back of the guard's head blocked my view through the small window in the hallway door. She was leaning against it, relaxing while no one was around. I had no way of knowing if there were more of them out there, or if it was just the one. My best guess was just the one, since that's how many were there when I was brought in.

Bracing the door closed with my foot so it wouldn't open, I turned the knob slowly, hoping it wouldn't make any noise. I thought I heard a small click, and the door moved when the catch released. The guard jerked forward. It was now or never. I pulled my foot away and yanked the door open.

I was faster than the guard and she toppled backward, falling flat on her back. I didn't give her a chance to react. Before she could move, I stomped on her chest, forcing all the air out of her lungs. Straddling her, I pressed on her windpipe until she blacked out. She barely had the chance to fight.

I dragged her back to my room, locking her in. The thought had been to steal her uniform and pass myself off as a guard, but there was no way it would work. She was too big for me to fit into anything she wore. Instead, I grabbed her stun gun, leaving the shock stick behind.

The elevators were clearly marked. I was on C1, the lowest you could get, by this elevator at least. The way the hallways curved, I could believe it. I pressed C5, where Bryson's living quarters were, and waited for the door to open. The stun gun went into my pocket.

The doors opened to a hallway that looked like the one I had left, maybe a little wider and less curved, but the same cables and junction boxes on the wall.

There was only one way to go from here. I turned left and hugged the inner wall, hearing voices before I saw anyone. Two of them, a man and a woman. I peered around the curved wall. Two guards stood in front of a set of doors. It was the only way forward. I put on my best game face and strode ahead.

Fake it till you make it.

The guards stood at attention immediately, staring down the hall as I approached. They made me stop three meters away.

"What's your business here?" the woman asked.

"I'm here to see Bryson Searls. Ms. Peters said he would be down here." I didn't know if it was going to work, but at the mention of Ms. Peters' name, both guards stood a bit straighter.

"Do you have your access document?" one of them asked.

"Yes." I took a step forward, reaching into my pocket. The male guard popped the restraint on his taser. I would have to take him out first. Before he could make another move, I lunged, driving the stun gun into his chest and kicking out at the other guard. I got lucky, surprise was on my side.

My foot caught the woman below her knee, kicking her leg out from under her. I left the man and drove my heel into the back of her neck, feeling it snap as I was tackled from behind.

Ground fighting had never been my strongest area. I was too small to have a lot of strength. If the guard managed to get me down, this was over. I leaned into the wall to keep myself upright and spun around. The guard pressed forward, a shoulder aiming for my head. I didn't have time to duck. I jabbed the stun gun forward, catching him in the armpit, and pulled the trigger.

He dropped as he lost control of his legs. His shoulder grazed my cheek. I followed him to the ground, pressing my advantage as long as I could. When the stun gun ran out of power, he didn't get up. I could see he was still breathing.

I wasn't sure what to do. I couldn't leave him behind, and I had nothing to tie him up with. He was just doing his job, and he would do it again if I left him here. I unclipped the knife from his belt and hovered it above his carotid artery. I hesitated, but I knew I couldn't leave a guard at my back. I plunged the knife in and pulled it out again, just like I'd been trained to do. Blood pumped from the wound.

It was different in real life.

Behind the double doors, it looked like an apartment complex. Each door had a lock similar to what I'd seen when I was drafted, the lights glowing red. Beside each keypad was a card swipe.

I searched the guard's bodies, careful not to look in their faces or step in the pool of blood. The woman had a card in her vest. I pulled it out and went to the first room, swiping it.

The door popped open, startling an older man leaning on a cane in the middle of his room. I held my fingers to my lips and left his door open a crack. I swiped the card in the next door, pushing it open to two people sitting on the bed. They were holding hands and not paying attention to anything. I recognized one of them.

"Bryson." He turned to look at the door, surprise on his face. The girl let out a small squeak. "Shh." I stepped in and leaned the door closed, making sure the latch didn't engage. All I needed was to lock myself in here with them.

"Who—"

Bryson jumped up and pulled me into a hug. The girl didn't look impressed. "It's so good to see you. Did my dad send you? When do we get out?"

I pushed him away and looked out the door again. "Quiet. How long have you been here?"

"About two weeks. Since I left—"

The girl stood up and approached us.

"This is Kris, the one I told you about that rescued me from Kadokawa."

The girl looked me up and down, as though surprised I could have done anything of the sort.

"Kris, this is Ailsa. We . . . we've been working in the lab together."

I nodded at her before turning back to Bryson. "We've been working with your dad ever since you left the restaurant."

"So how do we get out?"

"I don't know. There's a shuttle leaving this evening that was supposed to take me, but I have no idea who they are. The guy I was with knew. He's dead." I was surprised at how calm I felt about it. Maybe because I didn't know him that well. "Do you know a way to the shuttle port?"

"I've been there once. I could figure it out. But we're not going to get past the outer door. They leave a guard on duty all the time."

"Two, now. I already took care of them."

FOURTEEN

SOCAL SAT CITY 2—FRIDAY, JULY 7, 2141 1:35 P.M.

BRYSON AND AILSA heard the door lock activate. Ailsa scampered back to the bed, farther away from the door, and huddled by Bryson. Her face had drained of all color. He grabbed her hand and held it.

"You said you wouldn't leave me behind," she said.

He awkwardly rubbed her forearm. "I won't. It's okay. They're probably just coming to take us back to the lab."

Ailsa nodded, her eyes glued to Bryson. The door didn't open.

"Maybe it's another glitch. I know what's causing them. The glitches," Bryson said, hoping to get her mind off the guards. As soon as he said the words, he realized he'd hit the core of her terror.

She looked at him like he was crazy.

"I do." Bryson pressed on. "I was trying to get data off the memory key I wrote when Kadokawa had me. The key must have been swapped, and—"

"Bryson." A female voice cut through his confession. He twitched and looked at the partially open door. Ailsa gripped him tighter, her fingernails cutting into the back of his hand. The person at the door stepped into the room, closing it gently behind her. He knew her . . . It was the girl that had rescued him from Kadokawa! He jumped up, yanking his hand from Ailsa's grip, and ran to the door, pulling the girl into a hug.

"It's so good to see you. Did my dad send you? When do we get out?" It was only when she looked out the door that her name popped into his head. Kris!

She ignored his question, following up with one of her own. "How long have you been here?"

"About two weeks. Since I left—" He felt Ailsa grab his arm, partially hiding behind him. It made him feel stronger than he was. He introduced them, stuttering over their relationship.

Kris ignored him again, opening the door a crack and peering into the hall. "Come on. I'm not sure how much time we have." She stepped out of the room.

"You have a plan to get us off the city?"

Kris explained it to them as they headed to the exit.

The door to the first room Kris went into opened, and the old man with the cane walked out. He made a beeline for the double doors, completely ignoring the bodies. As he passed Kris, he gave her a tip of his head and carried on.

"What about the others?" Ailsa asked.

Kris handed her the card and she ran back down the hall, swiping every door and pushing them open. When she came back, Bryson turned, yelling as loud as he could.

"The doors are open. We can get out."

Kris pulled him through the doorway before he could see if anyone responded.

Bryson stepped over the guards' bodies without a word. Ailsa balked, her hand over her mouth, before following.

The constant thrum of ventilation stopped, followed by the steady vibration of the city. Ailsa froze in the middle of the hallway. A low moan escaped her lips. Bryson felt the panic start to well in his chest as his feet slowly lifted from the floor. The loss of power had hit the gravity generators. The thought had barely entered his head when his weight came back.

"We have to get to a shuttle, now," Kris said. She jerked him forward just as his fingers wrapped around Ailsa's wrist. They stumbled down the hallway and waited by the elevator.

It was the only way out, and it was taking too long! The old man must have taken the damn thing up.

Bryson yanked his arm free of Kris's grasp and took a step back. "Wait! Was it you that swapped out my memory chip for one with the virus?"

"Virus?" Ailsa asked.

"I was about to tell you when she came in," Bryson said. "The chip Ms. Peters took from me contained a virus. When I tried to find my data, I let it loose. I think it's what has been causing all the problems."

The elevator dinged and Kris shoved them inside, hitting the close button as fast as she could.

"Kai swapped the chip when he made you sleep. The information on it is part of the reason we've been looking for you."

"I knew it!" The revelation cut through his fear. As the elevator doors closed, he heard the ventilation systems kick back in. "That thing is destroying the city. We need to evacuate!"

"That's what we're trying to do," said Kris.

He grabbed Kris's arm, realization dawning on his face. "I need to get back to the lab. I have to destroy the data. All of it, the computers, the pads, everything. Before they have time to get it."

"There's no time. This whole place could shut down at any second."

Bryson's head cleared. He stood straighter and let go of Kris. "I have to. We're—humans—aren't ready for this yet. Look what's been done over just the hint of it already. Maybe man isn't supposed know how to travel through space."

The look on Kris's face said she thought he was crazy.

"Look, I know we can do that now. But if we can get almost anywhere instantaneously, what kind of damage do you think we would do?" He stopped. "Shit. They already have a ship built, with engines and our latest shielding. If that thing launches . . ."

Ailsa stepped forward as the doors opened on the promenade. Her entire body was vibrating but the color had come back to her cheeks. "I can get to the lab," she said. "Can you get to that ship?"

Bryson let the question hang in the air. He looked into her eyes and saw the same determination in them he had seen in the lab. She still looked scared, but she looked ready as well. She was probably stronger than he was. "Maybe. It's a couple of floors down in the military section."

"We'll never get in there," Kris said.

"I have to try."

"Let the virus finish what it's doing then. You said it would destroy the city."

"I can't. What if the safety systems contain it, or it can't get past a critical firewall? I can't take that chance."

Ailsa pushed them out of the elevator. He watched as the doors closed.

SOCAL SAT CITY 2—FRIDAY, JULY 7, 2141 1:41 P.M.

The promenade behind us was in chaos. Through the narrow view the hallway offered I could see people running toward the shuttle port, forcing their way past anyone who was slow. Now might be the only time we could hide amongst them and sneak onto a shuttle.

I turned back to make sure Bryson was following me. He was already getting on another elevator. I ran and slipped through as the door was closing.

"You're fucking insane!" I had no idea why I followed him.

Bryson kept his eyes on the numbers flashing over the door. The elevator slowed and I moved behind the control panel, out of sight of anyone waiting for the door to open. I held my breath.

In stark contrast to the promenade, the hallway was empty. Bryson stepped out and started jogging down the corridor. I followed him. Red lights flashed every ten meters and the overhead ones were dim, making the hallway seem to swim and shimmer.

"Where are we going?" I asked.

"There was a door we went . . . we went through to get to the ship."

He was obviously not used to exercise of any sort. We'd barely gone twenty-five meters and he was already out of breath.

"There's a guard . . . it's a checkpoint . . . of some sort . . ."

I grabbed his arm, pulling him to a stop. "How the hell are we supposed to get past a checkpoint?"

"I . . . I don't know." He had his hands on his knees, trying to suck in a breath. "I didn't think that far."

"No fucking kidding."

Bryson took off again, stopping only a few meters away. He stepped backward and looked into an open door before racing to the next one and doing the same. I caught up to him and looked into the rooms.

They were exactly the same.

"It's one of these two," he said.

"You have a fifty percent chance of getting it right. This hall can't stay empty forever, so make up your mind." The thought of being caught in a military area chilled me to my core. If we were lucky, they'd question us. If we weren't . . . With all the systems failures, they might shoot first and ask questions later. Bryson picked a door and walked in. I followed, pushing it almost closed. There was no handle on the inside.

The room was small, with only a desk and another door with no handle in the opposite wall. Above it, a light glowed red.

"How did you plan to get through?" I asked.

"I told you, I didn't think that far ahead. I thought I could bluff my way in."

"How did it work last time?"

"There was a guard with a gun. Ms. Peters said a number and the door opened."

"Well there's no guard here now."

"I can see that!"

I searched behind the desk. Maybe there was a release button for the inner door. I even crawled under the damn thing. I didn't think the guard opened the door for them.

"What did she say when you walked in?"

"Five four zero six three."

I repeated the numbers, lowering the tone of my voice to more closely match hers. Nothing happened. "You're sure those are the numbers?"

"Numbers are what I do."

"Well, they're not doing anything. Did she say anything else? A phrase before or after the numbers?"

"I can't . . . no wait! She did. Let me think."

"Make it fast. We can't have much time."

"Just let me think."

I stood quietly and watched his lips move. His forehead scrunched in concentration.

"I think she said her last name, the numbers and that she was with me. And the light over the door was white."

I tried to modulate my voice again. "Peters, five four zero six three. I'm with Bryson Searls." Nothing happened. I tried again with the same results. "Are you sure that's what she said?"

"No, the last part was different. I think she said she was accompanied by Dr. Bryson Searls."

I tried one more time. Nothing. "This isn't working. We need to leave."

"That light was white," he said again, ignoring me. He moved to the door we came through and pushed it shut.

"What the fuck?" I pried my fingers in the door's seam, trying to get a grip on something that would open it. It was like trying to climb wet limestone, slippery and painful. We were stuck. "There's no way out now."

Bryson pointed at the light above the door.

It had turned white. I tried one more time. "Peters, five four zero six three. Accompanied by Dr. Bryson Searls." The light above the door turned yellow and pulsed. "Did—"

He held up his hand and pressed a finger to his lips. His mouth counted up silently. When he reached ten, the door popped open.

I ran to it before it changed its mind, sliding my fingers through to open it a crack.

SOCAL SAT CITY 2—FRIDAY, JULY 7, 2141 1:53 P.M.

The hangar was a flurry of organized activity. From the small slice I could see, uniformed men and women rushed everywhere. There were one or two people in regular clothes, but none of them were dressed like me. A group by the ship in the middle of the hangar were wearing white lab coats. Though the ship towered over the people below it, it didn't even make a dent in the space available. I pulled my head back into the room.

"We'll never make it. There are enough people out there to stop an army."

Bryson stood over me and looked through the crack in the door as well. I moved out of his way, the sudden feeling of being confined bringing on the sharp edge of panic. He swore under his breath.

"What do we do?" he asked.

"We get the hell out of here and try to get on a transport with the rest of the fucking station. That's what we do."

He glanced at the door we came through. "We can't go back."

He was right. I'd already tried to open the door we'd used to get in. "How did you get out last time?"

"This way. The guard had the outside door open for us."

"How the hell did he do that?"

Bryson gave me a blank look.

I leaned my head against the wall. Think dammit. Think! It looked like there was only one way out of this mess. "Okay. We don't have much choice, do we? We head out there and try to look like we fit in. We'll stay as close to the wall as we can and look for another way out. All those people didn't get in through this room."

"If we're in there we can get to the ship."

The bastard had only one thought on his mind. "And do what?"

"They followed my design, I can get in and destroy it." He took another look through the crack. "We won't want to be in there when it happens though. In fact, if they powered on the engines, we don't want to be anywhere near the city."

"You'd kill all these people?"

Bryson stared into my eyes. "If I have to," he said. "We can try to set off an alarm. A lot of them should get out."

He opened the door and stepped through before I could say another word. I followed him. I'd had one goal in my head for so long, maybe I'd become too focused. What if Bryson was right? Either way, I wasn't getting him off this piece-of-junk city until he either realized the job was hopeless or we succeeded.

Once he was in the hangar, Bryson froze. He obviously had no idea what to do next. Against the wall right by the door were some bright yellow and orange safety vests and a pad. I grabbed two of the vests, shoving one into his hands before slipping mine over my head. I held the pad, willing my hands to stop shaking. The disguise wasn't much, but it was the best we could do.

There seemed to be a regular flow of people by the right-hand wall. Maybe it was a way out. With the door behind us locked, it might be the only way. We moved toward the ship.

"You're sure this is what you want?" I asked.

Bryson nodded. "What are they going to do? Kill me? They still need me."

"Sure they need you. They'll probably shoot me on sight. And think about it, they have a working design and a ship to go with it. How important are you at this point?"

His step faltered. "I let Ailsa go to the lab to destroy everything there. If I don't do this, what kind of person would I be? If she succeeds and I fail, her work was wasted."

"And if you die?"

He looked at me and down at the pad in my hands. Tears had formed in his eyes.

"This is right. I know it's right, and for the first time, I know I need to follow through. Don't stop me."

"Then let's get it done."

I lowered the pad and he moved toward the ship. I fell in line beside him. Sometimes there were things more important—bigger—than yourself.

Or your family.

The closer we got, the more I realized the size of the ship was deceiving. The hangar was so large, it made the ship look smaller than it really was. By the time we were directly under it, I was in shock.

Some of the people gave us strange looks, but let us pass. A group of armed men approached us, and I looked at the pad again, bending down by an access port in the floor as if to verify it was the one we were looking for. I fought to look natural, like I belonged. Every movement took so much effort, I was sweating. The men passed us by without a second look.

Now, though, we stood out like grass on Level 1. Everyone here was either in a white lab coat or uniform. I wasn't sure how long our ruse would work. We maneuvered under the belly of the ship. It was so high, I wouldn't have been able to touch it even if I stood on Bryson's shoulders. We almost made it to the stairs leading into the ship before we were stopped.

"What are you two doing here?" The soldier in front of us carried his weapon at the ready.

"We—"

Bryson interrupted me. "We're looking for access port eighty-seven in grid two-H."

"I don't know where that is."

"It's a good thing we do then. You're standing on port eighty-six. Eighty-five is that one." He pointed behind us. "That makes eighty-seven over there." Bryson pointed to behind the soldier, right by the stairs.

"I'll have to verify that. You wait right here."

"You go ahead," Kris said. "The power fluctuation readings we're getting from there are big enough to destroy half this ship. But we'll wait."

The soldier looked at both of us. He seemed unsure about what to do, before finally falling back to his initial decision. "You'll have to wait."

Bryson nodded and gave me a nudge. What the hell did he expect me to do? He held the pad up as if to show me something and traced his finger on the screen. It looked like he said *hit him*. He was crazy.

The soldier reached for a comm unit attached to his belt. Bryson gave me a push and I lurched forward, grabbing onto the guard for support. I could tell by the look in his eyes that he wasn't buying any of this anymore.

Well, fuck.

I swung out and hit full speed with my fist in his throat. He fell without a sound. A whistle echoed across the deck.

Bryson grabbed my arm and dragged me to the stairs. We were halfway up when a familiar voice called down.

"If it isn't my two favorite people. Kris Merrill and Bryson Searls."

FIFTEEN

KADOKAWA SAT CITY 2—FRIDAY, JULY 7, 2141 2:28 P.M.

THE SQUADRON ANDREW had ordered to be ready hadn't had a chance to stand down before SoCal 2 started exhibiting problems again. He hadn't heard from Okinawa, which was surprising considering he'd disobeyed a direct order by calling Admiral Hamil. He left his quarters and went back to Operations. The hush that fell when he walked in was different this time. Maybe it was him, but it felt like it was filled with more respect than his title gave.

Mori came rushing up. "*Kaishō-ho*, SoCal 1 and 2 are both having problems. From what we can detect, things are escalating quickly. SoCal 2 has already shut down its primary docking bay twice in the last ten minutes. It looks like they can't launch any shuttles."

"Have they ordered an evacuation?"

"Not yet, but our source says the people are doing everything they can to get out. Two emergency pods have already left the station. A rescue ship picked them up and brought them back to the city."

"Have they docked?"

"No, they are waiting for the landing beacons to come back on."

Andrew sighed. Good. There was a chance that at least some of the people would make it off. As long as the ships couldn't dock.

"There's one more thing. Without the ability to launch the shuttles, there aren't enough escape pods for everyone. Not even close."

"And the military dock? Still functional?"

"Yes."

"What do they have in inventory? Enough to get everyone off?"

"Intelligence reports say they barely have enough for the military staff. No room for anyone else."

Andrew felt the inexorable draw of the conflict he had hoped to avoid ever since he'd read Natsumi's message. He'd already disobeyed orders when he contacted the admiral earlier. Was he really prepared to take the final step? A battle raged in the back of his mind between his orders and what he knew was right. He turned back to the large display and stared at the faltering city.

"*Kaisa*."

"Yes, *Kaishō-ho*."

"Bring your second-in-command to my ready room."

The smaller man saluted and spun on his heels. Andrew watched him go. The next few minutes would decide the fate of himself, possibly his entire crew, and those who remained on SoCal 2. He was about to not only disobey his commander's orders again, but also Admiral Hamil's warning.

The ready room was in the corner of Operations, close to the entrance. He marveled again at how good a job Meridian had done in laying out the station. Even Kadokawa 1 didn't flow as well.

Meridian had spread military control throughout the city, interspersing it with the required residential and economic sectors. To them, it was for resiliency in case of war. If a portion of the city was damaged, any one of the other military sections could take over command. He looked at it differently. Military and family life did not often go hand-in-hand, but if you wanted soldiers who had a home to go to, a place where they could put aside their duties for a while, you ended up with staff who would do extra when you required it. Only the immediacy of this war had made him send family off-station.

Mori and *Kaisa* Tahn walked into the ready room, standing at attention until Andrew asked them to sit. She looked like she had just woken up. Mori had no doubt brought her up to speed on the way back.

The truth was, Andrew was scared. Not for his life, not even for the lives of those who served him here. He was scared for the future of Kadokawa. He had no children to pass the future on to, but many did. Was he able—was he capable—of making the right decision for all of them? Did he know what the right decision was?

It was time to get straight to the point. "I have had a direct order from Okinawa. Earlier today, I requested permission to extend an offer of help to SoCal. They are obviously having issues they cannot resolve. *Kaishō* Aiko responded to me directly. Under no circumstances was I to do so." Neither of the *Kaisas* moved. Andrew pulled out a chair and dropped into it. He was so tired, it felt like his life was draining from him.

But he had made up his mind.

"I am about to disobey that order. The people of SoCal are in need, and Kadokawa has built itself around helping the people of this planet, no matter who or where it was required. That single-minded purpose is the reason I joined the military. That purpose has made me who I am today, and I cannot turn my back on it. Or the people of SoCal.

"I will be ordering all of our fighter craft back here and sending out personnel carriers and hospital ships. We need to evacuate SoCal 2 before it collapses. I need to know where you and the rest of the men and women stand."

A long silence filled the room. Andrew felt his own heart pounding in his temples.

"I'm afraid I need an answer fairly quickly."

Mori was the first to respond. "I am with you, *Kaishō-ho*. I think you know the Operations staff are as well. We may have some issues lower down the ranks, but I believe we can contain them."

Andrew let out a sigh. One down, one to go.

Kaisa Tahn sat for a long time before she answered. Andrew knew exactly what she was thinking. Was saving the people of SoCal worth destroying her career?

"I cannot speak for the people who work my shift, *Kaishō-ho*, but I will stand with you as well. Thirty years ago, you rescued my little brother from the rubble of an earthquake in Korea. He lived, thanks to Kadokawa and to you. I will not turn my back on the kindness I saw that day."

Tension flowed from Andrew's shoulders, quickly replaced by a flood of relief. Having his two *Kaisas* behind him went a long way to having everyone else agree. "Thank you. If—perhaps when—I stand trial for treason and insubordination, I will make it clear you were simply following my orders. Your records will remain clear from what we do here today."

He was the first to leave the room, followed closely by Mori and Tahn. She left Operations, though Andrew doubted she would go back to bed.

He raised his voice loud enough for the entire bridge to hear.

"*Kaisa* Mori, withdraw our fighters from the front line and have them dock. Send out as many personnel carriers as we have, and three hospital ships. Have more standing ready in case we need them. Inform the pilots that if we need to dock, they are not to connect to any internal SoCal systems. For any reason. All docking procedures are to be done manually. Both cities are having system failures. We don't want any of their problems affecting us. Monitor everything. If they connect to any systems, refuse them docking rights when they get back. Open a line to Rear Admiral Hamil."

"Yes, sir!"

It had begun.

SOCAL SAT CITY 2—FRIDAY, JULY 7, 2141 2:31 P.M.

They moved Bryson and me into an office off the hangar deck. I was surprised they'd kept us together. Not that it would make much difference if they'd already decided what to do with us. We were strapped into wheeled chairs using old-fashioned metal handcuffs. A cuff for each arm and, if my restraints were the same as Bryson's, a single one looped under the wheeled feet. No zip ties to get out of this time. The handcuffs limited our movement. We could shift in our seats, but we could only move our hands and feet as far as the chain let us.

We sat in the chairs facing two large windows overlooking the hangar deck. On the other side of the glass everyone ran around, the previously organized people now looking lost and confused. The only thing not moving was the ship and two soldiers positioned outside our door. The only way out of the office was through them.

I couldn't see any way to get out of this one.

On the hangar deck I saw Ms. Peters talking to some guy

wearing the same uniform as everyone else. She was giving him a good dressing-down, and he just stood there, replying to whatever she said. It didn't seem to faze him at all. My guess was he was fairly high up the organizational ladder.

She waved her arms in the air. He said one more thing and turned to leave. When she started talking again, he kept on going. Definitely someone important. She watched him go for a while before turning and heading toward us.

I leaned into Bryson. "Don't say anything," I said. "Nothing you say can get us out of here any faster, all it can do is mess up Ailsa. Understand?"

He gave me a shaky nod. His face was white, and I could hear him trying to control his breathing. His entire body vibrated in the chair. This guy wasn't going to make it if he didn't get his shit together.

He closed his eyes. "For Ailsa," he whispered.

The color didn't return to his face, but his breathing slowed and the trembling became less noticeable. Good. The more control he had before she got here, the less damage he could do if he lost a bit of it.

Ms. Peters didn't keep us waiting for long. A soldier opened the door and closed it behind her. She looked flustered. Spots of red sat high on her cheeks, and her eyes almost sparked with barely controlled energy. I smiled when she wasn't looking, calmer than I had been since we'd been caught. She was off-balance. When someone was on the edge, they tended to make poor decisions. We needed to make sure those decisions went our way.

"Bryson," she said. "I thought we had an agreement?"

Her voice was calm and under control. I berated myself for being so optimistic. This was a dangerous woman. Bryson stayed quiet. Good for him.

"Nothing to say? Maybe we need a bit of persuasion."

Bryson started shaking again. Her threat scared him to the core.

"Talk to me, Bryson."

"I . . ." His voice faded away.

He stared at me with a pleading look.

"So, this girl has more control here than I do? Is that what you think?" She waited for a response. When none came she turned to look at me.

"And how about you? Will you be talking to me today?"

I didn't answer, keeping my eyes on Bryson. Out of the corner of my eye, I saw her move closer. Bryson's gaze flicked over to her and widened. I didn't have time to do anything before the back of her hand hit my face. The blow wasn't powerful, but it stung, bringing tears to my eyes.

I looked at her then, blinking away the tears. She was rubbing her hand. The impact had hurt her. That meant it wasn't something she was used to doing. She *was* on the edge. The urge to rile her up more, to push her over, call her a fucking bitch and lash out, washed through me. I shoved the giddy feeling aside, knowing it wouldn't work. It was what she wanted. Staying quiet was doing the job just fine. She leaned in closer.

"What was that? Were you going to say something?" Her voice stayed calm and controlled. "Come on, tell me what you're thinking. How much you want to hurt me back."

I glanced at Bryson. His eyes were huge and a string of snot ran down from his nose. He wasn't going to make it. I did what Ian would have done; I smiled and winked at him. It seemed to work, at least a little bit. He leaned back in his chair and gave me a lopsided grin. It was pretty shaky.

Ms. Peters straightened and took a step back. "Well, this isn't working, is it? I'll tell you what I'm going to do to you, dear girl. I'm going to have one of those men come in here and hurt you. I know you're pregnant, so I'll make sure they're careful. You don't need your legs or arms to give birth. Not even your sanity, really. When you're lying on the floor in a pool of your own blood, I'll bring in a doctor. He'll fix you up enough for you to stay alive. He'll put you into a coma until you're due. We'll pull you out when the baby's ready, let you experience the birth. I'll even let you hold him for a minute." She leaned in closer. "Then I'll take him away. Raise him as my own."

"Why? Because you're too stupid to raise your own son? That was his picture on your display, wasn't it? Where do you keep him so he doesn't learn about the piece of shit his mother is?" I'd let her words get to me, let the fear and the anger wash through me until I couldn't control it anymore. I knew I'd lost this battle the second I opened my mouth. The look on her face was almost worth it.

"How dare—You have no right—" Ms. Peters' face flushed red and she looked like she was struggling to get herself back under control. "It was trash like you that took him from me, that ended his beautiful life before he'd even had a chance to enjoy it." She straightened, staring down at me with a loathing I could almost feel. "I'll take yours. Teach him to hate the people below Level 6, teach him how to make them do his bidding, like they do mine. Every day I'll show him your picture and tell him how you killed his father. He'll grow up hating you and everything you stand for. Too bad you won't be around to see it."

The more she spoke, the more I wanted to be free for just a second, to wrap my arms around her ugly face and twist until I heard the snap of her neck. No one, *no one* was going to raise my little Ian but me.

"No!" Bryson couldn't keep his mouth shut. He pulled against his restraints and looked at me "I can't do it. I'm sorry. I can't—"

"Don't you see it doesn't matter?" I asked. "Nothing you say will help now."

Ms. Peters grinned. "Are you sure of that, Bryson? Tell me what you were planning on doing to the ship, and I'll let her live. Let her son actually see the person he'll hate more than anyone else."

I shook my head. Bryson fell back into his chair, his eyes wild.

Ms. Peters' lips pressed together. "Fine."

Klaxons went off on the hangar deck. I flinched, taking my eyes off Ms. Peters. Smoke billowed from the far corner, coming from behind the ship.

"Now what?" Ms. Peters went to the door. "Watch these two. If they get out, I'll see to it you're kicked out of the military and forced to work on Level 1 for the rest of your short, miserable lives." She stormed out.

One of the soldiers came in and double-checked our restraints. Satisfied with what he saw, he left and closed the door. They turned their backs to the window and watched the smoke cloud grow.

When I was sure they weren't watching us, I leaned close to Bryson. "Do you have a thin piece of metal or a pin on you?"

Bryson shook his head.

"Anything hard and flexible?"

He shook his head again. "Wait, I have a memory chip."

"Too small, and not strong enough." I looked around the room for something to help me. If only I still had my bobby pins. On the desk was the pad I had grabbed when we'd entered the hangar. "Is there anything in the pad that is strong and flexible?"

Bryson thought about it for a second. "Maybe. The shielding on the back panel may work. It doesn't have to be thick to block what the pad puts out, though. Will it do what you want?"

"It has to." I rolled to the desk. The soldiers were still looking at the smoke that was filling the hangar. I leaned forward as much as I could, barely catching the edge of the pad with my chin. I dragged it across the desk until it fell into my lap. So far so good. "I need your help. We need to break this thing open. You grab one side, and I'll grab the other. Try to fold it in half. Don't drop it!"

I moved the pad between our chairs. If we dropped it, it was gone. Neither of us could pick it up off the floor. Bryson grabbed an end and we tried folding the pad. It snapped with a soft pop, breaking much easier than I'd thought it would. Bryson let go of his end and the pad slipped from my fingers. I lunged as far as I could and pinched. The handcuffs dug into my forearms, but I had it!

I dropped the pad in my lap again and turned my back to the window, picking away the pieces of plastic. Bryson kept a lookout. He was right, the entire back was covered in a thin layer of metal. I pried a fingernail under it until it lifted, and carefully peeled it off the plastic. It was way too thin for what I needed, but it was more than big enough. I only hoped that if I folded it a couple of times, it might do the job. By the time I'd folded it five times, I had a heavy-duty strip about one centimeter by five. It would have to do.

I took the folded metal and spun back to Bryson. "Move your wrist so I can see the ratchet on your cuffs." He shifted and I slid the metal shim into the locking mechanism along the teeth. It stopped when it hit the lock. I put my thumb on it, keeping a steady pressure on the metal while I slowly tightened his handcuff. The lock ratcheted and the shim slipped in deeper. The cuff didn't relock. The metal strip held the locking mechanism out of the teeth and the handcuff sprang open. I breathed easier. This was working.

I took a quick glance out the window. It was still chaos.

"Give me your other hand." Bryson spun his chair and I repeated the process, talking my way through it so he knew what I was doing. His cuffs fell into his lap. "Okay, now me."

"What about my feet?"

"Me first. If they catch us, I have more of a chance of stopping these guys than you do."

Bryson nodded. He missed the push of the shim on the first try, tightening my handcuffs even more. I figured he had one chance left before it would get too tight to work.

"Slow and steady. You can do this."

He sucked in a breath and held it, repeating what he had done the first time. The cuff sprang open and the shim fell to the floor. I reached down to pick it up.

I didn't even have time to free my other hand before the door to the office jumped open.

SOCAL SAT CITY 2—FRIDAY, JULY 7, 2141 2:45 P.M.

I launched myself from the chair, tripping over my leg cuffs. My shoulder slammed into the door with all the speed I could get and the chair fell on top of me. The door smashed into the first soldier. Momentum was on my side and I felt more than heard a crack. He slid to the ground. The door burst inwards, slicing into my cheek, and I scrambled back on my hands and knees, dragging the chair with me.

The second soldier jabbed his shock stick at me. I scuttled farther backward. The stick sparked against my shirt, barely missing. My legs were free of the chair, but still shackled together.

I didn't have time to think. Instead I moved, scrambling onto my feet and swinging the chair between us. He kicked it out of the way, forcing me off-balance.

Bryson unlooped his foot cuffs from the chair and hobbled behind the desk. He was useless in here and he knew it. The shock stick swung. I fell back, kicking out with both my feet. I felt the impact of the stick, sending it flying as I landed on the overturned chair. My back arched and I rolled away, twisting my shoulder as the chair moved with me.

The soldier jumped and I rolled back, struggling onto my hands and knees. A heavy boot swung toward my face. I wasn't going to win this one.

I twisted, and the heel scraped my ear. I waited for the next blow. The soldier spasmed, falling to a knee beside me. Above him, Bryson held the shock stick, a look of grim determination on his face.

Before he could strike again, the soldier lunged, knocking Bryson backward. He grabbed the shock stick and swung with his other hand, hitting Bryson in the temple. Bryson folded in on himself.

The distraction gave me time. I untangled the cuffs and jumped to my feet, picking up the chair and swinging with everything I had left. A wheel caught the soldier's face, spinning him around before he crashed into the window.

He fell, pulling the chair with him. My shoulder tore, pain searing through the muscles as the chair spiraled where my arm was still attached. I collapsed on top of him.

My shoulder was on fire and blood dripped from the cut on my cheek, but it was over. For now. Adrenaline was the only thing that was keeping me going. It surged through me, pushing me through the pain. I hobbled to Bryson's still form. He was alive at least.

It took me a few minutes to search the guards for the key to the cuffs. My hands shook so badly, I didn't think I was going to be able to unclip it from the loop in his pocket. Still shaking, I freed my one hand and both of my feet. When the last cuff sprang open, I almost cried. Bryson was sitting now, leaning against the wall and staring at the bodies on the floor. I unlocked the cuffs on his ankles and pulled him to his feet with my good arm, and together we left the office.

We stopped a few meters outside the door, not sure which way to go. Bryson pointed at the smoke-covered ship as the floor lurched under our feet. People screamed and the random movement changed to a steady stream heading to our left. I looked ahead of the mob. Doors swung open as everyone pushed past the security staff manning them. I dragged Bryson behind me as I followed.

The smoke cloud enveloped us before we reached the exit, smelling strangely sweet. Without letting go of Bryson, I lifted the collar of my shirt, covering my mouth and nose as best I could. We merged with the crowd close to the exit. People bumped into my shoulder and I almost cried out.

We were practically blind.

People shrieked and shouted, creating more panic, more of a rush to get somewhere safe. We pushed into the hallway, sandwiched between the mass moving too slow in front of us and the frenzied rush from behind. The floor fell away from our feet again and a sudden hush fell.

Someone whimpered as I fell, my knees almost buckling as I met the floor moving back up, like jumping in an elevator. I kept my grip on Bryson. There was no way I was letting go. I pulled him along, fighting to get to the emergency stairs leading up to thc promenade.

The stairwell slowed us down even more, and the only thing keeping us moving was the crush of bodies behind us. The smoke was gone here, but I still couldn't see anything through the flashing red lights and people. I stepped on something soft and looked down. A man had been trampled; the only thing holding his body together was the skin stretched taut over jutting bones. I kept on going.

We exploded through the door to the promenade, almost pushed to the railing around the central courtyard. I dragged Bryson away from the throng of bodies, away from the shuttle port. We hunkered down by a bench overlooking the trees that still rose majestically toward the ceiling, unconcerned with what was going on around them. I struggled to catch my breath, finally letting go of Bryson's hand to probe my shoulder.

"We'll never get to a shuttle, if they're still flying," I said.

"There's no place else to go."

He was right. We'd left the only other docking bay I knew of on this piece-of-junk city. I scanned the crowd between us and the transports. We had to try. "Okay, ready?" He nodded and we stood, ready to charge through the fray.

At that exact moment, every drone flying through the promenade fell silent, dropping like bombs into the crowd and down to the lower levels. I crawled under the bench, and Bryson tried to squeeze under with me. I counted to ten after I heard the last impact and crept back out. No more drones flitted through the trees above us. A few people in the crowd were hurt, blood dripping from defensive wounds as they tried to protect themselves from the falling machines.

"Hey, bitch!"

The scream rose above the sound of the crazed crowd. People stopped and turned. All but one continued the mad dash to the shuttle port. The scream had come from behind me, but Ms. Peters stood in front. I spun, ignoring her as she was dragged away from us by the mass of panicked flesh.

Janice drove toward us, a look of pure hatred on her face.

"This is your fault. All of this." Her hands waved crazily around her. Blood ran from a gash on her head, partially running into one swollen eye.

A sense of calm filled me, and my mind processed everything as fast as it could. She'd be blind on that side. My damaged shoulder would be facing her though. I stood my ground. This needed to be taken care of, or we might never make it.

"Get to the shuttle port." I didn't turn to see if Bryson had listened to me, didn't check if he'd seen Ms. Peters. I wouldn't give Janice the opportunity to attack me when I was distracted. I was in no condition to fight anyone, but I couldn't let her know. Taking a few steps back, I put the bench between us. Janice stopped her advance.

A blur separated from the crowd, charging toward me. I twisted out of the way, losing Janice's position.

Ms. Peters ran past me. Shit. She was after Bryson. I followed the motion, hoping I could delay Janice in the press of people. All I saw was a blinding flash of light as something hit my face under my eye, right where the door had sliced me open. The last I saw of Bryson, he was pushed against the railing by a demon in a red business suit.

A second punch followed the first. I dropped, rolling under the bench and coming out the other side. Janice launched over the top, tackling me on the ground. I jerked her off me, my shoulder screaming in agony, and sprang to my feet. She used the back of the bench to help herself up.

I took advantage of it, kicking out her supporting arm. She fell on top of the backrest, slowly sliding to the floor. I stopped her descent, pressing her neck against the hard back of the bench, elbowing the base of her skull until she was too hurt to fight back.

I put all my weight on her head, holding her there until she wasn't moving any more.

Where was Bryson? Blood pounded in my ears as I scanned the crowd. He stood by the railing, leaning over it, his feet almost lifted off the floor, fighting being pulled over. Ms. Peters clawed at his arm, one hand twisted in his shirt in a death grip. I fought through the crowd.

Reaching over the railing, I pried her fingers open. The material tore. She made one last desperate lunge, grabbing Bryson's hand. He jerked back and her grip slipped, sending her to the floor below. I pulled Bryson from the edge and looked over. She lay awkwardly at the bottom of one of the trees, not moving.

The crowd surging toward the shuttle port had thinned slightly. I dragged Bryson behind me as I pushed through them, adrenaline driving me through the pain and exhaustion.

"I . . . I killed her," was all he said.

It wasn't my job to console him.

When we reached the front of the crowd, he stopped, grabbing the back of my shirt. People in uniform were separating the crowd into manageable groups and loading them onto shuttles.

"Those are Kadokawa uniforms," Bryson said.

SIXTEEN

SOCAL SAT CITY 2—FRIDAY, JULY 7, 2141 3:06 P.M.

THE FLOOR of the shuttle port shook and people screamed, surging forward again despite the Kadokawa soldiers. Bryson pulled me farther back. I wanted to grab him, to drag him with me, but my shoulder roared as the joint stretched, bringing tears to my eyes. It was easier to follow him. He let go when he reached the wall.

"I can't get on there."

"They don't even know who you are. Look around you, this place is falling apart."

"I . . . I can't . . . I can't be someone's slave anymore."

"Then stay here and die. I give up."

Bryson grabbed my arm, stopping me from leaving. I screamed in pain. No one noticed or cared.

"I'm sorry," he said. "I—"

"Shut the fuck up." My voice was harsh and raspy. "Either follow me, or stay here. Those Kadokawa soldiers are too busy to care about you or me or anybody right now. All they want is to get as many people onto those shuttles as they can."

He looked like he was about to fall apart. I stepped in front of him.

"What if Ailsa's on one of those shuttles?" I asked. "Do you want me to tell her you were so scared to get on one that you chose to die here? I can do that for you . . . let her know."

"You really are a deep-down bitch, aren't you?"

I laughed, the reaction surprising me. I had thought those exact words about Dispatch over a year ago. She'd believed she was helping me back then as well. Bryson had to make up his mind. "Look, I'm sorry. I'm not staying here." I walked back toward the shuttles, cradling my arm. Every step sent shards of pain radiating from my shoulder, and the right side of my face felt paralyzed. He caught up with me as I waited in one of the lines.

The shuttle in front of us took off and the line almost disintegrated into a riot before everyone noticed another taking its place. I stepped forward when it was my turn, Bryson right behind me.

We were herded on board and told to sit. I slid over to a seat by the window. Outside, I could see more people streaming toward the shuttles. Would there be time to get them all? Would there be enough shuttles?

The adrenaline rush left me, filling me with weakness and pain. Nausea creeped into my bones. I pressed my head against the cold viewport and closed my eyes, listening to the sobbing and soft whispers of the other passengers.

"Where will they take us?" Bryson asked.

"I dunno," I mumbled.

"Do you think we're going back to one of their Sat Cities?"

"I dunno. I doubt it."

"Back to San Angeles, then?"

I lifted my head from the cool plastic and looked at him. The man was a mess, even more shaken than when we had fought our way out of the hangar, or when he'd dropped Ms. Peters over the railing. I'd seen him stand up to the challenges we had faced. I knew he had it in him. He just had to hold out a bit longer.

"Relax," I said. "The Kadokawa Sat Cities are too small to take all of us, and I doubt they want to shove us all on the other side of the planet from where we live. They'll put down in San Angeles somewhere." I truly believed it.

We left the city when the shuttle was full. Men and women stood in the aisles. Bryson left his seat, offering it to a man with a cane. The man took it without question. I recognized him. He was in the room beside Bryson on C-5. He gave me a tense smile when we left the shuttle port, floating out into space.

Out the viewport the city looked peaceful, with beacon lights flashing and shuttles drifting away in an orderly fashion. Behind the massive globe of the city floated Earth, the west coast of North America basking in warm sunlight. If I shut out the sounds of the other people, I could almost imagine everything was okay. Maybe it was because I desperately wanted it.

The shuttle shot upward, though I didn't feel anything. I realized it wasn't us that was moving.

The city dropped in its orbit.

Flashes of released oxygen, frozen in the coldness of space, exploded from the city in a huge geyser, propelling it closer to Earth.

The space around SoCal 2 exploded with shuttles launching, abandoning those people left behind to save the ones already on board. The Sat City began to spin.

Jets fired around its perimeter and the speed of the spin increased. Another chunk of the city on the space side exploded outwards, sending shrapnel deeper into the blackness. The satellite accelerated toward Earth, thrust by the blast. I thought I could almost hear the groan of stressed composite and metal, impossible through the vacuum of space.

The city went dark, every beacon, every shuttle port at the same time. It looked like it had stopped moving, but I knew once its descent had begun, nothing could prevent it. Not in this condition. The shuttle fired its thrusters, pressing me into my seat, distancing us from the doomed city. The satellite plummeted out of my view, still moving uncontrollably. The cabin filled with silence as the thrusters stopped and we coasted through space.

We made a slow turn until what was left of the city spread out below me, outlined by the beauty of Earth under it. Another chunk of the satellite blew off, venting more air into deep space, and the city plunged closer to Earth.

A blinding flash filled my viewport, and SoCal 2 was gone.

In its place, millions of pieces of debris filled the view. I knew some of them had to be human. The old man beside me leaned closer, peering through the window with me. He brushed my shoulder and I cringed.

"Sorry, miss," he said. "I wanted to say thank you. I thought I was going to die in that room."

"What happened?" I asked, still staring at the empty space that used to be living, breathing people.

"A failsafe. One of the cities falling back to Earth would be catastrophic. No one would survive the aftermath. So each city has a failsafe. It's not connected to the computers, the explosives aren't even connected to each other. Each one has its own sensors. If the orbit drops below 20,000 kilometers, they blow."

I tore my gaze from the explosion and stared at him. "How do you know that?"

He laughed. "Same way you know how to get your job done, I suppose. You learn."

We waited in the cramped shuttle for hours as the space around us slowly cleared of traffic. The old man beside me slept. I stared out the viewport. Those in the aisles eventually found a place to hunker down. The shuttle started its descent. Hopefully heading to San Angeles.

As we sank into the atmosphere, the ocean came into view, sparkling in a sunset of deep reds and vibrant oranges. Below us, the coast of San Angeles looked the same as it had when I'd left. Chatter among the passengers was more rumor than fact. Stories of SoCal 1 being destroyed, of them not being able to evacuate. A half million lives lost.

If it was true, we were landing in a world that needed more help than it ever had before.

LOS ANGELES LEVEL 7—FRIDAY, JULY 7, 2141 7:23 P.M.

As we were coming down, the pilot announced over the speakers that we were scheduled to land at the San Diego shuttle port. Bryson offered a small smile when he heard that. The smile got bigger when the pilot came back on and said we'd been rerouted and would be landing in Los Angeles instead.

The sky above the shuttle port was filled with transports marked in the Kadokawa colors. In the distance, I could see even the SoCal Air Base was busy. Our shuttle landed at the end of a runway, settling down and turning off its engines. It looked like we took the last bit of real estate left. We were asked to wait a bit longer as buses came to take the old and those that couldn't walk to the terminal.

The rest of us made our own way across the tarmac. The smell of the ocean and the fresh air cleared my head.

Inside the terminal there were already aid stations set up, tables with food and water, others where people could check to see if their loved ones had arrived. People were either working or milling around, looking lost and dazed and confused. I was sure some of them hadn't set foot on Earth in years.

A woman touched my elbow. She wasn't wearing a uniform, but below the red cross on her armband was a small Kadokawa logo.

"Your face. It is bleeding. Come, we can take a look at it," she said.

I followed as she led me through the crowds. Bryson stayed right behind us. A corner of the terminal had been cordoned off and separated into a triage area with small, curtained-off examination rooms. The woman dropped me off and went to find another person that needed help.

There were no serious injuries. A few broken bones and contusions. Those that made it onto the shuttles were the lucky ones. A nurse cleaned my face and glued the cut together. They put my arm in a sling and recommended I get it X-rayed and taken care off. I told them I would.

Bryson called his dad. Traffic was so bad, we agreed to meet him outside the shuttle port grounds. I was surprised when Kai and Pat showed up with him. It didn't take long for the story to come out. SoCal 1 had self-destructed shortly after SoCal 2. They didn't have the benefit of Kadokawa nearby to send transports.

Close to half a million people had called SoCal 1 home. Among them were the top brass, the ones that controlled the company. With the loss came the rapid disintegration of SoCal's control in San Angeles. The Level 6 up-ramps were still being blocked. Doc Searls was able to use his access to bring people up. Level 5 had been reopened almost right away. The soldiers had abandoned their posts, letting the masses back in. Chaos was starting to take hold.

It was only expected to get worse, and both IBC and Kadokawa had brought in extra forces to help police the situation. Kadokawa had gotten to the southern part of the city, while IBC had taken control of the north. At first, people had called them vultures, going after the carcass. Now, only a few hours after the fall of SoCal, IBC had proven the people right. There had already been arrests and killings.

Kadokawa had done things differently, and the violent outbreaks seen in San Francisco and San Jose weren't happening down here.

We ended up at Doc Searls' Level 6 offices. He took care of my shoulder and gave me a place to sleep. I tossed and turned most of the night listening to Bryson and his dad talk. Healing the wounds they'd nurtured for so long.

Sleep finally came, and I didn't wake up until late the next morning.

LOS ANGELES LEVEL 7—SATURDAY, JULY 8, 2141 10:41 A.M.

While I slept, the city went crazy. Kadokawa brought in troops, taking control away from IBC. There was still fighting just south of San Francisco as IBC was trying to hold on, and a few of SoCal's military bases remained under siege. The President of the United States complained, calling it an act of war. No one listened to him. Especially when a few of the independent cities offered to help Kadokawa, including Denver and Minneapolis, and sent people and supplies.

It was a difficult declaration to make stick when Kadokawa stopped most of the looting and chaos and started working with the insurgent cells to supplement the food lines, even adding new locations to help bring sustenance to the people of San Angeles. Canada had created a route for medical supplies and more food, supplementing Kadokawa's work. All communication barriers had been dropped.

Kadokawa had set up checkpoints at any access between all the levels, keeping people from flowing upward and creating more havoc. They promised that within the next few days, they would begin opening access up again. I wasn't sure if I believed it, but in the short term, things seemed to have settled down a bit.

When asked, the man in charge simply said it was what Kadokawa did. I had always thought the corporations were all alike, but now I was wondering if it was because my view had been limited. The man, someone by the name of Andrew Ito, had more to say.

It had been Kadokawa that was fighting with SoCal, but apparently there had been some recent shake-ups in the organization, and they were now being run by a woman. One of the original Kadokawa line. The first thing she had done was replace the military leadership, supposedly to bring it more in line with how Kadokawa used to be. I didn't pay too much attention.

All I knew was that, even while fighting their own internal problems, they had come to San Angeles and SoCal 2 to help.

Bryson took off before I woke up, heading to the shuttle port to register his name, hoping Ailsa had done the same. It would take a few days for the volunteers to sort through everything, find out who had died on the Sat Cities and who had lived. It would take longer than that to bring families back together.

I had breakfast with Pat and Kai. Both of them were still mad at me for taking off, for being on SoCal 2 when it had all fallen to pieces. I think they were too relieved to show it much though. Instead, we talked about the changes that were taking place, whether Kadokawa was setting itself up to keep control of the city, or whether they were actually telling the truth. I voted for the former, but Kai disagreed. He'd seen some of the good Kadokawa had done in the past. I wasn't holding my breath.

The weight of everything that had happened since Ian died bore down on me, bringing me back to the reality that was my life. I wanted time to be alone, time to think of what I had done in the last day. I borrowed Doc's car and went down to Level 5, back to the greenhouses. Soldiers stopped everyone going down, checking their IDs—driver's licenses mainly, not the SoCal trackers—and issuing return passes to let us back up. It felt good to be somewhat anonymous.

I didn't head straight for the greenhouses, taking a small detour instead, heading back to the drugstore I'd stolen from a few short weeks ago. I'm not sure they believed me when I told them why I was there, but they took my money anyway. It was a short drive to the greenhouses after that.

The Kadokawa logo on the *shinrin-yoku* sign caught my eye as I walked past it, and I couldn't help wondering how common it would become in San Angeles, how ingrained Kadokawa would be.

Entering the greenhouse was like walking into a sanctuary. The sounds of the city muted and the rich smell of soil and green life filled the air. The place seemed empty. I couldn't even find a worker picking up fallen leaves or patching a spot of bare soil. Everyone was at home or at the food kitchens, waiting out the changes as best they could. Hoping for the best.

I didn't take my shoes off this time. I went straight to the tree and sat by the scarred trunk, the tiny carved heart still healing. I didn't talk either. I relaxed, enjoying the silence and the solemnness of the trees. Letting it wash through me.

How I wished Ian could see me now. I had family again. *Real* family. Not that Pat and Kai weren't, but somehow Auntie was different. She was my dad's sister, and that changed everything. It made me think how important the ties of family were. How important keeping the connections alive would be.

I didn't want to end up like Doc Searls, wishing things had been different. He and Bryson had a chance to heal—to reconnect. If Ailsa made it off of SoCal 2, maybe a chance for grandchildren. It felt good to look toward the future with hope.

With no SoCal and no Meridian following me—trying to kill me—anymore, I didn't need or want the name ACE had given me. In the back of my brain, I'd always associated *Merrill* with being a fugitive. I wanted the name I was born with, and I wanted my son to carry that name forward. I hoped Ian would understand.

I was Kris Ballard, daughter of Henry and Mei Ballard. My son would be a Ballard as well. Ian Henry Ballard. It had a nice ring to it.

A young child squealed, waking me up from a dreamless sleep. I watched as he ran through the trees, falling and laughing and getting back up. His parents followed close behind, giving me an apologetic smile as they passed. I rested my folded hands on my tummy and smiled back.

Things were changing. Whether they would stay that way or fall back into their old habits was impossible to say. But right now, here, I was happy.